PRAISE FOR
H. MITCHELL CALDWELL

COST OF DECEIT

"Readers will cheer this polished, highly enjoyable legal thriller. Caldwell gradually raises the tension level until the plot verges on thriller. Fans of courtroom drama will savor this peek into the inner workings of an attorney's mind while puzzling over the alleged villain's guilt."

> — EDITOR'S PICK, BookLife

"The dramatic dynamic of the trial is comparable to the action that occurs outside the courtroom as one proceeding gives way to another and tensions rise. A most enjoyable read from start to conclusion. 5 STARS."

> — Philip Zozzaro, Los Angeles Book Review

"H. Mitchell Caldwell's COST OF DECEIT is a well-structured and easy-to-read legal thriller with believable characters, an engaging story and insight into the criminal court system."

> — *Indie Reader*

COST OF ARROGANCE

"A complex courtroom drama, anchored by sharply drawn characters. In Caldwell's legal thriller, a law professor decides to represent an inmate on death row and finds it to be a daunting case. Caldwell's work shines in his ability to make the intricacies of the law accessible to laypeople while still satisfying those with legal experience."

> — *Kirkus Reviews*

"This book is a must-read for any fan of courtroom thrillers. There is no stone left unturned when Jake Clearwater takes on a case. Author Caldwell certainly knows his subject matter and I look forward to reading more courtroom fiction by this author."

— Kristi Elizabeth, *San Francisco Book Review*

"As a former prosecutor myself, I appreciated how the book accurately portrays trial proceedings, including a realistic approach to cross-examination and an insightful view of the different ways prosecutors and defense attorneys approach a case and present their evidence."

— Darren Shulman, Ohio Lawyer, *Ohio State Bar Association Journal*

"A gripping novel about a former top prosecutor turned esteemed law professor who takes on a case to challenge the death sentence for a vicious, confessed, and convicted murderer. The trial details are accurate and dramatic reflecting the author's real-life experience as a prosecutor who now teaches law. I lost a night's sleep—I couldn't put it down."

— John Sharer, trial lawyer, Gibson Dunn & Crutcher, member of the American Board of Trial Advocates

"Pepperdine/Caruso law professor H. Mitchell Caldwell has written a chilling legal thriller around the retrial of a convicted murderer facing the death penalty."

— Norm Goldman, *Bookpleasures.com*

"Caldwell's strong and charismatic protagonist Jake Clearwater is the new Perry Mason, and I can't wait to read the next entry in the series. Highly recommended!"

— Eric Petersen, *The Internet Review of Books*

For my sons, Lee and Eric

COST OF MALICE

A JAKE CLEARWATER LEGAL THRILLER

H. MITCHELL CALDWELL

COST OF MALICE
Published by Nine Innings Press

First Edition 2024
Copyright © 2024 by H. Mitchell Caldwell

Cover design: Eric Labacz

ISBN: 978-1-7375123-6-3 Paperback Edition
          978-1-7375123-7-0 Hardcover Edition
          978-1-7375123-8-7 Digital Edition

Library of Congress Control Number: 2024901654

Author services by Pedernales Publishing, LLC
www.pedernalespublishing.com

10 9 8 7 6 5 4 3 2 1

Printed in the United States of America

v13

PROLOGUE

September 3, 2016

"Honey, it's late. I'm not excited about you driving to Pomona this time of night. Can't it wait till tomorrow?"

"Mom, I promised my sorority sisters. I want to show them my new truck." She wore the determined look of an eighteen-year-old experiencing the flush of autonomy. "I'll be fine. I'll be back in a couple of hours."

"It's just that your father and I worry about you driving clear down there at night. It's not the safest area."

"It's only fifteen miles. It's not like I'm driving somewhere crazy like Las Vegas."

Her mom replied with an indulgent teenager-placating smile.

Tracie gave her mother a hug. "I'm a safe driver. I'll be back before you know it." And with a cheek kiss, she was out the door and into her bright showroom-red extended-cab Toyota.

Donna made the first reluctant call to Tracie's cell four hours later, at precisely 1:00 a.m. No answer. She left a voicemail. Nothing. She called again at 1:15 a.m. Nothing. She called the sorority house five minutes later. Tracie had never arrived. The sisters assumed she had changed her mind and stayed home. Frank called the Pomona Police Department. No reports involving a red Toyota with paper plates. He called the Los Angeles County Sheriff's Department. Nothing.

The Switzers made the twenty-minute drive from their home in Norwalk to the sorority house, desperate for a place to start looking. No one at the sorority house had seen Tracie or heard from her. Calls and texts went out from twenty phones. Was she meeting a boy? Had her truck broken down?

Unspoken prayers flew from her frantic parents for their precious daughter. Donna and Frank drove around the campus in ever-widening circles, looking for the truck. More calls to the Pomona PD, to the LA County Sheriff's. Nothing.

At 5:00 a.m. they drove the fifteen miles home, praying against all common sense that her truck would be at the curb. It wasn't. The worst night of Donna and Frank's lives dissolved into the worst possible morning. Tracie's truck was found on a turnout on the road to Mt. Baldy, ten miles from campus. Tracie's body was in the passenger seat. Her throat had been cut.

CHAPTER 1

Fall 2018. Two years after the murder of Tracie Switzer.

Nancy Seah quietly stepped into the back of my first-year criminal law class and took a seat. She hadn't been invited, but it was common knowledge that my classes were always open to anyone who cared to venture in. It's against school policy, but what the hell. I momentarily paused, gave her a quick look, and resumed the class discussion of involuntary manslaughter. When I wrapped up, Seah remained seated while the last of the students filed out.

"Nice class, professor." She grinned as I walked to her. "Attentive group. I'm not surprised. I already knew your communication skills were good." Seah was tall and erect, with gray-streaked hair. Her pantsuit was creamy white, cinched with a wide red belt. I would put her in her early sixties. She exuded dignity and authority as befitting the number two in the LA District Attorney's office.

I grinned as I reached her seat in the back row of the cavernous classroom. She stood, and we shook hands. "I don't usually get such distinguished visitors. I'm sure your focus is not on involuntary manslaughter."

"No, it's not." She cocked her head and with a trace of a smile said," I'm here hunting."

"Hunting?"

"For a top-flight prosecutor."

Uh oh.

I understood. She'd been trying to recruit me into the DA's office for the past two years. "You've got twelve hundred prosecutors in your office. Most of them pretty good," I said with a good-natured smirk.

"Many of them are, or should I say were." She cocked her head. "And that's why I'm here. There's been a mass departure of our best senior trial lawyers over the past year. I'm concerned about our depleted talent pool."

Surprised, I nodded. "Didn't realize it had reached that level. I did get a text from John Wills yesterday that he was leaving for a civil firm. I figured John would be a lifer in the office." Wills had sat second chair to me last summer when I had taken leave to prosecute Sheriff's Lieutenant Max Cort.

"John's resignation surprised me too." She hunched her shoulders in a what-are-you-going-to-do? gesture. "Hated to lose him. But the money out there in the private sector is good, and what we pay can't compete."

"But that's always been the case. Why now, and why are so many jumping ship?"

She shrugged. "We've done exit interviews. Some are being recruited by civil firms, some are hanging their shingles as defense lawyers, and a surprising number are leaving the state. Cost of housing, a more laid-back lifestyle, I guess." She shook her head. "We've always had attrition, but never on this scale. It's alarming."

"There's always new talent coming up through the ranks," I commiserated.

"My problem is at the top end. I need more aces. We can't afford to have the office outgunned. Especially when some of our former aces are now taking on a number of higher profile criminal defenses."

"So this is a recruiting pitch?"

"It is. And I'm not just talking to you but to a number of other top trial lawyers." She gave a tired laugh. "But not with much success."

"Nancy, you know I just came in last summer to try Cort. That was the extent of our deal, of my commitment." She and the DA himself had recruited me to temporarily join the office with the understanding that it would only be for the Cort prosecution. Sheriff's lieutenant Max Cort was prosecuted for murdering his wife and then concealing her body. Following a mistrial when the jurors could not reach a verdict, I was brought in for the retrial.

Seah put up her hands defensively. "You're absolutely right. You made no commitment beyond Cort."

"Besides"—I swept my arm toward the empty classroom—"as you just witnessed, I'm a law professor."

"I'm very aware of that. I'm also very aware that you loved every minute of being back in trial."

I gave her a skeptical look. "Except the part when a witness was killed and a gun battle raged outside the courtroom."

"Doesn't divert from what I'm saying. You know exactly what I'm talking about. I watched you. The courtroom is your element. I think that's where you belong."

Following an uncomfortable silence which I refused to fill, Seah continued. "I understand your work here at the law school is important, but it's not going to sustain you in the long term. You're a prosecutor through and through."

Was she right? I was still working that out.

I sat beside her and flashed back to the Cort trial. Max Cort was dead. And that was a good thing. Christie Cort and Willow Merkle were dead at Cort's hands, and those deaths were tragedies. Amazingly, for all the attendant national attention the Cort trial had received, it had now begun to fade to the back pages only a month or so later. New stories, new tragedies emerged to fill the void. Merci MacPherson, the brilliant lawyer who had defended Cort, was back in the San Francisco Bay Area. Duke, my pal and investigator of choice, was resettled back into his private investigation practice up north. Sherri Ossoff, the heroic district attorney investigator who had worked the Cort case with me, was promoted to chief DA investigator. And I was again in the classroom at Pacifico Law, teaching crimes and trial advocacy. And just to top things off, Lisa and I had gotten married.

"Nancy, you might be right. But I've carved out a different life here at the law school. Surrounded by twenty-three-year-olds, thirsty for learning. Little stress. Few deadlines. It's pretty much the perfect job."

Seah turned away and gazed around the classroom. "Jake, I think you like the stress, the deadlines, the constant hassle with judges and defense lawyers, and most of all, the trials." She turned back to me and, with a knowing smile, said, "How about that feeling you get when you stand and announce, 'Jake Clearwater for the People'?"

"Come on, Nancy." I put up my hands, exasperated. "Did you really think you could stroll in here, play to my ego, and that would be that?"

"Just hear me out. I've got what I think is a great proposition. Part one, you take a one-year leave of absence from Pacifico, starting this January after your current semester is over, and become one of our frontline prosecutors. One year," she emphasized. "And as an added inducement, I'll put you on the DA's Advisory Committee."

I sat back, caught off guard. "You'd make me one of the Elders?" The four prosecutors who comprised the Advisory Committee were euphemistically referred to as the Elders.

"I'm deadly serious, and I'm desperate. One of the four just retired. I'm throwing you a real bone here. Come on board."

The Advisory Committee wielded considerable power. They were the decision makers on all cases requiring special scrutiny. All murder cases throughout the sprawl of LA County were referred to the Advisory Committee. The committee decided which murder prosecutions would seek the death penalty, which were the worst of the worst. Even though California's current governor and his predecessor had placed moratoriums on executions, that didn't mean death penalty prosecutions stopped.

As a result of the moratorium, an inevitable backlog ensued. The most egregious murderers were still convicted and sentenced to death, only to languish in prison. If sometime down the line the moratorium on executions was lifted, then presumptively, executions would recommence. Meanwhile, California has stockpiled the most populous death row in the nation. It wasn't even close. Over seven hundred prisoners were incarcerated under sentence of death. In all likelihood, they would die of natural causes or take their own lives.

Some system we've built.

In addition to making all capital decisions, the committee members were also the final arbiters of other difficult and occasionally controversial cases. Cases that fell outside the typical. Some were high visibility, others on the periphery of criminal conduct. The committee was the nerve center of the district attorney's office. It was a hell of an inducement.

Her seduction was well underway.

"One year, you say?" My resolve to stay clear of the DA's office was wavering.

She nodded, knowing full well she had baited the hook just so. "And after a year, if you decide to return to teaching, I won't bother you again."

"Nancy, you just don't quit, do you?" I said, shaking my head in admiration.

"There's a reason I'm still chief of staff for my third elected district attorney." She stood and held out her hand to seal the deal.

I leaned back, avoiding her proffer. "Oh, no. I'm not making a decision on the spur of the moment."

She gave a what-else-can-I-say shrug and nodded. "I understand."

"Just so I have a complete picture. Salary and benefits?"

"You'd start as a level four with full benefits."

"It's enticing. But I need to think about it and talk to my wife."

She stared at me, surprised. "I didn't know you got married. Good for you, Jake." Then adding ruefully, "I tried marriage a couple of times, didn't work for me."

Was that last comment necessary or just plain inappropriate?

"Time for coffee?"

"Thanks anyway. I've got to get back to the office." As we were leaving the classroom, she turned and touched my shoulder. "If you accept, the committee meets once a month on the first Tuesday at 7:30 a.m. You can start with the meetings right away. I think you'll find them pretty challenging. We meet this upcoming Tuesday. Call me if you're coming in and I'll send you some files to look over."

CHAPTER 2

Back in my office, I primed my Keurig and called Lisa. Not surprisingly, I got her voicemail. As a middle school vice principal, her life was ridiculously busy. Our lives, in general, were unsettled. We were alternating weekends between her duplex in San Arcadia, ninety miles north of LA, and my third-story loft in Malibu. An hour-and-a-half drive separated us during optimum commuting hours. But it was at best a two-and-a-half-hour drive during our typical commuting times, late afternoons and early evenings into the teeth of the commute. Weirdly, it didn't seem to matter if the drive was north for me or south for Lisa. Commuting weekends between the two, with days apart in between, was becoming unsustainable. Solutions, however, were in short supply.

Lisa, my remarkable and talented spouse, could paint her world-class watercolors anywhere, but her position as a school administrator demanded forty to fifty hours a week in San Arcadia. Likewise, I was locked into Malibu and Pacifico, whether I accepted Seah's offer or not. Something had to give. I had noodled with the idea of moving back to San Arcadia and hanging a shingle so we could live under one roof. But the only law I know is criminal law. I couldn't probate a will, draft a contract, or work through a divorce to save my life.

Especially divorces. I tried that once for a former girlfriend.

Ugly, petty, never again. So if I hung a shingle, it would have to be exclusively as a defense lawyer. The big problem: I wanted no part of defense work.

As for pursuing a prosecuting position in San Arcadia, that was an absolute no-go. San Arcadia's district attorney, John Tice, and I harbored a mutual disdain. A disdain born while I was a deputy district attorney in San Arcadia under Tice, which grew even meaner after I left the office and successfully defended Duane Durgeon against capital charges. Tice had personally prosecuted the case. He was not a good loser. That had been my only foray as a defense lawyer. I wasn't built for defense work. Some attorneys were, and I admired that. Nothing is more stressful than being a criminal defense attorney.

Especially if you had an innocent client.

I thought of my work defending Durgeon as an aberration, an extension of my efforts to gain him a new trial following his wrongful death penalty conviction. Durgeon was to be the exception. Seah was right—I was a prosecutor at heart. Consequently, my options for moving north and living and working in San Arcadia were nil.

Likewise, Lisa's options were limited. She had worked diligently to become a vice principal, and there was no way she should give up such a hard-earned position. Seeing no immediate or even intermediate solutions, we kicked the can down the road and kept driving.

I called Tony Martin. "You free?"

"Sure, come on down."

I took my coffee and walked down three offices. Tony was short with a full head of silver hair. His thoughtful and sometimes deliberate demeanor was sometimes frustrating but always well-reasoned. He was a good friend and confidant. He was also my landlord. It was through his largesse that I was able to live in Malibu. My professor's salary fell short of sustaining a Malibu mortgage or lease. Tony and his wife, Eve, rented me the third-story loft of their three-story beach house. The loft had its own entrance, bathroom, and balcony. Tony was a man of independent means. I told him about the visit from Seah. He listened without comment until I had laid out the whole proposition. After a thoughtful pause, he said, "Let's deal with the personal side first. What about Lisa?"

"I called and got her voicemail. You know how busy she is. But from her perspective, things wouldn't change much. I'd still be working down here while she's up in San Arcadia. Of course, I'd have to get her blessing, but I don't see that being an issue. You know how supportive she is."

"I do. So, let's swing over to the practical. Pacifico?"

I had a commitment to the law school and Dean Chauncey. I was in the midst of my fall semester classes, teaching criminal law, criminal procedure, and trial advocacy. A heavy load—well, all things being relative, heavier than usual. I was covering criminal procedure for an ailing colleague. No matter my decision, I would, of course, finish the fall semester. "The dean will have sufficient time to make adjustments for the spring semester. I don't see him being an impediment."

He nodded in agreement. "Shouldn't be a problem."

"A couple of things really appeal to me," I said. "Being on the Advisory Committee focusing on capital cases and only making a one-year commitment are pluses. I like the idea of a test drive. And if things don't fit, I walk away after a year."

Studying my face, he said, "Whether you accept the offer or not, it doesn't change the fact that you and Lisa will still be living apart."

I put up my hands in frustration. "Yeah, I know."

Following another delayed response, Tony arched his eyebrows. "Seriously, back to being a prosecutor?"

"You know how much I enjoyed being back in the courtroom during the Cort trial."

"I do. I also recall how stressful it was for you."

I cocked my head. "Yeah, never a dull moment."

That evening, I decided to make the trek north to Lisa's place. I wanted to lay out Seah's offer in person and give Lisa a relaxed opportunity to voice any concerns. I was able to leave Malibu at four and got to Lisa's warm embrace a little after six. We shared a pretty good chardonnay and relaxed on her patio as I filled her in.

She was enthusiastic about the work of the committee. "You can really impact important decisions, especially death penalty decisions." We shared serious reservations about the efficacy of capital punishment.

"That's a big plus," I agreed. "But there are some downsides. I've got a comfortable schedule at Pacifico doing what I enjoy. But if I'm a prosecutor, I am either in the office or in a courtroom five days a week. There will be no six-week breaks over the winter holidays when, your schedule permitting, we can get away. Nor is there a twelve-week break over summer. It could cut into our time together."

"I don't see things being much more complicated or time-challenged than they are now. If that's where your heart is, I think you should go for it."

CHAPTER 3

Tuesday, October 5, 2018. 7:35 a.m. District attorney's conference room. There were four of us, fortified with Starbucks and pastries. Seah, the first among the four Elders, was our committee chair. She was dressed smartly in a dark tan Gucci suit and subdued neckwear.

She never seemed to have informal days. It came with the job.

Roger Hawthorne, a prosecutor with over two hundred trials under his belt, had thirty years in the office. He was a lifer; they'd carry him out of the office with his boots on. He was heavy set with a deep, commanding voice that was as blunt as a sledgehammer. From what I'd been told, jurors didn't always like him, but they usually agreed with him. He eyed me with thinly veiled hostility as I took a seat.

Who was this newbie inside our sacred club?

The third Elder was Leslie Mann. She started in the office the same year as Hawthorne and has headed up gang prosecutions for the past two decades. For her efforts, she had been targeted for execution by various gangs over the years. She remained unhurt and unfazed. She was short and Black with a modest Afro. She preferred bright colors and elaborate African necklaces. I'd also been warned that nobody crossed her.

It was a hardass, no-nonsense group.

Seah got us started. "Morning, everyone. I think both of you know Jake Clearwater. I'm sure you followed the Max Cort trial, which he took on for the office. He's coming aboard full time in January. And as of now, he'll be a part of our committee."

There were unenthusiastic nods. I suspected Hawthorne and Mann felt that my appointment to the committee hadn't been earned. I understood their lack of enthusiasm. It hadn't been earned. Without question, Seah had pulled rank to include me. She chose to ignore the cool—no, cold—reception I received, and carried on. "Roger, why don't you get us started?"

With a sharp, skeptical look at me, he began in a voice too big for the room. "Okay, we've got a tough one from our friends in the San Fernando Valley Bureau. What do we do with an eighty-nine-year-old man who plowed into people at a farmers' market, killing three, and injuring dozens of others?" I had read about the case. It had drawn serious media attention.

A long pause as we waited for Hawthorne to go on.

We didn't need a dramatic pause.

Finally, an irritable Seah said, "Give us some specifics, Roger. Don't dribble it out."

Hawthorne looked up from his notes. "It looks like he hit the accelerator instead of the brake."

"Drugs, medications, under the influence?" Seah prodded.

"Doesn't appear so," said Hawthorne.

"Eighty-nine?" Mann asked, shaking her head as if his age might explain everything.

Maybe it did.

"Let's see," said Hawthorne, distractedly checking his notes. It seemed as if he was not fully ready to brief us. Reminded me of an unprepared law student. "Yep, eighty-nine."

"Did he still have his license?" Mann again.

"He did," Hawthorne said. "What pushed this mess to us is that following the carnage, the old guy appeared completely in control of his senses but registered no remorse."

Three bodies? No remorse?

"Well, what exactly did he have to say for himself?" Seah again prodded.

"Nothing. He refused to discuss the matter with anyone and, when pressed, became belligerent. According to the responding officers, he was more concerned about the damage to his car than the trail of bodies and injuries in his wake."

As the new guy, I carefully ventured into the discussion. "Did the officers think he was just rattled and not fully understanding what had happened? Maybe in shock?"

Hawthorne gave me an appraising look. "I don't know. There's nothing in the report about the officers' impressions."

Seah asked, "Any history of traffic violations?"

Hawthorne again flipped through his notes. "A rear-ender a couple of months ago."

"Mechanical defects?" Seah again.

Hawthorne again checked his notes. If this had been one of my law students, I would have ridden him out of the room. "No report yet. But it's being checked out."

Mann pulled an I-don't-know face. "Eighty-nine. Do we do nothing and let the civil courts handle this?"

Seah shook off the suggestion. "Prosecuting a cantankerous old man is something I'm hesitant to wade into. But doing nothing sends the wrong message." She mused, "Three bodies."

"I agree," said Hawthorne, "we've got to weigh in on this. But before we do, and especially before we allow this to slip away into the civil courts, I suggest we order a full neurological workup of the old fella as well as a mechanical report on his car."

"I'm with you, Roger." Seah nodded in agreement. "I'd also like to take Jake's suggestion and have the on-scene officers offer their impressions. Let's push this back a month and see if we get some clarity."

Seah looked at Hawthorne. "I take it he's not in custody?"

Once again, Hawthorne leafed through his notes. "No, he's not. He's eighty-nine. The jail doesn't want him."

Seah followed up. "Even if we ultimately prosecute him, what then? I don't see someone this age being locked up. Hell, six months with this guy could be a death sentence."

Sometimes kicking the can down the road can be a good thing.

Seah looked around. There seemed to be a consensus. "Okay," she said. "Roger, get on top of this and we'll circle back at our next meeting." A not-so-subtle dig.

He nodded. Feeling her rebuke.

Seah turned to Mann. "Leslie, what do you have for us?"

"Here we go," she said, with a weary expression. "This is the case we've known was coming to our little group since it happened a few weeks ago." She checked her notes. "September 13." She looked up and began. "Devon Pouse, a sixteen-year-old from Excelsior High in the Valley, brought his semiautomatic handgun to school and shot and killed three other students."

"How could we not know about this? It was in every newspaper in the country," Hawthorne said, as he hunched his heavy shoulders and leaned forward. "This is as high-profile as it gets." He was more ready to engage than when he was briefing.

"Two momentous issues," said Mann, scanning our faces. "First, do we try Pouse as an adult or let him remain in the juvenile system? Second, should we even consider filing against the parents?"

No one spoke. Everyone recognized that our decisions on the two issues, especially concerning the parents, would generate considerable controversy, no matter which way we decided. This is the kind of case I envisioned when I signed on.

"Okay, Leslie, lay it out for us," Seah said.

"Just to reset." She cleared her throat. "Let's start with Devon Pouse. What do we do with a sixteen-year-old? Up until this, there had been no disciplinary issues. Pretty unremarkable, by all accounts. Apparently, guns and shooting are the norm with the Pouse family. Kay Pouse, Devon's mother, purchased a Glock semiautomatic handgun. Devon immediately posted photos of the gun on social media, saying, 'Just got my new beauty today.'"

"So, it's clear that the gun was purchased for the kid?" Hawthorne asked.

"That's a bit murky, but the kid seemed to think so," Mann answered.

Hawthorne grunted and motioned for Mann to continue.

"A week later, a teacher caught Devon searching for ammunition on the internet via his phone. He was pulled from class and his parents were called. According to the principal, the parents were too busy to come to the school. The principal opined that the parents didn't seem concerned. The principal confiscated the kid's phone and eventually sent him back to class. Later that same day, the mother responded with a text to her son: 'LOL, I'm not mad at you. You have to learn not to get caught.'"

"Amazing," said Seah, slowly shaking her head. "Don't get caught was her response? And that's seven days before the shootings? Did the school take any action?"

"No," said Mann. "On the day of the shooting seven days later, a teacher saw Devon with a drawing of a gun pointing at the words, 'I'm useless, help me. I hate them all.'"

"Neon lights should have been going off at the school," Seah muttered.

"You'd think," said Mann. "The kid was again brought to the principal, who again contacted the parents. This time, the principal insisted they come and get their son and schedule some counseling. The parents came, but for reasons unfathomable to me, the parents refused to take the boy home, and perhaps as surprising, the principal acquiesced. So Devon was sent off to complete his school day."

"Wait a minute," I said, shaking my head. I wanted absolute clarity. "The kid was sent back into his classes?"

"Remarkably enough, he was. And as Devon was being shuffled back to class, no one thought to check his backpack, which contained the handgun." The room went silent. We had all read the media reports, but these new revelations had been withheld.

Mann took a deep breath, almost as if apologizing for the hard facts. "A little over an hour later, Devon shot and killed three students."

Without waiting a beat, Hawthorne said, "Let's deal with the shooter first. I'm leaning toward finding him unfit for juvenile court and bumping him up with the adults." He was emphatic. "We've got three bodies and a semiautomatic weapon."

The DA makes the decision to determine if a minor will be dealt with as a juvenile or be tried as an adult. The decision is consequential. The state is charged with attempting to rehabilitate juveniles instead of punishing them.

How's that for an optimistic spin?

They are not packed off to prison but rather to juvenile detention centers. Adults, on the other hand, face hard prison time.

Seah held up her hand at Hawthorne. "Slow down, Roger. You may be right, but before we make the call, we need to undertake a careful evaluation. No knee-jerk decisions." She studied Hawthorne with a don't-dare-me look.

"Three bodies, Nancy!" Hawthorne dared.

Mann interceded like a third-party neutral. "Roger, Nancy's right. Let's take it slow and careful.

Hawthorne threw me a look and disdainfully asked, "How about you, Clearwater? Joining the chorus?"

What an ass.

"Yeah," I said, returning ire with ire, "I'd certainly like to discuss it." In the brief few minutes of this meeting Hawthorne had established himself not just as an ass but also a bully. I stared him down. I was apparently being forced to mark my territory early. I caught a faint grin from Seah.

Hawthorne sat back in his chair. That's the second time he had been called out. Was there some history here? Were these meetings typically contentious, or was this just episodic?

Or was Hawthorne just the blowhard ass he appeared to be?

Everyone in the room knew the factors in considering whether a juvenile should be bumped up and tried as an adult. Nonetheless, Mann felt compelled to read them out. "So, we have to consider the minor's level of criminal sophistication, whether he can be rehabilitated, his previous delinquent history, any previous attempts at rehabilitation, and finally, the circumstances and gravity of the alleged offense."

Unchastened and with no notion of how to read the room, Hawthorne said, "This is an unprovoked murder of three human beings. In my view, that makes it an easy call."

"Again, Roger, in the final analysis, you may be right. But we must work through the factors." Seah locked steely eyes on Hawthorne. He shrugged but didn't speak. Having made her point yet again, she turned to Mann and asked, "Leslie, criminal sophistication?"

Mann was ready and read on. "Criminal sophistication contemplates mental health, maturity, impetuosity, and the effect of familial pressure on the minor." She looked up. "In looking at these considerations, we've got to worry through the words and the drawing the school found just prior to the shooting. Seems as if he was calculating, even thoughtful. Were his words a warning that someone should have picked up on?"

"I think they were." I ventured into the fray. "Seems to me he was looking for help. Maybe someone to stop him." I considered my next sentence. Like the others, I had read the news accounts and had some familiarity with the facts.

"What I'm struggling with is why the school authorities did nothing. They saw his note and drawing. They had earlier caught him looking for ammunition. They could have sent him home. But because the parents insisted he stay at school, they ignored clear signs of danger. The school's conduct was, at best, questionable."

Seah shook her head. "Jake, I appreciate your observation, but at this point we're not evaluating the school's conduct or the parents' conduct. We'll get to those concerns later. Our first job here is to focus on whether this boy is to be tried as an adult. You drifted from that consideration."

Seah, taking charge. "As for the first factor"—she went on—"I believe he was lacking any degree of sophistication. Sophistication contemplates the ramifications of a person's conduct. How he might escape responsibility. From what little we know, it doesn't appear as if he thought about the consequences of his behavior."

"Was this just some dumbass kid contemplating the joys of his new toy?" Mann mused. "I'm conflicted on this first factor."

"Okay then, let's move to the other factors. Maybe we can get some clarification," said Seah, focusing the discussion.

"The next factor is his potential for rehabilitation," said Mann. "In other words, with counseling and therapy, will he mature?"

"That's real helpful," Hawthorne said with a sarcastic sneer.

"Let's throw him into a juvenile hall and speculate as to whether that'll straighten him out."

"Let's not be defeatist, Roger," Mann admonished. "He will certainly receive more counseling at the juvenile level than in a state prison."

"I'll concede that," said Hawthorne, with a slightly indulgent nod directed at Mann.

"I know this is not precisely on target," I asked, "but I'm thinking about how vulnerable this sixteen-year-old would be in prison. Leslie, how big is this kid?"

She studied her paperwork. "Not big. Apparently, he has not yet hit physical maturity. He's five-four and one hundred and thirty pounds."

"That's not a consideration," Hawthorne irritably pointed out.

"Well," I said matter-of-factly, "that's something I'm going to factor in, regardless of the stated considerations. This kid would be real vulnerable in prison."

Hawthorne grunted and shook his head.

Mann said, "Let's get back to the points we are to consider. The next two factors are pretty straightforward. They ask about delinquent history and prior attempts at rehabilitation. He's a first-timer. That weighs in his favor, and since he's a first-timer, there have been no prior attempts at rehab." She paused before moving on. "The final factor, as Roger keeps insisting, involves the circumstances and gravity of the alleged offense."

"I've said my piece here." Hawthorne didn't need to remind the group. "This was an unprovoked murder of three people. That's enough for me."

I looked deferentially at Seah and Mann before speaking. "Reluctantly I'm forced to agree. Even if he is in a bizarre family that encourages guns and shooting. Even if he is having anxiety issues, he would know you can't do what he did. I'm leaning toward trying him as an adult. Although I'm very concerned about his safety, should he be sentenced to prison? For me, the gravity of the shootings is too hard to get around."

Seah and Mann looked at me, then Hawthorne, and they silently nodded. There was no joy in the decision. Seah hunched her shoulders as if trying to shrug off the weight of the decision. "Let's take a break."

As I helped myself to coffee, Hawthorne came up behind me and put his hand on my shoulder and in a conciliatory tone. "Not a tough call."

"No, but still a difficult one," I responded.

He nodded and walked off.

An effort to welcome me?

Seah brought us back. "Okay, as difficult as that decision was, let's wade into the even tougher call. The parents. Leslie, I have a preliminary question. Do we know where the gun was kept in the house?"

"According to Devon's mother, in an unlocked drawer in the kitchen," Mann answered without referencing her notes. "I'm glad you asked. I looked up the safe-storage provision in California. Parents can be criminally charged if they keep an unlocked firearm on their property where children can access it. Seems we have a clear violation against the parents here."

I sat back in my chair, wondering if anyone would suggest that the parents only be cited for a safe-storage violation. When no one spoke, I felt compelled to weigh in.

"I trust no one is thinking about a safe-storage violation? A low-grade misdemeanor?" I asked incredulously. "We're not seriously considering allowing the parents to walk away with a slap on the wrist? We've got three bodies on our hands. I know I'm just getting started here, but we need to hold the parents accountable in these deaths. Looks to me that they did everything but fire the shots." I worked to keep my voice calm. "There's no question the school folks screwed up, but let's not absolve the parents."

Hawthorne was having no part of my argument. "Wait a moment," he blustered, "where are you coming from? Parents can't monitor their children all the time. And beyond that he was no child, he was sixteen." He stayed zeroed in on me. "Frankly, what did the parents know? The kid was looking for ammunition. That makes sense, and the family likes to shoot. What else do we have? Nothing. He didn't threaten to shoot anyone. He complained that he was confused. What teenagers aren't confused and muddled in their feelings from time to time? There were no red flags prior to the day of the shooting."

As I started to reply, Seah cut me off. "Roger, this isn't a situation where the parents were ignorant of their child's disturbances, and there was no significant notice of pending trouble. Seems to me that even in the hour or so before the shooting, these parents should have recognized the lethal combination of a disturbed and distraught teenager with immediate access to a semiautomatic weapon."

"This wasn't an act that materialized out of thin air," agreed Mann. "This was entirely preventable. The parents had several opportunities to prevent this tragedy and failed at every turn."

Before Hawthorne could respond, I jumped in. "Involuntary manslaughter requires that the defendant's conduct creates a high risk of death or even great bodily injury. The parents read his words, they knew he was disturbed, they knew he had access to an easily concealed handgun, which pushes me to involuntary manslaughter."

Hawthorne stood and paced. His face flushed with anger. He

took a moment to compose himself. "I couldn't disagree more. It's okay to have a gun in your house. It's commonplace for teenagers to say dramatic things and act out," he said through clenched teeth. "That doesn't mean they are going to kill. Charge the parents with failing to provide safe storage, but that should be the limit of their criminal liability. If the families of the victims want to sue the parents civilly, that's their prerogative. This case against the parents doesn't belong in a criminal courtroom."

I couldn't let it go. "I'm certain you've tried involuntary manslaughter cases. And I don't have to tell you that when an individual acts with gross negligence, with a kind of mean indifference that ends up with someone's death, that's involuntary manslaughter. That's what we have here. These parents acted with extreme carelessness and should be held accountable." I was in closing argument mode.

Hawthorne fought back. "Don't lecture me, rookie. You're damn right I've tried involuntary manslaughter cases, and they typically involve some dumbass doing very stupid things behind a wheel. Even if this group green-lights such a filing, it will not result in a conviction. Hell, the parents had no idea that gun was in his backpack."

Seah motioned for quiet. "Roger, looks like you're in the minority. They knew he was deeply disturbed after seeing that drawing and reading his words. They knew there was an unaccounted-for weapon which he could access." Seah concluded the debate. "Looks like involuntary manslaughter. Let's file it." Seah looked at me as if sizing me up. "Jake, by the time this case starts squaring up for trial, you should be on board. I'd like you to prosecute these cases against the juvenile and his parents."

Looking directly at Hawthorne, I replied, "I'd be pleased to."

Hawthorne wasn't done and in a more conciliatory tone said, "Let me make a suggestion. In addition to manslaughter, file a second count against both parents for violating the safe-storage statute. If you fail on manslaughter, you've got them for something."

Seah replied, "Roger, you know that's a no-go. If we give the jurors an opportunity to compromise their verdict, there's a good chance they'll go for it. We've got three bodies. We're all in on manslaughter."

CHAPTER 4

The following morning, as the sun was rising over the LA Basin haze, I trotted down to the Malibu Pier. Four upper division law students were waiting for me. Without a word, with only nods serving as greetings, we jogged into the cold surf, ducked under some small swells, and headed out around the pier. Vanessa Clemens, one of my favorite third-years, set a demanding pace. We rounded the pier, and the old grizzled fisherman who seemed a permanent fixture at the end of the pier waved us on.

I had been swimming the pier since I started at Pacifico. Three times a week, Mondays, Wednesdays, and Fridays. Several years ago, my first-year criminal law class had caught wind of my swims and all of a sudden, I had company. The tradition had continued. Vanessa and the other three were former collegiate swimmers who liked the idea of staying in shape with ocean swimming rather than Pacifico's Olympic pool. From my perspective, it was stimulating having swimming companions. But damn, the water was cold.

As we were drying off and doing our beach change, I asked the students how their classes were going. Evidence seemed to be the prime challenge. They had just moved into the Hearsay Rule and were fighting that elusive concept. I offered some pointers and invited them to my office to help any way I could.

Two hours later, I was in Auditorium C, in front of my sixty-five-student second-year criminal procedure class. We had just broken the seal on *Miranda*.

I started with Gerald, a bright and enthusiastic student sitting front and center. "Okay, Gerald, before we get into Chief Justice Warren's *Miranda* holding, let's first talk about the history behind the admissibility of confessions."

He was ready. "As we read the cases leading up to *Miranda*, it seemed to me that none of the other approaches in dealing with the admissibility of confessions were particularly workable."

I gestured with my hands. "Give me an example."

"There were the cases that excluded confessions once a suspect was represented by counsel."

"What's the problem with that approach?"

Without hesitation: "It had only limited applicability. Most confessions and other incriminating statements made by suspects occur before the suspects are represented."

"Why's that?"

"Suspects are frequently interrogated in the field or back at the station before they're charged or have a lawyer. From reading Warren's *Miranda* opinion, that involves the overwhelming number of cases."

I nodded approval and walked to the left of the class. "Teresa, let's build on that. What other approaches had been explored prior to *Miranda*?"

She hesitated just a tick. "There was a due process approach in which the courts would look to see if the confession was coerced."

"Coerced, how?"

"You assigned one extreme case in which a suspect was denied food and water and held under stressful conditions until he agreed to confess."

"What about cases that didn't involve such extreme measures?"

"As Justice Warren pointed out, the police may utilize any manner of interrogation techniques to elicit confessions, such as long interrogations intended to break down resistance."

"Was Miranda himself under coercion?"

Tough question.

She considered whether I was baiting her into a trap. Tentatively, she answered, "Yes."

"Okay, let's look at the circumstances confronting Ernesto Miranda himself. Lay it out for us."

"Okay, the police suspected Miranda had committed a rape but didn't feel they had sufficient evidence against him for an arrest. He was held for hours in a closed interrogation room until he signed a suspicious-looking document allegedly written by him, claiming he had committed the rape."

"Coercion?"

"It didn't appear that he had been beaten or even threatened."

I asked again, "Coercion?"

She sucked in breath. "He was isolated with several detectives over a period of hours."

"Coerced?" I repeated.

"Yeah, I guess one could argue that the circumstances might call into question whether his confession was coerced rather than the product of his free will."

I stopped within five feet of her. "Teresa, it's time to commit. Was he coerced?"

"Probably."

I smiled at her soft response. "Would you agree that the question of coercion might sometimes be difficult to ascertain?"

"Yes." She grinned back at me. "As you just demonstrated with your questions."

I looked around the room and landed on Erica, a shy woman who refused to make eye contact in what I believed was an effort not to be called on. I threw her a softball. "Erica, what approach did Chief Justice Warren and his eight colleagues come up with to solve the problem of coerced confessions?"

She stammered, looked down at her notes, and quietly said, "The police must give suspects a warning before their statement is admissible."

A weak start, stay with her.

"And that's the *Miranda* warning we are all familiar with, right?" She nodded. "But I want to back up. When must the warning be given?"

Another softball.

She hesitated, and then, in a low, uncertain voice, "Anytime a suspect is in police custody."

It was painful to draw her out, but she seemed to be holding up.

"That's part of it. How do we know when a suspect is in police custody?"

This was a tougher question. The Court's *Miranda* opinion didn't define custody. I gave her a minute to worry through an answer. To her credit, she looked up at me and, in a stronger voice, said, "It doesn't mean the suspect has to be under arrest. From what I gathered from the cases following *Miranda*, it seems to be anytime a person doesn't feel they can simply walk away from the police without being stopped."

Right on the screws.

"Spot on, Erica." I nodded approvingly and worked my way to the other side of the classroom. "Matt, let's follow up. So if a person gives a confession while in custody, is it inadmissible against her at her trial?"

Matt, one of the top students, was right on top of my inquiry.

"Not necessarily. In addition to being in custody, questioning by the police has to be underway."

"Shake that out for me."

"Sure. The Court said the confession would be inadmissible if it occurred during a custodial interrogation." I looked quizzically at him and motioned with my hands for him to further explain. "Not only must the suspect be in custody, but the police must be questioning him."

"So custody is not sufficient?"

"No, an interrogation must be underway."

"Interrogations sound pretty formal. Are we talking about taking the suspect to the station for formal questioning?"

"The way I understand it, any questioning at any time or place with a suspect who is in custody will bring the case within *Miranda*."

Natasha raised her hand. She was a tall, collected woman who didn't lack for confidence. "I'm a little confused. We keep using the term 'interrogations.' What if the cop asked a guy hanging around a convenience store at eleven p.m., 'What are you doing here?' Is that an interrogation?" She was referring to a hypothetical situation I had used earlier in the semester in discussing reasonable suspicion.

I ricocheted the question to Matt. "Matt, an interrogation?"

"Probably. Subsequent cases have told us that an interrogation occurs anytime a cop asks the suspect something that is reasonably likely to elicit an incriminating response."

"Natasha, does that help?"

Shaking her head, she said, "I remember reading that phrase and thinking, 'How do we know when a statement by a cop is likely to provoke something incriminating?'"

"Terrific question. Anyone want to pick it up?" No immediate takers. I scanned along the back row and landed on Raul, one of the back-row denizens trying to stay off my radar. "Raul, help me out. How do we know when a statement from a cop will provoke something incriminating?"

He surprised me by standing, bobbing up and down like he was balancing on his toes. "We've been talking all semester about looking at the surrounding circumstances in an attempt to ascertain what someone might be thinking at any one time. Examine the surrounding circumstances," he said with complete conviction. "Seems that approach should work here. Look at the circumstances to figure out what people are thinking and why they are acting the way they do."

He seemed to be venturing off topic, but I let him go on to see if there was a point to be made. "A guy outside a store late at night might or might not be planning to rob. The cop by approaching and asking what he is doing might be attempting to get him to say something incriminating." He paused, groping for the right words. "The cop isn't just passing the time. From the surrounding circumstances, it's clear he's investigating a potential crime and his remarks are intended to get something incriminating."

He managed to tie it up.

"Well thought out, Raul." I stepped back to Erica. Now that the pump was primed, I wanted to follow up. "Erica, can you help us understand when statements made by the police may be an attempt to elicit something incriminatory?"

She was surprised I had come back to her. "Are you referring to the Christian Burial Speech case?"

That's what I was looking for.

"Give me the facts."

"Okay." She took a fortifying breath. I suspect this was the most Erica had ever spoken in a law school class. "A young girl was missing, and the police were pretty certain that the defendant Williams took her and murdered her. The girl's body had not been found. Williams was taken into custody, charged with her abduction and murder, and provided a lawyer." She hesitated, on the verge of hyperventilating.

Damn it, Clearwater, back off.

But as I turned to call on someone else, she continued, "For some reason, the police had to transport Williams to another city an hour or so away," she said, picking up momentum. "During the drive, the detective began talking to Williams and told him a winter storm was on the way that would cover the girl's dead body until spring. The detective said that the girl's parents wanted to find her body before it would be covered with snow so they could provide her a Christian burial. Williams broke down and agreed to lead the police to the girl's body."

Wow! The pump had indeed been primed.

"What do you think, Erica? Was the detective's speech conduct reasonably likely to elicit an incriminating response? Should the fact that Williams led them to the body be admissible under *Miranda*?"

She locked eyes on me. "The Court said it was an interrogation because Williams was susceptible to the detective's speech."

"From your answer, I'm not sure you agree."

"It seems like they're stretching things." She shook her head and actually smiled. "I guess I'm not sure the detective's comment would lead him to talk."

"Good job, Erica. There are a lot of people who would agree with you." I stepped back. "How about someone to defend the Court's decision?"

Several hands went up. "Jacob, what've you got?"

"The detective knew that Williams was a religious man and that he might be susceptible to the idea of a Christian burial. In my mind, that was a significant factor. The cop played to that, and I think that's what pushed this into an interrogation."

"So, if Williams wasn't a religious man, would this have been conduct that elicited his response?"

"I don't think so. It was the appeal to a religious man asking him to do the right thing." Jacob turned to the back of the room and looked at Raul. "Just like Raul said, looking at the surrounding circumstances gives us the insight we need." He nodded to Raul. "Thanks, brother."

Raul stood and saluted.

"Point taken," I said. "Williams pushes the envelope about as far as it can be pushed. I've got one more scenario. Let's go back to the scenario Natasha raised with our cop approaching a man hanging out late at night near the convenience store entrance. What if the cop doesn't say anything but gets right in the guy's face? And the guy blurts out something incriminating." I paused, letting the facts sink in. "Can mere conduct without words constitute custodial interrogation?"

A flurry of hands. I waved them off. "That's it for today. We'll pick it up next class."

Good to leave them with a provocative question.

CHAPTER 5

November 7, 2018. My second meeting with the committee. Seah had directed a case file to me to work up and present to my fellow Elders. It involved the two-year-old murder of Tracie Switzer, an eighteen-year-old student at Pomona-Pitzer College. The murder investigation hadn't quite gone cold and had recently resurfaced when a jailhouse informant claimed he had some information about the murder.

In preparing my briefing for the committee, I read the police report detailing the investigation. Switzer's body, with her throat cut, was found in the passenger seat of her pickup truck on a turnout on a mountain road. Five hundred dollars had been withdrawn from her account using her ATM card at 9:35 the night before her body was discovered. The ATM camera displayed a grainy image of what appeared to be a Black man activating the machine and taking the cash. From the poor quality of the photo, investigators had not been able to identify the man.

No physical evidence was developed from the scene of the murder. No fingerprints, no DNA. The investigation had stalled for nearly twenty-four months, until Dinold Melrose, a man in custody and awaiting trial for robbery, reached out to sheriff's investigators. Melrose claimed he could provide information on "that white girl in the pickup, killed on some turnout on a mountain road a couple of years ago."

Sheriff's Detective Armand Coolidge interviewed Melrose and was of the opinion Melrose's information may have some merit. Melrose was able to detail some specifics. Without naming names, Melrose claimed that while he and an unnamed friend were driving in the Riverside area on the night Tracie Switzer was killed, they had stopped at a liquor store and had run into a man Melrose knew from the area. The man asked Melrose to give him a ride to Pomona. Melrose claimed the man was a "crazy mean motherfucker" and didn't feel he could refuse.

During the drive, the man said he was going to sell drugs to some people he knew. Melrose said the man directed him to drop him at the Pomona Mall and then wait for him to return. Melrose explained that he complied out of fear. A half hour later, the man drove up in a red Toyota pickup and ordered Melrose to hand over the keys to Melrose's car and for Melrose to follow in the pickup. Melrose said the man complained he had trouble driving the truck. 'It's a goddamned manual.' Per the man's order, Melrose's companion remained in the passenger seat of Melrose's car. When Melrose climbed into the truck, he saw a woman lying facedown on the back floorboard of the extended cab. She was gagged, her hands tied behind her back.

Melrose, driving the truck, followed the man driving Melrose's car as they entered a freeway, drove east, and got off on some unknown mountain road. After a couple of miles, the guy pulled onto a turnoff, and Melrose followed in the truck. At the turnout, the man pulled the woman from the back of the truck, sat her in the passenger seat, and "quick as a flash" jerked at the woman's head. 'Spraying blood everywhere.' The man stepped away and threw something over the cliff. He ordered Melrose and his companion back into Melrose's car, and they drove off.

Detective Coolidge believed there were sufficient corroborating facts to negotiate a deal with Melrose to disclose the identities of the killer and Melrose's companion. Melrose and his lawyer wanted a one-year cap on his pending robbery and complete immunity on the Switzer murder.

In preparation for my report to the Elders, I drove to Pomona's sheriff's station. I wanted to meet Coolidge to get a better sense of the case. The tall, slender thirteen-year veteran of the sheriff's department, radiated competence, he didn't seem like someone who would be taken in by some jailhouse snitch, but I needed to fill in some gaps. "Detective, what information did Melrose provide that wasn't disclosed to the public?"

"The specific location of the murder, and that Switzer was found sitting in the passenger seat of her truck."

"Color of the truck?"

"It had somehow leaked out that it was a red Toyota."

"How about manner of death?"

"Melrose was vague about that. He said the suspect pulled on her hair and made a jerking motion at her. But that wasn't disclosed."

"Was that when her throat was cut?"

"As far as I can figure."

"How about any specifics about a possible motive, other than the money taken from the ATM?"

"Nothing, but the local paper surmised that it must have been a robbery gone bad."

"Fair assumption."

"Agreed."

I studied the grisly crime-scene photographs and asked, "What do you think, is this Melrose character the real deal?"

"I think so. But we've all been burned with these jailhouse snitches." Coolidge paused, considering. "I've worked this case since we found Tracie's body. Her murder has really stuck with me. Maybe I'm not as objective about trusting this guy as I should be."

"Can't blame you. I imagine you've dealt with the family."

"Yeah, nicest folks you'll ever meet."

I nodded my understanding. "Tell me about Melrose's pending robbery case. Solid?"

"Absolutely, and he's also got several dope knocks we can pile on to jack up his sentence. He's looking at some serious time. It's easy to see why he's willing to turn snitch."

"I'm stuck on giving Melrose immunity on the murder. He was driving Tracie's truck with her in the back. I don't care that he might have been intimidated. This guy doesn't walk clean from a murder."

Coolidge shrugged agreement. "Yeah, but without him I've got no way of moving on the murder."

"I understand," I said. "I'm going to take this up with the committee at our next meeting. I'll get back to you."

Following my briefing, I looked at the Elders. Hawthorne was the first to react. "I hate jailhouse snitch cases. I personally have been burned using these manipulative dirtbags. They'll do pretty much anything to get out from under some hard time. Seems like from what you've gathered, this Melrose character is looking at better than a decade on the robbery with the dope enhancers."

"I hear you, Roger," said Seah. "But on the other hand, there is a bit of corroboration, and it is a murder case."

"What has he really told us?" Was Hawthorne always a contrarian? The red pickup, which was disclosed in the media, as well as the location of the body on some turnout, which was also disclosed." He shook his head dismissively. "Did he say anything about the ATM robbery?"

"No," I answered. "According to Coolidge, Melrose said the killer ordered Melrose and the guy he was with to stay put while he walked off. So Melrose would know nothing about the ATM robbery."

"Jake, are you pushing this?" asked Mann. "I'm leaning with Roger on this one." She looked at Roger and shrugged. "Just not enough here. Jailhouse snitches are a low form of life, and it sounds to me that this snitch would have to be a big part of the prosecution case. He'll get chewed up at trial."

"I know this is only my second meeting," I said somewhat defensively, "but I do have years as a prosecutor under my belt. I've used snitches before, and for the most part, it's worked out. For what it's worth, I'd trade a robbery conviction for a murder conviction every day. Tracie Switzer was eighteen, a complete innocent. Wrong place, wrong time."

Seah weighed in. "Jake, I'm afraid I've got to agree with Roger and Leslie. There's not enough here to convince me that this snitch was even there. Without more, we've got to pass." She shook her head. "Unless your detective can come up with a lot more, this guy gets no deal."

Coolidge took it hard when I called. "Shit, we've got a stone-cold killer out there and we're afraid to make a move."

"I understand your frustration. I feel it, too. With some additional corroboration, we could take it back to the committee."

"Screw that!" he said bitterly. "I've been working on this case for two years. I've been dealing with Tracie's parents all that time." Long pause. "Thanks for giving it a shot."

Meanwhile, Melrose pled guilty to the pending robbery and was sentenced to ten years.

CHAPTER 6

Three weeks later, I received a message that Coolidge had tried to reach me while I was in class. I was hopeful as I returned the call. "Detective, what've you got?"

"I've got more corroboration on the Tracie Switzer murder."

"Great news. Let's hear it."

"Melrose pled and was sentenced, so now he's looking to get some reduced time. He and his lawyer met and returned with the name of the other guy who was there. Name's Glen Bridge. I was able to locate Bridge in Ely State Prison, Nevada's maximum security facility. Melrose claims that Bridge will be able to corroborate his account."

"Detective, I appreciate the effort, but how do we know that Melrose and this new guy didn't just get together and concoct the same story?"

Coolidge had already considered that. "Because this other guy, Bridge, stupid shit that he is, was arrested in Las Vegas two years ago for robbery just a couple of days after Tracie was killed. He's doing better than a decade. As far as I can make out, there was no connection between these two scumbags since the murder. No time for them to get their stories straight."

"Huh," I said, thinking this through. "This might work." My mind was racing. "Where the hell is Ely State Prison, anyway?"

"I Googled it. It's just north of the town of Ely, which is in the far east of Nevada, tucked right up against the Utah border."

"Not particularly convenient."

"Turns out there's an airport in Ely. And perhaps most surprising, Southwest flies there from Burbank."

"Let's go see this guy. This might be our ticket." I knew there would be questions from the Elders about this Bridge character. I wanted to see for myself.

It was a murder case, worth the effort.

Two days later, Coolidge and I were escorted into an otherwise empty visitor's room where Glen Bridge sat, his wrists manacled to a metal table. The drive from the airport had featured lots of scrub and not much else. In my Google search I learned the town of Ely claims it has "the loneliest road in America."

Now that's a distinction worthy of a billboard.

Our nine-mile drive from the airport to the prison was a testament to that auspicious claim. The prison was relatively new, distinctive only in its non-distinction. It had all the pizzazz of an Amazon warehouse.

Bridge was Black, slight and short with an Afro that overwhelmed his small head. His face was nearly cocooned inside his hair. He looked at us with frank surprise. He had no idea who we were or why we were there. Coolidge and I had agreed that he would take the lead. I was to be a mere spectator.

"Mr. Bridge, I'm Detective Coolidge with the Los Angeles County Sheriff's Department, and this is Jake Clearwater, a prosecutor from LA County. We're investigating a murder that took place a while back in Southern California, and we're here to see if you can help our investigation."

True to cons since time immemorial, Bridge's initial response was complete denial.

Of course it was. He had a long tradition to uphold.

"I don't know shit about no murder. You got nothing on me." He tried to raise his hands to signal his innocence but the manacles jerked his hands short.

Undaunted by Bridge's predictable denial, Coolidge put a small recorder on the table and clicked it on. "Mr. Bridge, we're going to record this conversation."

"You can record all you want. I don't know nothing 'bout some murder."

"Well, Mr. Bridge, you do know something and we're here to find out what that is." Coolidge spread his hands on the table. "And with some cooperation from you, we may be in a position to help you out."

"What do you mean?" His voice was suddenly and carefully hopeful. We had his attention.

"A couple of years ago. Pomona area. White girl."

Bridge gave Coolidge a wary look. "How'd you come up with my name?"

"You tell us," Coolidge said.

"No, you tell me."

"I've got a blast from your past. Dinold Melrose. Ring a bell?"

Bridge arched his eyebrows into his Afro. His wheels were turning. "I've still got ten more years in this goddamn place. What are you looking for?"

Talk about turning on a dime.

Bridge locked onto Coolidge and then me. He was figuring out the angles. "I'm listening. What can you two California people do for me in this Nevada stink hole?"

"If you give us some help on the murder, we might be able to cut some years off the time you're still looking at."

He guffawed. "'Might be able to' don't cut no ice. I need a lot more than that to turn snitch." Bridge was sensing an advantage.

"Tell you what, Bridge. Do you want to explore this a bit further, or do you want us to walk out of here so you can enjoy your time in this fine facility?"

"Bullshit!" He shook his head emphatically. "You two have come to the end of the world to see me. I don't see you walking away that easy."

This streetwise con had more savvy than I would have figured.

"You give us information about the murder and our next visit will be with your lawyer to work out a deal."

"You think you can knock off some years?" He looked skeptical. "These motherfuckin' cowboys in Nevada are tough."

"We can work with them," Coolidge said. "But first we need to know if it's worth our effort."

"Oh, it'll be worth the effort." He sat back as if he had accomplished something momentous. "It'll be worth it." Then he twisted his small head and pulled a face. "I get involved, I don't want no part of any murder rap. I need to steer clear of that."

"Like I said, we can work on that." Coolidge brushed past Bridge's concern.

"That'll be part of the deal?" Bridge pressed.

"Everything will be on the table."

"Di, huh?" He shook his head.

"Yeah, Dinold Melrose. I'm sure he sends his best."

"Figured." He looked off to his left at nothing, just absorbing the information. "That stupid sonofabitch. Di must have got himself jammed up."

Once again, a quick study.

"Yeah, I guess he did," confirmed Coolidge.

"What did Di tell you?"

"Enough that we're talking to you."

"What's he looking at?"

"That's not important to our discussion with you." Coolidge leaned into Bridge. "We need you to tell us about that night. We need names and details."

"Couldn't get enough from Di, huh?"

Coolidge's tone turned mean. "Don't be an asshole, Bridge. We're here talking to you. Figure it out! We need enough from you to convince us you were even there. Once, and if, we're convinced, we'll talk about a deal. Capeesh?"

Capeesh?

"What about the murder rap? I can't go down on that."

Couldn't blame him for coming back to the murder. He wanted some clarity.

"Like I just said"—Coolidge tapped the table with his fingers—"everything is in play. It's your move, so quit dicking around."

Bridge took in a deep breath. "Okay, but no names until we've got a deal."

"Convince us that we're not wasting our time."

"Let me give you a taste. Me and Di were driving around sharing a blunt when we see this guy hanging in front of a liquor store. The guy motions us over. Di pulls in, gets out and talks with the guy. Next thing I know, the guy's in the back seat and we're driving around."

"What's the guy's name?"

Bridge laughed. "Now you're the one dicking around. You want to hear what I have to say?" He delicately touched the table with his fingers, mocking Coolidge's earlier admonishment. "I'll give you other stuff, but no names."

"Go on," said Coolidge, with restrained professionalism.

Bridge nodded, his point made. "Like I said, we were driving around smoking and kickin' back when the guy told Di that he needed a ride to Pomona to sell dope. Di seemed to be okay with that. Once we were in Pomona, the guy told Di to pull over near some mall. The guy gets out and tells us to hang out there until he gets back. I thought it was strange, so I asked Di, 'What's happening?' Di says, 'I'm doing what he says.' So I asked him why."

"He said the guy is a mean motherfucker. He's always packing. That got me nerved out. I wanted to leave but I had no way to get back to Riverside."

"Then what?"

"Me and Di did another blunt and hung out. Next thing I know, a car pulls up behind us. At first I thought it was the police. All I could see was headlights. Me and Di were rolling down windows and tossin' stuff. Turns out it was him."

"Tell us about the car." Coolidge, crossing T's and dotting I's.

"It was a pickup. Red. He told Di to drive the truck. Said the manual transmission screwed him up."

"What do you mean screwed him up?"

"The dumbshit was having trouble driving a stick shift."

Coolidge gave me a look. That detail corroborated Melrose's account.

Bridge was there.

In an indifferent tone, as if nothing significant had happened, Coolidge urged Bridge to continue.

"Di got into the truck and followed us."

"So who was in Melrose's car?"

"Just me and the guy. He was driving."

"Anybody talking? Did you ask where the truck came from?"

"Not a chance. Not after Di had warned me about the guy."

"Where'd you go?"

"I don't know. After a while, we're in the mountains, and he pulls off on some turnout. The truck pulled in behind us. We get out. Next, I see the guy pulling some girl out of the back of the truck and shoving her onto the passenger seat of the truck. I'm wondering what the fuck. That's the first I'd seen of her. Then he grabs her hair and it looked like he hit her. I couldn't see real clear. Looked like her head fell forward."

"What happened then?"

"He comes back to us and told us to get into Di's car and we drove off."

"Left the truck there?"

"Yeah."

"Where'd you go?"

"Back to Riverside. When he got out he pulled a gun from under his shirt. 'You motherfuckers didn't see me tonight. Right?' We agreed and drove off."

"When did you find out the girl had been murdered?"

"I didn't. I just figured she was dead." He paused. "But you got to believe I had nothing to do with it."

"Right." Coolidge shook his head.

CHAPTER 7

I asked Seah to schedule a committee meeting for later that week to present the newly developed facts. When I explained to Seah that Coolidge and I flew to Nevada and interviewed Glen Bridge, Seah's eyes grew wide.

"You went to Nevada? This is the first I've heard of this. You haven't even started with the office yet."

How dare I not ask Big Sister for permission?

"That's right." I said matter-of-factly. "I needed to hear for myself if this guy witnessed the murder, and if he did, could he be trusted as a witness." I kept my eyes on Seah and finished, "I figured if Bridge panned out, we had two corroborating witnesses. With two, we've got a shot."

Seah sat back. "Next time, I'd like to be in the loop."

She was hung up on my trip instead of focusing on what had developed.

"Get over it, Nancy. It's a murder case," I said, with an unapologetic grin. "I wanted to have a clear idea if we could believe and trust this guy," adding, "I knew the three of you would question me about him as a witness."

At the meeting the next day, Hawthorne gave me an admiring look. "Good for you, Clearwater, I'm impressed with your initiative.

But as much as I admire your efforts, I remain skeptical. We don't know that your two witnesses didn't get together and concoct the same story."

"I appreciate your concerns, but Bridge is doing a twelve-year stretch in Nevada. He's been in custody in Nevada since September 8, 2016, five days after the Switzer girl was murdered. There doesn't appear to have been any time for Melrose and Bridge to work out corroborating stories."

Hawthorne nodded thoughtfully. "All right, I'm starting to come around. Two independent snitches could push this over the goal line." While Hawthorne appeared to be leaning my way, Seah and Mann had yet to weigh in.

"Wait a minute, guys," Mann cautioned. "Let's discuss the viability of a murder prosecution so heavily dependent on snitches. As you both know," she said, looking at Hawthorne and then me, "I'm in the gang prosecution business. Lot of our cases involve informants. Jurors don't like informants," she lectured. "Informants get crucified by defense lawyers." She stopped to assess how her words were registering.

Her arrogant professorial tone grated on me and, I suspect, on Hawthorne.

I responded caustically. "I don't need a 101 lecture on the difficulties in using informants." I lifted my chin, looking her in the eye. "I'm not a rookie."

She pulled back, not expecting the new guy to call her out. She studied me and slowly shook her head. "My apologies if I sounded a bit brusque," she said, without conviction. "I just wanted us all to be aware of the hazards of informant-based prosecutions."

Why in the hell did she think I flew to Nevada to get Bridge's story and assess his credibility?

I was about to respond when Seah cut me off. "Enough back and forth. Leslie, you were out of line. Maybe I didn't make it clear. Jake is a seasoned prosecutor and a hell of a trial lawyer. I'll have no more of anyone's disrespect toward any member of this committee." She gave Mann and Hawthorne hard looks. She waited to see if anyone dared cross her. No one spoke. "So let's move the discussion to the independent facts on which the informant testimony would hang."

Pointedly turning to me, "Okay, Jake, lay it out for us."

I let the moment linger for just a bit. I hadn't really experienced this side of Seah. She was the alpha, and her rebuke of Mann made that crystal clear. "First off, we have two snitches, which by itself is unusual and significant. Second, their accounts match up pretty well. And to Roger's point, they didn't have the opportunity to sync their stories. As for independent facts, we've got the distinctive location of the murder *on a turnout* in the mountains up from Pomona. That precise location was not disclosed to the media."

I stopped to field any questions. Nothing so far. "We've got the independent accounts of the suspect disappearing when the ATM was hit, including a time stamp from the machine. We've got two identical accounts of the suspect driving up in Switzer's truck. Both informants discuss that the male suspect told Melrose to drive the truck, and they offered nearly identical accounts of the male suspect cutting Tracie's throat." I looked at the three faces. "I'm certain there are more points of similarity, but those are just off the top of my head."

Hawthorne said, "Clearwater, like Leslie said, your witnesses are going to get pounded, but I think it's worth the risk going forward."

Hawthorne an ally?

Mann looked at me skeptically and, in an even tone, said, "It'll be a hard prosecution. But like you said, it's a murder case. I'll relent if you think you can make it." She looked deferentially over at Seah. "What do you think, Nancy?"

Seah nodded. "I agree, but working out deals for these snitches may prove difficult. Jake, I want you to get this group's okay before you commit to any deals. One other thing: getting Nevada to reduce their sentence on Bridge could prove dicey. We're stepping on another state's autonomy. But, with all that said"—she smiled at me—"if you can pull off a successful negotiation, you've caught yourself another case. You're going to be busy once you come on board in January."

CHAPTER 8

I started with Melrose's lawyer, Kathleen Course, a veteran deputy public defender. She seemed reasonable and capable. She was not some starry-eyed new recruit who demanded to go to the mat on every case. I laid out my position, making it clear that the terms were tentative until I received clearance from above. "A three-year reduction on the robbery he just pled on, we don't file the drug enhancers, and three years concurrent as an accessory on the Switzer murder."

She took it in without interruption. "How about five years cut from the robbery?"

She knew that was a no-go. But what the hell, push the envelope. Better to have tried . . .

I smiled at her effort and shook my head. "I just laid out the best offer you're going to get. We're talking robbery and murder. It's a good deal for Melrose. And let me add two more conditions. The other guy, Bridge, has to come on board. No Bridge, no deal."

Course gave a sardonic grin. "I understand. You can't make your case without both of them?" Not waiting for a response, she added, "You've got your hands full getting cooperation from Nevada in reducing Bridge's sentence. I've been involved in a couple of those interstate deals, lots of resistance."

"Melrose better hope I can pull it off," I responded. The other condition is full cooperation. Melrose makes me break a sweat. We're back to ground zero."

"That's understood," she replied. "I'll get back to you."

I got the name of Bridge's lawyer from Detective Coolidge and called. Norm Michaels was a conflict lawyer based in Las Vegas. He was a private counsel who picked up cases the public defender couldn't handle for any number of reasons. Bridge's robbery trial had occurred in Vegas.

After identifying myself and exchanging pleasantries, I laid out my proposal. Three years off his Nevada sentence and plead his client to three years as an accessory on the Switzer murder, the murder sentence to run concurrent with his robbery time. Once again, I cautioned that I was only authorized to make a tentative offer pending approval from my office. The offer, of course, was contingent on Nevada reducing his sentence. I made it clear that I would blow up the deal if Bridge was anything less than fully cooperative.

Michaels didn't push back and said he would travel to Ely and discuss the offer with his client. But he felt confident that Bridge would be on board. He cautioned, however, on whether the judge who had sentenced Bridge would agree to reduce the sentence. "I know that judge, and she's a tough woman and doesn't much care for anything California."

Warnings around every corner.

"Have you been involved in one of these interstate witness scenarios?" I asked.

"Not personally, but it's not so much the interstate clearance for a witness to testify that you've got to fight through, but getting the judge to reduce a Nevada-imposed sentence. That's where the fight will be. Wish you luck."

I emailed the deals I had discussed with the defense lawyers to the Elders. They were on board.

I went back to Melrose's lawyer first. Melrose wanted the deal. I set up a meeting at the jail with Melrose, his lawyer, and Coolidge to suss out the full story, including the name of the killer. Before he would talk, Melrose demanded to be put into protective custody. If word got out that he was snitching, he was legitimately concerned for his safety.

Couldn't blame him for that.

Coolidge agreed, and we were underway.

I looked expectantly at Coolidge and then Melrose, wondering if this lowlife was going to follow through. Sensing the moment, he hesitated and then said, "Jaxon Webb."

After we wrapped up the session, Coolidge and I walked back to his office, and he ran Webb to see if he was incarcerated, a fair guess for someone like Webb. He wasn't.

That would have made life too simple.

Webb's sheet showed several drug busts for which he had done minimal time, and a six-year-old assault with a deadly weapon conviction. He served four years. His sheet listed a Redlands address.

"No way it's still a good address," said Coolidge, "but it gives us a starting point." Coolidge still studying the printout, "Webb's wife Marrika, it seems, is in LA county lockup, awaiting trial on a fraud charge. Perhaps Marrika gets visitors. Maybe a little monitoring could prove fruitful. I'll let you know if he shows up to pay a visit."

Now that we had a suspect, I figured it would just be a matter of time before Webb was arrested, so I would continue negotiations.

Ever the optimist.

I circled back to Norm Michaels, Bridge's lawyer. He had

spoken to his client, and Bridge was ready to deal, but for a few concessions. I listened patiently while Michaels detailed Bridge's counteroffer. Without even acknowledging the terms put forth, I flat-out refused. "My initial offer has been approved, and it is our final and only offer."

I could sense Michaels smiling through the phone. "Okay, I had to give it a shot. Bridge wants the deal. What happens now?"

"Detective Coolidge will schedule a meeting with you and Bridge at Ely. He'll be looking for full disclosure."

"I understand. I'll wait for your detective to reach out."

Several days later, Coolidge called and reported that Bridge was as good as his word. He named Jaxon Webb.

My ducks were lined up, only awaiting word from Coolidge that Webb was in custody.

As if that was a foregone conclusion.

Nine days later, on Thanksgiving, I got the call. Webb had been arrested without incident when he showed up to visit his wife.

I had the stone-cold killer. The trick now was to convict him.

CHAPTER 9

It was early December, and classes were wrapping up. My swimming companions had remained steady. In fact, we picked up a couple more students willing to brave the cold Pacific three mornings a week. Lisa and I had come no closer to resolving our long-distance commuter marriage. Neither of us had any solution in mind. I will say that living apart for most of every week had only one upside. It made for wonderful greetings over the weekends.

Absence and all that.

At the December 5 committee meeting, Hawthorne reported back on the old man who had run his car into the farmers' market, killing three. The old guy had suffered a fatal heart attack, saving us the difficult task of what to do with him.

How's that for cynical?

Meanwhile, Seah reported that Devon Pouse had been arraigned in adult court and charged with the murders of his three classmates. Devon's preliminary hearing was scheduled for January 5. Even though he was charged as an adult, he was temporarily placed in a juvenile facility pending the prelim. Our decision to bump Devon up to adult court was condemned in some circles and praised in others. I was delighted that I wasn't on any of the social media sites. I'm sure they were blowing up.

Seah also reported that on the same day as Devon's arraignment for murder, his parents were arraigned on three felony counts of involuntary manslaughter. From what I understood from my media-savvy colleagues, that decision sent seismic waves across the internet. Not surprisingly, the NRA was apoplectic, referring to the prosecution of the parents as "an affront to the American way of life." I'm not certain how this was an affront to the American way of life, but if the NRA said so, it must be so. Their judgment in matters like this was always spot on.

Conversely, gun control advocates applauded the decision, calling it historic. Hyperbole stacked on hyperbole. The decision wasn't historic but rather in my view, common sense. Parents buying their troubled sixteen-year-old a semiautomatic handgun and then refusing to recognize that their son might well act out was criminally negligent. That failure of basic common sense caused three other families to lose their children. The preliminary hearing was set for January 19. The Pouses were not in custody. They were not flight risks.

Hawthorne sat back with his hands behind his head. "Well, we've poked the hornet's nest with that ill-advised filing. The Second Amendment folks are going to be camped outside the courtroom for that spectacle. Jake, you might consider a bulletproof vest under your trial suit."

"Dammit it, Roger, that's enough!" Seah's face was red with rage. "What a terrible and stupid thing to say! Bear in mind that wasn't just Jake's decision but the committee's." Staring needles at Hawthorne, she continued, "If you ever say something like that again, you will not only be off this committee but out of this office, do you understand me?" Her intensity vibrated around the room.

Hawthorne put his hands up defensively. "Don't go off on me. I wasn't serious."

Unappeased, Seah said, "Sure you weren't. Consider this your first and last warning."

Hawthorne looked off but had the sense to shut up.

Seah held her look on Hawthorne for an uncomfortable moment. No one spoke. Finally, she said, "Let's take up the Webb murder case."

The death penalty was on the table, since Tracie Switzer had been kidnapped and her truck stolen, all in the commission of her murder. Murder in the commission of felonies like kidnapping and robbery constituted special circumstances, allowing us the option of capital charges.

However, the zeal to file capital charges had diminished in recent years. Absent multiple murder victims or particularly gruesome circumstances involving torture, the committee, and therefore the DA's office, was out of the death penalty business. Webb, if convicted, was looking at a lifetime in custody without the possibility of parole. A lifetime being caged in a twelve-by-eighteen-foot cell was worse than death. Days, weeks, months, and years with no hope.

Hawthorne, an avowed advocate of the death penalty, was conspicuously quiet. Discretion being the better part of valor?

The preliminary hearing on Webb was set for April 6. I volunteered to handle the case. Seah pulled a face and observed, "Jake, we do have other prosecutors in the office. Your calendar for the upcoming year is filling up."

"I've helped work this case up. I can handle it." The cold-blooded unnecessary execution of Tracie Switzer had burrowed deep under my skin.

CHAPTER 10

I hired Vanessa Clemens, a third year who was also one of my swimmers, to clerk for me. She had a light semester and could invest the time. Her first task was to become conversant with the Uniform Act to Secure the Attendance of Witnesses from Without a State in Criminal Proceedings.

How's that for a tidy title?

That would start the process toward hopefully getting Bridge into a Los Angeles courtroom. And from what I kept hearing, that would be the easier obstacle. The second and more significant obstacle would be getting the Nevada sentencing judge to agree to the three-year reduction of Bridge's Nevada sentence. As I had been warned, states are historically resistant to outside interference with their criminal justice decisions.

Vanessa had done her homework. "It's pretty straightforward. First, we draft what the Uniform Act calls a certificate, setting forth the basics of the case and why Bridge is a material witness."

"How detailed? Is it a full-blown trial brief or more of an overview?"

"From what I've been able to find out, it doesn't require an extensive factual layout. It seems that we must establish how Bridge fits into the trial and how essential he is."

"Doesn't sound too demanding. You've got Detective Coolidge's reports, including the interviews with Bridge and Melrose. Are you comfortable drafting the certificate?"

"Yeah," she said tentatively. "As long as it's only a draft. I don't want to screw this up."

"Of course," I agreeably assured her y. "Who do we send the certificate to?"

"The language in the act is a little vague, but from some follow-up research I did, it gets sent to the sentencing judge. Once that judge approves, they notify the Nevada Department of Prisons, authorizing the transfer. The prison department coordinates with the California authorities to arrange for the transfer."

"Okay, anything else I need to know now?"

"I don't know how important this is, but the certificate has to specify how long the prisoner will be required in the requesting state. It looks like a pretty tight window."

"That makes sense. How much notice does Nevada need to get started on this?"

"I don't know, but I'll find out."

"Thanks, Vanessa, good work."

As she was getting up to leave, she added, "Oh, I forgot to mention, the requesting state pays all costs associated with the transfer."

"Seems only fair. We're doing the asking."

Vanessa had a draft of the certificate on my desk the following day. She was diligent as well as smart. It supplied all the essential information and was artfully crafted. Without making any edits, I had her file it with a Judge Elon of the Nevada State Court. Five days later, I was surprised by a call from Judge Elon's clerk, asking me to hold for the judge. After five minutes on hold I seriously considered hanging up, but then Elon came on.

"Mr. Clearwater, I've got your certificate requesting that I modify Inmate Bridge's sentence and authorizing his temporary release to the California authorities to testify." Her voice was husky and raspy, almost like she had a speech impediment.

"Thank you for contacting me, Your Honor. It's a pleasure to speak to you."

In an acidic tone, "This is business, not a social call."

Pleasantries be damned.

"Okay," I carefully replied.

"I sentenced Bridge to twelve years, which he so sorely earned, and now I get this request for you to cut time from his sentence. I'm not pleased with your request." When I judiciously didn't reply, she went on. "Are you aware of the circumstances of Bridge's offenses?"

"I'm not. Only that he was sentenced for robbery."

"Robbery was but the tip of the iceberg. He inflicted serious injuries on his victim. Injuries which the victim will bear the rest of his life." She let that resonate before continuing. "As a result of a negotiated disposition, the aggravated assault charges were dropped, and I sentenced him to twelve years on the robbery."

"I understand."

"I don't think you do. I wanted to sentence him to a longer term, but because the victim was very reluctant to testify, I was forced to accept the terms of the deal. From my perspective, Bridge got off easy, and now I receive your request to cut off even more time. I hope you fully understand my reticence to reduce his sentence."

I'd been warned.

I hesitated, making certain she was finished. "I hear you, Judge. May I fill you in on the other side of the equation?" I paused to see if she would let me go on. She did. "I know you've read our brief and the dry facts therein, but let me give you a more specific account. The man I'm prosecuting randomly kidnapped and robbed an eighteen-year-old college freshman. Stole her truck, drove her to an isolated location, and cut her throat from ear to ear, for no discernible reason."

I paused, letting my side of the equation sink in. "Inmate Bridge just happened to be along during that girl's execution. He took no part in the murder. Without question, Bridge is a lowlife and has very well earned his prison time. But I can't convict her murderer without his testimony."

There was a long silence before Elon asked. "He's absolutely essential?"

"He is."

"What are the prospects of a successful prosecution? You trying the case?"

"I am the trial prosecutor. And I'm going to be straight with you. My prosecution is heavily dependent on Bridge and one other lowlife snitch. But I'm hopeful I can get a conviction and bring some small level of relief to the parents who lost their girl."

"Will Bridge be implicated in the murder?"

"Yes, part of the deal is he will receive three years as an accessory to murder, his time to run concurrent with his Nevada time."

"So, he'll serve no additional time on the murder?" She sounded disgusted.

"That's correct."

I could hear Elon blowing out her breath. Here it was; the case would hinge on Elon's answer.

"This just isn't right, but I'm going to reluctantly grant your request and approve the sentence reduction." She paused. "Murder trumps robbery and assault. Convict this sonofabitch."

"Thank you, Your Honor."

"My clerk will get you the paperwork. Good luck, Mr. Clearwater."

CHAPTER 11

Wednesday, December 20, our long-awaited honeymoon trip. Great Exuma, Bahamas. I made a promise to myself to leave my cases behind me, to not think about them, and to just completely relax. A promise easy to make but difficult to follow. My mind kept pulling Webb and the impending Pouse trials front and center. My gorgeous wife and a week in the Bahamas were the counterpoints. And by the second day, I was a Bahamian. Thoughts of mean trials awaiting me were lost in snorkeling crystal waters, kayaking glassy seas, fishing for big boys, and making love with my stunning and passionate wife. The week was a magnificent blur. Thoughts of crimes and trials slipped into the ether.

Our last Bahamas morning fell on Christmas. We snorkeled off a breakwater. Almost without warning, clouds filled the sky, quickly followed by rain. We swam ashore and, with the gentle rain keeping us company, leisurely walked back to our Airbnb. Lisa took my hand and bowed, inviting me to dance. We danced in rhythm with the sound of the rain soothing our slightly sunburned bodies. I spun Lisa around twice and dipped her.

We had agreed to not give each other Christmas presents. We both failed. I had purchased an intricate gold bracelet which I had secreted in the luggage. Lisa gave me gold cufflinks. She instructed that I only wear them when I'm in trial.

Lisa called her dad to wish him a Merry Christmas. I called Tony and Eve to do the same. We drove to a church in town and took in the celebratory atmosphere. The choir's version of "O Holy Night" was mesmerizing. A wonderful Christmas service.

When we emerged from church, the storm had passed. The sky was as blue as ever, and the ocean was back to its translucent self. It was Christmas, and it was time to leave the magic of the Bahamas and fly back to reality.

CHAPTER 12

On January 2, at our first Elders meeting of the new year, I was sworn in as a deputy district attorney by Seah as the other Elders looked on. This time it was for more than just last summer's Max Cort trial. I was part of the team, the family.

The brief formalities having concluded, we got down to business. Hawthorne was up and prepared to brief us on a potential capital case. He cleared his throat in an old man's gross hack that put everyone on edge, checked his notes, and began. "Mean case. Very mean case." He hacked again. "Caesar Ramirez and his wife Cathy Ramirez have been arrested for the murder of their eleven-year-old nephew, Oscar. Apparently, Caesar kicked the child to death while his wife looked on."

I sat back, uneasy.

The killing of children pulling on a special place.

"To fully come to grips with this case, we need to go back a year or so. Oscar and his thirteen-year-old brother, Felipe, were living in Riverside with their mother, Murielle. She had serious addiction problems and all that comes with that. However, she was self-aware enough to realize she could no longer care for her sons. She reached out to her older brother, Caesar, who was living on welfare with his wife, Cathy, in a donated trailer in the rural area of western Oregon.

I leaned back. *How could this not go wrong?*

Following another cringe-worthy hack, Hawthorne continued. "Murielle, the mother, was hoping that her brother and sister-in-law could provide a home for the boys, perhaps unaware that neither was employed and were surviving on welfare and the occasional charity of others." Hawthorne shook his head at the apparent absurdity of the Ramirezes as a refuge for the boys.

"I'm going to pause the narrative to give you a bit more on Caesar and Cathy Ramirez. It will have a bearing on how we ultimately view this case. Neither one has so much as a high school education, and from what the investigation has determined, neither has held a job for more than a few months throughout their entire lives. It should also be noted that Caesar is a small man, and Cathy is a very large woman, weighing in at better than three hundred pounds on a five-foot, two-inch frame." Hawthorne gave us a knowing look as if that information would prove useful. I figured he would tie it back in later.

"Okay, back to the narrative," he said, in a somber tone. "The boys were shipped up to Oregon, and not surprisingly, things didn't go well. The investigator reported that neither Caesar nor Cathy had ever raised a child. However, they were of the mind that if you spared the rod, you spoiled the child. And as you'll see in the autopsy photos of Oscar, the kid was beaten long, hard, and often."

Hawthorne paused for emphasis. "According to the coroner's report, Oscar's injuries were horrific. I looked at some of the photos and nearly lost my lunch." He paused again. "Now, this is coming from me, a longtime prosecutor, who has prosecuted every conceivable inhumanity. Every part of this kid's body was beaten to the point that he could no longer digest food. He was wasting away. The coroner concluded that the immediate cause of death was blows to his emaciated midsection, which broke several ribs and punctured his lungs, causing him to bleed out. The coroner opined that the boy was in critical condition suffering from sepsis prior to the final blow.

Silence ensued until Seah dared to ask, "What about the other boy, the thirteen-year-old?"

"That remains a bit of a mystery," Hawthorne said. "Cathy claims that he ran away with an older man a month or so after arriving in Oregon." Hawthorne shook his head skeptically. "When pressed, Cathy suggested that Felipe was probably gay and had willingly gone off with the man."

"What?" said Mann shaking her head. "That's too crazy."

Hawthorne nodded in agreement. "Especially since the Ramirezes didn't report the boy's disappearance to the Oregon authorities."

"So how did they end up back here in Southern California?" Seah asked, prompting Hawthorne to move through this ugly briefing.

"I'm getting there, Nancy." Using his hands, he motioned for her to be patient. "Seven months after the boys had been packed off to Oregon, Caesar and Cathy decided to move to Southern California, specifically Rialto, out in East County. They somehow managed to rent a two-bedroom duplex, again relying on county charity. And it was from there, this past Thanksgiving, that Caesar called 911 to report that Oscar wasn't breathing"—Hawthorne paused—"but it was too late."

Hawthorne took a swallow of his coffee and again gave one of those unsettling hacks. "During the interviews, Caesar claimed that he had disciplined Oscar by putting him in a closet. Later, when he went to check on him, Oscar was unresponsive."

Hawthorne stood and, carrying his coffee cup, stepped to the Keurig and concluded, "That is the short, tragic life of Oscar Ramirez." He added, "God only knows what happened to the other kid."

No one spoke. We were taking it in.

"Okay," said Mann, breaking the silence. "Why do we have it? We've seen"—she made air quotes—"'discipline cases' leading to death before. As tragic as it is, we typically file involuntary manslaughter charges and be done with it. I'm not sure why this committee is looking at this one."

Hawthorne, carrying coffee back to his seat, started to answer, only to be interrupted by Seah. "Roger, let me weigh in."

He gestured with his cup. "Please."

"Thanks. When our supervising deputy in East County sent this case to us, she wanted us to take a very close look. She was of a mind that we should consider capital charges, with torture as the special circumstance against both the husband and wife."

"Capital charges?" Mann interjected with surprise.

Before anyone else had an opportunity to voice any questions, Hawthorne was back. "Like I reported initially, the injuries to Oscar evidence torture." He pulled the autopsy report from the file and began reading. "'A large abrasion present on the left cheekbone. An abrasion over his left eyebrow. Older abrasions over his right eyebrow. Many injuries show scabbing. A split in his lip. A U-shaped injury to the face is usually the result of being hit with a cord. Behind the ears on both sides are recent injuries. Multitudes of different injuries are present beneath the chin region, approximately twenty of them, most of them healing or scarring. Abrasions to the ear itself. Scarring consistent with approximately twenty different injuries to the front part of the ear consistent with being struck with a cord. Discoloration through his midsection that extends down to his thighs, which is consistent with significant infection.'"

Mann held up her hands cutting Hawthorne off. "That's sufficient, Roger." With a deep sigh, "I get it."

"Let's not forget," Hawthorne added, "like I said earlier, this child was so beaten, he couldn't eat. His organs were shutting down."

No one spoke. We were all grappling with the horrific facts. How could someone do this to another, especially to a child?

"Okay," I said, breaking the silence. "I'm good on considering torture as a special circumstance against the husband, but what do we do with the wife?"

"Okay, let's talk about that." Hawthorne nodded to me. "When I heard East County wanted us to consider filing on both of them, I reached out to a Detective Everly, the lead on the investigation, to get a better feel for the case. He had conducted the interrogation of Caesar, and although Caesar admitted that he administered the punishment, he was adamant that Cathy was at the heart of the kid's death. Everly believed that she was the dominant partner in the marriage. That she was the instigator. He said, and I quote, 'Cathy ruled the roost.' Everly's confident that even though she was essentially sedentary, due to her bulk, she was in charge, and nothing happened in their home without her assent. Caesar, during the interview with Everly, said, 'She told me when to discipline Oscar.'"

"Roger, can I stop you for a minute?" Mann said. "Is Caesar turning on his wife? Are they at odds with one another? Has anyone questioned the wife?"

"When she was arrested, she refused to make a statement. However, according to the detective, he sensed their relationship was on the rocks."

Mann followed up. "Now that I have a better sense of the relationship, I see a problem. How do we get around spousal privilege if we can only implicate her from his confession?"

Hawthorne, who had had time to consider the case, responded. "Leslie, I appreciate your concerns. Caesar did the hitting and kicking, but Cathy was up to her eyeballs in the torture. She may not have struck a single blow, but according to Caesar, she was complicit in the torture. It appears she directed when and how severely Caesar would beat the kid. She aided and abetted. She was a full-on accomplice in the death of Oscar."

"Okay," Mann asked, "but how do we prove that?"

Hawthorne responded, "The mere circumstances are most likely sufficient to incriminate them both. Up in Oregon, they lived in a trailer, close quarters. Their duplex in Rialto, close quarters. How could they both not be involved? Especially considering Cathy was dominant in the relationship. This certainly doesn't appear to be a situation where an overwhelming male partner intimidates and has his own way with everyone in the home."

"Leslie," Seah nodded in agreement, "as you know, there are duties that arise under certain circumstances. A person in Cathy's position, an aunt who has voluntarily taken over the care of a child, has a duty to exercise care for that child. Given the acceptance of care and the nature of the living arrangements being so tight, it would be difficult for some defense attorney to argue she was unaware of Oscar's circumstances and didn't violate her duty of care for the boy."

Mann put up a hand in an I'm-thinking-about-it motion. "I understand the argument, but if we're going to file capital charges, I'm hard-pressed to see a jury convicting this woman and then putting her on death row." She looked at us and waited for anyone to disagree.

"I'm really torn on capital charges," Seah said. "I'm okay with capital charges against the husband, given the torture, but I'm apprehensive about going after the wife. I've heard the arguments and remain unsettled."

Again, no one spoke.

Mann, patting her lips thoughtfully, said, "Would it be acceptable to you three to push off our decision until our next meeting? I'd like time to reflect carefully before we act. Because of the severity of the beatings, which evidence torture, this obviously has death-penalty implications, and I find myself in a vengeful mood after hearing the terrible injuries to this child, but I want to make certain that we're acting with the dispassion required of us."

Hawthorne nodded his head. "Fair point, Leslie. Let's kick it over a month. They're in custody, and there's no harm in pushing this decision back."

CHAPTER 13

It was only my first week in the office, but I already felt the stressors. Just like when I was a prosecutor in San Arcadia. I was no longer in the abstract academic world of criminal law, criminal procedure, and trial advocacy, but in the actual world of crimes, motions, and trials. It felt good. The stressors were invigorating, if not a bit overwhelming. I had bitten off two serious cases. Actually, it was three, considering that the Pouse shootings involved two separate prosecutions: the sixteen-year-old and his parents. And then there was the prosecution of Jaxon Webb.

Devon Pouse was first up. His preliminary hearing was set for January 12. There's an old saying among criminal law practitioners that prosecutors could indict a ham sandwich. Indeed, in taking a case to a grand jury, prosecutors pretty much have their way. The defense is not represented, and convincing a majority of the grand jurors by a simple preponderance of the evidence that a crime has been committed and that the defendant is most likely the culprit is not a particularly difficult task.

Likewise, preliminary hearings only require a simple preponderance of evidence. The difference at a preliminary hearing is that the defendant is represented, and a judge is the decider. Nonetheless, prosecutors rarely have problems succeeding at prelim. In California, prelims, as opposed to grand juries, are used almost exclusively to determine if there are sufficient facts to proceed to trial.

I took a good look at Devon Pouse before his prelim. He was listless, sitting quietly with his head down. He was thin, his face ravaged by acne. The jail-issue uniform bagged at his shoulders and knees. His lawyer tried to engage him but, from what I could see, got no response.

For the prelim, I called the investigating officer and the coroner. During their direct examinations, I laid out the broad strokes that were sufficient for purposes of the prelim. Defense counsel Julia Wesson, a seasoned criminal defense lawyer hired by Devon's parents, didn't dispute whether Pouse shot anyone but used the opportunity, during her cross-examinations of my two witnesses, to probe and discover if there were any potential weaknesses in my case. As far as I could determine, there weren't. This was about as open and shut as a case could be.

At the conclusion, the judge found I had met my burden of proof and bound the case over for initial appearance and arraignment at the trial court on March 10. The judge as per Wesson's request ordered that Pouse's confinement be continued in a juvenile facility instead of the men's jail. The upcoming prelim of his parents would be much more challenging.

Defense counsel Wesson cornered me outside the courtroom. "Mr. Clearwater, I've tried talking to this kid, and I'm not convinced he is aware of the consequences of his conduct. He won't talk to me. It's as if he's in a shell. I'm not certain he's competent to stand trial."

From what I had observed, I wasn't surprised. I figured some manner of mental defense would surely factor into the defense of Devon Pouse. "What are you suggesting?"

She shrugged. "I've got him scheduled for a psychiatric evaluation, but my more pressing concern is his lack of responsiveness to all that is swirling around him. As I said, he may be incompetent to stand trial."

I chewed on the idea, thinking through Devon's listlessness during the prelim.

"Incompetent in the sense that I don't think he is aware of what's happening to him." She went on, "As things stand now, I don't believe he can assist in his own defense." Which is the standard for determining competency. An incompetent individual cannot stand trial.

"Should we put him back on the calendar, asking for a competency hearing?" I asked.

"That's what I'm thinking. I'd like to set it up sooner rather than later."

"I've got no problem with that. Let me know when."

Maybe this kid suffered a psychotic break. I recalled the words he wrote on the day of the shooting. "I'm useless. Help me. I hate them all." The consequences of a finding of incompetence have long-term significance. An individual found incompetent could be confined in a secure mental facility until and if he regains his ability to assist in his own defense. That could involve months, even years.

Later that day, Wesson called me. She had set up a competency hearing for January 16. My calendar was starting to fill up.

That afternoon, I received a call from Suzelle Frost, my former student and now a deputy public defender. "I heard you were doing the DA thing. Do you have time to have lunch with a former student?"

I couldn't help but grin, hearing her familiar voice. "I've been here all of a week. What took you so long to reach out?" She had been one of my favorite students. We had become close when I took an earlier leave from Pacifico and defended Duane Durgeon against capital charges up in San Arcadia a couple of years ago. At that time she was a third-year student and she'd assisted me, and she'd been a huge help in successfully defending Durgeon.

"You were on my mind," she replied.

"How about Tuesday?"

"Philippe's at eleven-thirty, before the crowd descends?"

"It's a date."

CHAPTER 14

It was a San Arcadia weekend, and Sunday morning, we were having coffee at Lisa's kitchen nook before we were off on what Lisa promised was a not-too-strenuous hike in the surrounding foothills. Lisa was a dedicated trekker. I was in pretty good shape but couldn't keep up with her when she was seriously hiking. She picked up on a conversation we'd had the night before about the case against Devon Pouse's parents. She remained unconvinced that the parents should, as she described it, "pay for the sins of their son." I thought that was an inaccurate description.

Standing at the counter, spreading jam on toast, she said, "Given the proliferation of guns in this country, is it reasonable that we should hold parents accountable if their adolescent, unbeknownst to them, gets his hands on one of their guns?" I started to respond, but she raised her hand in a let-me-finish gesture. "I read recently that by some estimates, there are over four hundred million guns in the hands of Americans. It just seems inevitable to me that some of them are going to end up in the hands of impetuous teens."

"You're right, there are a lot of guns out there. In my view, way too many. And, again, in my view, there should be consequences for adults acting unreasonably in failing to keep guns from kids."

She shook off my statement, handed me toast, and sat down across from me. "My dad, even to this day, keeps a rifle under his bed and has done so for as long as I can remember. He never locked it up, even when there were kids in the house. Should he be responsible if one of his children got the gun and shot someone?"

"A lot of folks keep guns in the house for protection. I get that. But my argument against the Pouses isn't about that. This wasn't a single-shot rifle like your dad's, this was a semiautomatic weapon. A military weapon. And it wasn't a rifle, but a handgun. Something easy to conceal. Not securing that kind of weapon, a weapon their teenager was fixated on, and not owning up to his clearly disturbed mental state, was, in my view, reckless conduct on their part."

She sipped her coffee and gave me a skeptical look. She was far from conceding. "So from your assessment, the kicker was the parents not recognizing that Devon was disturbed and potentially volatile?"

"In part, but don't forget the type of gun. This was a military-type weapon. This wasn't your dad's single-shot rifle."

She rested her chin on her steepled hands, a posture I found endearing, even in a disagreement. "I don't know, Jake. I can't see this couple going to jail for this." A thoughtful pause. "Maybe allowing the victims' families to sue the parents civilly for the deaths of their children, but not locking them up."

I'd made my case the best I could but still couldn't convince my personal jury of one. That didn't bode well. How could I convince the twelve in the box if I couldn't convince Lisa?

"You may be right. There's no guarantee that the jurors will agree with me." I shrugged. "I could lose. This is by no means a straightforward prosecution. But I feel duty bound to pursue it." I hesitated, feeling frustration welling, wrestling with whether to go on. In a tone harsher than I intended, "Lisa, three innocent boys are dead, their families devastated. Those parents didn't just allow it to happen—they did everything but pull the trigger again and again and again!"

She jerked from her chair, surprised that I had escalated the discussion. "Hold on, mister. We were having a civil conversation. Don't you dare raise your voice at me."

I dropped my head and leaned over the table, my hands contritely extended. "I'm sorry. That was senseless of me. I've agonized over this case. My emotions got the better of me. Forgive me."

She shook her head, got up, and tossed her toast in the sink. "I'm going for that walk by myself."

And with that, she was gone.

Well played, Clearwater.

The rest of that weekend didn't get much better. I drove back to Malibu that afternoon instead of staying over. Her choice, not mine.

A long week followed. By Thursday, she grudgingly accepted my apologies. I wasn't all the way back, but I could see a path.

On the Tuesday before the Friday preliminary hearing of Devon Pouse's parents, I was in court as Julia Wesson moved to have Devon declared incompetent to stand trial and requested the court order a psychological evaluation. I didn't oppose her request. The court accordingly ordered an evaluation and ordered us back in two weeks to determine if Devon was competent to stand trial. Accordingly, Devon's arraignment was pushed back to March 30. The judge again ordered that he be held at a secure mental-health facility.

I met Suzelle for lunch. It was delightful catching up. She still looked about fifteen. She was thin and blond, with her hair pulled into a tight blond ponytail, just as she had worn it during law school.

She had a number of misdemeanor trials under her belt, almost a veteran. "I've been assigned my first felony trial, set for next month."

"What's the charge?"

"Drug distribution. They busted him with a meth lab in his house."

"Surprising that it came to your office. Usually, drug offenders have trial counsel lined up. Do you have the rare itinerant drug guy?"

"You mean alleged drug guy?" She smiled that disarming, sweet smile that I so enjoyed.

"My mistake, *alleged* drug guy." I smiled back.

The time passed too quickly and we were on our way back to the courthouse, with promises to not wait so long to see each other. She would be a top defense attorney in short order. She was smart and dedicated to her craft.

Friday, January 19, 2019. The preliminary hearing on the three counts of involuntary manslaughter against the Pouses. It was a brawl, far from that imaginary indicted ham sandwich. On the street fronting the courthouse news vans lined the curb. Banners one would expect of the Second Amendment crowd were on full display.

From my cold dead fingers.

I had to fight through the protesting crowd to enter the courtroom. A woman wearing a MAGA cap confronted me and screamed something I couldn't understand. A bailiff pulled her away and held the door for me. The room was full and raucous. I was the object of derision as I made my way forward.

Judge Merritt had been assigned the case. From what some

prosecutors had told me, he was a ditherer. He was indecisive and could be bullied. Not everyone was cut out to be a judge.

To compound the volatile atmosphere, Don and Kay Pouse had hired Sam Hardy, an antagonistic, bombastic lawyer. Hardy's reputation was well known throughout the LA legal community. Civility was not in his DNA, and he blustered his way through cases. Yelling, theatrical posturing, and even intimidation were his well-honed tactics. He was huge, at least six-foot-eight, and had to be north of three hundred pounds, with a bald block of a head. Always on the offensive, always completely confident that his side of any case was righteous. Lawyers are sometimes referred to as sharks, and if that were true, Hardy was a twenty-foot Great White.

Would I need a bigger boat?

Throughout the prelim, the bailiffs had to order silence. Hardy challenged and objected to pretty much every question I asked. Judge Merritt made little attempt to rein him in, and not surprisingly, Merritt appeared cowed by Hardy's onslaught and the intimidating crowd. I patiently slugged through the direct examinations of my investigating detective and the coroner. Hardy's cross-examinations were vicious. I did the best I could to protect the detective with objections but didn't get much support from the judge. A prelim that should have taken an hour went on all morning.

At the conclusion of the evidence, Hardy slammed into my case. More bombast. Words and phrases like "outrageous" and "prosecutor overreach" even characterized the decision to file criminal charges as part of a far-left liberal conspiracy targeting the Second Amendment. When Hardy temporarily ran out of breath, I made my points, discussing the reckless behavior of the parents that led to the deaths of three high school kids, emphasizing the military-type weapon, the parents' failure to secure the gun, their failure to recognize the obvious distress of their son, their failure to get Devon help, and their failure to take him home after each incident.

Hardy was having no part of my argument. "This is not and never has been a criminal matter. If there is any breach of responsibility, it can only be dealt with in the civil courts." He briefly paused to reload then practically screamed, "Judge, you have no choice but to throw this case out and send a message, a strong message, to this prosecutor and to the DA's office that we Americans will not tolerate filing criminal charges when there is no crime." He paused, drawing a breath. "Let's be very honest about the agenda of the district attorney's office. This is about an attempt to restrict the Second Amendment and intrude into the sanctity of the family."

The full house voiced their assent at Hardy's oratory, only to be quickly admonished by the bailiffs. The courtroom had an unhinged feeling.

I felt I was riding a small boat in heavy seas.

In a weak, barely audible voice, Judge Merritt, caught up in Hardy's bombast and perhaps sensing the groundswell from the gallery, agreed with Hardy and dismissed the case. The gallery exploded. Sam Hardy, their hero, had carried the day. Justice for Don and Kay. Redemption for the Second Amendment. If Hardy hadn't been so huge, I think they would have carried him on their shoulders as they paraded out of the courtroom.

Merritt actually dismissed the case. So much for the ham sandwich analogy. I was shocked. Perhaps I shouldn't have been. In my career as a prosecutor, I had never failed to succeed at a prelim. I knew this case was going to be challenging, but surely I could nurse it through the prelim stage. Roger Hawthorne's cautionary words from months earlier resonated in my head.

Dammit. A wave had washed over my boat.

Fortunately, jeopardy does not attach at a prelim. There was no double jeopardy issue. I could refile and run it again. Maybe next time the case would be assigned to a judge with a backbone. But who was I kidding? This was always a case on the margins.

I worked my way out of the courtroom and up to my office. I closed the door and slumped in my chair. Was Lisa right? Was Hawthorne right? Was the judge right? No! Dammit, I was determined to run the prelim again.

Would the Elders support that decision?

CHAPTER 15

I was still reeling from Judge Merritt's decision that afternoon as I was making the Friday drive to San Arcadia for a Lisa weekend. Lisa called when I was a half hour out, and without a greeting or any preamble said, "Russ, my principal, has been suspended. Effective immediately, I'm the interim principal." She spoke with a mixture of concern and excitement. Russ Rosen, the JFK Middle School principal, had supported Lisa and encouraged her to seek a principal's position. Lisa liked him but had expressed to me over the past year or so, it seemed to her that Rosen had just been going through the motions. In her view, his efforts with his middle-school faculty lacked much commitment or energy.

"That's a bombshell!" was all I could utter as I collected my thoughts. "When did you find this out?"

"Ten minutes ago. The district superintendent just called me."

"Any explanation?"

"No. But he told me that I'm the acting principal, effective immediately."

"From what you told me about Rosen slowing down, maybe this isn't surprising."

"It is to me, Jake. There's no way the district office would know Russ had slowed down." She paused. "For all I know, he may think I had something to do with this."

"Come on, Lisa, he knows you've been supportive." I carefully considered my next statement. "You're the principal. Perhaps congratulations are in order."

"I don't want the job like this. Russ is my friend. I've told you he has always had my back." Her voice had a slight quiver. "I was hoping I would eventually be promoted, but on merit, not by default."

"I hear that. But sometimes, positive events can crop up under unexpected circumstances. This could be one of those circumstances. Once the powers that be see the job you'll be doing, I'm sure they'll remove the interim tag."

"Jake, you don't know that. You're talking without any real knowledge of how this might work." She paused, then, sounding exasperated with me, said, "Let's talk it through when you get here, okay?"

I had done absolutely no good.

She met me with an icy Corona and a distracted hug. "Let's talk on the patio." And she led the way. She had a serving plate of crackers and artichoke dip sitting next to a glass of chardonnay. I suspected the treats had been prepared prior to the superintendent's call. We settled into comfortable chairs in her small garden-like patio.

"Tell me what you are thinking."

"Okay." She heaved a big breath. "You're probably right that sometimes opportunities come in unexpected ways." She took a contemplative sip. "And maybe I should be grateful for this opportunity."

Maybe I did do some good.

"But . . ." I said.

"I'm sick about Russ. He's a good guy. Like I told you, lately he hasn't done the job he should've been doing, but not enough to get suspended." She tilted her head down. "That makes this bittersweet."

I nodded my understanding. "Was there any indication that this was in the wind?"

"Not that I was aware of. Yeah," she bobbed her head, "he was underperforming, but to anyone other than me and a few of the teachers, that wouldn't have been obvious."

"So what, then? You got no indication from the superintendent when he called you?"

"No, nothing."

"Have you spoken to Russ?"

"No, this all came about in the last hour or so, and I'm still processing. I wanted to talk to you before I do anything." It was out of character for Lisa to be at loose ends.

"So you don't know if this is about job performance or something else? Some other issue?"

"Nothing that I'm privy to."

"Maybe you should call him. After all, you're a concerned friend."

"I want to, but I don't want it to seem like I'm piling on or had anything to do with his suspension."

"Why don't you fortify with that glass of wine and then give him a call?"

Sound advice?

With a determined look, she leaned forward, downed the wine in three gulps, and punched in Rosen's contact. Remaining on the edge of her chair, she heard it ring six times before going to voicemail. She disconnected without leaving a message, then slumped back in her chair.

"Shit!" she uttered.

We sat in silence, looking at one another. Finally, I ventured,

"Can we talk about the positive side of this? You're a principal. You've got your own school."

"I do." She smiled halfheartedly.

"Any thoughts about what changes the new principal of Excelsior Middle School might bring about?"

Working hard to push the positive.

She thought this through while pouring herself another glass of wine. "There are a few things I could do to improve the school. Of course, nothing drastic or fundamental. But I could inject more energy and enthusiasm into the faculty. Russ wasn't much of a cheerleader." She stopped and considered her words. "No, that's not exactly what I mean. I'm not a cheerleader either. But I do have ideas about improving morale, and like I said, energy." Her thoughts were scattered as she still grappled with her conflicted feelings.

I wouldn't let her turn from the positive. Maybe I'm the cheerleader. "Now you're talking. You have, what, five months left of this school year to show the folks in the district office that you deserve the job. Shake things up!"

"Jake, you're the real cheerleader." She gave me a low-wattage smile. "I'll do everything I can to get the job permanently. That is, if Russ is not reinstated."

Despite my best efforts, the unexpected news cast a pallor over the evening. And I hadn't even told her about the Pouse prelim.

We had dinner at the wharf. Sand dabs for me, scallops for Lisa. While we were enjoying great food and great service, I ventured into the challenge of moving the conversation off the Rosen news. "The prelim of the Pouse parents went sideways."

She sat back, surprised. "From what you've always said, prelims are a matter of routine for you prosecutors. What happened?"

"As you and others have pointed out, this is far from a routine case. The judge wasn't buying my argument."

I think I detected a slight I-told-you-so glimpse before she said, "Sorry, Jake, so what happens now?"

"I'll take it back to the committee and see if there is a consensus to run it again."

"You think they'll agree?"

"I hope so. I'm committed to this case."

"I know you are, Jake," she said, with a wan smile.

I took a healthy drink of my Ketel One and nodded.

It was time to move on from Rosen's suspension and my prelim whiff to something more positive. Without a preamble, I launched. "Bruno Keys is in the southern tip of San Arcadia county and roughly halfway between San Arcadia and downtown LA. It's about forty-five minutes, halfway to each of our jobs. We could live under the same roof."

A quizzical look. My left turn caught her completely off guard. "What are you talking about?" It took a moment for her to shift from the challenges of our jobs. "Is this your unsubtle tactic to shift the dialogue?"

"It is."

"What if I'm not ready to move off talking about what has happened?"

"My apologies. I'm not being insensitive. But sitting here, there's nothing we can do about what happened to Russ. I know that is troubling you. I believe I understand your feelings. If you think it would help, we can talk about it some more. I'm all ears."

She paused and considered my response. "Thinking about what Russ must be going through right now, I guess I would feel guilty moving on." She pasted on a smile. "Bruno Keys?"

"Yeah, Bruno Keys."

"All I know about Bruno Keys is that it's an off-ramp when I'm driving toward LA."

"I checked it out online. It's beachy, secluded, and expensive."

I didn't yet know how expensive.

"And it's our halfway point. It could be the answer since we are locked into our jobs for at least the foreseeable future."

She gave a what-the-hell shake of her head. "All right, I'm listening."

"I was hoping you'd say that. How about tomorrow? Let's do some scouting."

We took the lone Bruno Keys off-ramp from the 101. The houses, some huge and beautiful, some ready to be razed and made into huge and beautiful, were perched above the Pacific, looking down on softly rolling waves. There were no commercial establishments, no restaurants, no convenience stores. Just the houses. As we drove the Bruno Keys frontage road, we saw an open house sign.

An omen?

The perky, assured real estate woman welcomed us into a beautiful split-level house and offered what smelled like freshly baked chocolate chip cookies. That homey touch.

Does that wonderful aroma help with million-dollar purchases?

She invited us to explore. Two bedrooms—a main and a guest room—two baths, two-car garage, twenty-two-hundred square feet, with a killer balcony overlooking the Pacific. The place was fully furnished; the owner had passed, and her children weren't interested in the furnishings.

Then I saw the spec sheet with the list price and nearly turned and walked out. I was expecting high, but not that high. Way out of range. I should have done a deeper dive. Lisa, however, was not daunted by the price. Lisa asked the agent, Sally, if she would excuse us so we could sit on the balcony and talk.

"I'm sorry, Lisa, I never would have suggested this area if I'd realized how expensive it was. I'm so out of touch. I thought there might be some more affordable places mixed in here."

"Jake"—she reached over and grabbed my shoulder—"I love this house. I want to buy it."

Talk about impulsive. Before I could respond, she said, "I make a lot of money with my paintings. We can afford this."

"We can afford this?" I sat back and echoed a bit idiotically.

"We can," she said, looking pleased with herself.

I'm sure my mouth fell open. Not a good look. I didn't bother trying to speak.

She patted my shoulder. "I've got enough to buy this place outright."

What?

Ignorance is a hell of a thing. I had no idea. I had been to a number of her shows and saw what her paintings sold for, but I had no idea she had accumulated so much. Even though we had been together for a few years and had been married for five months, we had never talked money specifics. I was astonished at her reveal.

Astonished? Dumbfounded! Out of touch!

Should I have known she had that kind of money? Probably. But the truth is, I've never spent much time thinking about money.

We sat in silence while this revelation settled on me. I then stammered out something stupid. "I don't know if I'm comfortable with this."

With an edge, she replied, "Well, get over yourself, handsome. I can only figure your male ego is doing the talking." She paused and, in a softer tone, said, "We are going to be married for a long time, and what is mine is yours."

I was still dumbfounded. "When you agreed to marry me, I knew it would be forever. But this money disparity is troubling." I took her hand. "I like to think of myself as a liberated male. But this has caught me by surprise." I stood and walked over to the railing, turning back to her. "I need to absorb this."

She joined me at the rail. "Maybe we should have discussed our finances at some point."

I gave a self-deprecating laugh. "Maybe." I took her hand. "Well, here we are. Can I make a suggestion?"

"As long as you're not leading with your out-of-date male ego." Again, with a satisfied smirk.

"I'm trying real hard not to. If we—you," I corrected, "pull the trigger, the house is in your name only." I put out my hands. "That's the only way my fragile male ego can handle this."

"Dammit, Jake, just be graceful." She shook her head, considering. "But if that's what it's going to take, I'll accept your terms." She stood gazing out at the ocean. "Let's do a little due diligence, as you lawyers call it, and check out a few more of what's available. I'm pretty sold on this one. But maybe we should scout the neighborhood."

Fifteen days later, after doing walkthroughs of two other houses and dickering the price down a bit, we—or should I say Lisa—closed the deal. We were scheduled to move in on February 22. A major decision in the wink of an eye.

CHAPTER 16

February 6, 2019. Committee meeting. There were no new cases to consider, but we had pushed the decision on Caesar and Cathy Ramirez to this date. But before we dug into that tragedy, I reported that Devon Pouse was found incompetent to stand trial. During his competency hearing, it was pretty clear the kid couldn't function. We didn't need the two psychiatrists who had examined him to confirm what was patently obvious. Devon would be held in a secure state hospital until he regained his ability to understand and assist in his own defense, if indeed that ever happened. The news didn't appear to surprise any of the Elders. There were nods and murmurs of understanding.

I was ready to discuss having another go at the parents, but Seah opted for an update on the Ramirezes. Hawthorne began by reporting that the investigating detective opined that the husband was not very bright and appeared to be easily manipulated by his wife. Even with that caveat, it was an easy decision to file murder against him. He might be slow-witted and easily manipulated, but he was cognizant enough to understand the consequences of his brutal conduct.

We then turned to the more difficult call of what to do, if anything, with Cathy. Hawthorne was urging that we file on Cathy. "Like I said at our last meeting, the investigators who first caught this case were convinced that the husband inflicted the physical abuse but she was in control of the household. They urged me to inform the committee that she is a manipulative sadist.

Mann took that in and said, "I hear that, but how do we prove she was complicit in the kid's death?"

"As I recall from our previous discussion, they lived in close quarters," Seah said. "Didn't they live in a trailer up north and then in a smallish duplex down here?"

"That's right, and neither worked outside the home. They were, as far as we know, always in very close quarters," Hawthorne said. "Nothing could have gone on in their household without the other knowing."

"I like the close proximity argument as well as the duty they owed to the boys since they were the caretakers," I said. "However, we can't count on any testimony coming from either spouse because of the spousal privilege."

I looked at Hawthorne. "Roger, have the investigators found any witnesses who might be willing to testify as to the nature of the relationship between husband and wife that could shed some light on their dynamic? Has he contacted any of the neighbors?"

"I don't know, I would assume so," Hawthorne answered. "I could reach out."

Seah once again took charge. "I'm not certain we are in any better position today than we were last month concerning the wife." That generated nods from Mann and me. "They're both in custody, so there's no compelling need to rush our decision. Perhaps we once again put this over a couple of weeks for further investigation along the lines that Jake suggested. Maybe someone from when they lived in Oregon or more recently in Rialto might give us the push we need to make a filing decision on the wife."

"I agree," said Mann. "Especially given the torture which

potentially elevates this matter to a capital case." She looked at Hawthorne. "Sorry, Roger, but we need more."

Hawthorne shrugged. "I'll, of course, accede to the will of the group. But for my money, I think we've already got enough."

Seah grinned at Hawthorne. "With what we know now, would you be willing to try this case?"

"In a heartbeat," he replied. "I would, and when, not if, we file capital charges against both, I've got it."

"With that declaration," said Seah, "we'll assign you the case when and if."

Seah turned to me. "Jake, I know you wanted to take up Pouse today, but I just received a text. I've got a fire to extinguish. Would it be acceptable to you to schedule a meeting two weeks from now to have further discussion on both the Pouses and Cathy?"

"Works for me."

CHAPTER 17

Tuesday, February 20, 2019, supplemental committee meeting. We were there to discuss a possible filing decision on Cathy Ramirez and whether to go forward on the Pouses in the wake of the judge's dismissal of the involuntary manslaughter charges at the prelim.

Hawthorne, as requested, had gone back to Sheriff's Detective Ron Everly for follow-up investigation on the Ramirezes. Hawthorne instructed Everly that the committee was specifically interested in focusing on Cathy. Everly recanvassed the neighbors and interviewed "everyone within shouting distance of the Ramirezes' duplex." Once again the neighbors claimed ignorance, even after he explained that the eleven-year-old boy who had been living there had been killed.

However, Everly's dogged diligence finally struck gold with Marj Butler, who lived across the street from the Ramirezes. Butler, an older woman who lived alone, had not been home during Everly's earlier canvas. When informed that Oscar had been killed, she became visibly upset and, after collecting herself, agreed to speak with Everly.

Hawthorne passed everyone a copy of Everly's interview with Butler.

Everly: Ma'am, may I record our conversation?

Butler: Of course. I'll tell you what I know. I'm not certain it will be helpful. Will I have to testify?

Everly: That's not up to me. But it would be important to make certain I get your comments down accurately. Like I said, we're dealing with the death of an eleven-year-old boy and could use your help.

Butler: I understand. I knew it was bad. I should have said something or done something. I figured somebody else would say something. We could all hear it.

Everly: Tell me what you heard.

Butler: That woman was constantly cursing and screaming at her wimp of a husband and the boy. Everyone could hear it. We knew there was something wrong in that house and none of us did a damn thing.

Everly: What kinds of things did you hear her saying?

Butler: It wasn't so much what she was saying but how she said it. And her language and abuse of both of them was God-awful. A couple of times I saw the boy sitting on the curb in front of their place rocking himself and crying. Once I saw him holding himself, like he was sick or nauseous. I gotta tell you, I'm ashamed I didn't reach out to him. I guess I assumed that some of my neighbors would do something. At least call the police. We talked about it but did nothing.

Everly: Did you ever see anyone hitting the boy?

Butler: No, but my friend Mellisa saw the man kicking the boy.

Everly: Where does Mellisa live?

Butler: Just across the way. I think she'll talk to you, especially now that we know the boy was killed.

Hawthorne then handed us his interview with Mellisa Donohue.

Everly: Ms. Donohue, I'm going to record our conversation regarding your observations of the residents of 13208 Coldbrook. Is that okay?

Donohue: You've already talked to Marj?

Everly: That's correct, but I'd like to get your observations.

Donohue: Will I have to testify?

Everly: I don't make that decision. But a child was killed and I'm sure you want to tell me what you know about it.

Donohue: Yes. I should have come forward earlier. I'll tell you what I know. That woman was awful. Screaming and cussing. I felt sorry for her husband but sorrier for the boy. The husband was an adult and could leave, but that boy was trapped, as far as I could see.

Everly: Did you ever see either of the adults strike the boy?

Donohue: A couple of times I saw him kick the boy. I mean really kick him. I never saw her hit him.

Everly: You actually witnessed the husband kicking the boy?

Donohue: I did.

Everly: Any yelling or screaming coming from the house?

Donohue: Plenty of that. Mostly her. Constantly berating both of them. As you can see, we all live pretty close together. Couldn't miss her yelling at them.

Everly: What kinds of things did you hear?

Donohue: Threats. When she got on one of her rages, she would threaten both of them. But as far as I could see, she rarely left the house. She could hardly move. She was grossly obese.

We had what we needed to make a filing decision on Cathy. Hawthorne was insistent we file capital charges with torture as the special circumstance. Against Hawthorne's strenuous objection, we rejected capital murder and filed second-degree murder against both. Murder two doesn't require the specific intent to kill, but rather only the specific intent to inflict great bodily injury. Kicking the kid would get us there. Aiding and abetting by Cathy, as well as her duty to protect a minor in her charge, would bring her into the murder.

CHAPTER 18

Once we made our decision on the Ramirezes, Seah looked at me expectantly. "Let's turn to the Pouses. What happened at their prelim. How did it go wrong?"

"I didn't do a very good job," I said. "I wasn't forceful enough in conveying the case to the judge."

"Wait a moment," said Mann. "That's not quite the version I heard. It was reported to me that a large hostile Second Amendment crowd intimidated Judge Merritt. You also had to contend with that jerk Sam Hardy."

Hawthorne let out a sardonic laugh. "Yeah, I heard about that. Hardy's a handful."

"We all know about Hardy," Seah added.

"With all that said, it was my prelim to lose and I lost it." I scanned the faces. "I strongly recommend we refile and let me run it again. I'm confident we can get it past the prelim."

Hawthorne, in a haughty tone: "I thought it was dead on arrival the first time around, and I think my point was proven, even at this early phase. Let's recognize reality and let it be. If you want to file against these parents, go after them for failing to properly secure a firearm and slap them with a fine." He shook his head. "Even if you get this by a judge at a prelim, it's never going to fly at a jury trial."

Mann ran interference for me. "Roger, we had this discussion last time. Nothing has really changed. From what I've learned, Jake was up against a hostile crowd, a weak judge, and a raucous defense lawyer who was playing to the crowd." Her tone bridged no equivocation. "I think we were correct in filing this case in the first place and I think we are correct in refiling."

Hawthorne wasn't about to roll over. "Leslie, let me repeat, even should the charges survive prelim, it will never result in a jury conviction. I'm not certain we can go ahead ethically. I, for one, don't have a good-faith belief that there is sufficient evidence to convict."

"Roger," I said, "I'll never guarantee a conviction on any case, but I'm convinced I'll be able to put on a strong case."

"Again," said Seah, scanning the faces, "we have a consensus. We are authorizing Jake to go forward." Then looking directly at me, she said, "Get 'em, Jake."

CHAPTER 19

I took off the Thursday and Friday of our move to Bruno Keys. Moving is usually stressful, but not this move. This move was a celebration. Lisa and I would be under a common roof. We would wake in the same bed seven days a week. We would have breakfast together and dinner together. No more of the unsettling weekends back and forth.

I rented an SUV to tote my belongings to our new home. My old Benz is fun but pretty much unfunctional for hauling. Other than my books, clothes, and assorted keepsakes, I didn't have much to move. My one treasure was the watercolor Lisa had painted of the two of us walking toward the Malibu Pier. I bequeathed my limited furniture, including my bed, dining table, and assorted chairs to the fortunate soul Tony and Eve would allow to move in.

By far the most significant loss would be their daily companionship. They had been my family. Moving away from them was the only downside to the move.

But life is constantly in flux, be graceful, Clearwater.

Of course there were the promises Tony and Eve and I made to one another, but reality doesn't necessarily reflect promises. Sure we would see each other, but not in the casual daily interaction we had enjoyed.

The other big loss was the thrice-weekly swims around the pier.

I wondered if my faithful swim companions would keep it up in my absence. I hoped so.

Lisa had contracted Meathead Movers. She had a whole household to move. Her furniture would be our furniture. Her kitchen and bath stuff would be our kitchen and bath stuff. By the time I arrived in Bruno Keys, the four young guys from Meathead, under Lisa's expert guidance, had arranged most of the furniture in place. I tipped them fifty dollars each and sent them on their way.

Above the fireplace, I hung the painting of us walking to the pier.

By four that afternoon, we opted to take a break and retired with a nice chablis to our loungers on the deck. There were still boxes to unpack, but they could wait. The sun was preparing to settle beyond the Pacific and, with some coastal clouds, made for a breathtaking departure.

The next morning, way too early, a man appeared at our front door. "Welcome, neighbor. My name is Zack Zagorski. I live right there," he said, pointing to the house to our west. He was short, thin, tan, and weathered, with a ZZ Top beard, tie-dye shirt, shorts, and leather sandals. He looked to be on the far side of seventy. He handed me a platter of cookies as I invited him in. "Snickerdoodles, homemade, one of my specialties."

"Nice to meet you, Zack," I said, as Lisa walked in, wearing her robe.

When he saw Lisa, he nearly swooned. "No need to introduce me to Lisa St. Marie. I've been a great admirer of her and her work for quite a while."

Lisa stared. "Zack! Zack Zagorski!" She stepped to him and gave him a hug. "I don't think you've missed one of my shows in years."

"And I never want to miss one." Turning to me, Zack said, "I have seven St. Maries hung in my house. I'm passionate about the joy and color in her work. The optimism expressed in every painting makes me feel good about the world."

I took him by the arm, walked him to the family room, and showed him the Malibu Pier painting. He smiled. "Yeah, I saw this in Carmel during one of her shows. I wanted to buy it." He flashed a suspicious look at Lisa. "You had it wrapped up before the show?"

Lisa laughed. "He forced my hand, Zack."

Turning to me, he said, "I don't blame you." Scrutinizing the painting, he asked, "Is that the two of you?"

"It is," I said. "Now you can see why I had to have it."

He shrugged and gave a knowing smile. "Makes sense to me."

"Come join us for coffee and some of your cookies," Lisa said. "I'm just making coffee."

"I don't want to be a bother." Clearly not meaning it.

"No bother," I said. "Lisa, take him out on the deck. I'll get the coffee."

When I stepped out on the deck, I heard Lisa say, "What a coincidence, moving in next to you."

Zack smiled. "No coincidence. I have always lived a charmed life, and you moving in next door is just further evidence of that."

If only we all had such an optimistic attitude.

Lisa grinned and took hold of his hand. "Moving here was meant to be."

He filled us in on Bruno Keys. He was a twenty-year veteran of the enclave and knew, for better or worse, everyone who lived in the twenty-five residences. Not surprisingly, as we soon learned, it was an eclectic and eccentric group; several actors I'd never heard of, a number of artists, and a whole lot of retirees.

Before he left, he invited us to his house that afternoon. "I always have people over on Saturday afternoons. Bring a bottle and join us. Great way to meet some of your new neighbors."

"Thanks Zack, I think that would be nice," Lisa said.

"Good. I'll leave you two to your unpacking. See you later." He then added, "This is no coincidence, Lisa. You and Jake were meant to be here."

CHAPTER 20

With the committee's blessing, I did indeed refile the three involuntary manslaughter charges against Don and Kay Pouse. And I was fortunate to draw any judge but Merritt this time around. Judge Amanda Brand was new to the bench, having been appointed six months earlier by the governor. She was young, most likely in her mid-thirties. She was stout and pale, with short, no-nonsense hair. She had been in Big Law, specializing in intellectual property. Not a background often seen in judges.

The money in Big Law was usually too good to leave.

I had no idea of her judicial personality. But again, she had to be a step up from Merritt. Hell, a second-year law student would be a step up from Merritt. The question was, would she be able to stand up to Sam Hardy? Hardy was as tough and belligerent as Vlad Putin.

Given their success at the first prelim, the pro-Pouse crowd turned out in even greater numbers for round two. Judge Brand, apparently forewarned of the potential for disruption, took the bench, surveyed the crowd, gaveled for order, and warned the full house.

"It's my understanding there were some disruptions the last time this matter was heard," she said, giving Hardy a sidelong glance. "I will not tolerate any such behavior in my courtroom." Scanning the packed gallery, she continued, "I will clear the courtroom of anyone disrupting these proceedings." She paused a beat, and added, "I hope my message is clearly received."

A man in a camouflage vest over his bare chest stood and yelled, "Don't threaten us! We have a right to speak out against injustice! We are American citizens!" There were several other voices raised in agreement.

Brand wasted no time. "Bailiffs, escort that man from my sight."

The bailiffs were immediately on him. As he was being led off, he took a final verbal swipe at the judge. "You can't silence all of us! We are patriots and this is our courtroom!"

"Anyone else?" Brand scanned the crowd. All was quiet until Hardy stood.

"For judicial proceedings to have legitimacy," he bellowed, "they must proceed in full view of the public. Your initial comments warning of conducting this hearing in a courtroom cleared of supporters of the defendants is an unconstitutional challenge of the people's right to witness events occurring in their public courtrooms."

Brand had fired her shot; Hardy was returning fire.

Brand, leaning forward: "Your point, Mr. Hardy?"

Stepping around counsel table and taking several steps toward the bench, which alerted both bailiffs, Hardy stopped and answered. "My point is that your comments evidence a bias—no, actually a hostility, against my clients. I call for you to recuse yourself from this hearing. Your lack of objectivity is plain for everyone to see."

That elicited several additional comments from the gallery. Brand turned to her two bailiffs. "Clear those individuals from the courtroom!" Speaking to the gallery, she said, "You have been warned, now you are excluded."

As the bailiffs went about carrying out her order, she turned to Hardy. "Counsel, I'll deal with you after the courtroom has been cleared of those bent on disruption."

Brand was proving as tough as coffeehouse steak. I had the judge I needed.

Once the bailiffs had cleared the disruptors, Brand gave Hardy a surprisingly conciliatory whisper of a smile, and in an even tone, said, "Mr. Hardy, I will not recuse myself, and I'll expect you to participate in this preliminary hearing in a most professional manner." Hardy didn't acknowledge Brand's admonition but remained standing. Arching her dark eyebrows, she raised her voice. "Is that clear, Mr. Hardy?"

Hardy waited a defiant beat, then another. "I stand by my comments," he said, with his jaw jutting forward from his huge head.

"Then we are in accord, because I stand by my comments," responded Brand. They stared at one another.

This could be Tombstone in the 1870s.

I let the rancor settle and then broke the mean, uncomfortable deadlock. "Your Honor, may I call my first witness?"

I didn't want a shootout.

Brand broke off Hardy and looked at me. "Please, Mr. Clearwater."

Before I could call my investigator, Hardy interrupted. "I want it on the record that the courtroom has been cleared of some of the defendants' supporters. I also renew my motion that the judge has demonstrated a strong bias against my clients and has refused to recuse herself."

Nonplussed, Brand nodded agreeably. "The record will indeed reflect Mr. Hardy's comments." She cocked her head and continued. "May we now get on with the business of this preliminary hearing?"

Hardy wasn't through. "For purposes of this hearing only, I will stipulate to the shooting deaths that occurred on September 13 of last year. This hearing is not about my clients' alleged role in the shootings, but rather their conduct prior to those events."

Hardy's offer to stipulate caught me off momentarily off balance. He understandingly didn't want the blood and guts of the three dead kids to wash over his clients. He wanted to focus on the more "academic" issues embroiling Don and Kay Pouse.

It was clever. Stipulate out the blood and gore. Not a chance I would agree and accept his offered stipulation. The blood and gore, while not essential to my case, would help push the prelim where I needed it to go.

"I respectfully refuse," I said. "Your Honor, you need to hear the full range of this tragedy to fairly assess the defendants' involvement and culpability."

Without being invited to respond, Hardy said, "The shootings themselves are not critical to the question of the Pouses' culpability. Their involvement, if any, relates only to their conduct prior to the shootings. They are charged with involuntary manslaughter, reckless endangerment, if you will. Their involvement ended prior to the shootings. Consequently, testimony about the subsequent events is irrelevant and prejudicial in the extreme to the charges they are facing."

"Mr. Hardy, as you know, stipulations require agreement from both sides," Brand lectured. "It doesn't appear that the state is willing to stipulate. However, if you feel the testimony we hear is not relevant to this proceeding, I will entertain any objections as they arise during the testimony."

Hardy resumed his seat without speaking. Don and Kay Pouse sat at the defense table, wide-eyed at the confrontations between the crowd and the judge and then between Hardy and the judge. What must they be thinking? Were they supportive of Hardy's obvious belligerence toward the judge? Might they be having second thoughts as to their choice of counsel?

On the other hand Hardy had worked his magic at the first prelim. On a broader scale, were they feeling any remorse that three high school kids were dead? Any sense of guilt? Or were they convinced that their conduct played no culpable part in this tragedy?

I stood and called Sheriff's Deputy Jesse Blank. I made short work of the preliminaries, such as his experience and qualifications. This was a prelim and not a trial. I didn't need to showcase Blank for a jury.

"On the afternoon of September 13, 2018, did you respond to Excelsior High School?"

"Yes, I responded to a 911 call at approximately 2:55 p.m."

"Describe the scene upon your arrival."

"The school was in lockdown. There was no one around except an individual who identified himself as a custodian. He pointed at a building to my west."

"Then what?"

"I had my service weapon drawn and proceeded where he pointed. As I came around the building, I saw an individual slumped against a wall. There was a handgun lying loose at his side."

"Then what?"

"At gunpoint, I ordered him to lie on his belly."

"Did he comply?"

"No. He just continued to sit there."

With a nod, I urged him to go on.

"I approached and held him at gunpoint and retrieved the weapon."

"Then what?"

"My sergeant arrived and took over."

I then had Blank identify the gun and Pouse.

"I have nothing further from Deputy Blank, Your Honor." Like I said, bare bones at the prelim.

"Mr. Hardy, any cross?"

Hardy, from a seated position: "You described Devon as unresponsive. So I take it he didn't interact with you in any way?"

"That's correct, sir."

"Did he put up any resistance at all?"

"No sir."

"I have nothing further."

"Call Sergeant Rick Hence," I said.

After he was sworn in, I established his rank within the sheriff's department and established that he arrived on scene at 3:00 p.m.

"Describe the scene upon your arrival."

"There were three officers present. They had taken the suspect into custody but they had not yet secured the scene and in particular the boys' restroom. Since there were reports of shots coming from the restroom, I was concerned there might be others in there."

"What did you then do?"

"From a defensive position I yelled for anyone inside the restroom to come out, and I got no response."

"Go on."

Hence took in a deep fortifying breath. "I pushed open the restroom door and identified three bodies."

"Objection!" Hardy shouted. "This is precisely what I was concerned about. What he saw and did after the shooting has no relevance to the charges against Don and Kay Pouse."

Brand said, "This is a manslaughter case. Certainly the deaths of the victims have relevance to such a charge. Overruled."

What a difference a competent judge makes.

Without having to repeat the question, Hence answered, "I ordered the arriving EMTs into the restroom to confirm the deaths."

"Objection! Lacks foundation for this witness to opine on the condition of any persons."

It was a worthless objection. Even though it was correct. This was a prelim, not a trial. The objection was designed to delay and harass. It set the tone for Hardy's approach to the hearing.

Brand gave me a shrug. "Mr. Clearwater, please rephrase."

"Sergeant, describe what you saw."

"There were three nonresponsive adolescent males. The floor and walls were covered in what appeared to be blood."

"What did you do next?"

"I cleared the responding EMT's to enter the restroom."

"And then?"

"After the scene was secured I went to the vehicle in which the suspect was being held and read him his *Miranda* rights."

"Did he acknowledge that he understood his rights and agree to talk with you?"

"Objection!" Hardy's objection boomed off the walls. "Counsel knows he's a minor. He can't waive without the consent of his parents!" Hardy was correct; I simply wanted to establish that Pouse seemed stunned and bewildered by events.

Hence answered before Brand ruled on the objection.

"He did not respond. He looked at me and then hung his head."

Brand admonished Hence. "You know better than that, Sergeant. That won't happen again. You will wait for my ruling."

Hence contritely nodded his understanding.

"Objection overruled."

"What did you do next?"

"I instructed my personnel to question anyone who might have information. After the forensic team completed their processing, I instructed the school's principal to release the school from lockdown and send everyone home."

"Did you examine the firearm found on Devon Pouse?"

"It was a Glock 19 semiautomatic handgun."

"You described it as a semiautomatic weapon. Describe what you mean."

"Objection! Lacks expertise."

Like I said, delays and roadblocks are the playground of contentious defense attorneys.

Brand waved off the objection. "He's a sheriff's sergeant with years of experience. Sergeant, you may answer."

"Sergeant, what does semiautomatic mean?"

"A semiautomatic weapon is any weapon where, when the shooter pulls the trigger, one bullet is fired and a new bullet is automatically loaded into firing position."

"No need to cock the gun between shots?"

"That's correct. A shooter can fire multiple shots in mere seconds."

"Your Honor, I have no more questions of Sgt. Hence."

"Any cross-exam, Mr. Hardy?"

"Not at this time."

"Call Investigator Otto Cipolla."

"Investigator, please fill us in on your background."

"I'm an investigator with the LA County Sheriff's Department. I was assigned as lead investigator on the murders that took place at Excelsior High."

"Okay, let's get right to it. During your investigation did you learn how Devon Pouse came into possession of the Glock handgun used in the shooting?"

"Yes, the gun was purchased by Kay Pouse, the suspect's mother, on August 31, 2018."

"What else did you learn of events prior to the shootings?"

Cipolla checked his notes. "The gun was picked up by Kay Pouse after the three-day waiting period, on September 3. On

September 6, one of Devon's teachers caught him online searching for ammunition for the gun. The school called the parents and reported the incident. The parents refused to come to the school and discuss the matter. According to the principal, no disciplinary action was taken by the school or the parents."

Hardy was up again. "This witness is speculating as to whether the parents took any disciplinary measures."

"Without some foundation of the investigator's knowledge, the objection is sustained."

"Did you learn of Kay Pouse's reaction to Devon's conduct in searching for ammunition?"

"Objection. Calls for hearsay."

"Again, Your Honor, as you and counsel are well aware, the investigating officer can testify at preliminary hearings concerning his investigation. Furthermore, the statement I am about to elicit is a party opponent admission and therefore admissible around the hearsay rule." Statements made by a party to the lawsuit, such as a defendant, are admissible by the opposing side as exceptions to the hearsay rule.

"Overruled. You may answer."

"Kay Pouse texted Devon, 'LOL, I'm not mad at you. You have to learn not to get caught.'"

Judge Brand held up a hand. "Investigator, repeat what the text said."

Cipolla repeated, "'LOL, I'm not mad at you. You have to learn not to get caught.'"

"That's what I thought you said." Brand snapped a quick look at Kay Pouse.

I let the point linger. "Let's move seven days forward to September 13, the day of the shooting. What did your investigation reveal?"

"A teacher saw Devon with a drawing of a gun pointing at the words 'I'm useless, help me. I hate them all.'"

"To your knowledge, what was the school's response?"

"The parents were again summoned to the school. The principal strongly advised the parents that they take Devon home and arrange for counseling. The parents refused and Devon was sent back to his classes."

"This was the same day as the shooting?"

"It was." Then he added, "Devon's backpack was not searched."

"How long after the meeting with the parents did the shooting occur?"

"Just over an hour."

"Thank you, Investigator Cipolla. I have no more questions of this witness."

Hardy's cross-examination went on ad nauseam. He went to great pains to cast blame on the school authorities, especially the principal. He had some rope there; the school's failures were certainly relevant.

Truth be told, the conduct of the school officials was negligent. Just not, in my view, criminally negligent.

The only tools I had in attempting to reel Hardy in were "beyond the scope of direct examination" and "asked and answered" objections. But even when my objections were repeatedly sustained, Hardy was undeterred. Brand showed remarkable restraint and, for the most part, let Hardy have his way.

CHAPTER 21

Following the lunch recess, I called Dr. Miles Foreman, a deputy coroner. As Foreman was ready to be sworn in, Hardy stood and said, "For this hearing only, I'll stipulate to the coroner's report. There's no need for his testimony at this time."

Brand looked at me. I was surprised. I hadn't expected any reasonable conduct from Hardy. "That's acceptable, Your Honor." I already had the blood and gore testimony. "The report establishes that the three boys died as a result of multiple gunshot wounds." I looked at Hardy. "Will the defense also stipulate that the bullets that killed the three victims came from the weapon fired by Devon Pouse?"

Hardy nodded. "For the purposes of this hearing only, the defense will so stipulate."

With the stipulations, I rested the state's case, figuring that would wrap up this hearing.

I was mistaken.

"Mr. Hardy, anything from the defense?" It is a true rarity for a defense lawyer to call witnesses during preliminary hearings, recognizing that nearly every prelim results in the defendant being held to answer for the charges and the case moving on to trial. Defense counsel typically won't expose their defense strategy at this early phase of the process. But again, Hardy was cut from a different piece of hard leather and, as demonstrated during the first prelim, had won a dismissal.

He surprised everyone in the courtroom, including me. "Yes, Judge, the defense calls Julia Conklin." Conklin was the Excelsior High School principal. I had not subpoenaed her, but obviously Hardy had.

Here we go, I thought. Hardy is going to try and deflect blame from the Pouses onto the school and its principal. But this was not the trial, this was just the prelim. Why would Hardy play a critical defense card now? Perhaps he harbored a sense that Judge Brand might find insufficient evidence, as had Judge Merritt at the first prelim, and knock the case out. Alternatively, even if he didn't succeed at this prelim level, I could only figure that by deflecting blame from his client, he was sending a message to me and the DA's office that, should this case survive the prelim, it would go down to defeat if they dared to take it to trial.

He was swinging for the fences.

Hardy's investigator ushered Principal Conklin into the courtroom. She was a large woman with wispy blow-away gray hair, probably in her mid-fifties. She looked frayed, tired, anxious, and ready for retirement. And, I imagine, when she received Hardy's summons to appear and testify, she wished she had retired a year ago.

Conklin was sworn in and Hardy was on her. "You were the principal of Excelsior High School from August 31 through September 13, 2018, correct?"

Conklin's voice was high-pitched and anxiety-scratchy. "Yes."

"As the principal, you have authority to discipline students, isn't that right?" Hardy's first two questions improperly led Conklin. Typically, lawyers cannot ask leading questions during direct examination. However, if the witness is deemed hostile to the examiner's position, the examiner can lead. I didn't bother objecting; this was the prelim.

"Yes," she answered warily.

"And discipline can take several forms, correct?"

"It can." Her voice unsteady.

"One type of discipline you can mete out is to suspend a student, isn't that right?" Hardy's questions were fast on Conklin, barely time for her to answer.

"It is."

"And that is at your discretion?"

"Yes, if I feel it is warranted." Her first mild pushback.

"So, to be clear, you can send a student home if circumstances warrant?"

"Again, depending on the circumstances."

"As a principal, one of your most serious concerns is the safety of your students, faculty, and staff?"

"Of course." Conklin was shrinking into her seat. She clearly knew what was coming and had no ability to head it off.

"Guns in particular are a serious concern of any school principal, aren't they?"

In a tremulous voice, "We have a zero-tolerance policy." That response wasn't going to inoculate her from attack.

Hardy bore in. "On September 6, you learned that Devon Pouse was caught online searching for ammunition, correct?"

Conklin wrapped her arms under her ample bosom. "It was brought to my attention."

"That concerned you, didn't it?"

"Yes," she said with surprising conviction, "and I called his parents and explained the situation."

"But you didn't talk to Devon about his conduct, did you?"

"No," she leaned forward to explain, "like I said, I called his parents. I was hopeful they would come get their son and arrange for some counseling."

"Back to my question." Hardy was relentless. "You didn't talk to Devon, did you?"

Excellent technique by Hardy: when a witness evades the question, come back to it and drill it home.

She remained sitting forward, eyes fixed on Hardy. "I believe I answered that question."

"You called his parents because anything to do with guns on a high school campus is a serious concern?"

"Of course it is." She put out her hands as if explaining to a particularly dense student. "That's why I called his parents. I was concerned."

"But not concerned enough to interview or talk to Devon?"

"I called his parents." Her face a grim mask.

"You didn't order anyone to check Devon's backpack for a gun?"

"No, I didn't know he had access to a gun."

"But for all you know, he could have had a gun in his backpack?"

"I certainly didn't think so," she snapped.

"Despite Devon's conduct, you didn't take any disciplinary action regarding him on that day?"

She took a deep exasperated breath. "Like I've repeated several times, we called his parents to take him home and hopefully arrange for some counseling."

"None of your staff, counselors, or teachers followed up with Devon on any of the seven days from this incident to the day of the shootings?"

"I hoped his parents had taken appropriate action." Conklin was holding her own.

"But you never contacted either of Devon's parents to ascertain if they had gotten him any counseling or therapy?"

"Counsel, you've covered that."

Hardy bore in. "So to be clear, to your knowledge, no one at the school followed up with Devon or his parents during those seven days?"

"Not to my knowledge."

"And during those seven days from the incident we are discussing up until the shooting, Devon was allowed to come to school and attend his classes, correct?"

"He was."

"On the day of the shootings, one of your teachers reported to you that Devon had drawn a picture of a gun, isn't that right?"

"Yes."

"And along with that picture, Devon wrote, 'I'm useless, help me. I hate them all.'"

"Yes, it was very disturbing."

"Disturbing?" Hardy bellowed. "It was downright scary, wasn't it?"

"That's why I once again called his parents."

"At this point you had very serious concerns about Devon's mental health?"

Conklin tightened her jaw. "That's why I called his parents. I wanted them to take Devon home and arrange for some counseling."

"You would agree with me that Devon's words evidenced some mental instability?"

"It was pretty clear that he was troubled and needed some counseling."

"Devon's drawing of a gun and his earlier effort to purchase ammunition were a serious concern to the health and safety of everyone at your school, correct?"

Conklin hesitated, checking her irritation, and said, "Again, that's why I called his parents in and urged them in the strongest of terms to get him some help."

In his most incredulous tone, Hardy said, "It fascinates me that you let this kid remain at school after you saw that drawing and read his words. And to be clear, you even sent him back into the classroom."

"The parents wouldn't take him home," she punched back.

"So you made the decision to not remove him from campus before the shootings, but rather sent him back to class?"

"I was in a no-win situation. The parents would not take him home, and I didn't believe I had sufficient facts to call in the police."

"You had the authority to remove him from the school, but instead you let this obviously disturbed sixteen-year-old return to a classroom with other students?"

Mistake. Hardy had gone too far. If it was that obvious to Conklin, it should have been obvious to his parents.

"Regretfully, I did."

"One last thing, Principal Conklin. Devon had his backpack with him that day, didn't he?"

"You know he did."

"It's not what I know, it's what you knew then." Hardy gave Conklin a hard look. "You didn't have anyone check his backpack for weapons before you sent him back into the classroom, did you?"

"I wish we had."

"We all wish you had."

Hardy had brutally laid bare the monumental failures of Principal Conklin. Hardy's message to the DA's office was loud and clear. Don't take this to trial.

Brand asked if I wanted to cross-examine the witness.

I briefly considered. "Yes, just a few questions." Maybe I would send a message of my own.

"You may proceed."

"Ms. Conklin, did you play any role in purchasing the semiautomatic handgun used to kill the three boys?"

"Objection! This is completely irrelevant to this hearing."

Brand let a small smile sneak out. "Mr. Hardy, you put Ms. Conklin's conduct at issue. Your objection is overruled."

"Of course not," Conklin answered, without me repeating the question.

"Did you have anything to do with leaving that weapon in a place in the Pouse home where this sixteen-year-old could access it?"

"Objection! Again, irrelevant."

"Again, overruled."

"Shall I repeat my question, Ms. Conklin?"

"That's not necessary. I had nothing to do with how Devon got hold of the gun."

"On September 6, the day Devon was caught searching for ammunition, did you call his parents and report his conduct?"

She looked at the Pouses and said, "I did."

"Did you ask them to come to the school and discuss the situation?"

"I did." Still fixed on the Pouses.

"Did they come?"

"No."

"So, despite your efforts to get the parents to school and discuss Devon's conduct, they didn't come to school?"

"Objection. Counsel's leading the witness."

Brand sat back, cocked her head, and with just a touch of condescension, said, "He is, Mr. Hardy. But this is your witness, and this is cross-examination, where leading questions are not only permitted but preferred."

Hardy, embarrassed, sat down without a word. For someone like Hardy to be embarrassed was a singular moment.

I went right back to my question. "So, despite your efforts to get Devon's parents to school to discuss his conduct, they refused to come?"

"That's right."

"Principal Conklin, following the ammunition incident, did you have any knowledge that Kay Pouse sent her son a text which read 'LOL, I'm not mad at you. You have to learn not to get caught.'"

"I only heard about that after the shootings."

"So to be clear, you had no knowledge of Kay Pouse's message until after the shootings?"

"That's correct. I never looked at his phone before turning it over to the police."

"On the day of the shootings, just an hour or so before the shootings, did you urge the defendants to take their son home?"

"In the strongest terms possible."

"During that conversation, did you inform them that earlier on the very day of the shootings, he had drawn a picture of a gun?"

"I showed them the drawing."

"Did you also show them the words he wrote?"

"I did, and again I urged them to take their son home and arrange to get him counseling."

"And did they agree?"

"No, they refused."

I let the answer linger. "Thank you Ms. Conklin. Your Honor, I have no other questions of Ms. Conklin."

Brand turned to Hardy. "Very well. Any redirect examination, Mr. Hardy?"

"It's not necessary." Hardy shrugged as if my cross-exam didn't hurt. "But I have comments before you make your ruling."

"Go ahead, Mr. Hardy."

Hardy unfolded his huge bulk from his chair and launched his argument. "These parents bear no criminal responsibility for the conduct of their son. They purchased a completely legal firearm. They are a family, like many American families, who enjoy hunting and target practice. And like many of us, they feel the need to protect their family. In purchasing the gun, they were pursuing constitutionally protected conduct.

"It could be argued that since their sixteen-year-old somehow got his hands on the gun, they may be considered careless, perhaps even negligent, matters best handled in the civil courts, but that establishes no criminal conduct on their part." A long pause as Hardy measured his words. "Let's be clear, this is just another effort to curtail the rights guaranteed under the Second Amendment."

Hardy paused again but was far from finished. "Now let's turn to September 6, when Devon was using his phone to look at ammunition. I'm hard-pressed to connect Devon's conduct to any criminal acts by his parents. As the principal testified, the parents did not come to the school that day. Criminal conduct?" he asked rhetorically, and shook his head. "Maybe poor parenting, but criminal conduct?"

A dismissive shake of his head. "Let's turn to the day of the shootings. There is no evidence that Don or Kay Pouse had any knowledge that Devon had the gun in his backpack. Again, where is the criminal conduct? Lousy parenting at worst, but criminal behavior? Never."

There was yet another long pause, as Hardy leaned over his notes.

"Mr. Hardy, does that conclude your remarks?"

"No." He slapped counsel table. "No, it does not. Let me speak as to why I called the school principal. The school, especially the school's principal, was in the optimum position to prevent the shootings. They are the professionals charged with keeping our kids safe while in school. They have the training and experience to recognize behavior that presents a threat. The principal and her staff failed in monumental ways on both September 6 and all the days leading up to and including September 13. They had the obligation to suspend Devon indefinitely and even to order psychological counseling as a condition of his return to school. They're the experts."

He slapped the table again. "They saw the signs and yet just sent him back into a classroom. Without question, *they* were best positioned to avert this tragedy, not the parents." Hardy finished to a courtroom filled with his congregation on the edge of their seats. He was preaching to his choir. Fortunately the choir didn't have a vote.

When it was clear Hardy was done, I stood. "Your Honor, may I be heard?"

"It's not necessary, Mr. Clearwater." She turned to Hardy. "Mr. Hardy, a lot of what you say is most likely true. But the school is not the defendant here. My role is to focus on whether these defendants engaged in reckless, life-endangering behavior, as required for involuntary manslaughter. And, after considering the evidence presented today, I find that they did engage in reckless, life-endangering behavior. Accordingly, the defendants are bound over for trial." She checked the calendar. "Arraignment in the trial court is set for May 30, 2019."

"You're making a major mistake!" Hardy was outraged. "You're dragging these parents through more weeks of misery and anxiety, for a trial in which they will be acquitted. You need to reconsider."

"Mr. Hardy, I've made my ruling!" Brand responded, in a take-no-prisoners voice. "Is there any other business we need to take care of here?"

"No there is not." Hardy wouldn't quit. "But I encourage you to follow this case through trial and realize what a thoughtless decision you've made here today."

"You are edging very close to contempt, Mr. Hardy. It's time for you to leave my courtroom."

Hardy huffed but didn't speak. He noisily packed his papers and escorted the Pouses out of the courtroom.

I had cleared the first hurdle, the ham-sandwich hurdle. Judge Brand was on board, but going forward, she would have no say in the matter. Hardy would be waiting for me at trial.

That figured to be a walk in the park.

CHAPTER 22

The March committee meeting was pushed back two weeks until March 20, due to scheduling conflicts. When we met, Hawthorne, without any preamble, dropped a bombshell. "The Ramirez investigators found Oscar's older brother, Felipe. His body was stuffed into a fifty-five-gallon drum, encased in cement."

The stunned silence ricocheted around the room.

Hawthorne, who had had time to take in the news, let the shock play out before going on. "As if this case wasn't already gruesome enough."

"Okay, Roger," Seah said, in a soft, sad voice. "Tell us what you know."

"Yeah, okay, here goes. Three days ago, a neighbor living several duplexes down from the Ramirezes' complained of a foul smell emanating from the carport where the Ramirezes had lived. She called the fire department and they responded and narrowed the smell to a fifty-five-gallon drum. The firefighters identified the smell as something decayed and called the sheriff's office. When the sheriff's forensic folks began chipping at the cement, they found human remains. Suspecting the body might be the missing boy, they matched his DNA to the child's mother."

"My god," uttered Mann. "Just when you think you've heard

the worst this world can throw at you." She closed her eyes and dropped her head.

Following the initial shock, the Elders had questions. How had the smell only become noticeable after the passage of so much time? Where was Felipe killed, Oregon or California? If Oregon, why had the Ramirezes brought the drum with Felipe's body back to California?

The first question was answered by the forensics people: Cement is an effective insulator, and since the body had been double-wrapped in industrial trash bags and then encased in cement, the noxious fumes had been well concealed.

The second question was answered by Caesar himself. After Felipe's body was discovered, investigators went back to Caesar, and in the presence of his lawyer and after again being *Mirandized*, he agreed to speak, against the advice of his lawyer.

Hawthorne read aloud from the exchange transcript between Caesar, his lawyer, and Detective Sherman:

> Sherman: I'm recording this conversation. Mr. Ramirez is with his attorney, Ms. Goldman. Mr. Ramirez has waived his *Miranda* rights and agreed to speak to us. Mr. Ramirez, we identified Felipe's body, found in a drum located in the carport where you resided at the time of Oscar's death. What can you tell us about Felipe's death?
>
> Ramirez: Felipe was killed while we were still living in Oregon.
>
> Sherman: How was he killed?
>
> Goldman: Caesar, once again, I'm advising you to not speak to the investigators.
>
> Ramirez: I gotta get this off my chest. Felipe was disobedient and disrespectful from the time he arrived. He refused to go to

school. He was disrespectful and disobedient, especially to my wife.

Sherman: So what happened?

Ramirez: Like I told you before, I tried punishment with both of the boys.

Sherman: What kind of punishment?

Ramirez: I told them to do chores around the house, but when they shirked, I used my belt. That's the only thing I could do. I never meant to kill anyone.

Sherman: Let's back up. Did Cathy approve of punishing the boys?

Ramirez: It was her idea. Especially when they disrespected her.

Sherman: How did they disrespect Cathy?

Ramirez: Cathy is heavy and has a hard time getting up. A couple of times, one of the boys would slap her on the leg and run off. Felipe called her Shamu. We couldn't let that happen.

Sherman: Tell us how Felipe was killed.

Ramirez: It was the same old, same old. Felipe wouldn't eat dinner, saying the food was garbage. So Cathy told him to go scrub the bathroom. When I went to check on him, he was just leaning against the wall, doing nothing. I warned him with my boot, but when I checked up on him again, nothing. So I did what I had to do. I punished him.

Sherman: How did you punish him?

Ramirez: I grabbed him by his neck and the seat of his pants and slammed his head into the wall.

Muffled crying.

Sherman: Mr. Ramirez, I know this is difficult. Do you need some water?

Ramirez: I'm okay. I guess I knocked him out, so I picked him up and carried him to his bed. The next morning, he was dead. I didn't mean to kill him.

Sherman: Why did you put the body in a drum?

Ramirez: Cathy said it was just an accident but that the police wouldn't believe us. She told me to get rid of the body. So I put him in an old freezer behind the trailer. Then I got some quick-dry cement from the Walmart and put him in the drum with the cement.

Sherman: Was Oscar aware of what had happened to his brother?

Ramirez: Probably. They slept in the same room. But he probably didn't know what I did with Felipe.

Sherman: Was Cathy aware?

Ramirez: Oh yeah.

Sherman: Caesar, why'd you bring the drum with the body back to California?

Ramirez: Pretty stupid, huh?

Sherman: Well, weren't you afraid that eventually it would smell?

Ramirez: I wrapped it up real tight. I guess I figured with the cement and all, it wouldn't smell.

Sherman: Caesar, you want to talk about Oscar?

Goldman: Caesar, you've already talked too much. I strongly advise you to stop the questioning.

Ramirez: I need to explain what happened. They were accidents.

Sherman: Okay, tell me about Oscar's death.

Ramirez: It was Thanksgiving. Cathy's brother and his wife brought over a real good dinner, but Oscar refused to eat. It was disrespectful. Cathy warned him, but he wouldn't eat and kept hunching over. I sent him to his room and put him in a closet and told him to stay there until he acted right.

Sherman: You need water? Some time?

Ramirez: Just let me get through this. After her people left, I checked on him and he was standing up like he was trying to get out. I got angry and knocked him down and then kicked him in the chest with my boot. When I returned, he wasn't breathing.

Sherman: What happened then?

Ramirez: I wanted to call 911, but Cathy said no.

Sherman: So what did the two of you do?

Ramirez: Cathy got in our car and drove off. I called 911, but it was way too late.

Sherman: Caesar, thanks for setting the record straight. Anything else you want to share?

Goldman: Dammit Caesar, that's enough. This is over.

After Hawthorne finished reading, we all sat in silence.

Finally, Seah spoke. "This just gets worse and worse."

Mann was the first to offer her thoughts. "As awful and sickening as this is, I still don't see this as a capital case, despite the torture these two put the kids through. I see this as a breakdown of a system that allowed the Ramirezes to do what they did."

A breakdown?

She paused and stated the obvious. "Ramirez's sister should never have put those two boys in their hands."

"How was she to know?" I said. "Looks like she tried to do the best she could, given the state of her life. As it turned out, she made a terrible decision, but how was she to know?"

Seah weighed in. "What jumps out to me is how incredibly unsophisticated the Ramirezes were. As awful and tragic as this is, I agree with Leslie. Despite the gross abuse, I don't see this being a capital case. There is no premeditation here. They didn't mean to kill those boys. This is a murder two case. They had the specific intent to inflict serious bodily injury but not the intent to kill. This is murder two."

Hawthorne shook his head. "You folks are going soft on me. This is a capital case. We may not have premeditation, but we've got two killings during the course of torture. As everyone in this room knows, that's a special circumstance." He paused. "The jurors will be repulsed, just as we are. I can put them on death row."

"Two comments," I said. "First, we only have one death in our jurisdiction. Felipe was killed in Oregon and his death is their prosecution. Second, as to capital charges, if the only question is *can* we get them on capital charges, the entire system is broken. The question should be, *should* we get them on capital charges? These people, as Nancy pointed out, are unsophisticated rubes. The death penalty is reserved for the worst of the worst. For those vicious enough to knowingly go into their vile deeds fully aware of what they were doing."

I turned to Hawthorne. "There is, in my mind, little doubt that you could convict and get death, but that's not what we are about. We are about working toward the right result, and that doesn't include filing capital cases. We already decided on murder two. We put both of them away for years."

"Roger? Final say," offered Seah. "But I'm with Jake, and I think Leslie is as well."

Mann nodded.

"Okay. I will, of course, go with the will of the committee." Scanning the faces, he said, "I think the three of you are wrong, but I concede."

CHAPTER 23

I took the next Friday off to help with the last of the unpacking. Lisa knew where she wanted everything; I was the grunt following orders and muscling things. I knew my strengths, and they were far from interior decoration. My only creative input had been to hang Lisa's Malibu Pier watercolor the first day. We laughed and worked until things were where they were meant to be. Much of the furniture that the previous owner left behind, we parked in the garage, waiting for a Salvation Army pickup. We kept a beautiful rolltop desk and armoire that was left behind and moved them to the second bedroom.

Lisa was several weeks into being principal. She was pleased that the faculty and staff were supportive. Still no word from Russ Rosen. She had called him several times, only to leave voicemails. That Friday afternoon, we drove back up to San Arcadia, trying to catch Rosen at home, but got no response. A number of newspapers had accumulated in his driveway. We picked them up and stacked them next to the front door.

Likewise, I got a bag I kept in my car for groceries and gathered his mail. We walked around to the back, but all the blinds were closed. I walked over to the house to the west of Rosen's, but no one was home. Lisa went to the east and reported back that the neighbor hadn't seen him for more than a week.

"Jake, I'm worried for him. We need to do something."

"I agree. Let's contact the San Arcadia Police and see if we can get some help."

In the lobby, I asked for Sgt. Laske, a man I had worked several cases with when I was a San Arcadia DDA. We had become friends. Laske was in and emerged to meet us in the lobby. "Jake, it's good to see you." I got a big smile and an enthusiastic handshake. He was short and muscular, dressed casual in tan pants and a white polo shirt.

"Jeff, this is my wife, Lisa St. Marie."

He gave her an appreciative look and stuck out his hand. "Very nice to meet you. Jake's a lucky man." He smiled and turned back to me. "You still at Pacifico?"

"Yes and no." I smiled. "I'm on a one-year leave from teaching and currently working with the LA DA."

"Sounds complicated." He grabbed me by the shoulders. "It's really good to see you. Dammit Jake, you should do a better job of staying in touch."

Laske had made some effort to get together with several calls after I had left the office, but I hadn't held up my end. "Sorry, Jeff. I dropped the ball. No excuse, other than Tice had practically run me out of town."

"Well, things haven't changed much. Tice is still Tice, and we still have to deal with him." Tice seemed to have that effect on everyone he worked with. Laske looked at Lisa. "Sorry, just catching up on some old business. Jake and I have been in the trenches together a few times."

He slapped me on the shoulder and, in a not-quite-disparaging tone, said, "Although representing Durgeon put a strain on our relationship for a while," he paused, "turned out Jake was right. Durgeon wasn't good for the murders."

"I understand," Lisa said. "I was living in San Arcadia during the Durgeon trial. I know how difficult it got."

He nodded his understanding. "So Jake, what brings you to my doorstep?"

We filled him in on Russ Rosen's situation. Laske looked at Lisa. "He have any family or close friends we can reach out to?"

"Not that I know of. He's single and a bit of a loner. We never socialized. I don't know much about his personal life." She gave Laske an apologetic shrug. "Sorry I can't give you more."

Laske rubbed his ruddy, clean-shaven face. "Two weeks is a while. Maybe a welfare check at his residence is in order. I've got your number; I'll call when I have something to report. We'll check it out this afternoon."

"Thanks, Jeff. Appreciate the help. Lisa and I just bought a place at Bruno Keys, so no more excuses about getting together. Maybe get you and Marsha down for some drinks and barbecue."

"I'd like that." More handshakes. "I'll call once we've checked on Mr. Rosen."

That afternoon, Laske called. I put him on speaker. "We did a welfare check. No one home. Place doesn't look like anyone has been there for a while. The residence doesn't appear to have been disturbed. My guys noted there were no suitcases found in the home and it appears Rosen's clothes and personal items are gone."

"So what happens now?" Lisa asked.

"From what we know, no laws have been broken and it doesn't appear that he was a victim of any nature. I followed up with the school district and spoke to …," he paused "…Frank Bennett, the school superintendent. He told me that he had contacted Rosen on January 19, informing him that he was indefinitely suspended, effective immediately."

"Did he say why?" Lisa asked.

"No, he said it was a confidential personnel matter."

"That's all he would say?"

"Yeah, pretty cryptic. I explained that he's been out of touch for two weeks and that people are concerned. He doubled down on confidentiality."

"Can you force the district to disclose what's going on? I asked. Something may have happened to him."

"Bennett told me there's nothing he can do without a warrant to disclose the specifics of his suspension. And as you know, Jake, I can't get a warrant without cause." He paused, waiting for a response, but added, "In light of his suspension, he could have packed up and taken off. A vacation? There are explanations."

"That doesn't seem like the Russ Rosen I know." Lisa was frustrated.

"I've seen situations where folks just take off, sometimes even abandoning their families and jobs. I don't know what to tell you. Doesn't seem we have a lot of options right now."

"So, that's it?"

"I can initiate a missing person investigation. But without more info, that probably won't be fruitful."

"That's a start, Jeff," I said. "What I'm hearing from you is that unless we can establish some nexus from his suspension to his disappearance, we can't force the school district's hand. And without that information, we don't have any leads to run him down."

"I'm afraid that's right."

"Thanks, Jeff. We appreciate you looking into this. Would you please keep Lisa and me apprised if you learn anything?"

"Will do. Good talking with you and Lisa, Jake. I wish it was under different circumstances."

CHAPTER 24

April 6, 2019. Preliminary hearing of Jaxon Webb. Remarkably enough, the assigned judge was James Merritt. That's right, the judge who had been steamrolled by Sam Hardy during the first prelim of Devon Pouse's parents. I wondered if he had grown a backbone since that prelim. I still harbored ill will.

Tracie Switzer's parents, Donna and Frank, and Detective Coolidge were waiting for me in the hallway outside Department 505 of the Clara Foltz Criminal Courts Building. Coolidge introduced everyone. The Switzers were a handsome couple, both dressed as if interviewing for jobs at high-end firms. Donna took hold of my hand. "Detective Coolidge told us you were instrumental in getting Tracie's case to trial. Thank you." Her eyes glistened.

"Mrs. Switzer, the one to thank is Detective Coolidge. He stuck with this case and never quit. He is responsible for getting us this far."

"We know about his dedication." She reached over and patted Coolidge's arm.

"Mr. Clearwater, is there anything you need from us during this hearing?" Frank Switzer asked.

"No, not today. I'm not sure if the two of you are familiar with preliminary hearings. We don't put on our full case today. Just enough to convince the judge that we have a case. So today, I'm going to need Detective Coolidge, one of the two guys who were in the car that night, and a coroner."

"Detective Coolidge filled us in," said Frank Switzer.

"Okay. I'm sure he's warned you that I need to use some crime scene photographs to establish Tracie's death." I studied their faces. "That can be hard. You may want to step out during that time."

Donna nodded, working to keep her emotions in check.

I turned to Coolidge. "I assume Melrose is waiting in the wings."

"He is. He's also nerved out, having to face Webb."

"Tough," I scoffed. "No one's going to work up any sympathy for him." I nodded toward the door. "Okay, let's go get 'em." The four of us pushed through the courtroom door.

Webb, wearing his county-issue orange overalls, was already seated and talking to his lawyer, an older woman I didn't know but assumed was a public defender. This was my first look at Webb. He was thin and looked fit, with braided hair to his shoulders. When he turned to look at me as I was settling in at my table, his eyes were narrowed, which gave him a sinister look.

Webb's lawyer broke off and came over and introduced herself. "Brenda Tuck." We shook. She had the weary look of a deputy public defender who had been dealing with defendants for decades. I'd seen that look before, during my San Arcadia DA days. Burnout, the scars and fatigue of her difficult job. Representing those accused of crime day in and day out takes a vicious toll.

Only strong and dedicated advocates can hang in there and keep punching back when most of the time you're on the losing side. Thank god there were lawyers willing to take on such critical roles in our justice system. Tuck wore her easy-care hair short and was dressed in a baggy gray pantsuit. "I'll be handling the Webb prelim."

"Jake Clearwater. Nice to meet you."

She stepped back and took a good look at me. "Hey, you're the prosecutor from the Cort case." She gave a halfhearted grin. "That was quite a spectacle."

Spectacle? Odd comment. I don't think it was intended to be disparaging. Think the best, until proven otherwise.

"Yeah. Spectacle is one way to describe it," I laughed.

"I imagine one case like Cort is enough for a while," she said. "No fireworks this time around. Just another murder case the public has no interest in."

I looked over my shoulder at the Switzers. "Tracie Switzer's parents are here; that's enough of the public for me."

"Sorry, I didn't mean to be flip. Apologies." She looked over her shoulder at Webb. "He's a piece of work."

"What do you mean?"

"Just hard to work with, but what's new."

Our brief conversation broke off as Merritt assumed the bench in the sparsely populated courtroom. As Tuck had commented, this was just another murder case. The public was not particularly interested; unless there was some celebrity involved or multiple murder victims, it was just another trial.

The case was called, and when I made my appearance, Merritt looked at me for the first time. "Counsel approach," he ordered. "Ms. Tuck, good morning." Turning to me, he said, "Mr. Clearwater, we meet again. You were on the Pouse case?"

"I was." My voice was neutral.

He looked at me as if expecting some comment. When I offered none, it became awkward. He filled the vacuum. "I understand you ran that prelim against those parents a second time."

"I did." My face also remained neutral.

"I see," he said. "Were you able to put on any additional evidence the second time?"

"No. The second judge properly found I had met my burden."

He chewed on his bottom lip. "Are you implying that I got it wrong?"

I leaned toward Merritt. "The second judge got it right."

His face tightened and took on a reddish hue. In a tight voice, he replied, "Okay, let's hear your case today, Counsel. I trust you will be able to put on sufficient evidence this time."

A weak rejoinder intended to end our acrimonious exchange.

"I will, just as I did during the Pouse prelim." Neither of us was going to retreat.

Merritt paused, calculating whether to extend the exchange, maybe trying to formulate a comeback. Either he had had enough or he couldn't think of a rejoinder. He looked at Tuck. "Any motions before we get underway?"

"Nothing for the defense," Tuck said, eyeing us both, wondering about our back-and-forth.

"Nothing for the prosecution."

With that, Tuck and I returned to our counsel tables. I'd only been in the office a short while but had already developed an adversarial relationship with a judge. I will not be pushed around, especially by someone I believe to be weak and unqualified.

I called Detective Coolidge to the stand and laid out my case. We began with the ATM robbery by producing the bank records and the grainy video of an unidentified Black man at the machine. We then moved on to the murder scene and I introduced photos of Tracie Switzer's body in the truck. The Switzers remained in the courtroom but with eyes averted. I then had Coolidge describe his contacts with Melrose and Bridge, as well as the negotiations for reduced sentences.

During Tuck's cross-examination of Coolidge, she bore in on the plea deals and made it clear that the only percipient witness at this hearing was a snitch working to reduce his prison sentence. Fair point but not critical at this early prelim stage.

I then called Dinold Melrose to the stand. He was the more convenient of the two snitches. Bringing Bridge in from Nevada at this phase was not practical. Between Coolidge and Melrose, I had enough to get through the prelim—assuming Merritt wouldn't once again scramble my eggs.

Melrose, resplendent is his orange overalls, shuffled to the witness stand, accompanied by one of the bailiffs. From the moment he entered the courtroom, he never raised his head. He wanted no part of the angry stares directed from Webb.

Following Melrose's mumbled assertion of the oath—something I'm certain he took to heart—I began. "Mr. Melrose, why are you here testifying?" I stood as far from Webb as I could. I wanted Melrose to direct his testimony to me, away from Webb's menacing glare.

In a low, barely audible voice, he replied, "I was there when the girl was killed."

"Okay, let's back up and work through the events of that night and early morning. When did you first see Jaxon Webb on the night of September 3, 2016, the night Tracie Switzer was murdered?"

"I don't know. It was pretty late," he said, eyes riveted on his knees.

"Would you say it was around nine or ten that night?"

Leading questions are appropriate during cross-examination, but not during direct. He nodded without speaking.

"Mr. Melrose, you need to answer out loud so the court reporter can record your response," I mildly admonished.

Again, he nodded his head and said in a halting voice, "Yeah, that's right."

"Who were you with when you first saw them?"

A long, uncomfortable silence.

Was this guy going to go south on me?

Finally, he answered, "Glen Bridge."

"What were you and Bridge doing before you encountered the defendant?"

He gestured with his hands, still looking down. "We were just driving around, smoking, minding our own business."

"Where did you first see the defendant that night?"

Head still down. "I seen him outside a liquor store."

"What city was that?"

"Riverside."

"Did you know the defendant before that night?"

"Yeah, I'd seen him around."

"What was the interaction between you and the defendant that night?"

Long pause, no answer. I repeated, "Did you give him a ride?" I was trying to pull teeth, one molar at a time.

"Yeah, me and Bridge give him a ride." This second reference to Bridge was interesting; he was trying to divert as much of the blame from himself as possible. I'm not sure that cut any ice with Webb.

"So to be clear, there were three of you in your car: Bridge, the defendant, and yourself?"

Again a silent nod, and then a "Yeah."

Another tooth.

"Did the defendant tell you he wanted to go to Pomona?"

"Objection, Your Honor. He keeps leading the witness. This is supposed to be the witness's testimony, not the prosecutor's."

How's Merritt going to handle this?

Merritt: "I agree, Ms. Tuck. However, I find that the witness appears to be intimidated and reluctant to answer, so I'm going to overrule the objection and give Mr. Clearwater some license here."

Was this a makeup call for the pathetic job he did during the Pouse prelim?

Melrose answered without me having to repeat. "He told me Pomona."

"Did the three of you arrive in Pomona?"

"Yes." In a louder voice. Head still down. It was disconcerting talking to the top of his head.

"Tell us what happened when you arrived in Pomona."

Melrose looked up at me for the first time. "He told us to wait and then walked off."

"The defendant told you to wait?"

"Yeah, that's what I said." He snapped as if I was the source of his anxiety.

"What happened next?"

"After a while, he drove up in a small truck." He slid a quick glance at Webb and flinched from Webb's intense stare. He looked back at me and said, "He told me to get in the truck and drive."

"Let's back up, Mr. Melrose. How long was the defendant gone?"

"I don't know, maybe a half hour or so."

"Describe the truck he drove up in."

"It was a red pickup."

"And then what?" I stepped up closer to him. I wanted him to focus on me to blunt Webb's intimidation.

"He gave me the keys and told me to drive the truck."

"Did he say why?"

"He said it was a stick shift. He was having trouble driving it."

"So what happened?"

"He took off in my car and I followed."

"You followed him in the red pickup?

"That's right."

"To be clear, he was driving your car, and you were driving the truck?"

With a bitter edge, "That's what I said."

Melrose tried to pour himself water, but his hands were shaking so bad he couldn't manage it. The nearest bailiff poured him some water. As he brought the plastic glass to his mouth using both hands, some water shook onto his overalls.

"Where did you follow him?"

He flashed another look at Webb and then back to me. "What's the question?"

"Where did you stop?"

I was working to get another molar.

"Some turnout in the mountains, I don't know where."

"While you were driving, you saw Tracie Switzer in the back of the cab, didn't you?" I again led, wondering if Tuck would object. I was working to keep the narrative clear for Merritt.

"There was a white girl tied up." He stayed locked on me.

"She was tied up lying on the floor in the back?"

"Yeah."

"Did that concern you?"

Long pause. "I knew I was in deep shit."

"What do you mean?"

He looked at me as if I was stupid. "Something bad was happening."

"Did you try to help her?"

"No. I didn't want to piss him off."

"What happened at the turnout?"

He shot another glance in the direction of the defendant. "What'd you say?"

"What happened at the turnout?"

He cupped his hands over his face and mumbled through his hands, "He pulled her out from the back and put her in the shotgun."

"The defendant pulled her out?"

"Yeah."

"Could you see if she was still tied up?"

He shook no.

I let the inaudible response pass. "Go on, what happened next?"

Melrose steadied himself with a deep breath. "He swiped at her neck with something."

"What do you mean?"

Melrose looked at me, confused. "He cut her and then threw something over the cliff."

The choked sobbing from Donna Switzer was the only sound in the courtroom. Her head was buried in her husband's chest.

"Mr. Melrose, is the man who cut her throat in this courtroom?"

Without looking at Jaxon Webb, he pointed in the direction of the defense table.

"May the record reflect that the witness indicated the defendant Jaxon Webb?" I said.

"It shall," ruled Merritt.

I had what I needed for purposes of the prelim. I didn't bother with questioning Melrose about his consideration for testifying. I was sure Tuck would cover that on her cross. This was not the time to prick boils—hard facts that cut against my case. Every case that goes to trial has boils. At trial, I would prick the huge boil that he was only testifying for sentence reduction. Didn't matter at prelim.

Tuck didn't disappoint. She dwelled on Melrose's criminal past and went into excruciating detail about his deal to testify against Webb. It was fair game, and I offered Melrose no protection. He had made me work too hard. He could swing in the breeze, for all I cared. I had what I needed from him for the prelim.

After Tuck had verbally eviscerated Melrose, Merritt looked at me to call my next witness.

"The state calls Dr. Felix Wardlow."

Tuck stood. "Your Honor, on behalf of Mr. Webb and for purposes of this hearing only, the defense will stipulate as to the cause of death."

"Thank you, Ms. Tuck," I said, appreciating the gesture. "To be clear, the stipulation is that Tracie Switzer's throat was cut with a sharp object which led to her death?"

Tuck: "That's correct. For this hearing only."

I remained standing. "The people have no further witnesses, and submit that there is sufficient evidence to hold the defendant to answer for the murder of Tracie Switzer."

Merritt looked at Tuck, inviting a response.

Tuck spoke. "The only percipient witness is, as you heard, of very low integrity. We would have to believe this man in order to allow this case to go forward. The corroboration for his testimony is extremely scant and in my view doesn't support the convicted felon's testimony."

Merritt replied, "Ms. Tuck, this is a prelim, not a trial. The prosecutor's burden is simply a preponderance. I therefore find sufficient evidence to bind the defendant over to stand trial on one count of murder. Initial appearance and arraignment in the trial court is set for May 30. And with that, we are adjourned."

Merritt got this one right.

I sat across from Melrose in the courthouse lockup. "That was a terrible job of testifying. I'm half inclined to revoke our deal and just rely on Bridge."

"Screw you! That dude is going to do everything he can to have me killed before trial. He's a mean motherfucker. He scares the shit out of me. I'm dead man walking."

"Two things. First, you're in protective custody, and second, you testify like that at trial, our deal is off."

"If I'm alive at his trial, I'll do better." He paused. "If I'm alive."

CHAPTER 25

April 16, three months after Lisa's principal, Russ Rosen, had been suspended and disappeared, he called Lisa. He told her that his suspension had been for good cause. He explained that he was a gambler who had taken the school's discretionary funds and lost them betting on basketball in Vegas. Rosen said he was out of the country and would not be returning. She tried to engage him further, but he cut her off, wished her success as the principal, and hung up.

She called me and then called Laske. The mystery of Russ Rosen was no longer.

We sat on the balcony that evening, and Lisa talked through the Rosen interlude. She was having a tough time coming to grips with the Rosen she thought she knew and the Rosen who had absconded with school funds and gambled them away. At least now she wouldn't harbor any guilt, thinking she had somehow contributed to his dismissal.

The May committee meeting of the Elders focused on a double homicide in Long Beach. A husband found his wife having sex with another man and shot and killed them both while they were *in flagrante*. The question for the committee was whether to allow the defendant husband to plead to two counts of voluntary manslaughter, avoiding murder charges. Following a careful review of the circumstances, we agreed. The case was the textbook definition of the heat-of-passion defense, which is at the heart of voluntary manslaughter. The defendant, instead of looking at a sentence in the range of twenty years, would serve between five and eight years for each killing.

May 30, 2019. The second appearances and arraignments of Don and Kay Pouse and Jaxon Webb were set on the same day in the same courtroom. Sam Hardy wasn't present for the Pouses' appearance and arraignment. Most likely he was too important to appear for a simple arraignment. His surrogate entered pleas of not guilty on behalf of the Pouses and requested a trial date in August. Since the Pouses were not in custody, no doubt Hardy felt no urgency to bring things to an early boil. I didn't oppose an August 28 date.

The Webb case would most likely go earlier since, unlike the Pouses, Webb was in custody. As anticipated, Brenda Tuck entered a not guilty plea on behalf of Webb and requested an expedited trial date for her in-custody client. I didn't oppose. I was looking forward to a trial instead of more prelims and more committee meetings. The court obliged and assigned the case to Department 612 with a trial date of June 18. That was a surprisingly short setting, but neither Tuck nor I objected.

On June 4, Hawthorne put on the preliminary hearing on Caesar and Cathy Ramirez, and they were both held to answer.

I had my focus. Jaxon Webb. Now that I had a trial date, I called Vanessa Clemons and asked her if she would like to sit in on the trial to assist with motions, witness coordination, and whatever else might come up. I knew she would jump at the chance. Although she was a second-year student, she had a light schedule. She had time. I didn't have to ask twice.

It was time to begin putting together my case. There were a number of considerations. Since my case was almost entirely reliant on the testimony of Melrose and Bridge, the challenge was how best to support their testimony. I explained to Vanessa how we needed to weave the independent facts to corroborate the snitch testimony leading to Tracie's murder.

On a whiteboard in my office, Vanessa helped me list the key testimony from Melrose and Bridge and the best way we could corroborate their testimony with independent facts. It took a while but, amid numerous cross-outs and additions, we came up with six points of corroborating testimony; whether the corroboration would withstand scrutiny was very much an open question. I had pushed this case, and the committee had let me run with it. Now it was time to see if I could get the result I had lobbied for. The corroborating points were:

1. Donna and Frank Switzer's testimony that Tracie left home at approximately 9:00 p.m. for her half-hour drive to the university corroborated Tracie's presence in Pomona in her red pickup truck near the university at approximately 9:30 p.m.

2. Snitch testimony establishing Tracie's presence in Pomona at approximately 9:30 was also corroborated by the grainy ATM video footage showing an unidentified Black man using Tracie's ATM card and taking money from her ATM account at 9:37.

3. Tracie's contact by the unidentified Black man was also corroborated by the ATM video.
4. Snitch testimony that Tracie's truck was used to transport her to the mountain turnoff, the scene of the murder, was corroborated by Tracie's truck at the scene of the murder.
5. Snitch testimony that the murder occurred at the turnoff was corroborated by Tracie's body at the scene of the murder.
6. Snitch testimony that Webb cut Tracie's throat was corroborated by the coroner.

As Vanessa and I were composing the list, I remained concerned with how scant the corroboration was. For better or worse, it is what I had.

I next considered how best to present my case. Should I start with Melrose and Bridge's testimony and then set forth the underlying corroboration? My concern was that the snitches would not just get discredited but clubbed during cross-examination before I could present the rest of my case. Would our case be so tarnished that I might lose some of the jurors? I needed all twelve.

A counterintuitive approach, at least from a chronological standpoint, would be to start with the grisly scene of the murder, followed by the coroner's graphic testimony detailing and displaying Tracie's cause of death. That approach would, I hope, rivet the jurors' attention before I went back and laid out the snitch testimony with its corresponding corroboration. As I laid out the options, Vanessa favored the counterintuitive approach. At this early phase, I was leaning that way, but I needed time to marinate the idea.

I doubted that Tuck would have Webb testify. Webb had a six-year-old assault-with-a-deadly-weapon prior conviction and had served four years. If he testified, I could impeach him up with the prior. The jurors would never hear of the prior if he didn't testify. The prior would only be admissible as to Webb's credibility and if he didn't testify, the prior was rendered irrelevant. Tuck knew there was a price to pay for keeping her client off the stand.

Even with the judge's instruction that the jurors not consider why an accused opted not to testify, the jurors would hold it against him precisely for not doing so. The Fifth Amendment privilege is all well and good, but human curiosity would have the jurors speculating why, if he didn't do it, he didn't take the stand and so testify. This was a conundrum faced by defense lawyers since time immemorial.

That put Tuck and Webb in a tough spot, virtually reducing the defense options to having someone else offer an alibi for Webb or having to rely on Tuck successfully attacking the credibility of Melrose and Bridge and then claiming there was insufficient evidence to overcome reasonable doubt.

Had I been defending Webb, I would not put him on the stand. Furthermore, if Tuck and Webb attempted to conjure up some alibi, Tuck would have to disclose the alibi and we would have time to investigate it and hopefully discredit it. It would be interesting to see how Tuck would defend.

CHAPTER 26

I called Lisa at work and suggested we both leave work early and meet at home for a walk on the beach and then dinner at the Shores. She couldn't get away. Frank Bennett, the school superintendent, wanted to meet.

"Any idea what that is about?" I asked. "Certainly, the Rosen situation has been exhausted."

"Probably just more follow-up."

"Let me know when the meeting is over."

"I will. I'll get out of here as soon as I can."

"I'll be waiting. I'll make late reservations at the Shores."

She called around four, her voice strained and agitated. "I was ambushed. It wasn't just Bennett but also your friend, Laske."

"Ambushed? What are you talking about?"

"Yeah, I was ambushed by Bennett and Laske."

"Laske was there?" I was groping to make sense of what she was saying.

"Yes, your good buddy, Laske." Her tone bitter.

"Slow down. What the hell happened?"

"They questioned me—no, they interrogated me—about Rosen and his discretionary fund." Her voice quivered with anger. "Since I was the vice principal, what did I know about the funds? Did I have anything to do with the money?"

"Sonofabitch! Laske was doing the questioning?" I was struggling to control my anger.

"In addition to being ambushed, I got the whole story today."

I gritted my teeth. "Okay. Lay it out for me."

How dare Laske interrogate Lisa?

"Apparently there was close to $12,000 in the principal's discretionary fund. Money raised through a couple of school fundraisers. The money was earmarked to purchase laptops for the school's library," she said, her tone bitter. "Several months back, the librarian noted that the computers never arrived and asked Rosen about it. Rosen put her off, claiming some kind of ordering glitch. I didn't know about any of that.

"Months later, the librarian again asked Rosen about the laptops. Rosen again claimed some snafu. The librarian grew suspicious, called the district's purchasing coordinator, and learned that no order had ever been placed. When eventually confronted by Bennett, Rosen owned up to gambling away the money. Hence the immediate suspension. But before the matter was referred to the police, Rosen was gone."

"Rosen confessed, so why are they questioning you?"

"Bennett said there is a separate checking account for the principal's fund and that there are two people authorized on the account. The principal and vice principal."

"Were you even aware that there was such an account and that you were on it?"

"That's the first I ever heard of it. Complete surprise."

"So how'd it end with Laske?"

"Laske said there would be a follow-up investigation and that they might have to talk with me again," she said contemptuously. "At that point, I'd had enough and told them to get out of my office."

"Those assholes." I was livid. "Laske will never contact you again. He has me to deal with. As for Bennett, I don't know. He's your boss. I don't want to screw up your relationship with him. But if you give me the go-ahead, I'll rip into him as well."

"I thought Laske was your buddy."

"So did I. He's now my target. You okay to drive home? Should I come get you?"

"I'm rattled. But I'm okay to drive."

"Okay. We'll fix this."

I immediately called Laske. He was gone for the day. There was no target for venting my anger. I left my office and seethed on the drive home.

Lisa beat me there. She met me as soon as I got out of my car. "Jake, I'm not going to stand for this. Even if Bennett somehow denies me the promotion to principal, he and Laske will not hear the end of this."

"No, they're not. I'm going to be in Laske's office first thing tomorrow, and we are going to have a real heart-to-heart."

She paused, stepping back and registering my anger. "You think it's best to confront him while you're angry?"

"I don't know if that's best or not, but that's what's going to happen."

Laske strolled into the sheriff's station about 7:00 a.m. the following morning. I was waiting for him in the lobby.

"I kinda figured you'd be here."

"Damn right I'm here. You ambushed my wife."

"Come on back to my office. Let me explain," he said in an irritating, placating voice.

He closed his office door and remained standing.

"Superintendent Bennett has been bugging me about the

missing funds, suggesting that others may be involved. He insisted I question everyone in the front office at the school. We didn't just talk to your wife, but to everyone in the front office. The secretary, two counselors, and the librarian."

"No courtesy call to me?" I was not in the least assuaged.

"Jake, come on." He held his hands palms down trying to reason with me. "You know full well that would not be appropriate during an investigation. I had to follow protocol. Your wife was in the school's inner circle. Her name was on the discretionary fund account. Of course, she had to be questioned."

"Bullshit! You could have contacted me and set up an interview. This could have been done in a civilized manner without subjecting Lisa to a surprise and stressful interrogation. What'd you think, that springing a surprise interrogation would somehow shake a confession out of her? "

"It was hardly an interrogation." His earlier conciliatory tone now had some grit. "It was in her office, and the questions were soft, not intimidating. Jake, we're going to have to disagree on this. You're overreacting. Bennett and I came to her school and questioned everyone who might have any information. This was as far from an interrogation as it could be."

"You can rationalize this any way you want. You screwed up and my wife had to pay for it."

"Have it your way." Laske's voice had escalated to a harsher timbre. "I'm going to finish the investigation and determine if anyone other than Rosen had anything to do with this."

"You're not going to have any contact with Lisa without my presence." I stood to leave. "I trust that is abundantly clear!" I slammed out of his office.

CHAPTER 27

June 18. We drew Judge Millie Cochran for the Webb trial. I checked around the office and learned she had an excellent reputation as a thoughtful and fair-minded trial judge. She was a large Black woman with a friendly demeanor. She set a hearing for motions to be heard on June 11, with jury selection to start the following week.

Following the pretrial hearing, I asked and received permission to join her in chambers. I introduced Vanessa to the judge and defense counsel Tuck. I explained that Vanessa was a second-year student keenly focused on working in the criminal justice system and would be sitting in on the trial.

Judge Cochran shook Vanessa's hand. "Which side of the criminal justice system are you favoring?"

"I don't know yet. I'm still trying to figure that out."

"Well, I think this should be a real learning experience," Cochran said. "Perhaps watching this trial may push you one way or another."

Tuck smiled and added, "Just because you're sitting in with the prosecutor, don't let that influence any career decisions. I've been a deputy public defender for sixteen years. There is a real need for competent, dedicated PDs."

"Professor Clearwater talks a lot about the critical role of defense counsel," Vanessa said. "If I had to pick which side I might eventually go with, I'm leaning to the defense."

"Professor Clearwater?" Cochran cocked her head.

I explained my arrangement with the school and the office.

"I assume you teach trial advocacy."

"Among other things."

Cochran took that in. "I hope Ms. Tuck and I will get passing grades during the trial," she said agreeably.

"Your Honor, I'm here to learn as well as advocate."

"Okay," Cochran said, wrapping things up. "I will see everyone next week as we get underway."

During the pretrial hearing, Tuck moved to exclude Webb's prior assault conviction. Cochran made the correct decision to exclude the prior as too prejudicial, except in the event Webb testified. If he testified, I could use the prior to impugn his credibility. No surprise there.

Tuck also moved to limit the photographs taken at the scene as well as the autopsy photographs. I displayed the photographs on Cochran's desk, and the three of us, with Vanessa watching, went through them one by one. The judge ruled that I could use two photographs depicting Tracie's body at the scene and several others depicting how the truck was situated on the turnout. I was also permitted two autopsy photographs of Tracie's cut throat. And other than housekeeping bits and pieces, we were set to begin. It was all very civilized. Tuck and Cochran were both veterans who knew their business.

During voir dire—the questioning of the prospective jurors—the following week, Tuck focused on two concerns: racial considerations and sympathies. Since Webb was Black, she used her voir dire in an attempt to ferret out any racially related concerns of the twelve prospective jurors. Of course, no one would admit any racial ill will they harbored, so Tuck took an indirect approach. She used the answers of the two African-Americans in the jury box as to biases and situations they had suffered to set up her questioning of the other jurors. Tuck's questioning was clever, but I'm not certain it bore much fruit. Most non-Black folks so inclined either don't recognize their own racial biases, or if they do, they have become adept at covering them up.

Tuck's second effort was to harden the jurors against allowing sympathies toward Tracie Switzer and her family. Tuck went so far as to display Tracie's high school photograph on the PowerPoint and then identify Donna and Frank Switzer sitting in the front row. The Switzers displayed no emotions while the center of attention. Tuck got all the expected assurances from the prospective jurors before yielding the floor to me.

Some might have thought Tuck's efforts were counterintuitive, but I thought them clever. The jurors alerted to the sympathies might strive to keep them in check. Tuck, in her low-key, thoughtful approach, was an able adversary. The contrast to someone like Sam Hardy couldn't have been more stark. I most feared the Tucks over the Hardys—thoughtful and cerebral versus bombastic and confrontational.

"Ms. Tuck—" I nodded at her as I began my voir dire questioning, —"thank you for leading such an excellent discussion." Turning to the jurors, "Let me double down on both points Ms. Tuck made. Race has nothing to do with this case. There is no evidence that the race of the defendant or of the victim played any part in this tragedy.

"This is about whether a man kidnapped, robbed, and murdered the victim. Let me say that again: there will be no evidence that race played any part in this. So please, let your deliberations be guided by the facts and only by the facts." I worked that idea through the group, questioning their ability and willingness to view the evidence through a race-neutral lens. Clearly an impossible task, but nonetheless a necessary endeavor. For what they were worth, I got assurances from the prospective jurors.

"Ms. Tuck also led us through a thoughtful discussion of how sympathies can influence decisions. And she's right, it's going to be hard for each of you to hear some difficult testimony and see some disturbing photographs of Tracie Switzer and occasionally glance over to her parents and not sympathize with them. We're all human, and we may think, but for the grace of God, that could have been my child, my sister, and I could be in a courtroom experiencing what the Switzers are experiencing. But we must try our best not to project our sympathies. Like I said before, this is a fairly straightforward case: did that man murder the victim. Nothing more, nothing less."

I again went through the group, eliciting assurances, and there were the inevitable follow-ups. Two of the prospective jurors were dismissed because they candidly admitted they would be susceptible to their emotional reactions.

"If I could indulge your attention for one last point." I smiled. "I promise this won't take long." I received several nods of acceptance. "Some of the evidence that you will hear will come from what we call snitch testimony, also referred to as informant testimony." That caught some surprised looks. It was time to start pricking boils. And, oh my, Melrose and Bridge were massive boils.

"That's right, snitch testimony." I paused. "Let me explain. The only eyewitnesses to the crimes against Tracie were two men who were with the defendant that night. Both of these men are felons, men who have agreed to testify only if they receive some time off from the prison sentences they are currently serving for crimes unrelated to the murder of Tracie Switzer. As the prosecutor, I have to rely on these two men to complete my case against the defendant.

"The question is, will you good folks agree to listen to their testimony and consider their testimony in the full context of this trial and not instantly dismiss what they will say because of who they are? That's a difficult question. All I'm asking is for you to listen first and then judge the value of their testimony."

I let that provocative gambit rest a minute before looking directly at prospective Juror Number Four, a distinguished-looking Black man dressed in a subdued three-piece suit. "Sir, will you be able to listen to my full case first and then assess the testimony of these two men in the larger scope of the trial?"

Juror Number Four thought that over. "I would be reluctant to convict anyone on evidence I had questions about."

"Of course you would. But what if I backed up their testimony with underlying supporting testimony completely separate from their testimony?"

"That would help. But I would have to be convinced there was reliable support for that kind of testimony."

"Thanks for that." I nodded agreeably. "Would you also agree that sometimes criminal acts aren't witnessed by law-abiding folks, but sometimes only by those who we generally view as disreputable?"

He nodded. "I would have to agree with that. But again, I would want some reliable support for that kind of testimony."

"Thank you sir, you've done a lot of my heavy lifting." I nodded to him. "How about the rest of you? If the testimony of these"—I paused—"informants is backed up by the circumstances and the testimony of others such that you believe beyond a reasonable doubt that the defendant did what the state has accused him, would you be able to convict?"

I worked that proposition across both rows of prospective

jurors and received qualified assurances from all but one juror. It was from a young Black woman. "I don't have a serious problem with informant testimony, but I'm concerned that this Black man can get a fair trial from all these white folks." she said with conviction. "We've been hearing these kinds of promises of equal justice for centuries. I'm not buying it."

She had to go. But I didn't want to use one of my five precious peremptory challenges on her. I needed to follow up and show that she could not be a fair and impartial juror so I could challenge her for cause. There are no limits on cause challenges.

I nodded my understanding. "I respect your concerns. Of course we can't ignore centuries of abuse and discrimination. But my focus is much narrower. In this trial, will you be able to deliberate and put your concerns aside and judge this case only on the facts and the law?"

"I'm skeptical, but I will do my best." Her candid response had made my case for a cause challenge.

I made my cause challenge, which Cochran surprisingly denied. When I later exercised one of my peremptory challenges on her, Tuck asked to approach the bench. "With all due respect, Your Honor, I must make a *Batson* motion. Counsel's challenge is against one of only two Black jurors. As this court is aware, when prosecutors excuse members of the same race as the accused, that raises some serious concerns."

The Supreme Court's *Batson* decision maintains that any systematic exclusion of members of the same race or ethnicity as the accused is unconstitutional. The procedure requires the judge to make an initial decision as to whether on the surface the prosecutor's challenge has a discriminatory intent, and if so, the judge is required to ask the prosecutor to justify the challenge on race-neutral grounds.

I looked at Tuck. "I'm surprised you feel compelled to go this route. You heard her comments during voir dire. She told us she has real concerns."

"Counsel, direct your comments to me, not opposing counsel," Cochran admonished.

"My apologies, Your Honor," I said. "May I respond to the challenge?"

"Please."

"First, there has been no systematic effort to exclude Black jurors. She is the only one I'm challenging. Furthermore, she candidly conceded that the race of the defendant would be difficult for her to overcome. Leaving her on would have been tantamount to conceding the trial. Her response leaves me with no choice."

Turning to Tuck, Cochran said, "Ms. Tuck, I've got to agree with Mr. Clearwater. I don't see this as an effort to exclude Blacks, but rather a legitimate race-neutral challenge by the prosecutor. The motion is denied."

The jury, consisting of three Hispanics, one Black, and eight Caucasians, was eventually sworn in.

Cochran set forth the schedule for the balance of the week. "We'll start with opening statements at ten o'clock Wednesday. I apologize for not meeting tomorrow, but several other matters have dirtied my calendar."

That afternoon I gathered Detective Coolidge and Vanessa in my office to discuss logistics. I was going with Plan B, starting with Coolidge, the scene of the murder, and the photographs taken at the scene. I would follow up with the coroner and those graphic photographs establishing the cause of death. I would not need Melrose or Bridge for the first day or so. Vanessa had coordinated the transfer of Bridge. Coolidge had made plans to bring Melrose in on Thursday or Friday. I didn't expect the trial to take long.

With plans in place, Coolidge took off, and Vanessa and I

walked three blocks to Philippe's for their incredible sandwiches. As we sat, Vanessa had questions. "I was confused by your voir dire. You reemphasized what Ms. Tuck had already discussed with the jurors."

"I understand your question. It might have seemed counterintuitive." I dabbed just a little horseradish on my roast beef. "Let's start with my question to you. What's our biggest problem?"

"That's pretty clear. How reliant we are on the snitches."

"Exactly. My goal during voir dire is to present as the fairest prosecutor imaginable. Almost over the top. Those jurors need to like me and trust me that I'm not going to sell them a bogus case. I need to have them believe two cowardly felons in order to convict a stone-cold killer. I've got to be way above reproach, so when it comes to the hard sell at closing argument, they're going to listen to me. You've heard me talk about being the good guy, the white hat. This is the white hat on steroids."

She nodded her understanding. "That makes sense. You've got a tough sell with our snitches. I get it." Swallowing some Arnold Palmer, she thought things over. "You accomplished what you needed. They were with you."

CHAPTER 28

The courtroom was again sparsely populated. The Switzers, with what appeared to be some grandparents and friends, were clustered in the seats behind me and nearest the jury box. There were several Black faces in the seats behind the defense table. There were four or five people scattered in the gallery. It was indeed a far stretch from the overcrowded Cort murder trial I had prosecuted last summer or from the packed crowds during the Pouse prelims.

As the bailiff called court to order, my stomach did its familiar roll. Didn't matter if I was starting a low-grade misdemeanor trial or a murder case, the roll always preceded opening statement. I'd come to view that stomach churn as a positive. It put me on hyperalert; I never felt as keen or energized as during that stomach roll. I knew that once I got underway, that adrenaline-focusing surge would propel me. When I first started teaching law classes, I wondered if the stomach surge would hit me in front of eighty law students. It didn't. There was a rush, but not as intense as a trial rush.

I rose, nodded at the judge and Tuck, turned to the jurors, and began my opening statement. "A young woman was senselessly executed because she was in the wrong place at the wrong time." I paused and looked over at the Switzers. "A family, a mother and a father, left to grieve for the loss of their eighteen-year-old daughter. A sweet girl, a college freshman." I stepped back and looked at Jaxon

Webb. "This case is also heartbreaking because it was so senseless and violent and was carried out without any remorse, without any pity."

I moved forward and squared myself in front of the jury box. "I suggested to you during voir dire that no one wants to hear about the savage murder of an innocent, that you would be repulsed and would rather not have to think about or deal with such a mean situation." I offered a what-are-you-going-to-do grimace. "Well, here we are, and together we are forced to deal with this tragedy."

Using a clicker, I illuminated the word INTIMIDATOR on the PowerPoint. "The night of the killing, the defendant didn't have access to a car. You're going to learn that he forced two men, who you will hear from, to drive him from Riverside to Pomona. Near the university, the defendant ordered the driver to pull over and then, in very clear terms, told the two men to remain there until he returned. They complied because they feared the defendant. The defendant then set off on a hunt."

I clicked, and the word HUNTER was illuminated. "That's right, the defendant went hunting. He didn't have a particular target. Rather, anyone and everyone who crossed his path that night was in jeopardy. He spotted a young woman alone, and the hunter had his prey."

Tuck was on her feet. "Objection to the words hunter and prey— prejudicial and argumentative."

"Mr. Clearwater, reel it back a bit," Cochran admonished.

I nodded at Cochran and, without breaking stride, continued. "It was eighteen-year-old Tracie Switzer. Earlier on the day Tracie was murdered, she went with her dad and bought a brand-new red Toyota extended-cab pickup truck. She'd been working part-time to save up for the truck, and with a little financial assistance from her parents, she got her truck. And, not surprisingly, she wanted to show her new truck to her sorority sisters. So she made the drive to Pomona on that tragic Sunday night. She never made it to the sorority house."

I clicked again. THE ROBBERY was illuminated. "He—" I pointed at Webb—"intercepted Tracie, took her captive, forced her to turn over her ATM card and password, and took $500 from her account."

I next illuminated KIDNAPPING. "Somehow, in his mind, it wasn't enough to scare her and take her money. So he gagged her, bound her, and stuffed her into the back of the cab of her own truck. He then drove the truck back to the two men he had ordered to wait for him. Turns out the defendant was having trouble driving Tracie's truck because it was a manual transmission. So he instructed one of the men to drive Tracie's truck while the defendant drove the car with the other man. The defendant drove the freeway to the Mt. Baldy exit with the red pickup right behind him."

I stopped and slowly walked the length of the jury box. They were with me. Perhaps hoping my story wouldn't have the terrible ending they already knew was coming. Without looking at the PowerPoint, I illuminated THE EXECUTION. "The hunter pulled off onto a turnoff and stopped the car. The truck was right behind him. He then walked to the passenger side of the truck, pulled the bound-and-gagged eighteen-year-old from the back of the cab, and positioned her in the front passenger seat. He looked over at the two men standing by the car, pulled Tracie's head back, and cut her throat. Nearly decapitating her."

I stood, eyes downcast, without speaking, and then slowly walked to the counsel table and sat. The only sound was the soft sobs of Donna and Frank.

Judge Cochran waited a beat and, looking at Brenda Tuck, nodded, inviting her to make her opening statement.

I had deliberately violated one of my own rules. I had not

pricked the boil concerning the disreputable felons. Having introduced jailhouse informants during voir dire, I didn't bring them up during my opening. I wanted nothing to divert the focus from Webb. I wanted the senseless murder to be the centerpiece. I didn't want distractions. In hindsight, that could prove to be a mistake. I was second-guessing myself even as I sat down.

Tuck nodded to the judge and made her way to the jurors. "Good morning, ladies and gentlemen. My name is Brenda Tuck. We've already had an opportunity to meet during jury selection. We just heard a dramatic statement from the prosecutor. A young woman was killed and the prosecutor is convinced the killer is Jaxon Webb. While there is no doubt a young woman was killed, there is grave doubt about who killed her. Let me tell you what you didn't hear from the prosecutor."

This is where I would pay a price. Dammit! It only remained to see how dear that price would be.

"The only alleged witnesses to the killing of Ms. Switzer are convicted felons who are selling their testimony for years of reductions in their prison sentences. That's it!" she said emphatically. "No other witnesses. None! The prosecutor's case is one hundred percent dependent on two lowlife snitches. You didn't hear anything about them from the prosecutor, and it's easy to understand why— because he knows that is a crippling weakness of his case. Let me fill you in about these two characters, these two snitches"—she spat out the word—"and what they have done to earn their various prison sentences in the first place."

Contempt dripping from her mouth, she went on. "First up is Dinold Melrose. He is currently residing in a California prison, serving twelve years for robbery. Robbery, as we all know, is a violent crime. It isn't just about stealing and taking someone's property. No, robbery is much more than that. It is about using *force* and *intimidation* against another to get their property. This absolutely essential prosecution witness has agreed to come into this courtroom and swear under oath that he is giving honest testimony in exchange for getting back three years of his life."

Tuck paused and shook her head at the absurdity. "That's right, his prison sentence will be cut by three years as payment for his testimony." She tilted her head. "A pretty good deal, actually, a great deal. They're cutting over a thousand days off his hard prison time. Testimony bought and paid for."

My case was paying the price for not pricking the boil.

"Let's move on to the other best witness the prosecutor could conjure. This character's name is Glen Bridge, and like Melrose, he is an armed robber. A brazen robber. He entered a high-end Las Vegas jewelry store in broad daylight, smashed the glass counter with a heavy hammer, and grabbed up as much valuable jewelry as he could. In the process, an employee was struck with a shard of glass, causing that man permanent injuries. Consequently, he was arrested. but Glen Bridge went to trial denying his guilt. He took an oath, much like the one he will take in front of you, claiming his innocence. But the jurors saw through his lies and convicted him."

Stepping in close to the jurors, Tuck continued, "That Las Vegas trial judge, recognizing Bridge for what he is, sentenced him to twelve years in Nevada's maximum security prison. But like his fellow snitch, his sentence will be cut by three years for coming before you and taking that same oath and testifying in this trial."

Damn.

Tuck looked over at me. "These are the guys the prosecutor is one hundred percent relying on to convince you of Mr. Webb's guilt. I'm convinced that after you hear the evidence presented by the state, you will be struck by the untrustworthy testimony the prosecutor is trying to sell and tell him we don't convict on the backbone of felons and liars."

It was short, focused, and effective. She had no case of her own—so attack the prosecution case and wrap yourself in the presumption of innocence.

"I screwed up," I said to Coolidge and Vanessa back in my office during the recess. "If I had to do my opening again, I would have done it differently. I would have followed my own good advice and pricked the boils that were Melrose and Bridge."

Dammit!

Vanessa, my loyal student, came to my defense. "But you really drew the jurors in with the hunter, executioner language." She was trying to defend something not worthy of being defended. In a split decision, round one went to Brenda Tuck. The problem for me, however, was that by the end of trial, I needed a unanimous verdict. I couldn't make another mistake like that. This case was problematic enough without unforced errors.

I leaned back in my chair and said, "What Tuck didn't do was offer up any alibi for Webb. That's a serious concession. It signals that she has no case of her own. Her only avenue will be to successfully attack our case. It also confirms Webb will not be testifying."

As Vanessa fired up the Keurig, Coolidge stood at the window, staring out at Second Street. I went on. "She's going all-in on attacking the snitches. I understand her strategy. But before jurors acquit someone, they generally like the defense to point the finger elsewhere." Nonetheless, her opening was solid. Tuck's years in the trenches had honed her craft. She was a formidable opponent.

CHAPTER 29

Wednesday afternoon, the bailiff called the court to order. Judge Cochran looked at me. "Mr. Clearwater, your first witness, please."

"Call Detective Armand Coolidge."

He was dressed in his civilian attire, a dark blue blazer over light blue pants. He personified competence and earnestness. He had a deep Sam Elliott voice, which only amplified his presence.

Following the oath, we got underway. "Detective Coolidge, fill us in on your professional background."

He nodded. "I've been in the sheriff's department for thirteen years, coming up through the ranks. I've been a detective in major crimes for the past five years."

"Major crimes?"

"Primarily homicides, but occasionally I am called in on other matters."

"Before we turn to the specifics of this case, I want to back up and discuss your experiences in homicide investigations. Are you always working with law-abiding citizens in homicide investigations?"

"Objection, relevance?"

"Mr. Clearwater, care to respond?"

"Ms. Tuck spent pretty much all of her opening remarks

castigating the use of informants. I'd like leave to explore that area with a witness qualified to discuss the matter."

Cochran nodded her understanding. "Go ahead, overruled."

"Detective, do you have my question in mind?"

"I do."

"Please answer."

"It's not generally the so-called law-abiding citizens that are critical to many investigations. Homicides can occur anywhere, under a multitude of different circumstances. Many homicides happen outside the view of the more reputable people. We frequently deal with less-than-savory people in our investigations. The facts drive the investigations. My job is to follow the facts. That's just the nature of my work."

"Detective, have you personally relied on witnesses in your homicide investigations who were not"—I groped for the word—"of pristine character?"

"Of course. One of the realities I've learned in my experience is that you have to take the witnesses as you find them. The circumstances are not always ideal."

"Detective, what is a snitch?"

"A snitch is a term we use for a witness who is testifying for some personal benefit."

"A personal benefit, like a reduced charge or a reduction in their sentence?"

"That's right. Sometimes it's only by using snitches that we can get to the bottom of things."

"In dealing with snitches, how do you determine when you can trust their testimony?"

"Corroboration. I will never rely on snitch testimony unless I can corroborate what they are telling me."

"How do you go about corroborating what these folks tell you?"

"I always examine the surrounding circumstances to determine whether there are underlying facts or circumstances that support what I'm being told by the informant."

"Generally speaking, when do you reach the point where you have sufficient corroboration to support snitch testimony?"

"Objection. May we approach?"

Cochran motioned us up. "Ms. Tuck?"

"Your Honor, he is about to backdoor in the detective's opinion that there is sufficient corroboration in this case. That would call for an improper opinion."

I said pleasantly, "I'm not going to solicit the detective's opinion."

Tuck was not put off. "He may not use the word 'opinion,' but he's leading right up to the edge."

"Ms. Tuck, I can't sustain an objection for a question not yet asked." Cochran gave a quick nod, inviting no more discussion of the matter.

We stepped back. "Detective, let me ask my question again. When do you reach the point where you have sufficient corroboration to support such testimony?"

"It's got to be pretty compelling. I would not ask a prosecutor to go forward on a case that was reliant on informant testimony unless I was first convinced it was reliable."

Tuck was up. "Can we approach?"

Standing at the bench, a frustrated Tuck once again explained her concern. "Just like I said, he's trying to backdoor in the witness's opinion that the detective believes there is sufficient evidence in this case to believe Webb is the killer."

Cochran wrinkled her forehead and looked at me. "Very clever, Counsel." Cochran gave me a sardonic look. "Ms. Tuck has a valid point. It seems as if the last answer could be construed as the detective's opinion in the larger context of his work in this case."

I had what I needed. The jurors were savvy enough to connect the dots. "I'll submit, Your Honor."

Cochran motioned us back and struck the detective's answer and admonished the jurors to disregard the answer.

Tough bell to unring.

I resumed. "Detective, I mentioned earlier that snitches testify expecting something in return for their testimony."

"Yes sir, they do."

"Let's explore that." I moved halfway up the jury box. "Two individuals are going to offer their testimony in this trial as to what they witnessed. What will they receive in return for their testimony?"

"Both Dinold Melrose and Glen Bridge are serving prison sentences. In exchange for their testimony, they will each have three years cut from their respective prison sentences."

"In your experience as a homicide detective working with informants, is this arrangement unusual?"

"Objection! Beyond the witness's expertise."

"Sustained. Move on, Counsel."

I nodded, acknowledging the court. "Detective, let's change tacks. Let's talk about your investigation as the lead investigator in the murder of Tracie Switzer. Let's start with your initial involvement."

"I was called out on the early morning of September 3, 2016, to Route 120, which is on the way to Mt. Baldy."

"Describe the scene when you first arrived."

"There were several first responders from my office. A late-model Toyota extended-cab red pickup was on a westside turnout. A female was seated upright in the front passenger seat of the Toyota. It appeared her throat had been cut." He delivered his answer in his best Joe Friday voice: Just the facts. No emotion, no embellishment.

"From your subsequent investigation, were you able to identify the victim?"

"She was Tracie Switzer."

"In addition to Ms. Switzer's throat being cut, what else did you note concerning her body?"

"She was soaked in blood." Coolidge looked off and took a breath. Hard memory. "Her hands were bound at her back. There was a gag in her mouth."

I glanced at Donna and Frank; they were huddled into one another. "During your investigation, did you learn what the murderer had used as the gag?"

"Yes, it was a pair of Tracie's panties."

"How do you know they were Tracie's?"

"She wasn't wearing any, so I made that assumption."

"Was there any indication she was sexually molested?"

"No."

"Other than the sheriffs and EMT vehicles, were there any other vehicles on the turnout?"

Briefly consulting his report, he replied, "A Mr. French was present, sitting in his vehicle, when I arrived. He reported to me that he had pulled onto the turnout at approximately 6:00 a.m. He explained that he was a photographer. He had intended to photograph the sunrise."

"To your knowledge, was a coroner called?"

"Yes, two deputy coroners arrived shortly after my arrival."

"I assume the victim was pronounced dead at the scene?"

"She was. I then had the forensics team go to work on both the victim's truck and the surrounding area."

"Why the truck?"

"I'm always hopeful that usable evidence such as fingerprints and DNA will be found."

"What did you later learn about the results of the forensics analysis?"

I knew Tuck wouldn't make a hearsay objection because she knew forensics had found nothing usable. The truck had been thoroughly wiped down, and they found nothing of consequence in the surrounding area.

"Why the surrounding area?"

"Being thorough." Coolidge shrugged.

"Detective, how did you identify the body?"

"We ran the registration on the truck, and from that, we were able to contact the victim's parents. Her father"—he looked over at the Switzers—"later made a positive identification of his daughter, Tracie Switzer."

"In the aftermath of Ms. Switzer's murder, were you able to identify any suspect or suspects?"

"Unfortunately, the case pretty much went cold until nearly two years later."

"Let's pause a moment. Was there any useful evidence at that time?"

"All we had was ATM footage of what appeared to be a Black man withdrawing $500 from Ms. Switzer's account."

"From that footage, was it possible to view the person making the withdrawal?"

"No, it was not clear enough."

"So, your investigation was at a dead end?"

"Pretty much."

"Let's move forward nearly two years. Tell us what happened."

"An inmate in the Riverside County jail informed the authorities that he had some information, and I'm quoting here, 'about some white girl killed on the road to Mt. Baldy.'"

"Objection, hearsay."

"Mr. Clearwater?"

"This is not offered for the truth of the matter asserted but rather to explain the detective's subsequent conduct." Tuck's objection was worthless. Maybe she just wanted to break up my direct examination.

"Overruled."

"Did you follow up?"

"I did. I had been frustrated with this case since it happened. I felt the tip was worth exploring."

"How did you even learn of this person's statement? It was from Riverside County instead of LA County."

"There is a lot of interagency cooperation. Some folks in Riverside were aware of this open case."

"Who was the inmate?"

"Dinold Melrose. He was in jail awaiting trial on a robbery charge."

"You interviewed him?"

"I did."

"Based on that initial interview, did you believe he might have witnessed Tracie's murder?"

"He supplied enough information that I felt I needed to look into it further."

"Did he give you the name of the killer?"

"No. He wouldn't give that up until there was a deal. Something to benefit him. After I told him it was a no-go, he gave me the name of another man he had been with that night."

"Who was that?"

"Glen Bridge, a guy he said he used to hang out with."

"Did you follow that up?"

"I did, and I learned that Bridge was incarcerated in a Nevada prison."

"What was the next step in your investigation?"

"I needed to talk to this other man to see if there might be some validity to Melrose's story. So I flew to Ely State Prison to interview Bridge."

"Tell us about that interview."

"Bridge was reluctant to talk at first but eventually confirmed much of the specific information supplied by Melrose. Their accounts were in sync with each other and the independent facts I was already aware of."

"Are you referring to corroborating facts?"

"Correct."

"Were you concerned that these two men had gotten together and tailored their accounts of the murder?"

"That certainly crossed my mind. But in this case, I learned they could not have gotten together on their accounts."

"How so?"

"Bridge committed a robbery in Las Vegas five days after Tracie was murdered and has been in custody from the time he was arrested at the scene of the robbery." Coolidge put up his hands as if that answered the question. "There was little chance he and Melrose had gotten together to concoct some story."

"Objection. The witness is speculating, Your Honor."

"He certainly is," Cochran commented. "I'll sustain as to the last portion of the answer and strike that portion from the record and admonish the jurors to disregard that statement."

"Following the conversation with Bridge, what happened next?"

"I conferred with you as the deputy DA assigned the case and assisted in working out an arrangement whereby once Melrose and Bridge testified, they would receive time off their prison sentences."

"Was the arrangement contingent on Mr. Webb being convicted?"

"No. Only on their testimony."

"And, here we are." I nodded to Coolidge. "Detective, I'm going to call you back to the stand later in the trial and question you about the facts your investigation revealed that corroborate the testimony of Melrose and Bridge."

Turning to Cochran, "Your Honor, I have no further questions of Detective Coolidge at this time."

Cochran, noting that it was 4:20, looked at Tuck. "Ms. Tuck, would we be better served pushing your cross-examination until Friday morning? Unfortunately, I have a full calendar tomorrow."

"That's acceptable, Your Honor."

I was somewhat surprised that she was willing to leave the jurors with Coolidge's unchallenged testimony fresh in their minds.

CHAPTER 30

Friday morning. Judge Cochran greeted the jurors with a friendly good morning. Coolidge was already at the witness stand and was reminded that he was still under oath.

"Ms. Tuck?" Cochran invited.

"Thank you, Judge. Detective, this case, the murder of Tracie Switzer, had frustrated you for nearly two years before any arrest was made, isn't that right?"

"Frustrated?" Coolidge wagged a hand side-to-side. "Maybe it was so senseless and savage, it weighed on me. I very much wanted to catch the killer."

"You had spent quite a bit of time with Ms. Switzer's parents, getting to know them?"

"I did some follow-up with them to keep them apprised of the investigation."

"Actually, it was more than a routine follow-up, wasn't it?"

"Like I said, I kept them in touch with the investigation. I felt deeply for their loss."

"During those two years, this case had become personal for you, hadn't it?" Tuck fully understood that the question on cross was more important than the answer. She had what she wanted here.

"I wanted to apprehend whoever was responsible. They"— he nodded at the Switzers—"lost their child."

"Because it had become personal for you, you may have lost some of your professional objectivity, isn't that right?"

"Absolutely not," Coolidge said, nonplussed.

"You wanted to get Tracie's killer so badly that when you first heard that some jailhouse snitch claimed he had some information, you very much wanted to believe him, didn't you?"

"Counsel, you are trying to paint a picture that's not there. I did what any reasonable investigator would do. I followed up."

Tuck, ignoring the answer, continued. "Because this case had gripped you on a personal level, you very much wanted that snitch's information to be worthwhile?"

"Of course I did. I was trying to catch a killer." He paused and appeared to be thinking through his answer and then added, "Would you have me ignore an investigative lead in a murder investigation?"

"Objection," Tuck said. "The last answer was nonresponsive to my question. I ask that it be stricken."

Smiling slightly, Cochran replied, "It was responsive to your question. Objection overruled."

Undaunted by her failed objection, Tuck plowed ahead. "You're not denying that you felt a personal interest, are you?"

"Objection!" I'd had enough of this line of questioning. "Your Honor, I've been patient, listening to this line of questioning. It has become redundant and only marginally relevant."

Tuck responded without being invited. "When an investigator loses his professional objectivity and allows his personal feelings to color and shape his investigation, that investigation loses credibility. I submit that this detective's work and judgment have been compromised. It is critical that I explore his biases."

Cochran was visibly angered. "Ms. Tuck, I will not have speaking objections in my courtroom. You will ask permission to speak from this point forward."

Yet despite Cochran's dressing down, Tuck's uninvited reply allowed the jurors to be privy to the exchange instead of it taking place in the sidebar, allowing Tuck to spell out her point to the jury with clarity.

Cochran sustained my objection and signaled with an irritated gesture for Tuck to continue.

"Isn't it true, Detective, that if any fact was subject to two interpretations, one pointing toward Mr. Webb's guilt and the other pointing to his innocence, you would view that fact as incriminating?"

"No. That's simply not true," said the exasperated detective. Tuck was getting under Coolidge's skin.

"Let's explore that. After Mr. Webb was arrested, you viewed the grainy ATM video we've already heard about, correct?"

"I did."

"And after viewing the video, you believed it could have been a Black man, even though it's difficult to make out the race of the man, isn't that correct?"

"Possibly."

"Well, we'll let the jurors decide once they've seen it. But let's move on. After Mr. Webb was arrested, you professionally and personally believed that was Webb's image, even though the image is grainy and difficult to make out, correct?"

"Yes, after the arrest."

"That didn't answer my question. I want it clear on the record that just by watching the video, you couldn't make out Mr. Webb's visage."

Coolidge repeated his answer. "I came to believe it was Webb after his arrest."

Tuck let Coolidge's answer rest for a moment. Again, she had made her point. "Let's turn away from your personal perspective and talk about jailhouse informants, or as you have referred to them, snitches. You would agree with me that oftentimes people in custody come forward, claiming to have some knowledge useful to law enforcement, agree?"

"I agree."

"You would also agree that in your experience, most of the time snitch information is provided, it turns out to be worthless, isn't that right?"

"I wouldn't say most of the time, but I'll agree that sometimes it doesn't pan out."

"Fair enough. These jailhouse informants often lie to get some kind of deal, some benefit?"

"That's where corroboration comes in. We're not going to believe these people without sufficient corroboration to back it up." Coolidge was holding the line.

"Would you agree with me that jailhouse informants sometimes catch a fact or even a couple of facts from God knows where and then try to embellish what little they know into a whole story?"

"I'm sure that probably happens sometimes."

"Let's circle back to this case. There was a newspaper account of Ms. Switzer's murder, wasn't there?"

"There was."

"That account described her body being found in a Toyota pickup truck on a mountain turnout, didn't it?"

"I'd have to go back and check."

"Would you take my word that the *Riverside Press-Telegram* so reported?"

Coolidge shrugged in agreement.

"Is it possible that a man in custody, awaiting trial for armed robbery and looking at a long prison sentence, might be motivated to take what facts he was aware of and spin it into a whole fabricated scenario?"

"So, are you suggesting that the informant holds onto facts he learned from a news report two years earlier to later work an angle?"

Nice pushback from Coolidge.

"That's exactly what I am suggesting. Hold onto that info. You might never know when it might come in handy."

"Counsel, that's quite a stretch."

"Well, let's stretch it out a bit further. Your two jailhouse snitches appeared to be companions, right?"

"They were together on the night Tracie Switzer was murdered."

"Isn't it possible that before the snitches parted ways, they conjured up a story and agreed to support each other's account as kind of a backup plan, should they find themselves looking at hard time?"

"Like I said, Counsel, that's a stretch."

"You would agree both snitches were looking at hard time, weren't they?"

"I'll agree to that."

Tuck had made her point and seemed to reflect on its import before proceeding.

"I've got one more line of inquiry, Detective. The prosecutor, Mr. Clearwater, was your point of contact with the district attorney's office on this case, wasn't he?"

"That's right."

"So you reported the various steps in your investigation to him, right?"

"That's right."

"You also consulted him on some of the investigative steps, didn't you?"

"That's right."

"And just to be clear, the final decision on whether to file charges lies with him and his office, right?"

"That's right."

"And you would agree that one of the reasons decisions are made by the prosecutor instead of the police is to distance that decision from the police who investigate?"

"Correct."

"The system is built so that the DA, as a third party, can perform a detached, independent review of a case before it is filed?"

"That's one of the reasons."

"In fact, that's the primary reason, isn't it, Detective?"

"It's an important reason."

"Despite this rationale for an independent evaluation, Mr. Clearwater actually participated in your investigation?"

"No, he didn't. I consulted him, like I do in many cases. But he was never part of my investigation."

Tuck pulled a skeptical face. "Maybe I'm mistaken, but I thought this prosecutor sitting right here traveled with you to Ely State Prison to interview one of the jailhouse snitches."

"He was there solely as an observer."

Tuck with raised eyebrows and outstretched hands. "He was in the interrogation room with you during that initial interview with Bridge?"

"He was, but only to observe."

Tuck's face reflected her skepticism. "The filing decision as to whether to charge Mr. Webb with murder had not yet been made, had it, Detective?"

"You're trying to make it sound like he was active in my investigation."

Tuck brushed off the response. "Let me repeat my question.

The case was still under investigation at the time the two of you traveled to meet Bridge, true?"

"It was."

"And the prosecutor involved in that critical decision whether to file murder charges was sitting next to you in a prison interrogation room hundreds of miles away while the investigation was still very much underway?"

"As an observer. You're making it sound like there was something wrong with his input. Counsel, it was very standard procedure."

Tuck made a show of looking over at me as if I had kidnapped the Lindbergh baby. She then turned back to Coolidge. "You would agree with me that his presence in that room was unusual, in your experience?"

"No, I wouldn't."

Tuck began her walk back to her counsel table. "Detective, you've been most helpful."

We took our morning recess.

CHAPTER 31

Tuck had crossed the line. Her attack on me was groundless. Of course, prosecutors advise investigations. Happens routinely. But the jurors didn't know that. She had made my participation seem unscrupulous. She was groping for an issue at my expense. In my view, she had gone from being a thoughtful, fair-minded defense lawyer to a lawyer lowering herself into the muck for the sake of her client. Nonetheless, she had scored with her cross-examination, questioning pretty much every aspect of my case. I had no choice but to redirect Coolidge to rebut her assertions.

"Detective, the criminal defense attorney, through her questions, has called both of us out. Accusing us of colluding against her client. Let's—"

"Objection. I did nothing of the sort."

Cochran understood what Tuck had been about, and the judge was going to give me leave to respond. "I warned you, Ms. Tuck, I will have no speaking objections." Objections should be short and focused and consist of the word objection followed only by the specific objection. Anything beyond that is violative of courtroom protocol. "As for Mr. Clearwater's question, I think he has every reason to delve into your attack on the integrity of the investigation. Overruled."

"Thank you, Your Honor. Let's start with the investigation. In serious cases, is it unusual for prosecutors and investigators to confer in ongoing investigations?"

"No. As I was trying to say when Ms. Tuck was questioning me, it would be unusual if there wasn't some ongoing interaction between prosecutors and investigators. Happens every day of the week. It's extremely useful to have their input."

He hesitated briefly, formulating his thoughts. "As for evaluating the credibility of witnesses such as in this case, I'm appreciative of having a fellow professional give me input. And like I said"— here he directed his testimony to the jury—"when I interviewed Bridge, Mr. Clearwater was purely an observer and didn't participate."

"Do you know why I didn't participate in the interview with Mr. Bridge?"

"Of course I do. Since you would be prosecuting the case, should it proceed to trial, you couldn't call yourself to the witness stand. You had to remain an observer."

"The defense lawyer also questioned you about your interaction with the Switzers. She questioned your objectivity in working on this case. Did your personal feelings in any way interfere or compromise your investigation?"

"I was surprised that she insisted I was personally involved with the victim's family. I work heavy cases, serious crimes, frequently involving victims who were severely injured or even killed. I take every one of these cases to heart. I want the perpetrators brought to justice."

Looking over at Tuck, he continued, "Damn right I take my cases personally. Damn right I'm going to do what little I can do to help people like the Switzers get through their nightmare. An eighteen-year-old innocent was executed, and her parents were left to deal with her loss. The least I could do was keep them posted on the progress of the investigation. I apologize for nothing."

Tuck felt compelled to defend her turf. "Objection! Unduly prejudicial."

Cochran leaned back in her chair. "Ms. Tuck, seems to me you put this area of inquiry in play. The detective's comments were simply responsive. However, Mr. Clearwater, we've heard enough on this point. Move on."

"I have nothing further, Judge." I wanted Coolidge's last answer to cap off his testimony. We had righted the ship. I felt Tuck's attack had been blunted.

"Very well," Cochran said. "Let's take our lunch recess at this time."

Coolidge, Vanessa, and I retired with coffees to the attorney conference room just off the courtroom.

"Damn it, Jake," said Coolidge, "I wish you had protected me during her personal attack on me. And frankly, on you."

"Two things," I said. "First, she went too far and exposed herself as an attack dog. Jurors don't like that. Second, I knew on redirect we could counter her attack. And boy oh boy, did you let her have it. Your answer about caring about your victims has been the highlight of this trial so far. You killed it, Armand."

Vanessa weighed in, looking at Coolidge. "I'm just a second-year law student who has never watched a trial before. But I thought you were awesome. You came off as the defender of justice. I was watching the jurors, and they really like you."

A somewhat mollified Coolidge took the comments in silence. He finally nodded. "Are we putting the coroner on now?" I felt Coolidge was a bit embarrassed about lashing out at me and wanted to move the conversation along.

Vanessa said, "I called her. She'll be here at two o'clock."

CHAPTER 32

Cameron Soon assumed the stand and took the oath. Dr. Soon was of Chinese descent. If she was five feet tall, I'd have been surprised. She wouldn't break triple digits on anybody's scale. She spoke English like it was her third language, which I knew it happened to be. She spoke slowly and clearly, carefully enunciating every word. Folks with multiple languages always impress me, and from what I had learned about Soon during our prep, she was impressive on a number of fronts. In addition to her language skills, she was not just a medical doctor, but she also held two PhDs, one in microbiology and one in theology.

After she had been sworn in, Tuck asked to approach at the sidebar.

"I'm willing to stipulate to Dr. Soon's credentials and her testimony concerning the cause of death."

Cochran looked at me.

"Not a chance. This is a first-degree murder case. The jurors need to know all about the defendant's handiwork."

Tuck appealed to Cochran. "In light of my offer to stipulate, it is clear that counsel wants this testimony primarily to prejudice the jurors against my client. Graphic testimony will bring impermissible prejudice into this trial and compromise Mr. Webb's ability to receive a fair trial."

Cochran looked at me and, seeing that I wasn't moving off my refusal, said, "Ms. Tuck, you know as well as I do that stipulations must be agreed upon by both counsels."

I shrugged, acknowledging the judge's statement.

"Regarding your undue prejudice concerns, I've already limited Mr. Clearwater to two autopsy photographs. If at any time you feel the questioning is pushing too hard, I'll be receptive to your objections."

Returning to the far end of the jury box, my preferred perch while conducting direct examinations, I began. "Dr. Soon, let's start with your qualifications to offer testimony about the cause of Tracie Switzer's death. Please set forth your educational background."

"Your Honor," interrupted Tuck, "the defense will stipulate to Dr. Soon's expertise. We accept the good doctor as an expert."

Tuck's play was twofold. First, to demonstrate to the jurors how thoughtful and cooperative she was, especially in light of her mean-spirited cross of Coolidge, and second, and more importantly, to move as quickly as possible off the gut-wrenching details of a young woman having her throat cut.

"Mr. Clearwater?" Cochran looked at me.

"While I appreciate defense counsel's gesture, I believe it is in the best interest of the jurors to hear Dr. Soon's qualifications so they can best assess precisely how Tracie Switzer was murdered."

"Very well."

I carefully worked through her extensive educational background and her professional experience as a coroner. I then turned to her examination of Tracie's body during the autopsy.

"Doctor, based on your training and experience as coroner, were you able to determine Ms. Switzer's cause of death?"

"I was. To make the point as clear as possible, her throat was cut so severely as to nearly decapitate her." Soon had followed my suggestion in preparation for her testimony and didn't bother working through the details of the various muscles and tendons involved. Her testimony was graphically blunt.

I let that linger.

Of course I did.

"To a reasonable degree of medical certainty, did you determine the type of instrument used?"

"I could not, other than to say it had to be quite sharp."

I approached with the two autopsy photographs. As I walked past the jury box, I noted several jurors pulling back in anticipation of having to endure the photos. "Doctor, looking at these two photographs marked People's 3 and 4, do you recognize them as depicting the wound to Ms. Switzer's throat?"

"I do."

"Move 3 and 4 into evidence."

"They're received."

"Leave to display the photographs side-by-side on the PowerPoint?"

"Objection. Overly prejudicial. Everyone in this courtroom and certainly everyone in the jury box is well aware of the cause of death." Another standing objection despite the judge's warning.

"Overruled. Mr. Clearwater, you may proceed."

Even having prepared themselves for the gruesome nature of the photographs, some of the jurors immediately turned away. It was one thing to hear about the gaping wound but another thing altogether to see it. I felt no compunction about displaying the photos. One of my jobs was to have the jurors feel the full weight of the defendant's savage act.

There were subdued sobs from the Switzer family contingent.

"Dr. Soon, tell us what we are looking at."

"The photograph on the left is a view from the side, showing the depth of the cut. The second is from the victim's front, showing that the cut was nearly from ear to ear."

A compelling place to stop.

Not surprisingly, Tuck had no cross of Dr. Soon.

Cochran ordered the afternoon recess.

"Your Honor, before we recess, may we approach?" I asked.

"Certainly."

At sidebar, I said, "My apologies, but I anticipated that the testimony of Dr. Soon would exhaust the afternoon. My next witness is incarcerated and we can't have him here until Monday morning."

Tuck leaped at the news. "The defendant is in custody and objects to any delays."

Tuck was being a real ass.

Cochran smiled at Tuck's obvious gambit. "Mr. Clearwater, let's not make a habit of this. You had better be ready to go Monday morning."

"I will be."

Since Lisa had arranged to meet several friends for a Friday afternoon ladies happy hour, I drove to Tony and Eve's that afternoon, hoping to catch them at home. And sure enough, they were on their balcony, relaxed on loungers, with cocktails in hand. "Surprise," I said, trooping up the outside steps to their balcony. "Hope I'm not intruding."

Eve jumped up and gave me a tight hug. "Jake, we've missed you." She looked past me. "No Lisa?"

"She's up in San Arcadia, having drinks with friends."

Tony gave me a fist bump. "I'll get you a Modelo."

Eve motioned me to a lounger. Tony returned with the beer. That first hit was always the best. "Thanks, Tony."

Tony lifted his drink. "Salute, the return of the wandering warrior." Eve and I laughed. "We were just having an engrossing conversation about where to have dinner. Hope you can stick around and join us."

"Would love to. Who won, and where are we eating?"

"I won," Eve said, "and it's Sunset down by Zuma Beach."

"Works for me. That place knows how to prepare sand dabs," I said.

We had a delightful time catching up.

Lisa and I spent time hanging out at our new abode that weekend. We didn't leave the house except to venture over to our neighbor Zack's for his regular Saturday afternoon get-together. I did spend some time on the deck with my laptop, working through some ideas for my closing argument.

CHAPTER 33

"Mr. Melrose, the jurors understand that you're testifying in exchange for a reduction of your prison sentence." It was Monday morning, and we were underway. "The question I have for you is why they should believe your testimony. So let's start by you telling us a little about yourself to help these folks get to know you as someone other than an informant."

Melrose was dressed in his jailhouse orange jumpsuit. I hadn't bothered to put him in a suit. The jurors were fully aware of his status. A suit wouldn't change that. He was hunched deep in the witness chair with his head down, and in a halting, barely audible voice, he asked, "What you want to know?" This was a reprise of what I had encountered at the prelim. He was scared to death of Webb and, by extension, Webb's lawyer. The months since the prelim hadn't quelled his palpable fear.

"Try to relax, Mr. Melrose," I said, tamping my hands in a calm-down motion. "Let's start with your age and where you lived before you were sent to prison."

He took a fortifying breath. "I'm thirty-nine. I live in Riverside." Long pause. "Used to be with my girlfriend. My old girlfriend. She might still be in the apartment, I don't know. Haven't had any visits."

"What kinds of jobs have you had?"

Without looking up, he shrugged. "Not much. Job market not so good."

"Mr. Melrose, you are here to testify against Jaxon Webb. Are you fearful of the defendant?"

"Objection, irrelevant."

The judge looked at me, and I offered, "Mr. Melrose's credibility is on the line. His fear of the defendant could well affect how he testifies. The jurors need to know that."

"Overruled."

Melrose snuck a quick glance at Webb and nodded. "Yeah."

I glanced over at Webb. He was hunched forward, zeroed in on Melrose. He was spring-loaded.

"Bearing that in mind, do the best you can." Offering what reassurance I could. "Before we talk about the murder you witnessed back on September 3, 2016, I want to ask you about your understanding of what you need to do to fulfill your side of the arrangement in order to cut time from your prison sentence."

His shoulders tight against his neck, he began slightly rocking back and forth. "Gotta tell the truth."

"And what happens if you don't tell the truth?" I asked as if talking to a child caught stealing a candy bar.

"No deal," he muttered, almost under his breath.

"How is it that you remember what took place on September 3, 2016?"

Following another long pause with his head still down, he replied, "I seen a girl get killed."

"Okay, let's go back to the beginning of that evening. I understand you were out driving with Glen Bridge."

"Objection. Leading."

I certainly was leading, and I would continue to lead when necessary. It was essential to keep the narrative clear for the jurors.

"Sustained."

"Who were you with that night?"

"Glen Bridge."

"Who is he?"

"A friend. We hang out."

"What were the two of you doing?"

"Just driving around, hangin' out, smokin'."

"How'd the two of you encounter the defendant?"

"Seen him outside a liquor store."

"Did the two of you talk?"

"Yeah."

"What about?"

"Told me he needed a ride to Pomona."

"So what happened?"

Head on his chest, shrinking even further into the chair, he mumbled, "I didn't want to take him."

"But you did. Why?"

Another long silence. I looked over at the jurors. They were studying the unspoken interaction between Webb and Melrose.

"I figured he was packing."

"A gun?"

He nodded. "Yeah."

I let that rest before asking. "I understand. Tell us about the drive to Pomona."

He briefly looked up at me. "Not much to tell."

"The three of you were in the car?"

A grunt of affirmation. I let it pass. Sometimes a grunt is enough.

"Once you arrived in Pomona, what happened?"

Melrose had managed to work himself more or less upright. "He tells me to stop at some mall."

"Go on," I urged.

"He tells us to wait for him. Walks off."

"And did you and Bridge wait?"

A nod. Again, sufficient.

"Why?"

"Not going to fuck with him."

I let that sit. Counting two beats, I asked, "What happened next?"

"We did a blunt, sitting in the car."

"A blunt?"

"Yeah, a blunt," as if that explained it.

"A cigar with marijuana?" I asked.

"Yeah, like I said, a blunt." A bit irritable.

Good, he was with me.

"What happened next?"

"After a while, he drives up in a pickup."

"Describe the truck."

"Red, a Toyota, I think."

"Then what happened?"

"He told me he couldn't drive it, 'cause it was a stick." Melrose surprisingly added, "Told me to drive the truck. He would drive my car."

"Is that what happened?"

"Yeah," he answered, and snuck a quick glance at Webb. Webb continued giving him a steely, intimidating look. I again flashed to the jurors; they were taking in the exchange. Good.

"What happened then?"

"He drove my car. I followed in the truck."

"When you got into the truck, did you notice anything unusual?"

Another grunt and then, "A white girl was on the floor in the back of the cab." Melrose was making an effort to only look at me, not at the jurors, and certainly not at Webb.

"Describe how she was positioned."

But with that question, he stole another look at Webb before returning to me. "She was on her stomach. Hands tied at the back."

I paused and stepped forward. "Mr. Melrose, when you saw that girl, what did you think?"

He took a deep breath. "That I was in deep fucking shit." As articulate a description of his state of mind as I could have hoped for.

I let that linger. "Did you help her or talk to her?"

This is a boil that couldn't be pricked. This lowlife coward did nothing to help Tracie.

"I didn't do nothing."

"Why?"

"I was scared."

"Did she try to talk to you?"

"She was gagged. Made some sounds."

"Did you follow the defendant?"

"Yes."

"Where to?"

"Mostly freeway, then some mountain road."

"Where did the defendant stop?"

"Some turnout. I followed."

"What happened then?"

"We got out. I went to my car, where Bridge was."

"How about the defendant?"

"He gets the girl out of the truck and lifts her into the passenger seat."

"She was still tied up?"

He nodded.

"How far were you and Bridge from the truck?"

"Ten, fifteen feet."

"How was your visibility? Could you see what the defendant was doing?"

"I could see. I wish I couldn't have." His voice quivered.

"What happened?"

Trying to maintain. "He says something, I don't remember. Then he pulls her head back and pulls something across her neck." Melrose's head once again fell as he again squeezed in on himself.

I walked back to the counsel table and flipped through some meaningless notes. I wanted to park here and let the jurors feel the full impact.

"What happened next?"

"We drives off in my car."

"What about the truck?"

"Left it."

"The person who you saw slice the victim's throat, is he in this courtroom?"

Without looking at Webb, he pointed a shaky finger in Webb's direction. "That's him."

"Your Honor, may the record reflect that the witness has identified the defendant?"

"It will."

"I have no further questions."

"Very well, let's take our morning recess." Cochran gaveled.

Melrose was escorted back to his holding cell. I remained in my chair. I was spent. Getting through Melrose's testimony, all the while wondering if he would collapse before finishing, had sapped my energy. I finally managed the attorney conference room and coffee.

"Ms. Tuck," Cochran invited, after the break.

Tuck bounded out of her chair. Predator to prey. She marched behind my counsel table and halfway along the jury rail, stopped and, sizing up her prey, began nonchalantly, "Ah, Mr. Melrose, where shall we begin?"

Melrose folded himself even deeper into himself. It was tough for a big man to hide in the confines of the witness chair, but he was doing his damnedest to make himself small.

"Let's start with your character," Tuck continued. "You wouldn't say you're an honest man, would you, Mr. Melrose?"

Melrose, squeezing his head against his shoulder, mumbled, "Probably not so much."

"Probably," uttered Tuck with a smirk. "You're actually a liar and manipulator, aren't you?"

"Objection! Argumentative." I knew the cross was going to be brutal, but I had to offer Melrose some protection. This wasn't a prelim; this was in front of the jurors.

"Ms. Tuck, you know better than that. The objection is sustained."

Tuck didn't care about the objection. She knew precisely what she was doing, laying the groundwork for her broadside of Melrose.

"Okay, Mr. Melrose, let's step back and talk about your character."

Melrose straightened in his chair. "What do you mean?"

"Your character is what I mean. Your ability to be truthful and law-abiding." Tuck's tone had quickly turned mean and biting; nonchalant was in the dust. With a lowlife like Melrose, she didn't have to play nice. Given who he was, the jurors would most likely applaud any attack on him.

"I'm telling the truth."

Tuck, with a raptorial sneer, said, "Let's explore that. I note that among your various arrests and convictions, there is some credit card fraud." Returning to her table, Tuck picked up a sheaf of papers and studied the top sheet. "Two of those, I see. One in 2007 and one in 2010." She gave Melrose a hard look, commanding confirmation.

He complied with a shrug. "Yeah, guess so."

"That involves a criminal getting some person's personal information and using that information to illegally obtain money or property. Fair description, Mr. Melrose?"

There's a reason Tuck led with the fraud charges. Everyone, including all the jurors, was a potential victim of this type of crime. It hit home.

"Yeah."

"You didn't care that you were taking from innocent people, did you?"

"I tried not to think about that."

"But you knew you were hurting innocent people, didn't you?"

"I know it was wrong. I was hurting. Didn't have a job."

The wildebeest dodging in and out of the brush, trying to elude the lion.

"So you made it your job to cheat other people out of their money?"

"Wasn't running the thing."

"That's your defense, that somebody else was in charge?"

"No, it was wrong."

"So, to be clear, you lied about taking someone else's identity to get their money?"

"You could look at it like that."

"Mr. Melrose, is there any other way to look at it?" Tuck's look again demanded an answer.

"Guess not."

"Mr. Melrose, not only were you lying while stealing other

people's money and property, you were also manipulating the victims and the companies involved, weren't you?"

Melrose had worked himself out of his scrunched position and was sitting erect. "Like I said, I wasn't running that thing."

"Mr. Melrose, as you are sitting here as a witness for the prosecution, you're manipulating the system for your own benefit, isn't that right?"

"What you mean?"

"You're certainly not testifying because you think it is the right thing to do, are you?"

"You know I got a deal."

"Yes, you did. Let's move our conversation to that deal." Tuck stopped to make certain all the jurors were closely following. "Three years off your current prison sentence?"

He nodded.

"Three years works out to 1,095 fewer days in prison. Pretty sweet deal, Mr. Melrose."

"Still doing hard time," Melrose offered tentatively.

"Which you so richly deserve." That was over the line. Tuck had descended to the depths of TV law.

"Objection! Enough is enough," I said.

Cochran agreed. "There is a line, Ms. Tuck, and you just stepped over it. Sustained. And Ms. Tuck, I'll have no more of that!"

Without acknowledging the court's admonition, she continued, her teeth deep into the neck of her prey. "Let's discuss why you are currently doing hard time. Robbery?"

"I didn't do no robbery."

Tuck offered a quizzical look. "Didn't you threaten a clerk and demand money, and weren't you arrested immediately outside the store?"

"I never got away, so there was no robbery."

Stupid is as stupid says. Channeling Forrest Gump.

"Did no one explain to you that you don't have to get away to be guilty of the crime?"

"I don't know what you mean."

Putting her hands up in mock surrender, she said, "To be clear, you did plead guilty to robbery, didn't you?"

"That's what my public defender told me to do."

"To be clear, you threatened the clerk with violence if he didn't turn over the money?"

"Didn't even have a gun."

Tuck walked back to her counsel table and picked up what appeared to be a police report. "You told the victim that you had a gun, right?"

"Yeah."

"So you threatened him with violence to obtain money?"

"Yeah, but I didn't get away with it." As if that was an exonerating factor.

The stupid goes on and on.

"And you pled guilty and received ten years in prison?"

"Yeah, my public PD sold me out."

Tuck gave a dismissive wave of her hand. "Now that we've explored your criminal history and what that tells us about your character, let's talk about the testimony you just gave." Tuck's tone had eased a bit. There is a rhythm to cross-examination, and she was riding it.

Melrose nodded without audibly replying.

"Your buddy Glen Bridge was with you that night, correct?"

"Yeah."

"And after that night, you and Bridge discussed Jaxon Webb, didn't you?"

"I don't remember."

"Well, let's see what you do remember. You do remember seeing Mr. Webb at the liquor store in Riverside, right?"

He nodded. "Like I said."

"And you gave him a ride to Pomona, right?"

He nodded.

"So, just the three of you in the car?"

"Yeah." Melrose briefly glanced over at the malevolent face of Webb.

"And he told you to stop outside the Pomona Mall, correct?"

"Yeah."

"Mr. Webb then got out of your car and told you to wait for him, right?"

He nodded.

"After a while, Webb returned?"

"Yeah."

"He told you to get in the truck and drive because he was having trouble with the stick shift, correct?"

He nodded.

"You got in the truck, and that's when you saw a young woman tied up on the floor of the cab, correct?"

"Yeah."

"But instead of driving the truck, you got out and told Webb you were leaving in your own car, isn't that right?" This sudden change of direction caught Melrose and me by surprise.

Melrose looked as confused as I felt. After grasping the question, he straightened his body. "No, he would shoot me if I didn't do what he said."

Tuck was attempting to reinvent events by creating an alternate scenario. I was quickly calculating her tactic. The snitches were there at the beginning but not later on. And, of course, they didn't witness the murder. I no longer had to wonder where she was going to dig in. I was still processing as she worked to spin out her version of events.

Ignoring Melrose's denial, Tuck plowed ahead. "And after you got out of the truck, you told Webb you couldn't be a part of whatever was going on, isn't that right?"

"That what he told you?" Melrose's fear was somewhat abated by Tuck's surprising turn. "Because he knows what happened." Pointing at Webb.

"Then you and Webb got into a fight."

"Wouldn't fight him. He'd shoot me."

"After the fight, he drove off in the truck. And that was the last time you saw Webb that night?"

"You're making this up! We were with him the whole time!" He was upright, shouting at Tuck.

Again ignoring Melrose's outburst, Tuck walked back to counsel table and consulted a notebook. "Let's understand how, after you and Bridge got away from Webb, you two put together some facts you read about in the newspaper and spun a story about Webb's murder of the victim."

"Objection! Is there a question in there somewhere, or is this closing argument?"

"Sustained."

"Indulge me." Tuck was on a roll. "Assuming you and Bridge left right after Webb drove up, the two of you would have no story to tell. You two wouldn't have anything to offer for some kind of deal, wouldn't that be right?"

"That's wrong!" Melrose leaned forward, defending his turf.

In a reasonable, almost conversational tone, Tuck asked, "You read in the *Riverside Press-Telegram* that a murder victim was found the very next day after your interaction with Webb, correct?"

"Didn't read nothing!"

"In that article, you read that the murder victim was a young woman?"

"Didn't read no article."

Undaunted by Melrose's denial, Tuck stayed the course. "You read from that same article that she was found in her own vehicle, correct?"

"No."

"You read that the vehicle was a late-model red Toyota pickup."

Melrose shook no.

"And that her body was found in the truck on a mountain turnout?"

Again, Melrose shook no without an audible response.

This time, Cochran instructed Melrose to answer out loud.

He did.

Tuck then returned to her table and produced an article from the Riverside paper, walked over and showed it to me, and had it marked as Defense A for identification. The article was dated September 5, 2016, two days after the murder. She then approached Melrose. "You recognize that article, don't you, Mr. Melrose?"

"First time I seen it."

"Your Honor, will the court accept my representation that this article appeared in the September 5, 2016, issue of the *Riverside Press-Telegram*?"

I quickly considered. There was a hearsay objection available but which I would ultimately lose. An objection from me would look trivial and defensive.

Cochran looked at me.

"I'll stipulate."

The article went up on the screen. It set forth the salient facts Tuck had described. She let the jurors have time to work through the article.

Tuck nodded her head toward Melrose. "You didn't like Webb, did you?"

"Never did."

"You and Bridge got together after your encounter with him and, piecing together what you already knew with the facts you learned from the newspaper, conjured up a whole story?"

"We were there, we saw him." Melrose was frustrated.

"As a person who has been in and out of jails and prison, you know that coming up with a story and selling the believability of the story can allow someone to manipulate the system."

Frustrated, Melrose just shook his head.

"Isn't it true that you and your buddy, Bridge, figured that coming up with a story about a murder may prove valuable, should you ever find yourself once again in prison and need some story to help you out?" Without waiting for an answer, she continued. "You two weren't on the turnout that night, were you?"

"We was."

"It's curious to me, Mr. Melrose, that two years after the murder, you decided to suddenly come forward and offer your story to the authorities. Two years had passed."

"That's when I got arrested."

"Two years, correct?" Without waiting for an answer, Tuck gave Melrose one more incredulous look and retired to her table.

Had Tuck planted a seed of doubt in my case by punching a hole in the leaky vessel that was Dinold Melrose?

"Mr. Clearwater, redirect?"

I nodded to Cochran. I pulled an arrow from my quiver. "Leave to post that article again?"

"Go ahead."

Once it was up, I said, "Mr. Melrose, I want you to carefully read that article." I hoped he could read.

"Okay," he said, as he studied it.

I waited for him to finish. "Mr. Melrose, does that article indicate the manner of death?"

"What you mean?"

"Does it say how Tracie Switzer was killed?"

He looked at the article again, smiled broadly, shook his head, and said, "Nope, sure don't."

Thank God he could read.

"Does it say she had her throat cut?"

Melrose, again shaking his head: "Nope."

I let the moment pass before asking, "Mr. Melrose, were you and Glen Bridge on that turnout and did you see the defendant murder Tracie Switzer?"

"Yes."

I put up my hands, palms out to Melrose and then to the judge to indicate I had nothing further.

Cochran looked at Tuck. "Any recross-examination, Ms. Tuck?"

"Briefly, you don't know if there were any other articles that reported the murder, do you?"

"Objection. Asking the witness to speculate."

"I'm asking for this witness's knowledge."

Cochran hesitated, thinking through the objection. "Overruled."

"To your knowledge you don't know if there were any other articles disclosing information about the killing, do you, Mr. Melrose?"

"Not that I know of."

CHAPTER 34

Coolidge, Vanessa, and I sat in the courthouse cafeteria. They both had grilled cheese sandwiches, one of the safe bets in the cafeteria. I had coffee, just to have something in front of me. I never ate much during trial. Coolidge was buoyant. "I think we got him. Melrose did well enough. Tuck had no answer for how the snitches would know the cause of death."

"This thing is far from over," I said. "Despite what assurances the jurors gave during voir dire about not discounting snitch testimony out of hand, our reliance on snitches could come back and bite us." I took a sip of so-so coffee. "Melrose is such a slimy character. I could sense one or two jurors rejecting his testimony just because of the source."

"But we've got a lot of corroboration for their testimony." Vanessa was fully engaged. "Even if they dislike our guys, they can't ignore the corroboration, can they?"

"I hope you're right. The idea of using jailhouse snitches is repugnant to most folks. There's been a lot of press coverage concerning the misuse and even the outright corruption of jailhouse snitches." I studied her and Coolidge and took in a deep breath. "I'm the one who pushed this case to get it to trial, and from day one, I have worried about this very issue. I keep telling myself it's a murder case, and I didn't feel we had a choice but to go for it."

Coolidge remained optimistic, despite my concerns. "Next up, Bridge. He'll reinforce Melrose's testimony, and that should get us home free."

Had he heard a word I said?

"Armand, I'm glad you're here. You've believed in this case from the beginning." I slapped him on the back as I stood to go back into battle. "I appreciate the hard work you've put into this." I affected a smile and a more upbeat demeanor. "You two, don't get bummed out because of me. I always worry through trials. I'm always looking for cracks and warts. I think we're going to be okay."

Two o'clock on the nose, Cochran ascended her throne, and her bailiff called court to order.

"Your next witness, Mr. Clearwater."

"The state calls Glen Bridge."

A bailiff brought Bridge through a side door. Like Melrose, he was still garbed in jailhouse orange. I'd forgotten how small he was and how his face seemed buried in his Afro. His walk was spritely as he was escorted to the stand. He didn't exhibit the anxieties and fears that had nearly crippled Melrose.

"Mr. Bridge, we've had an opportunity to hear from Dinold Melrose this morning, so the jurors have a pretty good idea about what you are going to testify to. But before we get to that, I'd like you to introduce yourself, and tell us about your life before prison."

Bridge, in a voice too deep for his size: "I grew up in Riverside and lived there my whole life. I was married once, got two grown boys. Don't see them much. Wish I did, but I don't."

"Jobs, work?"

"Not much. A custodian job at Blue Star Plastics on and off over the years. They give people like me a chance." He hesitated.

"Probably not anymore, even when I finish my hard time. I think I burned that bridge."

"Tell us about your relationship with Dinold Melrose."

"Sure. We grew up together. Same school. Same kinds of trouble."

"What do you mean, same kinds of trouble?"

"Di and me, we've had our fair share of run-ins with the law. We were in a tough crew when we was teenagers." Then he added, "Seems like we never got around to living normal lives. Wish we had."

This guy was an intellectual giant when stacked against Melrose.

"Thank you for giving us a bit of insight into your background, Mr. Bridge. Let's move to your current difficult situation."

He cocked his head and offered a brief chuckle. "Yeah, my difficult sit-u-a-tion," he said, dragging out the word sarcastically. "You mean my hard time in a Nevada prison?"

"How'd that come about?"

"Actually it's kinda related to this case. When Webb"—he motioned at Webb, who was staring death lasers at him—"left us off that night after the killing, he threatened us to keep our mouths shut about what had happened." Keeping his eyes on Webb, he continued, "He threatened to kill us." He was not nearly as intimidated as Melrose had been.

"Did you take that threat seriously?"

"Damn right I did. A couple of days later, I packed my shit up and moved to Vegas."

"Why Las Vegas?"

"Friends there, some contacts. I needed to get out of LA. I needed a fresh start. I couldn't abide no death threat over my head." After a brief pause, he continued, "Tried to get Di to come with me. He wouldn't."

"You got in trouble right away in Vegas. What happened?"

"Like I said, I had some contacts. A couple of guys had set up a smash-and-grab at some high-end jewelry store. They said the security guard was cool. Said it was going to be easy." He shrugged. "I believed them. My mistake."

"What happened?"

"Me and two other guys was smashing counters and grabbin' up shit, when it seemed like half the Las Vegas Police Department was on us."

"I heard one of the employees got hurt."

"Yeah, caught some glass in the eye, blinded that eye."

"What were the consequences of the robbery?"

"I pled guilty to robbery and got packed off to Ely State Prison in eastern Nevada. And I've got to say, it's a mean joint in the middle of nothin'."

"How many years?"

"Twelve."

"What will you receive in exchange for your testimony in this trial?"

"Three years off the twelve."

"One more thing. Did you and Melrose discuss the murder you witnessed?"

"We did that night. We was nerved. But not after that. And like I say, I took off for Vegas."

"That night, September 3, 2016, tell us what happened."

He looked over at Webb, seemingly not apprehensive. "Di and I was out driving around, nothing special. Smoking some dope. Di pulls into a liquor store and gets out to buy some beer. He sees Webb."

"Is this in Riverside?"

"Yeah."

"Could you see what was going on between Melrose and Webb?"

"I seen them talking, couldn't hear what they were saying."

"What happened next?"

"Webb climbs in the back seat. Di said we was giving him a ride to Pomona."

"Were you surprised?"

"Nah, Di is that kinda guy. Always helping out."

"What happened next?"

"Once we got to Pomona, Webb told Di to pull over. We was outside some mall. Webb got out and told us to wait. I thought that was kinda strange. Then he walks off."

"Can you give us an estimate of what time it was?"

"I don't know, nine, ten."

"You and Melrose waited?"

"Yeah I asked Di, why we're waiting, and he says Webb was a scary guy who was always packing."

"Packing?"

He shrugged. "A gun."

"What'd you think about that?"

"Objection, not relevant."

"Overruled."

"Go on."

"Made me nervous. I didn't want to get shot."

"What happened then?"

"After we was waiting, he drives up in some small pickup and pulls right behind Di's car. He walks to us and told Di to give him the keys to his car and tells Di to get into the truck and follow him." Bridge, unlike Melrose, didn't have any trouble telling the story.

"Was Webb asking or telling?"

A sarcastic grin. "He was tellin', not asking."

"Describe the truck."

"It was one of them small pickups, that's all I remember."

"Color?"

"Maybe red. It was a while back."

"Go on."

"I got back in Di's car. Webb drove. Di was following in the truck."

"Did you and Webb talk on the drive?"

"Shit, no. No, not a word. Like I said, I was nervous."

"And then?" I motioned with my hands.

"We was on a freeway and after a while, Webb turned onto some road heading into the mountains."

"Which road?"

"I don't know, but we were climbing."

"Go on."

"He pulls off on some turnout and stops. Di pulled in behind him, maybe ten, fifteen feet back."

"What happened then?"

"Everybody gets out. Di walks over to me by the car. Webb goes to the passenger side of the truck, shoves the seat forward and pulls out some woman."

"Did you have any idea there was a woman in the truck?"

"Hell, no. I was having a hard time believing what I was seeing."

"Let me stop you right there. It was night, how could you see?"

"Headlights. Headlights from Di's car shining on the truck."

"After he pulled the woman out, what happened?"

"It was weird. Like I said, I couldn't believe what I was seeing. He forced her into the passenger seat. Then he looks over at me and Di and said plain as day, 'What am I going to go with this little puss?'"

I stepped back. Stunned. That's the first time I had heard that. I parked there and let several beats pass. "Those were his exact words?"

"That's what I'm saying. Never forget them."

I took a long breath. "Then what?"

Bridge, shaking his head, shot Webb a quick glance. "Then he pulls her head back and cut her throat." Bridge looked down. "It was like it really wasn't happening. Blood was everywhere."

The courtroom was deathly silent.

"Did you see what he used to cut her?"

"No, but whatever it was, he turns and throws it over the cliff."

"How far away were you and Melrose when this happened?"

"By the car, like I said, maybe ten, fifteen feet."

"What happened then?"

"I didn't say nothing. I think I was in shock. Felt like death was in the air."

"What did you see Webb do then?"

"He tells us to get into Di's car, and we drove back down the mountain."

"The three of you?"

"Yep. Back to Riverside."

"Was there much talk as the three of you drove?"

"No, but when we dropped Webb off, he pulls up his shirt and shows us his gun." Bridge hesitated, then added, "He told us to forget about what we saw."

"How'd you take that?"

"Objection, calls for speculation."

"I'm asking for the witness's state of mind," I responded.

"Overruled."

Without me having to repeat the question, Bridge said, "I took that as a death threat. That's why I got out of SoCal."

I stepped back and put my hands up, signaling to the judge that I was through.

The judge gaveled us into the afternoon recess. As I got up, I couldn't look at the Switzers. The heart-wrenching testimony had to be agonizing for them. Most likely they were in tears. I could feel my own raw emotions well up. I made my way to the attorney conference room. Coolidge and Vanessa followed me in.

"Can I get you two coffees?" Vanessa offered.

We nodded. The mood was somber. Bridge had testified to the same horror as Melrose, but somehow the impact was more jarring this second time around.

"That sonofabitch!" Coolidge had apparently felt it too. He was pacing the small room. "It was so fucking callous. He should die. Jake, this should have been a capital case."

At that moment, Coolidge's sentiment seemed right. Webb's statement, "What am I going to do with this little puss?" will ever be branded on my soul.

When we reconvened that afternoon, Tuck was much more subdued than she had been with Melrose. I think she felt the sense of despair that had permeated the courtroom following Bridge's testimony. I say despair instead of anger. A deep sadness seemed to hit everyone in the courtroom. The jurors looked weary, even depressed. No question they felt Tracie's pain, her family's pain, but also their own pain for having been blighted by this abomination.

I forced myself to shake off my despondency, focusing on how Tuck would react to the prevailing mood. Seemed to me that the same frontal attack she had used on Melrose wouldn't play well with Bridge.

She began from a seated position rather than the in-your-face approach she'd taken with Melrose.

"Mr. Bridge, you are required to relay a story of an unspeakable murder to get three years of your life back, true?"

"I guess that's right," Bridge agreed.

"Three years off the twelve for your armed robbery sentence?"

"Yes."

"Your testimony this afternoon is the price the State of Nevada is obligated to pay for what you are testifying to?"

"Objection. Unintelligible." It was all I could think to throw out there. It was an odd question, poorly phrased.

Cochran looked at Bridge. "Mr. Bridge, did you understand the question?"

"I think so. Seems to me that I'm the one who's paying. I'm doing the time."

"Let me be more clear. You're being compensated for your testimony?"

Bridge shrugged his narrow shoulders. "That's one way to look at it."

Tuck slowly stood and shook her head. "Jaxon Webb frightened you that night, didn't he?"

"Absolutely."

"In Mr. Melrose's words, he was a mean motherfucker." The expletive from Tuck's mouth was startling.

Bridge took it in stride. "That's right."

"You harbor real hate toward Mr. Webb, don't you?"

"I won't deny that. He forced me to leave my home. If I'd stayed in LA, I wouldn't be doing a virtual lifetime in a Nevada prison."

Virtual? Like I said, a genius compared to Melrose.

Tuck stood and moved closer to Bridge along the jury rail. "Now that we all understand your hard feelings toward Mr. Webb,

I want to move into your testimony." She paused and looked off as if trying to get the question just so. "Mr. Bridge, I accept the stories of you and Melrose up to the point when Melrose climbed into the truck. It was right then that I have serious concerns about what happened."

"Objection. This is no time for counsel to ruminate. A question would be appreciated."

"Ms. Tuck?"

Without acknowledging the judge, she asked, "When Melrose refused to drive, he and Webb had words, didn't they?"

Bridge flinched in surprise. "No, there were no words. There was no argument. Melrose was as afraid as I was at this point. No way we'd cross Webb."

"So here's where I'm stuck." Tuck leaned into Bridge. "If your and Melrose's shared accounts of the events had stopped right there, with you and Melrose driving off in Melrose's car, the two of you would have no murder story to tell, no story to negotiate with, isn't that correct?"

"What are you talking about?"

"And without a big story about murder and kidnapping, you and your running mate would not have gotten the deals you got, correct?"

"Lady, I don't know what he told you. We saw the whole thing."

Tuck ignored the answer and continued. "Isn't it true you and Melrose made up the rest of the story after Melrose read a newspaper account?"

"You're the one making it up," he said with an incredulous look.

"Everyone in this courtroom saw the article. Red Toyota pickup, mountain road, young woman bound in her own vehicle, young woman murdered. Lots of specifics, Mr. Bridge."

"We didn't make nothin' up, lady."

"The facts from the newspaper, along with you seeing the truck and Melrose seeing the victim, gave you and your buddy lots to work with, didn't it?"

Bridge was exasperated. "We didn't make nothin' up."

"It's curious to me that as soon as Melrose was arrested and looking at serious custody, the story suddenly materialized."

"No. No." Was all the frustrated Bridge could say.

"Melrose didn't need the story until he was arrested. You don't see the connection, Mr. Bridge?"

"Objection. Asking the witness to speculate."

"Ms. Tuck, you've made your point. Move on."

Tuck didn't acknowledge the rebuke. "I was initially puzzled why you didn't try to leverage the tale when you were first arrested, but then it occurred to me that you were in Nevada, not California. Nobody in Nevada would listen to you about some California murder, would they?"

"Again, she's asking the witness to speculate."

"Sustained. Ms. Tuck, I asked you to move on."

Undeterred, Tuck stayed with it. "Mr. Bridge, you would do most anything to cut your prison sentence in that isolated facility in the wasteland of eastern Nevada, wouldn't you?"

"Argumentative!" I'd had enough of Tuck's specious conjecture.

"Sustained."

"Judge, I'm through with this"— slight distasteful pause — "witness."

It was a so-so cross. Drawing a line from the point Webb drove up in the truck gave Tuck something to build on. And build she did, by suggesting that Melrose and Bridge had worked the facts to create a plausible scenario. Tuck was working reasonable doubt. Whether ethically or not was another question. She couldn't just make up a theory out of whole cloth. Maybe it had been Webb's suggestion. At any rate, the landscape had been altered. But I still had my ace in the hole.

"Your Honor, redirect?"

"Of course, Mr. Clearwater."

"Mr. Bridge, the criminal defense attorney has done her best to discredit your testimony. She referred to a newspaper article about the murder. Did you ever read such an article?"

"I don't know nothing about no article."

"Your Honor, leave to repost the article?"

"Go ahead."

"Mr Bridge, read the article and let me know when you've finished."

After reading, he looked up.

"Let me ask you, was the manner in which Ms. Switzer was murdered in that article?"

"I don't think so."

"Would it be helpful if you were to look at that article again?"

"Sure would."

"Your Honor, leave to once again display the article?"

"You may."

Bridge slowly reread and looked up at me. "Nothing about how she was killed. I told you all, we didn't make this up."

"Thank you, Mr. Bridge. I have nothing further."

Cochran looked at Tuck. "Any recross?"

"Briefly." She turned to Bridge. "You don't know if there were any other articles that reported the murder, do you?"

"Objection. Asking the witness to speculate."

Tuck responded, "I'm asking to this witness's knowledge. There's no speculation."

Cochran hesitated, thinking through the objection. "Overruled."

Tuck: "To your knowledge, you don't know if there were any other articles disclosing information about the killing, do you, Mr. Bridge?"

"Not that I know of."

"Your Honor," I said, as we reconvened the following morning, "I recall Detective Coolidge."

Tuck asked to approach. "What's the purpose, the relevance?"

Cochran looked at me.

"This is the investigating officer, and there are some loose ends I want to tie up. If counsel has objections as I proceed, she's free to object."

Cochran smiled good-naturedly at my response. "Thank you, Mr. Clearwater, for undertaking both the role of advocate and judge. But I agree with you. Ms. Tuck, feel free to object as you see fit."

Coolidge was once again sworn in.

"Detective, were you able to establish, independent of the informants' testimony, the approximate time Tracie Switzer was at the Pomona Mall?"

"Yes, both from my interviews with her parents confirming that she left home at approximately nine p.m. for the twenty-minute drive to Pomona, and from the footage of her ATM being activated at that time."

"Objection. Asked and answered."

"I don't think so," said Cochran. "Overruled."

"Detective, how close is the mall to the college sorority house?"

"A half mile."

"Let's move to the next point. Apart from the witnesses' testimony, were you able to establish that Tracie was in the company of a man around that same time?"

"Yes. Whoever activated that ATM had to get her card."

"How about corroboration that Tracie's truck was used to transport her to the mountain turnoff?"

"That was corroborated by her truck at the scene of the murder."

"How about corroboration that the murder occurred at the turnout?"

Without hesitation: "Her body was found in the truck at the turnout and there was blood on the ground in the vicinity of the passenger door where Tracie's body was situated."

"How about corroboration as to how Tracie was actually killed?"

"That was established by the coroner's testimony."

I put up my hands in a nothing-else-to-say gesture. "Detective, thank you for your diligent work in this case." Looking at Cochran, I said, "No more questions."

"Ms. Tuck, cross?"

Tuck shook her head. "I made my points earlier with this witness. The jurors know where I'm coming from."

"Very well." Cochran looked at me. "Mr. Clearwater, your next witness."

"Your Honor, the state rests."

"Ms. Tuck?"

"I have a motion to be heard outside the jury's presence."

The jurors were sent back to the jury room and Tuck made her obligatory motion to dismiss, maintaining I had not put on sufficient evidence to sustain a conviction. She went on for a while. There was no way Judge Cochran would take this from the jury. Tuck was making her record, in the event of a conviction, for an appeal.

When she finished, I stood to counter, but Cochran waved me down. "That won't be necessary, Mr. Clearwater. The defense motion is denied." She looked at Tuck. "Ms. Tuck, will there be a defense case?"

Tuck hesitated, I think signaling her displeasure at Cochran that the quick denial of her motion meant it was not taken seriously. "There will be no defense witnesses."

No surprise there. "Very well," said Cochran. "We will reconvene at two o'clock for preliminary jury instructions and then closing arguments."

CHAPTER 35

Following thirty-five minutes of Cochran reading jury instructions, it was time for closing arguments. Since Webb didn't testify, I had to be careful and steer clear of any reference to his silence. The Fifth Amendment prohibition against self-incrimination prohibited me from commenting on Webb's failure to testify. That would constitute reversible error and would lead to a mistrial.

I began by touching Detective Coolidge on the shoulder, then nodding to the Switzer clan clustered in the front row, before setting aside the podium and settling in front of the jurors. "I'm not going to spend much time before you this afternoon. I don't believe it's necessary. You've heard what you've heard. The facts couldn't be more clear. The hunter stalked his prey, captured his prey, and executed his prey. Unlike a predator in the wild who only kills for purpose, the predator in this courtroom killed for no purpose." I shrugged at the senselessness of it.

"As Judge Cochran explained, we—Detective Coolidge and I—bear the burden of proof, proof beyond a reasonable doubt, that the defendant committed first-degree premeditated murder. Premeditated? Did he think about murdering Tracie Switzer before he jerked her out of the truck and cut her throat? Premeditated. If he thought about it before he did it, he premeditated." I put up my hands. "Enough said about that."

"Let's briefly explore reasonable doubt. The critical word is 'reasonable.' Not some fanciful doubt, not beyond all doubt, not beyond a shadow of a doubt, but reasonable doubt. Defense counsel has done her level best in an attempt to manufacture doubt, hasn't she?" I cocked my head. "Let's circle back to the cross-examinations. First it was Detective Coolidge himself she lit into. Why? Because he cared about bringing to justice a stone-cold killer. He cared about the anguish Donna and Frank Switzer were suffering."

Some jurors turned downcast eyes to the Switzers. "Let's not forget that she also got after the detective and me for being careful and making certain we got the right guy. Let me ask the twelve of you, did her attacks against me or Coolidge raise any reasonable doubts?" I let my rhetorical question resonate. "Because of those attacks, are you going to walk this defendant out of this courtroom a free man?"

I shifted to my right, centering on the lone Black juror. "Let's discuss her crosses of Melrose and Bridge. She did what she had to do. She went after them. Of course she did. They are both disreputable men. But, and this is a big but, they just happened to be the disreputable men who witnessed a senseless murder. Detective Coolidge pointed out you can't pick your witnesses. You've got to deal with what you've got. The detective knew that, he knew these two would get ripped by some defense lawyer somewhere down the line. Did he accept their accounts straight up?"

I had my answer as two jurors gave slight imperceptible head shakes. "That's right, the detective built the case through corroboration. Corroboration is the glue here. When I put Detective Coolidge up on that stand the second time around, he laid it out. Wasn't every key point of their testimony confirmed by facts completely independent of their testimony?" Once again I let my rhetorical percolate. I invited their collective common sense to reach the conclusion.

I bowed my head and blew out some breath. "Folks, I'm not going to go through the corroborating facts. You don't need me to do that. I saw you taking notes. I don't need to tell you what you heard. I'll accept your recall." I took a step back, taking in the twelve. "I've been a prosecutor for a while, and there's a lot I've learned. One lesson is that oftentimes there is one fact, one piece of evidence, that stands out above all else and is frequently the reason jurors do what they do. We have the benefit of such a fact in this trial." I paused. "I'm sure some, if not most, of you know what I'm talking about."

There were some understanding looks and some questioning looks. "It came when the defense attorney was suggesting that Melrose and Bridge had made up their story from that newspaper account." I paused to let the collective memories of the jurors catch up with me. "But what wasn't in the account? I can see from your eyes you know exactly what I'm referring to. That's right. There was nothing in the newspaper about how Tracie was killed. Nothing." I let that settle.

"We may not like using jailhouse informants. It stinks. But what was the choice here? Do nothing? Or do we do what's right and deal with the corroborated testimony and make certain a killer is caught out?" I dropped my hands. "Let us challenge defense counsel to answer the question, 'If they weren't there, how did they know about how she was killed?'

"I'm confident you folks understand this case and will do the right thing."

Would Tuck take the bait of my challenge? Or was she too seasoned to allow my comment to dictate how she would proceed?

Following the afternoon recess, Judge Cochran said, "Ms. Tuck, you may proceed."

She stood, moved the podium back in front of the jury, and began. "As I was listening to the prosecutor's argument, a couple of things ran through my mind. One of those things was the prosecutor's effort over and over to appeal to your emotions. We all understand why. A young woman is dead, and her family is sitting right here in front of us. Our hearts go out to them. But the prosecutor didn't stop there with his appeal to your emotions. In addition to the sympathy card, he played the anger card. Those references to hunter, prey, execution—those were his efforts to rile you up, to make you mad."

She took a reflective pause. "When I hear those kinds of appeals, I know, I absolutely know, the prosecutor is afraid of the facts. Is afraid of the evidence. The emotional pitch is a cover for what's not there. The more time he spent pulling on your heartstrings and whipsawing you with anger meant less time talking facts, talking evidence."

Tuck stopped, pushed away from the podium, and moved to the far end of the jury box. She grasped the rail in front of jurors eleven and twelve, older women. "Let's talk about what this case is truly about. Snitch testimony. Prostituted evidence. I chose the word 'prostituted' deliberately. Because it has a mean, unsavory flavor. Like something spoiled, something rotten." Leaning into the two women, she asked, "Did you taste it, did you smell it?" The two ladies remained stoic.

She backed off and asked, "Am I wrong for suggesting this whole case is about bought and paid-for testimony from two truly untrustworthy and awful characters? During his closing argument, the prosecutor made the decision not to deal with that aspect of his case very thoroughly. Why?" She stopped, still locked on jurors eleven and twelve. "Because of reasonable doubt. Is it just possible that the snitches have cooked up a story? Could these two, both veterans of the criminal justice system, have worked and manipulated the detective and the prosecutor?

"The prosecutor ended his closing argument trying to trap me with what he thought was an airtight challenge. Well, Mr. Prosecutor, here's my answer. These two cons very well could have learned about the cause of death any number of ways. Let's explore that. It was two years earlier that the killing occurred. Think some information might have seeped out over a twenty-four-month period? Newspapers don't just write a single story about murder. There are follow-ups. How about the sketchy people these cons hang with? Could some salacious facts come up? Does that raise some concerns, some doubts? This reasonable doubt business is the backbone of our justice system. Are we really going to put our trust in the hands of these two felons who have every reason to manipulate the system for their unworthy benefit?

"You twelve are the last line of defense against these two jailhouse snitches getting away with their con. Don't let them. Send a message with your verdict. Tell the prosecutor to bring cases with legitimate evidence, not this piece of garbage." She stared at the twelve, nodded, and walked back to counsel table.

"Mr. Clearwater, rebuttal?"

"Absolutely, Judge." I stood and began from my table. "What do you do when the facts aren't with you? You try to minimize their importance. You try a workaround. The cause-of-death evidence is a nail in the hide of the defendant. It completely solidified this case. Defense counsel's response to that very specific testimony"—I put up my hands in a questioning motion—"could have been other newspaper accounts. Or, and I like this one, that information could have been circulating in the underworld."

I stepped back. "I don't mean to demean defense counsel's conjecture, but come on. Even if Melrose had acquired more information, how would he communicate it to Bridge? There was no time between the murder and Bridge landing in a Las Vegas jail, and from there, packed off to a prison in eastern Nevada. We've got to recognize counsel's remarks for what they are. Feeble attempts to disregard compelling evidence.

"I don't intend to be sarcastic, but this is an extremely important decision. A young woman was taken from us in the worst possible way by a predator without regard for the sacredness of life. Do what needs to be done." I took the jurors in one last time. "Thank you for your attention. I look forward to your validation."

Cochran gave the concluding instructions and ordered the jurors back in the morning to begin their deliberations.

CHAPTER 36

The following morning, I drove to Pacifico instead of downtown to the courthouse. I figured the jury would work on their deliberations most of the day and perhaps into tomorrow. I wasn't into sitting around and waiting. As for working the next case up for trial, I'd already learned that when a jury was out, I couldn't concentrate on anything else.

I had earlier emailed Tony and Howard, my two buddies on the faculty, that I would be coming in. We met in Tony's office for coffee and to catch up. Howard in particular was plugged into everything going on at the school. He took some bizarre delight in telling us that one of our recent faculty hires had not only taken up with a first-year student, but had managed to get her pregnant.

"You're kidding," I said, stupified. Pacifico has a hands-off policy when it comes to profs engaging romantically with students.

Sound policy?

Tony, who, like me, had not heard, asked, "How is the dean handling this? We've still got several months of the semester. He can't just fire this guy mid-semester."

Zero tolerance?

"Actually, that's exactly what he did," said Howard. "The guy is out. Chauncey divided up his classes, and a couple of us are doing a little overload to cover."

"You?" I looked at Howard, surprised.

"Correct. I haven't taught first-year torts in years. I'm having a blast. The first-years are so much more enthusiastic than the upper-division students. It's been invigorating."

Howard was brilliant across the board, as evidenced by everything from his Pulitzer Prize to being voted Prof of the Year pretty much every year. For him to slide from the lofty intellectual environs of upper-division constitutional law to first-year torts had to have been an adjustment. But apparently not for Howard. Those first-year students were learning at the feet of a master. If I had to guess, with minimal preparation, Howard could teach any class in Pacifico's curriculum, and most likely do so better than those of us regularly assigned those classes.

It was fun to catch up. I'd only been away for a couple of months, but I missed the daily camaraderie of my friends and the optimism and energy of the students. That said, I had no regrets about my decision to jump at Seah's offer and get back into trials. The Webb trial had been a rush. The uncertainty, the battles, and the sense of accomplishment had been exhilarating. I hoped the accomplishment business would happen. Jurors were unpredictable creatures.

"You said you had a jury out deliberating?" Tony asked. "What kind of case?"

"It's a rough murder case."

"Aren't all murder cases rough?" Howard asked.

"Some more so than others. This was a senseless execution of an eighteen-year-old college girl. My case was built around two jailhouse snitches, which was challenging."

"Oh, I imagine jurors don't much like snitch testimony," Howard said, wincing. "Are they going to convict?"

"I think so. I had solid corroboration for their testimony plus the gruesome nature of the murder. But I always worry about one or two holdouts."

My cell rang. Caller ID: Judge Cochran's clerk. "Yes, Maxine."

"We've got a verdict," she said.

I was astonished. "It's only been two and a half hours."

"I know that," she said. "Are you local?"

"I'm at Pacifico in Malibu. I can be there in half an hour."

"Hustle up. The judge doesn't like waiting."

"On my way." Turning to Tony and Howard, "Got a verdict. Gotta get downtown."

"Short deliberations," Howard observed. "Good for the prosecution."

Hope so.

I was the last one in the courtroom. Tuck, Webb, Coolidge, Vanessa, and the entire Switzer clan were in their seats. Even Cochran was on her bench. I caught an irritated look from her.

"Now that we're all here"—I caught another look—"let's bring in the jury."

As the twelve filed into their seats, I couldn't pick up any sense of how they had decided. No eye contact, no quick looks, nothing.

Cochran: "I understand, ladies and gentlemen, that you have reached a verdict. Will the foreperson hand the verdict sheet to the bailiff?"

The lone Black juror stood and handed the verdict sheet over, and the bailiff handed it to the judge. The judge took a solemn look, careful not to display any emotion, and then handed it back to the bailiff, who handed it back to the foreperson.

"The defendant will stand," ordered Cochran. Cochran nodded to the foreperson.

In a clear, resonant voice, he read, "We, the jury in the case of the State of California versus Jaxon Webb, find the defendant guilty of first-degree murder."

There was a quiet moment and then a collective release of breath from the Switzers sitting behind me. From the defense table, Webb stood and screamed at the jurors, "Fuck you! Fuck all of you!" He pushed Tuck to the ground before the bailiffs were on him.

Cochran ordered the bailiffs to clear Webb from the courtroom. As he was dragged out, kicking and screaming, expletives and threats streamed from his mouth.

Cochran banged her gavel, reasserting order. "Ms. Tuck, are you okay?"

"I am, Your Honor. I've experienced worse," she said, as she readjusted her jacket. Her years in the trenches had hardened her. I turned to Frank and Donna. Once Webb was removed, there were tears and hugs. They'd never get their precious daughter back, but it had to be some small relief to get the sonofabitch who had killed her.

Cochran: "Ladies and gentlemen, I want to thank you for your service. Even though this was a relatively short trial, it had its challenges. We in the justice system thank you for doing your duty and fulfilling your citizenship requirements. If you so choose, you may discuss this case with anyone, including the involved attorneys. You are now free to leave, with my thanks."

Once the jurors had shuttled into the hallway, Tuck and I remained at our tables. Cochran looked at her calendar. "Everyone is ordered back for sentencing on July 23."

There were lots more hugs and backslaps in the hallway. Coolidge embraced Frank and Donna. All three had tears running down their faces. Then jurors mingled with the Switzers. It seemed a cathartic experience for family and jurors alike. "Mr. Clearwater"— it was the foreperson—"I want to thank you for letting me remain on the jury. I know it took some guts leaving a Black man on the jury with a Black defendant, but it was the right thing to do."

"I appreciate that, sir. Thank you for your service."

Vanessa and I walked to Philippe's for a celebratory lunch.

Coolidge opted to go with the Switzers for their own lunch.

CHAPTER 37

July 3, 2019. Committee meeting. Hawthorne wasn't present. "Roger's been suspended, pending an internal investigation," Seah explained in a flat, emotionless voice, catching Mann and me flat-footed. "There have been a number of sexual-harassment allegations leveled against him. Until those are resolved, he is suspended and his cases are being reassigned."

After a moment of reflection, Mann remarked, "Didn't see that coming. Sometimes he was a bit of a contrarian at these meetings, but never inappropriately so."

"Any idea how long the inquiry will take?" I asked.

"Don't know. Meanwhile, we shall carry on. The DA is not inclined to appoint a new Elder until things shake out. Roger currently has four assigned cases. One is Ramirez. Jake, since you recently wrapped up Webb, would you be willing to take it on?" She looked at me hopefully. "Roger took it through prelim, so it's set for pretrial on July 11, and trial on July 18. I know it's short notice and I know it's a mean, messy case. But since you've been in on the discussions, you are in the best position to pick it up."

"Of course I will. Currently my only assigned case is Pouse. I need something to fill the idle hours," I said offhandedly.

Seah grinned at me. "Well, with the Pouse case against Hardy and the Ramirez mess, you're carrying some heavy weight."

"What about his other cases?" Mann asked.

"I'll take those to the chief trial deputy and have them reassigned to our felony panel." Seah looked at Mann and me. "Okay, let's carry on. In our committee capacity, we've only got one case to look at today. It was originally assigned to Roger, but I've read the reports and can brief it."

Mann and I settled back in our chairs to the new reality without Hawthorne. Even though he was occasionally a pain in the ass, his extensive trial experience provided valuable insight. His absence cast an unsettling pall. He was a heavy presence. The room felt out of balance.

Seah laid out the case. "An eighteen-year-old living day-to-day on the streets gave birth to a meth-addicted baby. The baby survived and was treated for withdrawal at USC General. Two days later, the mother somehow got her baby and slipped out of the hospital undetected. But five days later she returned to the hospital with her baby. The baby was dead."

"Oh no!" uttered Mann. "Homelessness and drugs." We sat reflecting on the scourges that felt overwhelming. Mann bowed her head and closed her eyes. She might have been offering a prayer for baby and mother.

Seah broke the silence. "Autopsy determined the cause of death was the methadone in the mother's system, coupled with malnutrition."

"Not a great surprise," I added for no one's benefit, including my own. "Do we know what the mother did during the days she had the baby?"

"No, the woman won't talk," answered Seah. "According to the investigator, she was so distraught as to be incoherent. They haven't been able to get a thing out of her."

Mann said, with mournful sarcasm, "This one pulls on the

heartstrings in every possible way." She took a breath. "I don't know what we do with this. A tragedy born of many of society's ills. The fact that this woman appears to have been living on the streets through her pregnancy sickens me."

"I agree," said Seah. She got up and paced. "Does this woman belong in the system? Are we doing any good filing involuntary manslaughter? Would that benefit society? Would that benefit this woman?" Seah's compassion played across her face.

"On the other hand," Mann gently countered, "a human being died. We have to account for that."

"This woman needs a roof over her head, adequate food, drug treatment, and counseling," I offered, without moving the needle on the best course of action.

"The idea repulses me, but Leslie is right. We have an individual responsible for a death," Seah said almost under her breath. "I think we have to file." Returning to her seat, "Maybe sometime prior to trial, the assigned deputy can work out some kind of solution not involving much custody." She put up her hands in a futile gesture. "God, I hope I don't sound like some cold-hearted bitch."

"No, you don't, Nancy," I replied and then added, "A baby died."

CHAPTER 38

July 11, 2019. Pretrial meeting in chambers with judge and counsel representing Caesar and Cathy Ramirez. Anna Goldman represented Caesar, and Marcel Serge represented Cathy. Goldman was a public defender and, from what I had gathered from my colleagues, was one of the go-to lawyers in her office. She had a mature elegance. In what I guessed were her early fifties, she was tall and slim, with beautiful auburn hair that brushed her shoulders. Even though this was an informal meeting in chambers, she was dressed for trial in a dark blue pantsuit with a gold necklace and matching earrings. Why she remained with the public defender's office was a matter of speculation. She could command sizable fees as a private defense lawyer. Perhaps she's a true "cause" lawyer.

Marcel Serge couldn't have presented a greater contrast to Goldman. He was on the conflict counsel panel, which doled out indigent cases the PD couldn't handle, generally because of conflicts between defendants, such as presented here. Typically, the PD would represent one defendant in a multiple-defendant case, and conflict lawyers would be assigned as needed. Serge, I had learned, was a hustler. He would take on pretty much whatever came his way. His reputation was to get appointed, collect a fee, and then plead his client out without going to trial. It was unknown if he could competently handle a trial, since there wasn't much history.

He was short and slovenly, with an unkempt beard and a sport coat that looked like it was off the rack from Goodwill.

Our judge was George Slater, a balding redhead of middle age with several bandages dotting his face. Probably from recent surgeries. I learned from Seah that he prided himself for his ability to "coax" settlements, sometimes with subtle urging, and occasionally with a big club. If a judge is intent on getting a disposition, some are not above flat-out extortion, such as threatening a defense lawyer with a disproportionate sentence if their client dares to go to trial and loses. Or threatening a prosecutor with a pretrial ruling which could adversely affect their case. Everyone in Slater's chambers that afternoon understood that a joint trial of the Ramirezes would involve, at minimum, five to seven days of much-in-demand trial-court time. I was certain Slater's directive from his boss, the county's supervising judge, was to achieve results short of trial.

Following pleasantries, Slater began with me. "Mr. Clearwater, I understand you are just recently with the DA's office."

"Yes, I'm taking a year leave from my post at Pacifico Law. I was a prosecutor in San Arcadia prior to my faculty position."

"Welcome," he said, while walking to his espresso machine. "Anybody interested?" he asked. "Good stuff." The three of us declined as Slater went about the meticulous business of preparation. Over his shoulder he asked, "What's your office's position in this case, Mr. Clearwater?"

Amidst the buzzing and moaning of the machine, I replied, "As you are aware, we filed second-degree murder against both defendants. We believe the husband intended to inflict serious bodily injury on his nephew, which resulted in the child's death."

With his back to me while still tending his machine, Slater asked, "And I assume Mrs. Ramirez is charged as an aider and abettor?"

"That's correct, as well as a caretaker who violated her duty of care for the deceased."

Walking back to his desk with his treasure in hand, he said, "Ms. Goldman, what a pleasure it is to have you back in my courtroom."

"Thank you. I always enjoy trying cases in front of you."

Pre-existing relationship. An attractive woman. Was there going to be a problem here?

Slater gave her an ingratiating smile before turning to Serge. "Mr. Serge, I'm not ignoring you. I'll get to you in a moment. First I want to get the measure of the prosecutor as to the husband." Focusing on me, he said, "What is your position concerning any kind of disposition regarding the husband?"

"Judge, I don't know that we have much flexibility. The nature of the injuries sustained by the eleven-year-old victim are grievous. My office feels the charges are appropriate."

Slater uttered a *hmm* before again looking at Goldman. "Okay, Ms. Goldman. I take it you have something to say?"

She nodded. "I agree with the prosecutor's assessment of the injuries. They are grievous." Pitching to the judge, she went on. "The concern I have is the husband's ability to fully comprehend what he did and why he did it. From my first meeting with him, I've had serious questions about his mental acuity. He appears to be quite slow. He has difficulty focusing on the conversation or even fully grasping the potential jeopardy he is in. I had him evaluated by a psychiatrist, and my initial impression was borne out."

Clever move, good lawyering.

Goldman turned to me. I was the one she needed to convince. "There is a reason he has never held a job of any consequence and is living on the edge of homelessness. In his day-to-day activities, he is performing at a fourth-grade level. He can barely read. And," she added for emphasis, "according to the psychiatrist, he is easily manipulated."

Slater nodded agreeably. "I assume you will make these findings available to Mr. Clearwater and Mr. Serge?" Slater said.

"Of course I will. I only received the results this week. I'm still considering the implications these results have for his defense."

"Mr. Clearwater, your reaction?"

"This is new to me. I'll have to see the report, and in light of Ms. Goldman's representations, I may have to have Mr. Ramirez evaluated by one of our psychiatrists." There was always a stable of psychiatrists willing to work with prosecutors.

Slater nodded at Serge. "Mr. Serge, your take?"

Serge, seemingly surprised to be included, hesitated and caught his balance before responding. "This also catches me completely by surprise." He paused, thinking it through. "The suggestion that the husband could be easily manipulated certainly could have an adverse impact on Mrs. Ramirez." His self-evident statement did nothing to move the discussion along. Serge was playing to form.

Slater sat back, sipping his espresso. "Given this development, perhaps we would all be better served to schedule another pretrial hearing." He studied his calendar. "Would three weeks be sufficient time to assess where we are?"

"Three weeks is unrealistic, since I need to have Mr. Ramirez evaluated," I said. "I suggest we put this over for at least five weeks." Having stipulated to a recent request by Hardy that the Pouses' trial be extended to early October meant that late August would still work for me.

"How about a month?" Slater countered.

"I think that's doable," I agreed.

"Okay." Slater again consulted his calendar. "How about we pick this up on Wednesday, August 15?" Having received nods, he asked both defense counsel, "Time waived?" Since both Ramirezes were in custody, a time waiver was necessary to avoid a speedy-trial motion.

They agreed.

As we stood to leave, Slater said, "I'm looking to get this baby off my calendar." He was confident he could bend the disposition to his will. My insistence that this was a murder and as such most likely would proceed to trial apparently carried little weight.

CHAPTER 39

August 7, 2019. Committee meeting. Seah confirmed what had been circulating around the office for days: Roger Hawthorne had resigned amid sexual-harassment allegations. Seah, as was her wont, refused to comment whether charges would be filed, beyond her earlier terse disclosure.

With that sobering news, Seah reported that there were no new cases for us to consider. She asked for an update on Ramirez. I laid out Goldman's reveal. Neither Seah nor Mann was surprised. "Looks like Goldman will be using the wife's conduct to lessen the hurt on the husband." She stopped to consider. "Could she be angling for a manslaughter lesser?"

"That has certainly crossed my mind," I said. "While I've been waiting for Dr. Ready's results, I've been thinking through how Goldman might work this." I studied my colleagues. "Cathy Ramirez is the principal, and the husband, her tool." I cocked my head looking for their reaction.

Seah obliged. "But does that get the husband off the hook? Or at least mitigate his involvement down to involuntary manslaughter?"

Mann considered. "If Ready confirms the defense findings, it could knock the husband down to invol. But I don't see this getting him off the hook."

"I agree," I said. "But Goldman may argue that it's possible this guy may not even have realized the damage he was doing. In his mind, perhaps he believed he was only disciplining the child."

"That's threading the needle," Seah said, shaking her head.

"And let's not forget about Felipe, the other nephew that they killed." Mann gestured with a dismissive wave. "Not just one dead kid, but two?"

"But Leslie"—I put up my hands and shrugged my shoulders— "the same defense applies to that death as to this one. Beyond that, I doubt very much if Felipe's death will be admissible. Slater most likely will knock it out under 352 grounds as overly prejudicial. If Goldman's theory pans out, it shifts even more culpability onto Cathy."

"Jake, you've had more time to think this through," Seah said. "Do we have any room for negotiation?"

"Again assuming Ready agrees with their shrink, here's the rub. One of our attack plans against Cathy is to pursue aiding and abetting. If we don't pursue murder charges against Caesar, the actual killer, will the aiding and abetting theory hold up against Cathy?"

"And following that chain of logic," Mann said, "if we reduce the charge against Caesar to involuntary manslaughter, then Cathy would only be culpable of the same. That is unpalatable."

I got up for coffee. "Even so, I'd still have her violating her duty of care."

While I was messing with the Keurig, Seah countered, "The husband can't get off lighter than the wife. That won't wash with any jury."

"You're right," said Mann. "I think we need to come back after we get Ready's report."

"Good idea. I'm scheduled to meet with Slater and counsel

August 15 for more pretrial discussion. So let's meet sooner rather than later."

Dr. Ready's report arrived the next day:

At the request of DDA Clearwater, I evaluated Caesar Ramirez regarding his ability to understand and perceive the nature of his conduct regarding his relationship and treatment of Oscar Ramirez during the seven-month period leading up to Oscar's death. Specifically, I was tasked with determining whether Mr. Ramirez understood that his treatment of his eleven-year-old nephew was life-threatening. I was also tasked with evaluating Mr. Ramirez's susceptibility to being manipulated, in particular by his spouse.

In preparation for my evaluation, I was given access to the case file, which included the police reports, the coroner's report, and the subject's custodial interview in which he admitted to inflicting fatal injuries to both Oscar and his brother, Felipe. I explained to Mr. Ramirez that I had been retained by the prosecution. Throughout the evaluation, he seemed agitated but agreed to proceed. When asked about his medical history, he explained that he has suffered throughout his life with headaches, including the period in which he was acting as Oscar's and Felipe's caretaker. He reported that he had never been evaluated or treated for same. He also indicated he had never been treated for any psychiatric issues.

As for family history, he reported that he was raised by his mother, as his father had abandoned the family when he was very young. The family lived on welfare throughout his childhood. He dropped out of school during the tenth grade. He explained, "I just didn't get any of that stuff. There was no point continuing." He worked a number of part-time jobs, including janitorial work and kitchen help. He continued to reside with his mother until age thirty-four, at which time he met and married Cathy Ramirez.

He described his relationship with Cathy as unequal. When asked to explain, he said Cathy, from the time of their marriage, was "in charge." He said she often made him feel like a child. "She told me what to do and I did it." When questioned about his nephews coming to live with him and Cathy, he expressed frustration. The boys, he explained, were disrespectful of Cathy. They made fun of how big she was and how she had difficulty moving. He felt it was his responsibility to discipline the boys. When asked if Cathy directed the discipline, he agreed that most often, his discipline followed Cathy's direction.

Following several additional pages of narrative, Ready offered his conclusions.

I find that Caesar Ramirez was capable of understanding the consequences of his actions. I also find he is an unsophisticated adult with the maturity level of a preteen, susceptible to impulses and to manipulation. However, he would have known that the injuries he inflicted on Oscar were severe and could have been life-threatening. In part, I base my conclusions on the earlier death of the older brother. Mr. Ramirez was aware that after the death of Felipe, his "discipline" was life-threatening.

I emailed Ready's report to Seah and Mann and suggested a meeting prior to my pretrial meeting with Slater and counsel. Two afternoons later, we met.

Mann shook her head. "Some help from Ready, but only some. It read to me that Caesar, as unsophisticated as he is, is savvy enough to lay off much of the blame on Cathy."

"That was my read as well," said Seah.

"I don't know about savvy, but I agree, he is a worthless putz who will go along with what a stronger personality dictates," I said. "Fortunately, we've got Ready's conclusions that he is capable of understanding the consequences of his actions. Especially, as Ready points out, after killing Felipe. But as I suggested before, the jurors are not likely to learn of Felipe's death."

I sat back. "However, even a person with a lack of maturity understands that beating someone to the point of torture has severe consequences." I looked at my two partners. "We're sticking with murder on both of them."

"You're pretty fired up, Jake," Seah said. "Judge Slater is going to lean hard on you to settle this for invol man."

Mann was shaking her head at my fervor. "Good for you, Jake. Hang tough with Slater. Murder, in whatever form it takes, is murder. Convict their asses." Her comments were way out of character for the reserved Ms. Mann.

Seah laughed at the unexpected from the quieter Mann. "Jake, looks like you've got your marching orders." She leaned over the conference table and gave Mann and me fist bumps.

Another first.

CHAPTER 40

August 15, late afternoon, Judge Slater's chambers. I accepted the judge's offer of espresso.

What the hell, I'm good with afternoon caffeine.

Slater settled behind his desk, sipped his drink, and focused on me. "Mr. Clearwater, I assume you have your own psychiatric evaluation at this point and can fill us in on your current thinking regarding a disposition."

"I've got the evaluation and, in compliance with reciprocal discovery, have forwarded it to counsel. The evaluation confirms some of the findings and conclusions of the defense's psychiatric expert's evaluation. However, it concludes that Mr. Ramirez did understand the potentially life-threatening consequences that could result from the injuries he inflicted." I turned to Goldman. "He may be immature and gullible and even manipulated, but he knew full well that the savage beatings he administered to this eleven-year-old boy could kill him." Turning back to Slater, I put my hands out in a what-can-you-do gesture. "My position, accordingly, has not changed. This is a murder case and will be prosecuted as a murder case."

Slater's face flushed. Any hint of cordiality had slipped into the ether. He put down his coffee. In a strained voice, he said, "This matter is not closed until I say it's closed. We, the four of us, are seeking an equitable disposition. I will not accept your conclusion, Counsel." He gave me a hard look, thinking to intimidate.

It didn't.

"We are going to continue to talk this through. Do I make myself clear?"

This was upper-division arm-twisting. I checked my temper and responded in an even tone. "I fully understand the function of this pretrial disposition hearing, but along with several of my colleagues, we have considered options short of murder. But it just doesn't work in this case. The defendant knew what he was doing, that he was essentially torturing this kid for months before finally killing him."

An exasperated Slater dismissively waved me off and looked to Goldman. "Ms. Goldman, I don't seem to be making much headway with this prosecutor. Would you care to weigh in?"

She nodded thoughtfully. "This immature, slow-witted man believed he was simply administering discipline. Was his discipline way over the top? Of course it was. But he had no understanding that his conduct was life-threatening."

She drew a breath, looking from Slater to me. "This case is about a childlike individual under the control of a domineering spouse. He simply didn't appreciate that his idea of discipline was going too far." She stopped again, thinking through her argument. "In tragic cases such as this, where there is no intent to seriously harm, and a person dies, we call that involuntary manslaughter."

The room went silent. I think Slater expected me to respond. I didn't. Sometimes, it's best to remain quiet. Finally, in a manner suggesting big brother imparting sage advice to little brother, Slater said, "Mr. Clearwater, I've been on the bench for twenty-five years. I've seen cases where parental discipline has gone too far. Jurors are not inclined to find that these cases constitute murder."

I carefully considered before responding. "Sometimes trials need to go forward despite the impact on a judge's busy trial calendar."

Gas on flames.

I was toeing the line on contempt. Probably the only thing that absolved me is that I had maintained a level tone.

Fully vexed, his face flushed, his shoulders tensed toward me, Slater demanded, "Who is your supervisor? Who do you report to?"

Through clenched teeth, I dropped my voice almost to a snarl. "I don't report to anyone. This is my case, my call."

"Don't get insolent with me, Counsel. You're walking a fine line." We had both moved to outright hostility. "Do you report to Nancy Seah?"

"I thought I made my position clear. This is my case."

Slater yelled through his open door to his administrative assistant. "Pat, get Nancy Seah over at the DA's office on the line."

We all sat uncomfortably silent until informed that Seah was on the line. Slater put her on speaker. "Nancy, this is Jim Slater, we're on speaker. I'm in chambers with counsel on the Ramirez case. Your deputy, who I'll inform you is on the very edge of contempt, will not engage in any reasonable disposition talks on this matter. I'm hopeful you'll intervene."

I held my breath. This was one of those moments. Would Seah back down from a threatening judge or would she remain the same tower of strength I had gotten to know?

Her first words obliterated any concerns. "Judge, with all due respect, Mr. Clearwater has the full authority of the district attorney at his back. It is his case to deal with as his experience and common sense dictate." She paused, waiting for a response from Slater. When none was forthcoming, she asked, "Is there anything else I can help with, Judge?"

Slater's mouth fell open before he switched from speaker and picked up his receiver. In a tightly controlled voice, he said, "Thank you for your time. Good day." As he hung up, he stared accusingly at the phone. He put his hands behind his neck in an effort to control his temper and, in a bitter resigned voice, said, "We're through here. Motions at 1:30 this Friday, August 17. We'll begin jury selection Monday the twentieth."

When I reached my office, Seah was waiting for me.

"Thanks, Nancy."

"There's nothing to thank me for. It's your case. Slater's an ass. Has always been an ass. Loves to throw his weight around. It was a pleasure to shut him down."

I laughed, releasing some of the pent-up stress from confronting the judge.

Nancy smiled. "He prides himself on disposing cases. We've had run-ins with him from time to time." She gave me a knowing look. "Now I don't need to warn you, he's a vindictive sonofagun. It's going to be a hard trial."

"I figured that." I gave her a reassuring smile. "I can handle him."

"I know you can, Jake."

CHAPTER 41

I had Detective Ron Everly at the counsel table with me during Friday's motion hearing. No Vanessa this time around. It was time for her to return full-time to school. The Fall semester was set to start. She had been a huge help during the Webb trial, but her studies come first.

The hearing was my first opportunity to see the Ramirezes since Hawthorne had conducted the prelim. Caesar was short and thin. He wore an ill-fitting suit that I'm certain Goldman supplied. Cathy was another matter. She was short and huge. Folds of fat covered her face. She wore a muumuu-style dress that seemed appropriate to her bulk. Her hair was pulled back into a tight bun, inches of gray showing at the part. The Ramirezes made a memorable pair.

Motions before Slater went about as poorly as anticipated. The primary defense motion was to exclude any mention of the earlier death of Felipe. Goldman made a compelling argument as to the overwhelming prejudicial impact such testimony would have on the jury. "If that comes in," she argued, "this trial is effectively over."

I countered, knowing I had little chance of success. "The defendants' treatment and killing of Felipe is important to establish that both defendants were on notice that their version of discipline was life-threatening and could lead to death. Furthermore, Felipe is an integral part of this trial. Both boys were sent up to Oregon, but if there is no mention of Felipe, the jurors will be led to speculate as to what became of him. He has to be accounted for."

"Your Honor, if I may respond to counsel's concern?" Goldman was ready. "I suggest that there be no mention of Felipe throughout the trial. Beginning with the two boys moving to Oregon. Let's only mention Oscar."

"With that suggestion, we are playing fast and loose with the truth," I countered.

Slater heard us out and, with a tick of triumph in his voice, granted the defense motion to exclude any mention of Felipe whatsoever. It was not an unexpected blow. And frankly, it was probably the right call.

The second significant defense motion was brought by Goldman and Serge, seeking to exclude Caesar's two interviews with law enforcement. In the first interview, which occurred shortly after Oscar's death, Caesar explained the circumstances of Oscar's death to a responding officer, including that Cathy decided when Oscar should be punished and how severe the punishment should be. Serge appropriately argued that the portion of the statement implicating Cathy violated the spousal privilege and should be excluded.

I agreed that any portion of Caesar's statement implicating Cathy should be excluded. However, the balance of the statement should be admitted. Slater agreed. Caesar's statement was admissible but would be sanitized of any mention of Cathy's involvement.

The second defense motion considered Caesar's interview with Detective Everly. Both Goldman and Serge argued that pursuant to *Miranda* and *Messiah,* Caesar's interview should be thrown out. However, I had solid ground under my feet. There had been a clear waiver by Caesar before he engaged in that interview. Slater, after hearing arguments, was forced to side with me and allow the interview to come in. Once again, however, any reference to Cathy was to be excluded.

Saturday afternoon lounging on the deck with Lisa should have been relaxing. She was reading *Where the Crawdads Sing*, which had her tearing up. I had just started Daniel Silva's latest Gabriel Allon venture, but I couldn't relax, couldn't focus. Voir dire was Monday morning and I was at a loss. I put down the book and went to the kitchen and made margaritas. Cadillac, with Grand Marnier.

When in doubt, drink.

I handed Lisa hers and she looked up with moist eyes.

"Fun book?" I gibed.

"Don't be a jerk." She sat up. "Just very sad. An abandoned child."

"That'll do it." I sipped my drink. "Speaking of sad, as you know, I'm just getting started on Ramirez. And it is unsettling."

"I'm sorry, Jake. I know it's a brutal case." I had discussed the case until I'm certain Lisa was tired of hearing about it.

"Do you mind if we talk shop for a minute?"

She put down her book and picked up her margarita. "Sure, go ahead."

"I'm struggling with how to approach voir dire. I've got to be careful. This judge is going to cut me off if I bleed much into the facts. I know the defense attorneys are going to park on the defendants' ignorance as to how to properly administer discipline. They go first, so I need to move the discussion back to the child's injuries and death. But, like I said, I know the judge is going to tighten the leash."

Lisa took a thoughtful sip. "Seems to me like common sense might be your talking point. Let the facts speak for themselves. Will the jurors be able to exercise their common sense when presented with the ugly reality of the child's injuries?"

I fell back on my lounge. Her comment struck gold. "You're right, I've been overthinking this thing. It really does come down to their collective common sense. I can work with that." I looked at her. "You've just saved me a whole weekend of struggle."

She lifted her margarita in a toast. "To common sense." I laughed and we clinked glasses. "Now that your mind is free of stress, let's take these drinks upstairs for a little afternoon delight."

She didn't have to ask twice.

CHAPTER 42

August 20, Monday morning. Goldman embarked on her voir dire. Not surprisingly, she presented well. She was dressed in a beige pantsuit that flattered her body. She wore an understated gold necklace with matching earrings. Not ostentatious, just tasteful. Her voice was soothing and thoughtful, oozing credibility. She effortlessly worked to gain the goodwill of the jurors, despite the challenge of a child's grisly death. She questioned the jurors on their child-rearing experiences and was able to elicit comments about the thorny issue of discipline, especially for an inexperienced caregiver. She received commitments from the jurors that because discipline could sometimes seem harsh, they would consider all the surrounding circumstances in assessing the discipline used by the defendants.

She then moved onto what she referred to as Caesar's "limited abilities." She got the jurors to agree that they would be able to fairly assess the conduct of Caesar, bearing in mind his mental and psychological limitations, as well as the pressures exerted on him by his poverty and also by his wife. It was a thoughtful and effective voir dire.

Serge, who I think had to wonder how he had ended up getting this far in a case, was now up to his neck in what figured to be a difficult trial. To his credit, he wore what looked to be a new suit, was freshly barbered, and, for the most part, handled himself competently during his voir dire. On behalf of Cathy, he built on the ideas that Goldman had discussed, and then he broached the topic of aiding and abetting. He questioned the jurors whether they could carefully evaluate whether a person not accused of participating in an act could be found guilty for the conduct of another. His questioning, however, became muddled, forcing me to object. Slater appropriately stepped in and cleared up any misconceptions.

By the time Goldman and Serge finished, it was nearly noon. We broke for lunch. Detective Everly and I walked down to the courthouse cafeteria. As we looked for a table, I spotted Suzelle Frost sitting alone. We walked over and invited ourselves to join her.

From the moment we sat down, I sensed something between Suzelle and Everly. To say that they hit it off was an understatement. I'm not one to say the sparks seemed to fly between the two of them, but from my vantage point, there was some definite chemistry.

So as not to be too obvious, Suzelle turned to me. "I understand you're trying a murder case against Anna Goldman."

"We are. She's very good."

"I know, she was my training deputy. I watched her in several trials." She bit into her sandwich. "Detective," she said, smiling, "what's it like being the investigating officer with the famous Jake Clearwater? I've heard stories."

I cut her off. "That's enough of that. Detective, let me tell you about this remarkable woman sitting with us."

"Please do."

I swallowed a bite of my ham and cheese. "She was my law student at Pacifico, was on the school's trial competition team, worked on a death-penalty appeal with me, and when the Cal Supremes overturned our client's conviction and granted him a new trial, sat second chair during the trial."

"I'm impressed," said Everly. "Did you win?"

"Damn right we did," Suzelle said, with a flourish.

"And now you're a deputy public defender." He was impressed.

"Happily so." Suzelle took another bite from her grilled cheese. She looked at me. "I'd like to sit in on your trial with Anna, but that's probably not a good idea. So I'll just have to wait and hear about it later."

"Probably a safe call." I stood. "Time to get back to our courtroom. Suzelle, when this trial is over, lunch at a real restaurant, my treat."

"I'd like that," she said, and, looking at Everly, "Maybe Detective Everly could join us?"

"I'm sure that could be arranged."

"Mr. Clearwater, you may proceed," Slater said, with only the thinnest facade of cordiality.

"Judge," I acknowledged, holding up my end of that thin facade. I took my time positioning myself with the jury. "As you know by now, I'm the prosecutor. I represent the State of California in this important trial. I've listened to the criminal defense lawyers ask you any number of questions about how you might feel about this case from the limited information you've been supplied. From their questioning, you've learned that an eleven-year-old boy was killed. You've also learned that he was in the care of the defendants, his uncle and aunt. There were also some questions about discipline, when and how to use it. And about the business of aiding and abetting. Every one of you gave thoughtful answers."

I repositioned myself over to the left side of the jury box. "I'm not going to ask any of you more questions trying to gain some insight on how you might actually decide at the end of this trial." I held out my hands, demonstrating my sincerity. "I'm not going to go through the process of speculating how you might favor one side or the other. I'm not going to engage in guesswork on which of you I should exclude from the jury."

Full stop, letting my words sink in.

"That's right, I'm not going to challenge any of you." Pause. "You know why?" I got some surprised looks. "Because I know what the evidence is going to establish." I shrugged my shoulders. "Instead of excluding any of you, I only ask that you use your God-given common sense in deciding this case. Can you all do that?" Acknowledging the mildly surprised smiles and nods, I went on. "Thanks for that. I'm going to let the evidence you hear and see, together with your common sense, determine your verdict." Turning to Slater, "Your Honor, the state passes for cause." It was the shortest voir dire I've ever undertaken. I hoped to hell I didn't have any loose cannons among the twelve.

"Very well, Mr. Clearwater." Slater gave me a curt nod. "Ms. Goldman, having already passed for cause, do you have any peremptory challenges on behalf of Mr. Ramirez?"

Goldman stood and briefly glanced at me before challenging a day-care worker. Another juror was seated, Goldman and Serge questioned her, and I passed.

"Mr. Serge, any peremptory challenge?"

Serge seemed befuddled. "May I have a moment, Your Honor?"

"Of course."

We waited while Serge and Cathy held an animated whispered conversation. I suspect Cathy, not Serge, was dictating terms. Finally Serge stood. "On behalf of Mrs. Ramirez, we challenge Juror Number Six." The juror worked for a homeless shelter.

Same process, another juror was called and was questioned by Goldman and Serge. Again I passed.

Slater scrutinized at me. "Mr. Clearwater, it's your opportunity, a peremptory challenge?"

"No, the state continues to accept the panel as constituted." That elicited several smiles from the jurors.

After several more rounds, we had a jury. I had never before accepted a jury without a single challenge. But I was confident that once Oscar's injuries were detailed, common sense would carry the day.

The jurors were sworn, and Slater took the afternoon recess, with opening statements to follow.

CHAPTER 43

"His injuries were so severe, he couldn't digest his food," I began my opening statement from a seated position. I slowly stood. "Let me say that again. The injuries to this eleven-year-old boy were so severe, his body couldn't process his food." I paused and inclined my head courteously to Slater and defense counsel as I moved to the jurors. "This boy was in the exclusive, sole care of those two." I gestured to the defendants. "The husband beat him and the wife told him when and how hard." I expected an objection, especially from Serge, but he was sitting on his hands.

He had that technique perfected.

"Now before we get into the grisly specifics, I want to briefly discuss some of the critical law the twelve of you will apply to the evidence. Typically we don't discuss the law during opening statements, but there are two pieces of the law that are essential for you to understand as you listen to the evidence.

"First is the concept of aiding and abetting. You heard a little about that business during voir dire. Judge Slater is going to instruct that if a person helps, aids, promotes, or even encourages another to commit a crime, that person is just as guilty as the person who committed the act in the first place."

I zeroed in on Juror Number Two in the back row. During voir dire, she identified herself as a law partner in a large downtown firm. I figured her for the foreperson. I could usually predict who the foreperson might be. If any of the jurors got hung up on the concept of aiding and abetting, she would be able to clear up any questions during deliberations. Frankly, I was surprised Goldman had not challenged her. Maybe Goldman was thinking there might be a woman-to-woman connection. I trusted that common sense would prevail over gender solidarity.

"The other piece of law you folks should keep in mind while listening to the evidence is a duty of care. A person owes a duty of care for another when they're in a caretaker position. Think mother–child. The caretaker is duty-bound, obligated to watch out for the person in their care. Failing to come to the aid of the person in their care is criminal." I let that sit for a beat. "That's important in this case, since both the defendants agreed to parent Oscar.

"Enough on the law. Let's cut to the facts. It started seven months before Oscar's death. Oscar's mother, Murielle Castillo, who you will hear from, realized she was incapable of raising Oscar. She will tell you she was fighting drug addiction and knew she was not in a position to properly care for her boy. In hindsight, she made a tragic mistake."

"Objection," Goldman said. "Counsel is arguing his case."

Slater nodded as if her objection was tiresome. "Probably so. Mr. Clearwater, move on."

Without acknowledging the objection or Slater's comment, I went on. "Ms. Castillo sent Oscar to live with her brother Caesar and his wife Cathy. She hoped she was doing the right thing for her child. She will testify that she knew the defendants lived in a donated trailer in rural Oregon. She knew neither Caesar nor Cathy had a job and they were living on welfare. But she will tell you she still sent him north, thinking it was better than she could provide. She was desperate."

I shook my head and slid to my right, taking in two elderly men with stern faces and double chins. "Detective Everly and I have arranged for the counselor at the Oregon middle school Oscar sometimes attended to testify. She will tell you that Oscar missed school several days a week. That Oscar looked frail and listless. She will tell you she saw bruising on the back of his neck and on his arms. When she asked Oscar about the bruising, he wouldn't say anything. She will tell you that in hindsight, she should've reported her concerns. She regrets that she didn't.

"Seven months after Oscar had been sent to Oregon, the defendants decided to move to Rialto, out in east LA County. Oscar didn't attend school after the move to Rialto. That was curious, but I'll leave it to you to determine why." I was foreshadowing. They would come to understand that Oscar's injuries were too obvious and would come to light.

"Objection! He's inviting the jurors to speculate."

Damn right.

"Mr. Clearwater, stick to the facts you expect to elicit."

I nodded agreeably. "Meanwhile, Cathy had been able to secure subsidized housing in a duplex. The family was getting by on various welfare programs." I added as an aside, "Cathy was good at working the system."

"During their time in Rialto, several neighbors witnessed some of the goings-on at the Ramirez duplex. Two of those neighbors will testify about what they saw and heard during that time. No need for me to detail their testimony, you'll hear it directly from them." Again foreshadowing, saving the punch for the live testimony.

"Then you're going to hear from Sergeant Paul Manchin, who responded to the Ramirez residence this past Thanksgiving evening. He and his deputies found Oscar's body lying in a closet. Sgt. Manchin interviewed Caesar that evening. Caesar told him that Oscar had refused to eat any of the Thanksgiving dinner. As a result, Caesar punished Oscar by putting him in a closet. An hour or so later, Caesar said he went to check on him, but Oscar wouldn't apologize for not eating dinner. Caesar responded by kicking Oscar several times in the chest and telling him to remain in the closet." I stopped, in part because in thinking about that trapped and helpless eleven-year-old, I could feel emotion welling up in me. I could feel my eyes moistening.

Get a grip, Clearwater. You're the damn prosecutor.

I walked back to counsel table and took some water. I cleared my throat.

Moving back to the jurors, I went on. "Caesar, by his own words, went back to check on the boy an hour or so later. But when he did, Oscar was dead." I plowed on, working to get through this. "The coroner will testify that the kicks to the chest cracked some ribs, which punctured Oscar's lungs, causing bleeding which led to his death." I paused, letting that take hold. "The coroner will have much more to say. He will detail the multiple injuries suffered by Oscar. Injuries were so severe that this boy couldn't even digest his food. Multiple injuries to his face, his head, his ears, his chest, his arms, his back, his legs, his privates. If this child hadn't died from the kicks from his uncle, the coroner will testify he would have died from the multiple infections to his body as a result of the beatings."

I locked onto Juror Number Two, the law partner, who was staring at the defendants. Her lips were compressed in anger. "Meanwhile, Aunt Cathy," I said sarcastically, "didn't just sit by." I shook my head. "No, she not only didn't stop the beatings, she encouraged them." I studied my jury. "I'm confident that, after the twelve of you hear the testimony, your common sense will guide your deliberations to a just verdict."

The sparsely populated courtroom was dead silent. I nodded without speaking and slowly walked back to counsel table and sat down.

Slater looked at Goldman. "Counsel, ready to proceed?"

"Your Honor," she said, "I'd like to make my opening statement tomorrow morning."

Slater, checking the time and noting that it was only 3:50, thought over her request and relinquished. "Very well, Ms. Goldman."

Slater turned to Serge, "I too request to put my opening over until tomorrow."

Of course, Serge following Goldman's lead.

Slater, to the jurors, "Ladies and gentlemen, we'll recess and resume at nine in the morning. I'll again remind you to not discuss this case with anyone and to steer clear of any media reports concerning this case."

CHAPTER 44

That evening, Lisa met me on the deck with a cold beer. She had white wine. We watched the sun slip beneath the horizon. "How were things at the middle-school asylum today?" I asked, as I stripped off my tie, slipped off my shoes, and stretched out on a well-cushioned lounge.

"It was a vanilla day. No parents at the door, no teacher requests or complaints, no rowdy twelve-year-olds, and most importantly, no Laske," she said, smirking. "I could use more vanilla days."

"Are we now using ice cream flavors to describe our days?"

"No, that would diminish ice cream. I'm using vanilla without reference to ice cream."

"Got it. My day was peppermint chocolate chip." That got a laugh.

"Do go on."

"Your suggestion about building my voir dire around good ol' common sense was inspired. I didn't overdo it and pretty much sounded that theme."

"I'm glad I could help. Did you get to your opening statement today?"

"I did. I think it went well." We sat in silence. "But after my opening, something I didn't expect happened. Goldman, the woman defending the husband, had time to do her opening but elected to pass until tomorrow."

Lisa put up her hands in a so-what motion.

"I had laid out what I thought was a compelling opening, and it seemed she needed to respond right away. Otherwise, the jurors are left with my take on events to ruminate about overnight. It was strange for her to not offer up some defense."

"But you've said she is a capable trial lawyer. Why would she do that?"

"That's what I was thinking about, driving home. At first, I thought maybe I said something that caught her off guard. But I don't think so. She may be trying the rope-a-dope."

"The what?"

"Rope-a-dope." I grinned. "Toward the end of Muhammad Ali's career, when he was up against a younger, more-fit boxer, he would let himself get pushed onto the ropes and cover himself"—I pantomimed holding my arms up to protect my head and torso—"letting his opponent punch himself to exhaustion, and then settling the matter later on. It was mostly successful."

"Okay"—she was thinking it through—"so she is going to hope you punch yourself out and then pounce on you?"

"Yeah, something like that. Maybe she doesn't feel she can go toe-to-toe on the facts, so she watches and waits and hopes for any cracks in my case. Maybe a key witness goes missing or a witness I was counting on screws up her testimony. Anything she can exploit. As part of that strategy, she might reserve her opening statement until after I've put on my entire case."

"I didn't know an attorney could reserve their opening statement."

"It's not done often, but if the defense feels they are up against a strong prosecution case and they don't feel good about their own case, it's a tactic that's sometimes used."

"Rope-a-dope, huh," she said thoughtfully as she sipped her wine.

Tuesday morning, the bailiff called us to order, and Slater motioned to Goldman. In reply, Goldman said, "Your Honor, on behalf of Mr. Ramirez, I'm going to reserve my opening statement until after the prosecutor's case-in-chief."

Rope-a-dope.

Slater, not looking at all surprised, turned to Serge. "Mr. Serge?"

"Likewise, on behalf of Mrs. Ramirez. I will reserve."

Serge, clutching onto Goldman's skirt tails. Can a skirt have tails?

CHAPTER 45

"All right, Mr. Clearwater, are you prepared to call your first witness?"

"Call Murielle Castillo." Detective Everly went and retrieved her from the hallway. As is typical, witnesses had been excluded from the courtroom. Oscar's mother was thirty-five, but her war with drugs aged her into her fifties. She made some effort with her makeup, but it's hard to cover up decades of self-abuse. She wore a too-tight blouse with a too-tight skirt. Her clothes might have fit pre-babies, when she was eighteen.

As she walked in, Everly had a grip on her arm. She eyed the jurors nervously and nearly tripped over nothing. Everly helped her maintain her balance. Sometimes I forget how nerve-racking it must be for individuals outside the system to walk into a courtroom, having to testify. I'd seen it during the Webb trial with Melrose.

I don't think it occurred to Murielle to look at the defendants. She seemed more concerned with keeping her footing. Watching her approach the witness stand, I had to feel for her. I had instructed her that she could only discuss Oscar without mentioning Felipe. She didn't completely understand why, but she agreed once I explained that the trial could go sideways if she mentioned Felipe.

Following the oath, I began. "Ms. Castillo, before we get into the events that led to Oscar's death, tell us a little about yourself."

I started with a softball, hoping to acclimate her to the strange environment of the courtroom and give her a chance to somewhat settle her nerves.

"What do you mean?" Her voice came out squeaky, tight and anxious. She self-consciously cleared her throat.

"Just tell us a little about yourself."

She heaved a heavy sigh. It was as if I had instructed her to bench press an offensive lineman. "Okay, I'm thirty-five. I'm not married. I was married to Oscar's father before he left." She put up her hands as if to ask, Is that enough? And then added, "Oh, and I work at the Goodwill store in Ontario."

"I know you've had some hard times in your life. It's important that the jurors learn about that so they can better understand your actions." But my effort to steer her into her history of drug use went awry. She turned to the defendants. "That was the hardest time in my life. My brother, my only brother, who I stupidly trusted, killed my Oscar!" Like the snap of a cold slap, anxiety had given way to anger.

I took two steps toward her and, with my hands, motioned for her to calm down. "Let's back up. Tell us about your life before Oscar went to live with Caesar and Cathy."

"Oh, I misunderstood you." She looked off, embarrassed, and leaned back into the witness chair. "My life has been a mess. I was a drug abuser. Everything bad, including Oscar's death, is about me and drugs. If I wasn't a druggie, none of this would have happened." She slowed, forming another thought and in almost a whisper, "Caesar and that woman killed him, but I sent him to them. God help me."

After waiting a beat, in a low, soothing voice, I asked, "Tell us about Oscar. What was he like, growing up?"

Faint smile, glistening eyes. "He was busy. He played with

other kids. I think he was pretty good at sports, but I didn't pay enough attention to really know." Tears formed and ran. Thinking about missed opportunities. She sucked in some air. "He was a good boy. He managed to get by without much help from me. I was a terrible mother."

"Objection," said Goldman. "May we approach?"

Slater motioned us up. "Your concern, Ms. Goldman?"

"This is offered for no reason other than to work up even more sympathy for the victim. It's playing to the passions of the jurors. It has no relevance."

Slater, instead of looking for me to respond, replied, "I think you're overreacting, Anna."

Anna, first name.

"I'm going to overrule the objection." Then to me, "Mr. Clearwater, don't park here." Slater being tolerant.

We retreated and I asked, "Was Oscar a disciplinary problem?"

"No. Like I said, he had to manage his own life because of me. But he was just on the edge of being a teenager, and I was afraid for him. Growing up in our neighborhood with no real supervision. That's why I called Caesar, hoping he could help raise Oscar."

"What was Caesar like before you sent Oscar to him?"

She cast a hard look at her brother before answering. "I don't know what happened to him, he was always a nice person, even when we were kids. I never saw him do nothing mean to nobody."

She shook her head bitterly and then flashed, "But then for no reason, he killed my boy." She continued to glare at Caesar and then, completely out of nowhere, screamed, "You sonofabitch, you murdered my baby!" She dropped her face into her hands and began sobbing. She managed to fumble around in her purse for some tissues and worked to collect herself. It was a hard moment.

"Murielle, are you okay to go on?"

She held up a hand. "I'm sorry. Give me a …." She just waved her hand.

"Take all the time you need. Let me know when you're okay to continue."

She blew her nose and dabbed at the mascara running from her eyes. She pulled herself erect and looked at me.

"Murielle, you've told us that you were in a difficult part of your life when you made the decision to send Oscar to live with Caesar and Cathy. Why then?"

Working to maintain her composure, she replied, "The drugs had taken over my life. I was afraid I might lose my apartment. My life was falling apart. I had no choice." Her voice was quivering. "I thought maybe after a couple of months, I could get myself together and bring back my boys."

My boys! Dammit! Here was the slip I was concerned about.

Goldman hadn't missed it. "Your Honor, we need to approach?" Goldman and Serge were up.

It was a long walk to the bench as Slater glared at me. In a whispered snarl, "Was my order excluding mention of the second boy unclear?"

"It was very clear." I shrugged. "And I so advised the witness. But given the emotional nature of her testimony, I have been concerned since you made your ruling that this might happen."

"Counsel, you and your witness screwed up." Slater was furious. The idea of a possible mistrial and burning even more trial days had him choking mad. Goldman started to speak, but Slater held up his hand to cut her off and looked up at the jurors. "Ladies and gentlemen, we're going to take a recess. You will retire to the jury room." After they had filed out, "My chambers," ordered Slater.

We settled in, no offers of espresso this time around. It was time for me to get worked over. Instead, Slater surprised me and focused on Goldman. "Anna, your thoughts?"

"I'm at a loss," she said. "I don't know how we fix this. But I hate the thought of a mistrial." She drummed her hands on her knees, a very unlikely nervous tic for this elegant woman. "I'm afraid an admonition from the bench will be insufficient." Admonitions to disregard were worthless and yet are often used to paper over errors.

"Mr. Serge, your thoughts?"

He nodded and said, "I'm thinking back to exactly what the witness said. 'Bring back my boys.' It was said at the end of her answer, and maybe it was not clear to the jurors what she meant."

His comment seemed counter to the defense position. But then Serge seemed counter to the defense position.

Slater grunted. "Maybe you're right. Maybe the four of us are hypersensitized to the concern." He looked at Goldman. "Anna, could that be? That they may not have understood the plural?"

I kept my mouth shut. My standing as to how to cope was tenuous to nonexistent.

Slater eyed Goldman, looking for a response. "Anna?"

"I don't know," she said cautiously. "But I do know if you instruct the jurors to disregard the statement, they won't. It will only magnify the problem."

The voice of experience.

"They're presumed to heed the instructions from the court," Slater offered, without conviction.

Goldman couldn't suppress a skeptical frown. "If you'll indulge me a quick antidote. Following one of my trials last year, which I lost, the defendant didn't testify. The judge carefully instructed the jurors not to hold the defendant accountable for asserting his Fifth Amendment right. When the clerk and I went back into the jury room to retrieve some documents after the trial, the white board still had the notes from the jury, and under reasons to convict, 'Def didn't testify.'" She cocked her head. "So much for directions from the court."

"I understand," said Slater. "But nonetheless…"

"After that, I moved for a mistrial, which wasn't granted, but I'm appealing." She looked at me. "Likewise, I'm forced to move for a mistrial here."

That was anathema to Slater, the ever-vigilant champion of moving cases in and out of his courtroom expeditiously. "Mr. Serge, I assume a similar motion on behalf of your client?"

"That's correct."

Slater then zeroed in on me. "Mr. Clearwater, we've got a serious problem. Any suggestions?"

I was surprised to be included. "I don't think the witness's lone afterthought of a statement tanks the entire trial." Even as I spoke, my brain was on overload. I stood and moved to the window.

Ignoring Slater, I turned to Goldman. "I've got a bold proposition. I'll dismiss the torture allegation, so instead of looking at the possibility of twenty years, I recommend the minimum sentence allowable, ten years. With good time, they're out in seven." Two thoughts were warring in my head. I wanted to avoid a mistrial, but more importantly, even if I convicted them, Slater might well impose the minimum ten years. That sucked the air out of the room.

By not accepting my offer, Goldman and Serge were risking significantly more time for their clients and when the graphic testimony from the coroner came in, that additional time was more than a possibility. On the basis of the case I laid out in my opening and the fact that neither defense counsel offered an opening statement, they had to know conviction was a distinct possibility. The Ramirezes just might be amenable to the offer.

Slater hungrily arched his eyebrows and, without a word,

looked at Goldman, his hard-fought effort to get a settlement suddenly back in focus.

Goldman ignored Slater and gave me an appraising eye. "I still say this is an invol man case."

"But," said Slater, pouncing on my offer, "that's not on the table. In light of what I've heard so far, the prosecution case looks pretty strong." This from the same judge who had earlier nearly wrenched my arm from its socket to settle for manslaughter. "At any rate, you and Mr. Serge are duty-bound to communicate the offer to your clients. I'll extend the recess while you do so."

Twenty-five minutes later, we were summoned back to chambers.

"Any success?" Slater to both defense counsel.

"My client may want the deal," Goldman reported. "But I'm going to need more time with him before committing."

Slater was almost giddy. "How about you, Mr. Serge?"

"Cathy is adamant. Doesn't feel as if she did anything wrong and wants to stay and fight."

I don't know who was more disappointed, Slater or Serge. For Slater, it meant the trial went on chewing up the same number of days as if both defendants were still going forward. For Serge, the prospects of going it alone without having Goldman to lead the way had to be paralyzing.

Worthless sonofabitch.

But Serge had an ace up his sleeve and he played it. "Judge, I should warn you that my client and I are at bitter odds. If we do go forward, I don't think I'll be able to continue representing her."

Worthless scheming sonofabitch.

"That's not on the table at this point," said Slater. "In light of developments, I will dismiss the jury for the rest of the day. Mr. Serge, I want to give you and your client additional time to consider the offer." Apparently, Slater had disregarded Serge's representation that he and Cathy were at odds.

I explained to Murielle Castillo that her gaffe had created problems and that the trial was put over. She wasn't pleased. But she reluctantly promised to return in the morning.

Still thinking through my offer, I left for home and stopped and bought cooking ingredients for the dinner I was going to prepare for Lisa. I needed a distraction. Orange chicken. Most of the ingredients were already in the house. I still needed two chicken breasts and garlic gloves. Using the recipe from *Joy of Cooking*, I had it ready by the time she got home. When she walked in, I scooped her up and carried her to the deck, where chilled wine was waiting. I slipped off her unsensible shoes and massaged her feet. Then we settled in and ate my brilliant concoction at the cocktail table on the deck. It was good, at least that's what she said. I filled her in on the eventful day of trial.

She had questions. "If the husband pleads but the wife doesn't, will you have to start the trial over?"

"No, at this point the only evidence I've put on is applicable to both. I'm pretty sure that's the way the judge will see it. The only possible glitch is the mother's comment referring to 'boys.' But I hope the judge is going to ignore that and plow ahead."

"How much actual time will the husband receive?" she asked skeptically. "He did kill two kids."

"If he goes to trial and is convicted, he could potentially receive twenty years, out in fifteen. He could save himself significant years with a plea. Even though I don't think the judge would slam him for the max, I'm offering him an out.

"So why are you letting him somewhat off the hook?"

"A couple of reasons. Oregon will most likely prosecute him for Felipe's death and he'll get additional time on that. And second, I don't trust Slater to impose more than ten years, even if I get a conviction. I'm dealing from a position of strength here."

"I see," she said thoughtfully. "But you don't think the wife will plead?"

"Probably not, at least that's what her pretty-much-worthless lawyer is indicating. Of course, her case, from my standpoint, is more problematic since she isn't the actual killer. But I think I can get her."

Lisa shook her head. "Your day was a lot more eventful than mine."

"Another vanilla day?"

"Pretty much, and that's a blessing."

"Before we move off topic, Serge, the lawyer representing the wife, is angling to get thrown off the case. He started to set the stage to bow out as Cathy's lawyer."

"But the trial is already underway. How can he do that?"

"I think he's going to claim irreconcilable differences with his client and basically beg the judge to let him off."

"Well," she asked, "would that mean you would have to start over?"

"That's up to the judge. But I'm betting not. We're three days in, and I'm sure the judge won't want to lose those days."

CHAPTER 46

Judge Slater's chambers, Wednesday morning. He made espresso for him and me. Goldman and Serge passed. Was I suddenly in good graces? I had, indeed, offered a deal.

"Anna, you first." He sat and sipped.

"Caesar wants the deal, as long as the sentence is ten, out in seven."

"I can do that," said a clearly pleased Slater. He turned to Serge. "And?"

"No dice. She's adamant. Beyond that, she wants to fire me for even suggesting she take the deal."

"You discussed the offer?"

"I did."

"Any chance that further discussion could prove fruitful?"

"Not a chance."

"Dammit, I was hopeful we could resolve this thing." I think he had finally resigned himself that the trial would go forth. "Okay, outside the presence of the jurors, I'll take the plea from Caesar and set a sentencing date. And then we try the wife separately."

Serge asked, "What will you tell the jurors about Caesar being out of the picture?" Curiously he didn't ask about Murielle's reference to boys.

On and on with his brilliant lawyering.

"I'll instruct them that going forward, each defendant will be treated separately. They won't know that he pled out."

"I understand," said Serge. "But before you bring the jurors back in, I'm requesting a hearing concerning my continued representation of Cathy Ramirez."

Slater was irritated and didn't try to hide it. But he had no choice; if there was a legitimate reason for terminating Serge's representation, he was obligated to hear it. Even though he most probably harbored the sense that Serge was being disingenuous and working every angle to get out. "Okay, I'll hear your motion at two o'clock this afternoon. I hope you're not wasting my time, Mr. Serge."

That afternoon, in a courtroom devoid of jurors and spectators, Slater looked expectantly at Serge. "Mrs. Ramirez and I have reached an impasse such that she no longer wants me to represent her."

Slater: "What seems to be the problem?"

"She feels I am not adequately representing her. She feels I'm just going along with whatever Ms. Goldman says."

Cathy was aware enough to recognize that reality. Frankly, if I'd been her, I'd also want a different lawyer.

Slater to Cathy: "Mrs. Ramirez, that is an insufficient ground to replace your court-appointed lawyer."

Cathy was having none of it. In a surprisingly high-pitched voice for such a large woman, she didn't back off. "This guy is doing nothing. I think he's afraid of going on without Goldman to tell him what to do. I want a different lawyer."

"You've got the only lawyer you're going to get. It's Mr. Serge or no one."

In a defiant voice, she replied, "Then I'll take no one. I understand from my so-called lawyer that I have a right to do that."

Slater looked at her as if that was perhaps the stupidest thing anyone could possibly do. "You do have that right. But that would be a terrible mistake, especially in a serious case such as this."

She gave an ironic chortle. "I can't do any worse than him. Bring it on."

Whoa, maybe this is a glimpse of the Cathy who had ruled the Ramirez roost.

Forty years ago, the Supreme Court in *Faretta v. California* held that a defendant has a constitutional right to self-representation as long as the defendant fully understands the consequences of going it alone.

"Very well," Slater said with a resigned air. "The prosecutor will take your waiver in a moment." He then ordered Serge and me to approach. Slater covered the microphone and, leaning into Serge, said, "Counsel, I'm going to appoint you advisory counsel for the rest of this trial, but when this trial is over, I never want to see you in my courtroom again. You're a disgrace." A well-earned shotgun blast to Serge's torso.

When a defendant exercises their right to self-representation, the trial judge has discretion to appoint a lawyer to act merely as an advisor to the accused. There are strict rules for advisory counsel. They don't sit at counsel table and they're forbidden to offer any assistance to the accused unless the accused specifically seeks their help. Slater was punishing Serge by making him stick around for the duration.

It is standard procedure for the prosecutor to administer the *Faretta* waiver of representation, since the burden to make certain the waiver was effective is on the prosecution. Under *Faretta*, once a defendant opts to self-represent, they can't later claim ineffective assistance of counsel as a basis for appeal.

A touch of common sense.

I carefully took Cathy's waiver. Dotting I's and crossing T's.

Prosecuting a *pro per* defendant carried with it some advantages, along with some concerns. Advantage: no lawyer on the other side objecting during my direct examination, no lawyer executing a thoughtful cross-examination of my witnesses. Disadvantage: the risk of creating an appellate issue if I, as the prosecutor, run roughshod over the defendant and give the appellate court a cognizable prosecutorial-misconduct issue. Disadvantage: jurors might feel it was no longer an even battle, and side with the underdog.

Although in this case I wasn't too concerned about the jurors feeling sympathy for Cathy.

When I finished taking the waiver, Slater denied the motion for mistrial based on Murielle's misstatement concerning "boys" and ordered Murielle back to the witness stand to resume her direct examination. It was strange not having defense lawyers in the courtroom; there was only Cathy Ramirez. And, of course, Serge. But he was essentially gagged. Cathy was wearing the same muumuu-type dress. She had a legal pad and two Pendaflex folders on the table. When the bailiff had called court to order and everyone stood, I noticed it was difficult for her to stand. Slater must have seen what I saw, and he told her she need not stand when addressing the court.

Slater welcomed the jurors as they were ushered in. He informed them that Mrs. Ramirez's case would be tried alone and that she was acting as her own lawyer. There were equal parts surprise and skepticism from the jurors. They had to realize there had been significant developments outside their presence.

Murielle Castillo was called back to the stand. Slater reminded her that she was still under oath and nodded at me to resume my direct.

"Ms. Castillo, I think we left off with you telling us that you felt you had no choice but to entrust Oscar to Caesar and Cathy. After you sent him to Oregon, I assume you spoke with Oscar from time to time."

"I tried to call each week."

"Did you always speak directly to him?"

"Sometimes. Mostly it was to Cathy, and she would put me off."

"What do you mean?"

"Oh, she would say that he's outside or he's doing some chores. It was frustrating. I would ask her how he was doing. She would always tell me he was fine. Going to school and such."

"During the times when you actually spoke to him, did he indicate everything was okay?"

"Yeah, but I think Cathy must have been right there listening. I couldn't tell if he was talking straight."

I nodded my understanding. "Did you travel up to Oregon to visit?"

"No, I wasn't able to. I was under house arrest."

"After they moved back to Southern California, did you see Oscar then?"

"I wanted to."

"What prevented you?"

Murielle hung her head. "About that time, I was sentenced for violating my probation and spent time in jail."

"What were you arrested for?"

"Selling drugs." Then adding, as if to explain, "It was the only way I could get the drugs I was using."

"So at no time while Caesar, Cathy, and Oscar were back in Southern California, did you see Oscar?"

"No, it just didn't work out."

"Were you aware that Oscar was in poor health at any time while he was in the care of the defendants?"

"No, I trusted them. I had no idea." She broke down again. Quietly sobbing.

I offered her a box of tissues I thought to bring. She wiped at her face and took a deep breath.

"Murielle, I know this has been difficult." Turning to Slater, I said, "I have no further questions of Ms. Castillo, Your Honor."

Slater motioned to Cathy. "Mrs. Ramirez, do you wish to examine the witness?"

Cathy nodded and, from her chair, asked, "Murielle, you couldn't care for Oscar, could you?"

"No," Murielle responded, with venom in her voice, "but at least I wouldn't have tortured and killed him."

Ouch, that's not what Cathy was hoping for.

Undeterred, Cathy was back at her. "You're a junkie and a whore, aren't you?"

"Objection, Your Honor." The quick, acrimonious exchange had gone far enough.

Slater looked disapprovingly at Cathy. "Do you have any other points you would like to make, Mrs. Ramirez?"

Slater displaying restraint.

"No, the folks sittin' over there"—Cathy motioned to the jury box—"know what to think of her."

"I assume there will be no redirect, Mr. Clearwater."

I put my hands up in a that's-enough gesture.

I had planned to next call the middle-school counselor from Oregon, but even though we had sent her a subpoena and plane ticket, she was a no-show. Investigator Everly had tried running her down, without success. I later learned she had been terminated for not reporting the possible abuse she noticed on Oscar and Felipe.

No surprise there.

It was late afternoon of an eventful day. Slater adjourned.

CHAPTER 47

Thursday morning, we got underway a bit late. There was an issue with Cathy, as she was being transported to the courthouse. From what the bailiff told me, Cathy was attacked by two in-custody women on the transport bus. Apparently the word had gotten out that Cathy was charged with murdering a child. Child murderers and pedophiles were at the extreme bottom of the jailhouse hierarchy. Robbers at the top. Maybe in some crude way, that made sense?

When she was finally brought into court, she was wearing jailhouse orange overalls to replace her muumuu, which apparently had suffered during the scuffle. Given Cathy's girth and stature, the legs of her county-issued overalls had to be rolled up to her knees. Despite the indignity of her attire, she didn't look any the worse for wear but for a red splotch on her cheek. Wouldn't surprise me if she got the best of the scuffle.

Once Cathy was settled in, Slater called in the jurors. He didn't inform them why she was dressed the way she was.

Nothing worthy of explanation? Go figure.

He invited me to call my next witness.

I called Marj Butler and we got underway. Butler was in her low eighties and carried herself well. Detective Everly escorted her in. She did not appear to be in the least intimidated by the trappings of the courtroom. She looked like one of those aged wonders who walked at least ten thousand steps a day. During our pretrial preparation, it was clear that she was as sharp as a barber's razor.

"Mrs. Butler, tell us a little about yourself, so that the jurors have some context to help evaluate your testimony."

"I'm a retired surgical nurse. I'm a longtime widow with two adult children." Her voice was robust.

"Mrs. Butler, you are here to provide testimony about what you witnessed in regard to the death of Oscar Ramirez. So let's start with where you lived in reference to the duplex the Ramirezes lived during the weeks and months leading up to Thanksgiving.

"Sure." She looked intently at the jurors. Eager to say what she had to say. "I lived directly across the street from them."

"How far would you estimate your house was from theirs?"

"I'm not really good with distances." She hesitated, then said, "But I would say it was about three first downs between my place and their place."

Three first downs worked. Watching football has its rewards.

I smiled, as did some of the jurors. "A first down is ten yards, so your place was about thirty yards from theirs?"

She gave a shrug. "To the best of my knowledge."

"In the months before last Thanksgiving, did you ever speak or interact with anyone who lived in the Ramirez residence?"

"No, and that's on me. Maybe I should've." She looked over at Cathy and shook her head disdainfully. "Maybe I should've called the police. Something."

"What did you witness that made you want to call the police?"

"I saw her," indicating Cathy with an accusatory nod "screaming and cursing at the top of her lungs at the man, who I thought was her husband, and the kid."

I walked over to my table and Everly handed me photographs of Caesar and Oscar. "Leave to approach, Your Honor?"

"Go ahead."

I handed her the photographs. "Are these the individuals you are referring to?"

"Yes sir."

"The record will reflect that she identified the photographs of Caesar and Oscar Ramirez. What was she screaming about?"

Shaking her head, she replied, "I don't remember, but I can tell you she was hopping mad and they wanted no part of it."

"What do you mean?"

"From the way they held themselves and didn't respond. They both looked intimidated."

"Where were they when she was yelling at them?"

"Right in front of their place."

"Did you witness the boy, Oscar, on any other occasions?"

"Yeah, one time in particular, I saw him sitting on the curb in front of my house, crying. He was holding himself and slowly rocking like he was ill or nauseous." She dropped her head, and in a low, despondent voice, continued, "I'll be damned if I didn't do anything to help. I was a nurse for thirty-two years. I should have done something. That boy was suffering."

I could feel the hostile vibe emanating from the jurors. And it was not solely directed at Cathy. This nurse, this person who had worked to save lives and provide comfort, had done nothing.

What is it that causes so many of us to not get involved? Are we not our fellow travelers?

I waited a beat, letting the hostility play out. "Judge, I've got no more questions for Mrs. Butler."

Slater looked at Cathy. "Mrs. Ramirez?"

From her seated position, Cathy leaned forward and, in that

unlikely squeaky voice, asked, "You never saw me hit anyone, did you?"

Butler shook her head before saying, "No, I didn't."

"You never heard me tell anyone, including my husband, to hit anyone, did you?"

Butler hunched her shoulders defiantly. "No, I just saw you screaming bloody murder at both of them."

Cathy put up her hands as if she had Perry Masoned Butler. "I'm finished."

"I assume no redirect, Mr. Clearwater?"

I put up my hands. "No."

"Your next witness." Slater was hustling us through this.

An afternoon golf date?

"Elsa Donohue."

Everly escorted her in. She could have been Butler's twin. Roughly the same age. She was smartly dressed in a pantsuit. She had beautifully coiffed silver hair. She, like Butler, carried herself in a confident manner. She also didn't appear to have any anxieties about testifying.

"Mrs. Donohue, were you living across from the Ramirezes in the weeks and months prior to last Thanksgiving?"

"I was, and like I told you yesterday during our meeting, I saw the boy being kicked by the man of the house."

"Mrs. Donohue, before we go there, let's step back. Are you employed outside the house?"

"Thirty-five years teaching second and third graders. Retired sixteen years ago. I live next door to Marj Butler."

I showed her the photographs. "You recognize them?"

"Of course I do. That's the man and that's the boy who were living in that house."

"Tell us what you witnessed."

Looking disdainfully at Cathy, she replied, "She was constantly screaming and threatening the man and the boy."

"How so?"

"I don't know but it was unsettling."

"Did you see any other interaction between the man and the boy?"

Nodding yes while still looking at Cathy, she said, "On two occasions, I saw the man, I assume he was the father, kick the boy. It wasn't some little nudge. He reared back and really kicked him." She paused, her confidence seeming to deflate. "I'm ashamed that I did nothing. I was a school teacher my whole life. We're trained to look for abuse and report it, and here I was, directly observing terrible abuse, and I did nothing." Her voice cracking with regret.

I allowed the moment to play out before continuing.

"Mrs. Donohue, on either occasion when you saw Mr. Ramirez kicking Oscar, did you observe Cathy Ramirez?"

"Both times, she was standing in the doorway of their house. She saw what he was doing."

"Could you observe her reaction?"

She took a steadying breath. "She just watched and did nothing." Another breath. "Not a day goes by that I don't berate myself for my cowardice. If I had done something, called the police or confronted that man, that poor boy might still be alive."

"By coming in today, you have done something," I offered, by way of consolation that, frankly, she didn't deserve. "Thank you for your testimony."

Slater looked at Cathy.

Cathy nodded and asked, "You never saw me strike Oscar, did you?"

"No, I didn't."

"You never heard me tell my husband to strike Oscar, did you?"

"No."

Slater could see I had no need to redirect. He thanked and excused Mrs. Donohue.

Following the morning recess, I called Sheriff's Sergeant Paul Manchan. With a determined military demeanor and close-cropped hair, he was not in uniform but in an off-the-rack suit that fitted his stocky but solid frame well. From my pretrial prep of him, I knew that he was a Marine veteran and had ten years in the sheriff's department.

"Sergeant Manchan, fill us in on your background."

"Yes sir. I enlisted in the Marine Corps out of high school. Did two tours in the Middle East before joining the sheriff's department. I've been with the department for ten years. I was promoted to sergeant two years ago."

"Thank you, Sergeant. I want to zero in on the evening of last year's Thanksgiving. You were on duty that evening?"

"Yes sir, I was." His continued deference to authority was a testament to his Marine background.

"You received a call from dispatch to respond to"—I checked my notes—"13208 Coldbrook in Rialto at 10:55 p.m., correct?"

"Yes sir."

"Who did you contact at that location?"

"Deputy Ahearn, the first officer on the scene, who informed me that a deceased child was in the bedroom of the residence and that a Caesar Ramirez was in custody."

"Did you ascertain from Deputy Ahearn why Ramirez was in custody?"

"Yes, Ahearn reported that immediately upon his arrival,

Ramirez was standing in front of his residence and blurted out that he had killed his nephew."

"Describe your actions at that time."

"I confirmed there was a body and that a coroner had been dispatched to the scene. I then took Mr. Ramirez into the kitchen of his residence and read him his *Miranda* rights."

"And?" I urged.

"He waived his rights and agreed to speak to me."

"What did you observe of Mr. Ramirez during the interview?"

"He was pretty shaken up and in tears throughout the interview."

"Did you record the interview?"

"I did, pursuant to department policy."

"Your Honor, leave to play the audio of the interview?"

"You may."

"Your Honor, in addition to the audio I have prepared a transcript of the interview. May I distribute to the jurors?"

"Go ahead."

Everly activated the recorder.

Manchan: Please confirm for me, Mr. Ramirez, that you received your *Miranda* warning and have agreed to talk with me.

Ramirez: Yes.

Manchan: Go ahead, sir.

Ramirez: We were having Thanksgiving dinner with my wife's brother and his wife. But Oscar refused to eat, even when my wife told him to. She was embarrassed and felt disrespected.

Manchan: So what happened?

Ramirez: Cathy warned him, but he still wouldn't eat. I grabbed him and shoved him into a bedroom closet. I told him to stay there.

Manchan: Then what happened?

Ramirez: After they left, I checked on him. He was still in the closet, standing and fiddling with the door. So I knocked him down and kicked him.

Manchan: Kicked him?

Ramirez: I had no choice. He had embarrassed Cathy in front of her brother. He had disrespected her again.

Manchan: Again?

Ramirez: He needed discipline.

Manchan: I see. After you kicked him, what did you do?

Ramirez: I told him to stay in the closet until he apologized.

Manchan: When did you next check on him?

Ramirez: Maybe an hour or so. When I did, he was dead.

Manchan: How did you know he was dead?

Ramirez: I knew.

Manchan: What did you do then?

Ramirez: I told Cathy and she freaked out. I didn't know what to do. I waited, then finally called the police.

Manchan: What about your wife?

Ramirez: She took the car and left.

Manchan: Anything else you want to tell me about Oscar's death?

Ramirez: Just that it was an accident. I was just trying to be a good father figure. I can't talk anymore now. Please believe me, it was an accident.

"Sergeant, is that an accurate account of the entire interview?"

"It is."

"Why didn't you follow up with Mr. Ramirez concerning the other times he administered his discipline on Oscar?"

"Pursuant to my training, once a suspect indicates they don't want to proceed any further, the interview must be terminated."

This guy was by-the-book. "Were you able to contact Cathy Ramirez?"

"The following day, she voluntarily came into the sheriff's office in Pomona and was taken into custody."

"Did you attempt to interview her?"

"Yes sir. She refused."

"Sergeant, did that conclude your involvement with this case?"

"Yes sir. From that point, the investigation was followed up by Detective Everly."

"Sergeant Manchan, thank you for your testimony." To Slater, "No further questions, Your Honor."

"Would you care to examine the witness, Mrs. Ramirez?"

Cathy stared at Manchan and shook her head no.

Slater recessed a bit early for lunch.

Initially, I had hoped to follow up Sgt. Manchan's testimony with James and Paula Armstrong, Cathy's brother and sister-in-law. But not surprisingly, they had refused Detective Everly's efforts to get them to cooperate. James told Everly that during the Thanksgiving dinner, Oscar looked fine, and he was sent from the table because he was being dramatic about not eating and deserved to be disciplined. Paula wouldn't even speak to Everly. I couldn't see any sense in subpoenaing them.

CHAPTER 48

My plan all along had been to finish my case with Dr. Anthony Reeve, a deputy coroner and forensic pathologist who autopsied Oscar. Reeve had agreed to come to my office at one o'clock to discuss any last-minute logistics. Everly escorted him in. Reeve looked like he belonged in the Neiman Marcus catalog. His custom-made worsted suit and his dark-blue silk tie with matching pocket square spoke of money and meticulousness. He had slight touches of premature gray at the edges of his full head of wavy dark hair. I didn't know what kind of car he drove, but if I had to guess, it was a Porsche Carrera. He was first cabin, through and through.

When Reeve walked into my bare-bones office, he must have groaned. I motioned him to one of my back-breaker chairs. Maybe I should have relinquished mine. We exchanged handshakes. Everly hadn't taken a seat. "Jake, I'm heading down to the cafeteria. Can I bring either of you back something?"

"I'm good." Turning to Reeve, "Doctor, anything?"

He gave a dismissive wave.

Cafeteria food? How plebeian.

"Enjoy lunch as best as possible in the cafeteria." I grinned.

"I'm planning on meeting Suzelle there."

Good for Everly, good for Suzelle.

Reeve and I discussed how his testimony would proceed. As the examination moved onto each area of Oscar's body, he would use the PowerPoint photographs he had prepared of each area of injury.

I couldn't help wondering why this guy was a coroner. His whole demeanor spoke of private hospitals and celebrity patients, not the coroner's basement at USC General.

Everly returned a few minutes before two o'clock and the three of us walked to the courtroom doors, where I left them until I called for Reeve.

I noticed Cathy had been supplied a new muumuu, unfortunately just as unattractive as the others.

Slater's bailiff called us to order. Slater looked at me.

"The state calls Dr. Anthony Reeve."

Reeve, not surprisingly, walked in as if he owned the place. Just on the edge of arrogance.

He was sworn in. "Dr. Reeve, why have you been called to testify?"

In a Vin Scully voice, he replied, "I'm a deputy coroner and forensic pathologist who performed the autopsy of Oscar Ramirez. I've been called to describe his injuries and the cause of his death."

"Doctor, before we get to the results of your autopsy, let's discuss what qualifies you to perform autopsies and offer your findings. Let's start with your educational background."

Out of my peripheral vision, I noticed Cathy had raised her hand to get the attention of the judge. Slater put up a hand for me to stop, and inquired, "Mrs. Ramirez?"

"Can I talk to you?" she asked while seated.

Slater asked, "Do you want to talk to me in the presence of the jury?"

"That's fine."

"Go ahead."

"Do we have to hear all about this doctor? I'm sure he's qualified."

Slater shrugged and looked at me. "Mr. Clearwater, seems as if Mrs. Ramirez is offering to stipulate to Dr. Reeve's expertise and experience."

"That's acceptable to me." His background was pro forma anyway, especially since his findings would not be disputed. There was no defense expert.

Cathy again: "Do we have to hear in detail about Oscar's injuries? After all, they weren't my doing."

I didn't wait for Slater's invitation to speak but kept my eyes on him and not on Cathy. Courtroom etiquette being what it was, always triangulate through the judge; never directly address the other side. "It's critical that the jurors learn about the type and extent of injuries suffered by the child."

"Mrs. Ramirez"—Slater at his most solicitous—"I'm afraid it is essential for the prosecutor to question the coroner about the injuries."

Cathy surprisingly wasn't through. "But any detailed talk would be unfair to me since I didn't hurt him." That's the second time she made the point that she didn't inflict the injuries. I didn't think that was accidental.

Was she sharper than I thought?

"Mrs. Ramirez," explained Slater, "the state's case is twofold. That you aided and abetted your husband in the murder of your nephew, and that you violated a duty of care to him. The prosecutor has every right to go into the specifics of the child's injuries."

She huffed her meaty round shoulders in defeat.

"You may resume, Mr. Clearwater."

Here's where I had to be careful. Despite how Cathy might be perceived by the jurors, it couldn't look like she was being unfairly treated. I didn't want any underdog sympathy seeping in through the back door.

"Doctor, Mrs. Ramirez, as you just heard, graciously agreed to accept your expertise. So let's move on to the autopsy itself. Have you done autopsies involving child abuse previously?"

"Yes."

"How often?"

"Counsel, too many to give an accurate number. Unfortunately it's quite common."

I acknowledged his answer with a slight nod. "When did you perform the autopsy on Oscar Ramirez?"

"November 28, 2018. Two days after death."

"During that autopsy, were photographs taken, documenting your examination?"

"Yes, standard procedure."

"Where did you start in your examination of Oscar's body?"

"We start at the top of the head and work our way down." Turning to Slater, "May I step to the PowerPoint?

"Of course," said Slater.

Reeve stepped to the screen and clicked onto a PowerPoint image labeled Exhibit 1.

"What are we looking at?" I asked.

Reeve produced a laser pointer, which he utilized to pinpoint his focus. "A multitude of injuries were present to his face. We see, first off, a large abrasion present on his left cheek and a number of injuries present to his forehead that are actually relatively recent, within twenty-four hours of death. He's got an abrasion over his left eyebrow, one at the hairline. He's also got some on his right cheekbone region."

"Doctor, how can you tell older injuries from more fresh or acute injuries?"

"When you scrape yourself, it goes through a healing process. For fresh injuries, there's usually blood present within the injury itself. It hasn't started to scab over. That's what we use as criteria to make those determinations."

He clicked to Exhibit 2.

"What are we looking at here, Doctor?"

"We see the left-hand side of the lip, depicting a split in the center and a similar injury on the upper lip on either side. There's also an abrasion to his left cheekbone and a fresher injury right above his eyebrow."

He clicked to Exhibit 3 and went on without any prodding from me. "This gives a better appreciation as to the multitude of injuries to his face. Most of the injuries show scabbing and scarring. As you can imagine on your own body how long it takes to form a scar, that's what we're dealing with here."

Reeve took a breath and, using the laser pointer, went on. "We see a patterned injury present to his face. It's a U-shaped injury. It's very classic to see this type of injury as a result of a cord, usually an electric cord. We have injuries to his ear, again older abrasions with scabs." Several jurors looked off. It was hard to watch.

Another click displayed Exhibit 4. "We are seeing here the multitude of injuries immediately beneath the chin. Most of them show scar formation, approximately twenty of them, most healing or scarring."

"Doctor, how long does it take to form a scar?"

"Usually greater than a month."

Illuminating Exhibit 5, Reeve went on. "We've got abrasions to the ear itself, consistent with a cord. Behind the ear are acute abrasions as well."

He clicked to Exhibit 6. "Moving down from the head area. These are abraded contusions present to the left side of the chest.

We also see curvilinear scars consistent with a cord. We have approximately twenty different injuries to the front part of the chest. Some of them fresh, and some well-healed and scarred over."

Clicking to Exhibit 7, "This depicts discoloration through the midsection that extends down to the thigh area. I don't really want to show the private areas right now."

Slater spoke up. "Let's stop at this point for our afternoon recess. We'll break until 3:25." I think Slater wanted to give the jurors a breather from the gruesome testimony.

Reeve, Everly, and I walked to the adjoining attorney conference room. "You're very thorough, Doctor."

"I try to be. This isn't my first time around. Your jury seems quite focused."

At 3:25, with everyone, including the jury, returned from the break, Slater said, "We are back on the record in the case of People v. Cathy Ramirez."

"Doctor, please put up your next slide." Exhibit 8 was displayed. I asked, "What is depicted here?"

"This is the back of the decedent. There are a multitude of injuries, just like the front of the chest area. The majority of the injuries are actually healing or scarred over."

"Please go on." He displayed Exhibit 9. "Tell us what we are looking at."

"This is the lower part of the decedent, a front view. Notice the greenish discoloration to the majority of the abdomen. We also see regions of purplish discoloration and greenish discoloration on each side of the scrotum. Right here at the base of the penis where it meets the scrotum, you can see kind of a red curvilinear defect. This is a large injury to his scrotum. He's got multiple injuries, bruises, abrasions, to the inner portions of his thighs on both sides."

Illuminating Exhibit 10, Reeve explained, "We're looking at

the decedent's buttocks, we've turned him over. We see a large area of whitish discoloration. This is cellulitis. It's an infection. There's so much injury here that this is just infected tissue, and the body is having difficulty healing because there is so much infection." Several jurors looked off.

"Doctor, can you tell us at what stages of healing these particular injuries are at?"

"Yes. At least a number of days, if not weeks. It takes a while for the body to try to heal those particular injuries."

"So Oscar would have been suffering from these injuries from days to weeks to months before his death?"

"Correct."

"Doctor, in your opinion, could these injuries affect Oscar's digestive system in being able to hold down food?"

"Certainly. With this kind of infection, when it's so rampant, a lot of those bacteria will get into the bloodstream, and it makes you very ill. That's called sepsis. Most people respond with nausea and vomiting and an inability to want to eat or keep it down. More likely than not, Oscar was in that state as a result of his injuries."

"Now that we've worked through Oscar's injuries, please resume your seat at the witness stand." Once he was settled, I asked, "Did you determine what actually caused his death?"

"He suffered broken ribs which punctured his lungs, causing him to hemorrhage. He bled to death, most likely from being struck forcibly in the chest region."

"Doctor, can you testify to a reasonable degree of medical certainty that this boy was abused?"

"Without question." In a matter-of-fact, clinical voice, he said, "This is one of the worst cases of child abuse I've ever witnessed."

"Doctor, can you testify to a reasonable degree of medical

certainty that, if left untreated, Oscar would have died from his various infections?"

"He would have."

I let his response linger before concluding. "Thank you, Dr. Reeve. You've helped us all understand what Oscar went through." Turning to Slater, "I have no more questions of Dr. Reeve. At this time, I move Exhibits 1 through 10 into evidence."

"Any objections, Mrs. Ramirez?"

"What do you mean?"

"Do you have any objections to the jurors viewing the various exhibits during their deliberations?"

"Of course I do. They don't matter. Caesar did all that, not me."

"I'll note your objection. The exhibits are admitted into evidence." Slater looked at Mrs. Ramirez. "Do you care to cross-examine Dr. Reeve?"

She shook her head and looked off, exasperated with Slater.

"Dr. Reeve, you are excused."

After Reeve took his leave, Slater looked at me. "Mr. Clearwater?"

"The testimony of Dr. Reeve concludes the People's case."

Slater turned to the defendant. "Mrs. Ramirez, this is your opportunity to put on any testimony you might have. Do you care to do that?"

Her head was down; she didn't look up or respond.

What must she be thinking?

Slater again: "If you are unsure of what to do, you are free to consult with Mr. Serge."

That got a reaction. She stared at the judge. "I don't need anything from him."

Sound decision.

"I understand that." Slater, ever so understanding. "Are you going to call any witnesses? That could include yourself."

A quizzical expression crossed her face. "How can I question myself?"

"I would allow you to testify in a narrative. You could take an oath and say what you want to say. I must caution you, however, should you testify, the prosecutor would then have the right to cross-examine you."

She shook her head emphatically, "No witnesses!"

Another sound decision.

"Okay, it's 4:15," Slater said. "We will adjourn for the weekend. As I mentioned at the beginning of the trial, Fridays in this courtroom are dedicated to nontrial matters. I'll see everyone back here at nine o'clock Monday morning. The same admonition to you folks: don't discuss this case or follow any reports on the media. Good afternoon."

CHAPTER 49

My plan for the weekend was to hang around the house. Lisa needed time to paint. There was always another art show on the horizon. My self-appointed task was to sand and varnish our Adirondack chairs, which I had brought from Malibu. They were showing the effects of beach exposure. Mindless work would allow my mind to drift into closing argument mode. I was thinking about Cathy Ramirez. She was present during Caesar's infliction of Oscar's injuries. She knew, she instigated, she bears responsibility. The horrific facts of Oscar's death would get me most of the way home. These jurors wanted to convict, but they needed the tools to get there. Aiding and abetting and the duty of a caretaker were the tools to tie her to Oscar's death. It was my job to make the concepts abundantly clear, allowing the jurors to finish the job.

Come Monday morning, I got in my early-morning run along the hard-packed sand below our house, donned my dark-blue closing-argument suit, tied my good-luck Gucci tie, fitted my gold cufflinks into my French cuffs, and made the drive to LA. I felt comfortable with that adrenaline surge I always experienced prior to closing argument.

I was greeted by Detective Everly outside the courtroom. "Time to close it up, Jake," he encouraged, as we settled at counsel table.

"I think we're good, Ron." I patted his shoulder.

Cathy was escorted in, leaning heavily on her cane. Her hair, instead of hanging limp and loose, was swept up in a stylish coiffure. Her muumuu had been replaced by a matching skirt and blouse. I had no idea how or who was able to bring about her metamorphosis, but she presented in an almost professional manner. I felt myself involuntarily nodding my approval. The change in her appearance was so stark, I couldn't stop myself from staring. She caught me looking and gave me a self-satisfied, almost confident smirk. Was she that oblivious? She had to know her prospects were bleak.

I turned to Everly, who was also staring at Cathy, and whispered, "She's going to make an argument." I paused and said. "I thought she might just roll over. But no, she's going to fight. Can't blame her for that."

"Looks that way," said Everly.

Our exchange was interrupted as the bailiff called court to order. Judge Slater ascended his throne and did a double-take on Cathy. He shot me a look as if to say, Can you believe what we're seeing? He ordered the jurors back in and I studied them as they settled and took Cathy in. To a person, there were looks of surprise.

Slater explained to the jurors that he would instruct them on the law, which would be followed by closing arguments. The court's instructions were delivered in Slater's monotone cadence, which exacerbated the jurors' impatience—they had sat through the evidence and were eager to get into their deliberations. Thirty-five minutes later, he finished and turned to me.

"Mr. Clearwater."

I nodded to the judge as I slowly stood. "Were you sickened by the coroner's testimony?" I got several nods. "Hard to imagine that something like that can happen. Harder yet to imagine that it could happen in plain sight. Cathy and Caesar weren't living in some cave or in some remote location. They were out there among us, and yet they were able to beat and torture this boy for at least weeks, if not months. How can something like that happen? How is it that no one saw something, reported something?"

I stopped and studied some of the faces. "How could this happen in plain view?" I noted slight head shakes from several jurors. I think they were puzzling through the same question.

"In my view, the saddest testimony we heard was not from the coroner, as sad and horrific as it was. No, the saddest testimony came from those two elderly neighbors. One a retired nurse and one a retired school teacher. They knew that they were witnessing abuse and probably even torture, and yet they did nothing. Those two women who, given their respective vocations, understood their moral duty to report. You heard their testimony, their regrets and shame for not doing what they should have done. One phone call." I repeated, "One phone call to the police or to social services—hell, to anyone—might well have saved Oscar's life."

I walked to counsel table, and Everly poured me some water. I stood still and looked off past Judge Slater before coming back to the jury. "Now, I'm not going to fixate on those two witnesses. Frankly, I think they somewhat symbolize how we so often fail to take action, even when our instincts tell us something is wrong." I shrugged. "We don't want to get involved. We don't want to interfere. What if I'm wrong? I'll look like a fool. I'll look like I'm meddling where I don't belong."

I lowered my head in understanding, raised it and continued. "Isn't that what we do, what we think?" My rhetorical elicited several discreet nods.

"But this was a child, a trapped child with no way out. No refuge. No savior. Children belong to all of us. We are all responsible for protecting our most vulnerable. For saving the kids." I took a contemplative pause. "I wonder if I had seen Oscar being kicked or sitting on that curb holding himself and crying, would I get involved? God, I hope so. But until we are personally confronted with such circumstances, we don't know for certain how we'll react.

I moved up close to the jury rail and dropped my voice. "What's abundantly clear is that there are monsters among us. Sometimes well concealed. But when their horrors are seen or felt, we must shake ourselves and do the right thing. I used the word monster. No accident. If Caesar had not finally kicked Oscar to death, he most likely would've died anyway. But let's be very clear, the beatings, the abuse would have continued, and he would have died the following week or month."

I stepped back and studied the twelve deciders. "Let's talk about the other monster sitting with us in this courtroom. Should she bear responsibility right along with her husband?" I focused on the two women jurors sitting front and center. "You all know she should. You all know that, deep in your souls. That's moral knowledge. But moral knowledge isn't enough. How do we bring that moral knowledge into this court of law? Judge Slater put forth the tools the twelve of you can use to bring Cathy Ramirez into this deadly web of abuse. First, the judge told us that if you find that she aided and abetted in the killing of Oscar, she is as guilty of his murder as Caesar. Second, he instructed that caretakers have a duty to protect those in their care. Those are the tools you folks can use to convict her.

"Let's examine aiding and abetting. There are three requirements. Did Cathy have knowledge of the crime? Did she intend to aid or encourage the crime? And did she actually aid or encourage? We know that Cathy, Caesar, and Oscar lived in close quarters. How could Cathy not know that Caesar was beating Oscar? And we also have the testimony of the two neighbor ladies. What did they tell us? One of them saw Cathy watching as Caesar was kicking the child. Knowledge?" I nodded.

"The second element in aiding and abetting is that Cathy had to intend to encourage or aid Caesar in his abuse. Did she intend to aid or encourage her husband? It's not always clear what a person is thinking at a particular time and place. What we need to do is look at the surrounding circumstances to gain insight as to a person's intent. What was all that yelling about? When she witnessed Caesar kicking Oscar, what did she do? But we're not talking about isolated incidents, we are talking about months of abuse. Was she on board with her husband beating Oscar? Did she intend that he should hurt the child?" Phrase the rhetorical and then let common sense finish the argument.

"The final requirement is that she helped, or aided, or at least encouraged the beatings." I offered a knowing look. "You folks heard the same testimony I heard. What do you think? Did she encourage the terror in that house? It's your collective call: did she aid and abet?"

I got several nods. They were with me. "If you find that she did, she is every bit as responsible for Oscar's death as Caesar.

"Judge Slater gave you one other tool to use during your deliberations. If a caretaker fails to exercise proper care for someone they're responsible for and that person is killed because the caretaker failed in her care, that person is responsible for the death. That's the duty of a caretaker, especially a duty owed to children. Now we learned that Cathy and Caesar agreed to take in eleven-year-old Oscar. In so doing, they assumed responsibility for his welfare. They were his aunt and uncle. For the life of me, I'm having a hard time figuring out what must have happened. How did their idea of discipline escalate to this obscene level? The failure of their duty of care makes them both guilty of murder." I took a step back. "Cathy was supposed to mother him, not murder him."

I took another contemplative pause. "My burden, which I willingly accept, is proof beyond a reasonable doubt. Note the word 'reasonable' in that standard. It's not proof beyond all doubt or even proof beyond a shadow of a doubt. It's proof beyond a reasonable doubt. It's using your common sense and coming to a reasonable conclusion. For instance in our case, is it reasonable to conclude that Cathy knew that Caesar beat Oscar? Given the close physical proximity in which they lived, and given the length of time over which the beatings occurred, could she be unaware? Or is it reasonable to conclude she was aware?" I stopped to let my explanation resonate.

"Likewise, in examining whether Cathy intended in any way to help or aid her husband, we need to use our common sense. Did she intend to aid or encourage him? The same analysis can be used as to the duty of care she owed Oscar. Could she be ignorant that an eleven-year-old boy living under her roof for months and months was beaten so severely that he couldn't eat, that his face was crisscrossed with scars and open wounds? Yet she did nothing. This kid couldn't eat. He couldn't even digest his food. Yet she had him punished for not eating."

"You folks recall how during jury selection I didn't challenge anyone. And I told you why. Once you had heard what I already knew you would, you'd use your common sense and do the right thing. And now we're finally there. You twelve have the facts and the tools. I trust you will do the right thing."

CHAPTER 50

"Thank you, Mr. Clearwater." Slater turned to Cathy. "Mrs. Ramirez, you may make a closing argument if you so choose."

In a caustic voice, she replied, "I guess I better, after all the crap he just said." She threw me a venomous look, and then back to Slater. "Do I have to prance around like he did?"

Prance?

"You may speak from where you are." Slater was being very careful. He knew some appellate lawyer would scour the record, looking to see if either he or I had unduly taken advantage of the unrepresented Cathy. "If you would prefer, I can have the bailiff arrange a lectern for you, or like I said, you can make your remarks from where you sit."

"My balance is not so good. Something to lean on would help steady me."

"You got it." Slater said. The bailiff moved a lectern from a corner of the courtroom and positioned it before the jury.

"Mrs. Ramirez, will you require any assistance in making your way over?"

"I've got my cane. I'm fine."

And with that, she worked her way upright and, leaning heavily on her cane, labored to the lectern. By the time she got there, she was breathing hard, and there were rivulets of perspiration on the back of her neck. Strands of her upswept hair were coming loose and falling wet across her face and shoulders.

Despite the gruesome testimony and photographs of the injuries she had helped orchestrate, it was difficult to not feel some sympathy for her. She stood alone, without her husband, without a lawyer, facing murder charges, and it was all she could do to remain upright while gripping the lectern. Hell, if I felt some pangs of sympathy for this pathetic creature, what must the jurors be thinking?

In that unlikely high-pitched voice, she asked Slater, "Can I just go ahead?"

"Yes, please go ahead."

"It started when Murielle called me and begged me to take in her boy." She started to say boys but caught herself. "She was a junkie and said she was going to lose her apartment." Cathy shook her head with disgust. "I didn't want any kids living with us. We were barely getting by. My worthless husband couldn't hold a job for five minutes. I had to reach out to some organizations to help us get by as it was. That was my work. As you can see, I'm not built for any kind of physical labor." She offered a slight, self-deprecating smile. "I'm not looking for pity. I just wanted to explain that we weren't really in a position to care for someone else's child, but we did."

I watched the jurors as they were studying this woman. Not surprisingly, they were locked in on her. How could they not? It was like driving by a car wreck. Can't help yourself.

"My stupid and worthless husband didn't know anything about raising a kid. He thought you hit them to make them toe the line. That was his answer for everything. Kid didn't put his dishes in the sink, whack. Kid ditched school, whack. It just became what he did. Sometimes he felt like the boy was disrespecting me, whack. That was his answer to everything."

There were grim faces in the jury box.

"I didn't hit the boy. I never hit the boy. Those two old ladies said they heard me screaming at them." Nodding. "Yeah, sometimes I did. Far as I know, yelling at someone doesn't leave a bruise or a scar. When I saw those pictures, I had no idea how bad hurt he was. When he refused to eat, I thought he was being a drama queen. Maybe looking for attention." That drew some mean looks.

"On the day he died, I had no idea what happened. Next thing I know is that he tells me the kid is dead. I freaked out. I had no idea what Caesar had done." She sucked in a lungful of air and rested her chin on her chest. She held that pose and stopped talking. Was she done?

Slater finally asked, "Mrs. Ramirez, does that conclude your remarks?"

She lifted her head, which was barely visible over the lectern. "No, I've got more to say. That lawyer"—pointing at me—"knows he can't prove I abused Oscar, so he's using some legal mumbo-jumbo to stick me in prison." She turned and studied me. "He can't prove a guldarn thing." Then back to the jury, "But he wants to put me in prison for the rest of my life. That ain't right. I been locked up for months, itching to say my piece. Now you've heard it. Don't send me to prison."

She turned to Slater. "I said my piece."

"Thank you, Mrs. Ramirez." He motioned for the bailiff to assist her in returning to her table.

When she was seated, he looked at me. "Rebuttal argument, Mr. Clearwater?"

I stood and scanned the faces of the jurors, with particular attention to Juror Number Two, the law partner. When she took in my look, she dropped her eyes and, with just the slightest of movement, signaled no. She had heard enough, as had, I suspected, the other jurors. They wanted to get on with it. "No rebuttal, Judge."

Got to read and listen to your audience.

Slater gave the concluding instructions. "It's nearly noon. I'm going to instruct that the jury be served lunch in the jury deliberation room so that they can get on with their deliberations." And with that, they were dismissed.

CHAPTER 51

I watched the twelve of them take their orderly leave. Not one of them looked my way. Sometimes there might be a quick glance, a discreet nod of assurance. Not this time; Number Two had already given her nod. Here's to trusting that she was right. Would she be the foreperson, as I thought? If so, could she bring any naysayers around?

At that point in my career, I'd tried a number of trials before jurors, and what I wouldn't give to be a fly on the wall during deliberations. Which arguments worked and which fell on deaf ears? Did they understand and follow the jury instructions? Were there outside considerations that came into play? Did they understand the limits of reasonable doubt? These questions and dozens more would largely go unanswered. Occasionally, following trial, some jurors may decide to discuss their reasoning, but mostly juror deliberations would remain a mystery to all but the jurors—the twelve people in that room.

After the jurors retired and I was packing up, Slater beckoned me to the bench and asked me to join him in his chambers. Just me. *Strange.*

When the two of us settled in, he withdrew a bottle of JW Black and poured us each a liberal dose. "May I call you Jake?"

I answered warily. "Your Honor, I'm not certain this meeting is appropriate. There's a jury out, the trial is still ongoing, we shouldn't be here ex parte."

"Jake, the trial is over."

First name.

"And we are not going to speak of anything of consequence. So relax and enjoy the moment." He saluted with his glass. "Congratulations on what I believe will be a successful prosecution."

"I appreciate that, Your Honor. It may be a bit premature."

He grinned nonchalantly. "Back here with drinks in hand, my name is Jim. As for premature, hardly. I've been watching juries for a long time. Not only will you get your conviction, but I'm thinking we'll have a verdict before five o'clock this afternoon." Again he raised his glass in salute.

"Jim," I reluctantly saluted back. "Here's to your skills at reading jurors. I hope you're right."

"I usually am."

Remarkable. Such an ego. Such a lack of self-awareness.

He sipped and elaborated. "Those jurors hated the defendant and were just itching to show how much they despised her and what she did to that child."

I quickly finished my drink and declined a second. Still concerned about the propriety of this meeting, I unfolded myself and stood. Slater stood and put out a hand. "I want to apologize to you. During our pretrial discussions, I had no full realization for how much these two monsters brutalized that child. I understand why you were so adamant in refusing to move off murder. You were right and I was wrong."

I was stunned. This jackass of a judge was apologizing? Was this an attempt to perhaps mend fences with Seah and the office?

We shook. "Judge, I appreciate your apology," I lied.

I took the elevator back down to the DA's wing of the Foltz

Building, straight to Nancy Seah's office. Her secretary waved me in. "I just had a strange encounter." I relayed my exchange with Slater.

"No shit!" That pretty much said it all.

I received a call from Slater's clerk at 4:45 that afternoon, informing me there was a verdict. There are few adrenaline rushes as profound as hearing the verdict. I thought it would be good news, but still . . .

As Detective Everly and I took our seats, I noticed that Seah and my other Elder colleague Leslie Mann had slipped in and sat together at the back of the courtroom. Everyone was present except Cathy. Slater made inquiries and was informed that Cathy refused to leave her cell. Slater, for the benefit of potential later appellate review, explained on the record her refusal to participate, then turned to the bailiff. "You may bring in the jury."

As they filed in, they were a loose, casual group, no tension.

Was that good news?

Slater went through the formalities, asking for the foreperson. Not surprisingly, it was Juror Number Two. "Madam Foreperson, was the jury able to reach a verdict?"

In a clear, commanding voice, she replied, "We were, Your Honor."

"Please give the bailiff the verdict sheet." Bailiff to Slater, who reviewed the verdict and then sent it back to Number Two. "Please read the verdict."

In a flat voice which belied the circumstances, she read, "We the jury find the defendant Cathy Ramirez guilty of the second-degree murder of Oscar Ramirez."

Relief enveloped me as I looked at Juror Number Two, who was staring at me. I gave a slight nod and got one in return. Everly and I shook. I thought we would be successful, but sometimes jurors can surprise.

Outside the courtroom, several jurors wanted to talk and ask questions. Just beyond stood Juror Number Two, patiently waiting. When the others had worked their way down the hall to the elevators, she stepped forward.

"Congratulations, Mr. Clearwater. I suspect this wasn't one of your more difficult cases." It was a statement, not a question.

I put out my hand. "What is your name?"

"Nora McGinnis. As you know from jury questioning, I work in corporate litigation at Gibson Dunn."

"To respond to your statement, this was not my most difficult prosecution. It helped me to have a smart lawyer on the jury." I smiled. "If there were questions about aiding and abetting or duty of care, I figured you could steer them straight."

"I haven't thought about those concepts since my first year of law school." She grinned. "As for my fellow jurors, no one had problems with either concept. You made them very clear. But that's not what I wanted to talk about." She eyed me narrowly. "There were two boys, weren't there?"

I tilted my head and smiled. "You caught that, did you?"

"I thought so. After the mother blurted out 'boys,' and then seeing everyone's reaction, it was clear to me that something went off the rails."

"You're right. The mother sent two boys: Oscar, age eleven, and Felipe, age thirteen."

"Why'd we only hear about Oscar?"

"Well, I need to back up. But before I do, did you share your thoughts about there being two boys with the jurors?"

"No, I didn't think that would be appropriate, and surprisingly, no one brought it up."

"Here's what you didn't hear. Felipe was also killed by Caesar."

"Oh my God." McGinnis covered her open mouth. "He killed both boys?" She was trying to make some sense of it. But there was little sense to draw upon.

"Just weeks before they moved back down to California, Caesar 'disciplined'"—I made air quotes—"Felipe by smashing the boy's head into a wall."

"So . . . Cathy and Oscar had to know?"

"I'm speculating here, but I believe they both had to know. But it gets even darker and more bizarre. Caesar hid Felipe's body in a fifty-five-gallon drum and encased his body in cement." McGinnis went silent, her face blanched. "And to top off the bizarre, Caesar and Cathy loaded the drum onto their truck and brought it with them when they moved to Rialto."

"How does that make sense?" she asked, her forehead wrinkled. "They were living in rural Oregon? Why didn't they dump the body up there?"

"I've been wondering about that ever since I latched onto this case," I replied, my palms face up.

"Can we sit?" She pointed to an unoccupied bench. Once we were sitting, she asked, "I assume the body was eventually discovered? Why didn't we hear about this?"

"The body was recovered, but since the murder of the older boy happened in Oregon, I had no jurisdiction. I wanted to bring Felipe's death into this trial as further evidence that the Ramirezes' conduct was anything but accidental."

She nodded. "But the judge ruled it too prejudicial?"

"Exactly."

We sat in silence until McGinnis said, "Fortunately, you didn't need that evidence. I assume the husband pled out during the trial?"

"He did. I offered him a low range and he wisely accepted."

"Low range being what?"

"Ten years, out in seven with good behavior."

"Not to criticize, but that seems light. Two dead boys."

"I made my best call at the time. This was never going to be a straightforward prosecution. It was hard to gauge how this case would come off to the jurors. The husband was a bit slow and seemed pathetic, and Cathy, as you heard her say, never hit Oscar." I shrugged. "Beyond that, I had a conversation with the prosecutor up in Oregon that she would go after both of them for Felipe's murder."

"I'm glad to hear that," she said. "Will Judge Slater sentence Cathy to the ten years the husband got?"

"Probably, although there is often a price to pay for going to trial and losing. It'll be interesting to see what the judge does."

"Will you argue for a greater sentence for her?"

"No, I'm not sure she should be punished more harshly than the husband. I'll probably hold my piece. In my mind, a person should not suffer a greater punishment by going to trial."

"How noble, Mr. Clearwater." She grinned.

I shrugged off the remark. "As we both know, sentencing is with the judge."

"Got it." She leaned back on the bench, her questions satiated. She gave me a long, appraising look. "Mr. Clearwater, it's been an experience. You did a thorough job of presenting your case. Your strategy during jury selection was, by my way of thinking, a bit risky, but it worked out. The jurors commented on it during our deliberations, and that held you in their good graces."

"That's good to hear. I've never done that before."

"Well, it worked for this trial." She stood and shook my hand. "I'm looking forward to talking about this experience with my husband, who happens to be a civil trial lawyer."

"Ms. McGinnis, having you and your experience on the jury gave me great comfort. Thank you."

CHAPTER 52

The high of the conviction was muted when I thought of the anguish those two boys suffered. Don't get me wrong, Caesar and Cathy deserved to be convicted and locked up. But the suffering those kids endured lingered. I meant what I said during my closing argument, that there were monsters out there, preying on the innocent. Many of them hiding in plain sight. How many other Caesars and Cathys were out there? How many other Oscars and Felipes? I worked to shake off my malaise on the drive home. I couldn't save the world. Hell, the number of abuse cases was overwhelming. The thought of so many unreported cases weighed on me.

I called Lisa on the way home and gave her the news. "Thank God you got that terrible woman. Congratulations, Jake." And after just a wisp of a pause, "I don't mean to sound vindictive, but I hope she has an awful time in prison. Maybe she'll learn what it feels like to be abused, to be at the mercy of others."

"I couldn't agree more. Interestingly, she refused to leave her cell to hear the verdict."

"That's because she's a coward. She had to know she was going down. Too bad you didn't get a chance to see her horrible face when the verdict was read."

Lisa was worked up. Seldom had I heard her so emphatic.

I told her I would pick up some Chinese takeout. We ate

on the deck and drank too much. I had already decided to take the next day off and was trying to convince Lisa to join me. She finally acquiesced, and we enjoyed a leisurely nothing kind of day in Bruno Keys.

Come Wednesday, I was back, and Nancy Seah invited me to her office. "Congratulations on Ramirez. Leslie and I heard the verdict but didn't have an opportunity to congratulate you afterward. You were surrounded by jurors."

I nodded my thanks. "It was a good trial to get through."

"You've had two emotionally draining trials. How're you holding up?"

"I'm good. Getting a little breather before tackling Hardy and the Pouses."

"I hear you. That's going to be a bloodbath. But like you said, some time to catch your breath. When does that go?"

"Three weeks from Monday."

"Meanwhile, I'm shorthanded. Would you mind briefing a case for the committee? We meet Tuesday."

"Sure," I agreed. "I'll still have plenty of time to get the Pouse trial geared up."

Tuesday, September 4, committee meeting. A new face was in the conference room, visiting with Seah and Mann. The newcomer popped up when I walked in. Seah made the introductions. "Jake, I want you to meet Harvey Wisk. He's been heading up our sexual assault unit for the last three years."

We shook. Wisk was rail thin. I mean rail thin. He stood close to six feet but couldn't weigh more than a hundred and forty. He had an infectious smile and a flop of blond hair that covered his ears. He was someone you wanted to like right off, even before you got to know him. Great eye contact. He exuded goodwill.

"Mr. Clearwater," he said with genuine warmth, "I understand you just got a conviction on a difficult child abuse case. Congratulations."

"Thanks. The name's Jake."

"Jake," said Nancy, "I was just telling Leslie that I've invited Harvey onto the committee. In addition to running our sexual assault unit, he is a terrific trial lawyer." She stopped and looked inquiringly at Wisk. "In fact, I recently heard you've never lost a trial. True?"

He shrugged, somewhat embarrassed. "I've been fortunate to only go to trial on strong prosecution cases. I don't think it's so much about me but rather about the cases I've tried." I detest false modesty, but I didn't sense that here. This was genuine modesty.

"Harvey, welcome to the committee," I said. "We could use another voice. You'll find working with Nancy and Leslie is an invigorating experience."

That caught a laugh from Mann. "Invigorating? Come on, Jake, you can do better than 'invigorating.' How about 'thoughtfully challenging' or maybe 'intellectually stimulating'?"

I pressed my hand on Mann's shoulder. "Yeah, Leslie, that's what I *meant* to say." That got a laugh. Seah fixed coffees for everyone as we settled in.

"Harvey understands what this committee is about and how we work on some of the most difficult and occasionally controversial cases." Seah scanned our faces. "Sometimes we disagree a bit, but in the end, we usually come to a consensus."

Wisk set down his coffee. "I heard that in the Pouse case, you really struggled to file invol man against the parents."

Seah pulled a face. "I'm surprised our discussion leaked out. We strive to keep our deliberations within the group. I'm disappointed that got out."

Mann shook her head. "I think we know how that got out. Hopefully that won't happen again." The unnamed culprit was, of course, Roger Hawthorne. Mann studied Wisk. "We encourage robust give and take inside these walls. But once a filing decision is reached, those discussions remain only with us."

"I understand," Wisk said, nodding.

"Okay, now that the ground rules are clear, I've asked Jake to brief us on a difficult stalker-murder case. From my limited understanding, no arrest has been made, and the investigators are stuck and have asked for our guidance on how to proceed. Jake, have you been able to get a handle on this?"

"I think so. I've read the reports and talked to the lead investigator. This involves severe stalking capped off by murder. And the prime suspect is the stalker. Problem is, there's not much other than his stalking to link him to the murder. So let me fill you in on the investigation and then we can offer the investigators what guidance we can. First and significantly, the victim's body has never been found. Prior to her going missing, the victim reported more than fifty instances of the suspect either physically stalking or cyberstalking her over a twelve-month period."

"I take it there is no question the suspect is the stalker?" Mann asked.

"That's very clear, and he even admits he was stalking her. But he won't own up to killing her." I paused. "Let me lay out what we know. Carol Olson, the victim, worked as a clerk in a Vons market in Sherman Oaks. Sometime in October two years ago, Brian Sock kept coming into her store and always in her line. He referred to her by name and would ask personal questions. She became increasingly concerned and told the suspect that she was happily married and didn't appreciate his attention. Sock was undeterred. Eventually Olson went to her manager, who cornered Sock and told him that he was no longer welcome in the store. Sock became incensed and stormed off.

"The following day, Sock was waiting for Olson at her car when she got off work. When she saw him, she went back inside the store and made her first call to the police. A deputy promptly responded and, after contacting Olson, confronted Sock in the parking lot. The deputy wrote up an incident report detailing his conversation with Sock. Sock explained that he was Olson's former boyfriend and just wanted to talk to her and clear up any misunderstanding."

"Any truth to that?" asked Mann.

"No. The deputy suggested that Sock leave, but he refused. The deputy then escorted Olson to her car and she drove off."

"Undaunted by the police presence?" asked Mann.

"Apparently so."

"Any reaction from the victim's husband?"

"There was no husband. She told him she was married to deter him."

"So much for that," Mann offered.

"The following day, Olson contacted an attorney and within days had a restraining order. Notwithstanding the order, Sock started calling and sending emails about how much he cared for her. Between the spring of 2018 and the end of summer, Sock continued to call and send text messages. He also started sending packages, which Olson didn't open."

"But it was a no-contact restraining order," puzzled Wisk. "Why wasn't it enforced?"

"That remains a bit unclear, from what the investigator told me. Kinda hard to believe, isn't it?" I said with disgust. "No action was taken, and in the fall of 2018, Sock left over twenty voicemails on Olson's cell."

"She hadn't changed her number?" Seah asked.

"Oh, this was the third changed number. But somehow he got hold of it. In one of those voicemails"—I looked at the police report—"he said that he had a lot of anger toward Olson. In another he said, 'I don't care if the police come and arrest me. I don't care if I go to court. And I don't care if I get seven years or seventy years.' In his final voicemail, he said, and I quote, 'I honestly don't care what happens to me, I've made my decision, I know this is very severe and stupid of me. But I'm already dead and jail is just the place to finalize the act.'"

There was dead silence in the room. Everyone was waiting for the other shoe to drop.

"The following day, October 18, Ms. Olson went missing. And now, nearly a year later, is presumed dead."

"His last message was close to a confession," Seah observed. "Okay, Jake, what do they have on this guy, other than his extreme stalking and that near confession?"

"Therein lies the rub. According to Investigator Nichols, not much." I stopped and looked at Seah. "I know this sounds all too familiar, but without her body, this problematic case is even tougher."

As I had earlier mentioned, a little over a year ago I had prosecuted a sheriff's lieutenant in the murder of his wife whose body had never been found. It made for a difficult trial. I had to prove beyond a reasonable doubt that there was a body out there somewhere and then prove beyond a reasonable doubt that the defendant was the killer. Essentially doubling my burden. No-body murder prosecutions were rare for good reason. Hard to get a conviction.

"Dammit, Jake," said Seah, "I didn't know that Olson's body hadn't been recovered when I asked you to brief this case. Maybe this is a little too close to home after the Cort trial."

"That's all right." I shrugged. "Here's the evidence Nichols has been able to put together on Sock. He has been in and out of mental institutions over the past fifteen years. He lives at home with his mother, Dad passed years ago. No steady employment. On October 18, Olson simply disappeared. Without a trace.

"Of course, suspicion immediately fell on Sock. He was brought in for questioning. He admitted he was infatuated with Olson but emphatically denied involvement. His mother was his alibi for the day Olson went missing. Not surprisingly, she said he had hung around the house the entire day. Nichols got search warrants for Sock's house, the surrounding half acre, and the family car. Nothing came up. And that's pretty much it. The investigation was stalled.

"About a month ago—bear in mind this is eleven months after Olson disappeared—another woman, working at a convenience store near the Vons where Olson had worked, called and reported that she was being stalked. Her name is Becky Swift. The stalker was Sock. Investigator Nichols was able to make the connection back to Olson's disappearance.

"Nichols noted the similarities between the stalking of Olson and Swift. Both working retail and then the gradual escalation to full-on stalking, including sending gifts. When Nichols questioned Sock about his stalking of Swift, Sock became agitated and said, "These women had better start respecting me. There are consequences to be paid." When pressed as to what he meant, Sock refused to elaborate.

"What a nasty character," Mann said.

I nodded agreement and continued. "Nichols again went back to Sock's mother, and this time she wasn't so supportive of her son. She told Nichols that she was mistaken about her son's whereabouts following the disappearance of Olson. She told Nichols that her son had been gone for three days and she had no idea where he had gone.

"Nichols then went back to Sock and told him that his mother said he had been gone for three days following the disappearance. Sock screamed, "'Goddamn woman. We'd be better off without any of the scheming bitches.'" He refused to respond to any follow-up.

"Nichols is convinced that Sock is good for Olson's murder. But he has hit a wall in his investigation. He's asking us for help."

Seah sipped her coffee and thoughtfully summarized. "We've got severe stalking. We've got damn near a confession the day before the victim goes missing. We've got three days of the defendant being unaccounted for, following the disappearance. We've got a withdrawn alibi. And we've got two rants against scheming women. Am I missing anything?"

"Nope. That's where we're at," I said. "Not enough to charge."

Mann weighed in. "Nothing found in the house, the car, or the surrounding grounds when they executed the search warrants?"

"Unfortunately not," I answered, and then added, to the group, "Thoughts?"

"I've got nothing to add," said Mann. "It's a weak circumstantial case at this point. I agree with the investigator, not enough to go forward. But I can't think of another angle for them to pursue."

"Clearly needs more," I said, with a come-on shrug. "I'm with you, Leslie, I don't know what to advise the investigator. I'm stuck."

Wisk broke into the discussion. "I'd like to have Investigator Nichols question this guy in the presence of his mother. Sock seems fragile, and mom seems like she's perhaps fed up with him. Maybe if he's confronted with the facts as Nancy just laid out, with mom being part of the dynamic, something might break loose. She did withdraw her alibi. Might be worth a try."

"It's a direction." I shrugged. "Getting the investigator in the same room with Mom and Sock could provide a break. Maybe. If the investigator can make that happen, I worry about *Miranda* problems, but we can sort that out later if something pops. Good job, Harvey."

"All right," said Seah. "Harvey, you take over the follow-up on this case. Jake and Leslie already have their hands full. And," she added, with a rueful smile at Wisk, "should it ever get to trial, you can put your perfect record on the line."

"I'd be happy to." Wisk gave us his infectious grin.

I had no other involvement with the case. As it turned out, the investigator was able to arrange a confrontation of sorts involving Sock and his mother. And as Wisk suggested, Sock made some incriminating statements. The case was filed and set for trial. Tough prosecution. Could Harvey Wisk keep his perfect trial record intact?

CHAPTER 53

On September 5, I received notice from Sam Hardy requesting that a continuance of the pretrial meeting scheduled for September 17 be pushed back to October 3, with trial commencing on October 17. He was engaged in a federal civil rights trial in Seattle. I also received notice that the trial had been assigned to Judge Jules Wagner.

From asking around the office, I learned that Wagner was a senior status judge in his tall seventies who was, as the need arose, called upon to handle overload cases. Wagner's reputation, as befitting his age and experience, was old school. He was said to run a tight courtroom. My initial inclination was positive. I wanted a tough, no-nonsense judge who wouldn't take any of Hardy's blowhard antics. I didn't oppose the continuance.

Meanwhile, I was thinking through how I would approach this delicate trial. More than most trials, voir dire and jury selection would be critical to success. Hardy's subtext, lurking just beneath the surface, was that this prosecution was an indirect attack on gun ownership and parental autonomy. Whereas I needed the trial to be about parental responsibility.

Given the turnout at both preliminary hearings, I knew Hardy and the Pouses would receive strong support from the Second Amendment crowd. They were sure to pack the courtroom and quite possibly present an intimidating presence to the judge and jury. At that first prelim, I had experienced firsthand how a weak judge could be cowed by Hardy and his ilk. However, at the second prelim, a strong judge had controlled the courtroom and kept Hardy in check.

The trial would play out one of two ways. If Hardy had his way, any evidence of the shooting would be excluded. He would maintain, as he had at both prelims, that any actual case against the parents ended prior to the shootings; once the parents left the school, any involvement by them had ended. Admittedly, his argument had a certain logic. The parents were not charged as shooters, and unlike my case against Cathy Ramirez, there were no facts that Devon's parents aided and abetted in the murders. I couldn't establish that they intended to aid their son in the murders. Hell, they were likely as surprised as anyone by Devon's murder spree.

In order to prove involuntary manslaughter, therefore, I needed to prove the Pouses' culpability by establishing that their conduct prior to the shooting was criminally negligent. Not negligent in the sense of what might have caused a vehicle collision. That involved simple negligence. I had to prove criminal negligence, which involves a sense of recklessness beyond mere negligence. Were they criminally negligent when they purchased the gun and essentially gave it over to their sixteen-year-old? Were they criminally negligent in allowing him unsupervised access to the gun? Knowing he had access to a gun, were they reckless on the day of the shooting in not pulling Devon from school?

I had done my workup. I knew every aspect of my case. My witnesses were lined up and prepared. I had met with every witness to discuss their testimony. Some, like the school principal, were nervous and fidgety. As she should have been. Could she have handled this any worse?

Wednesday, October 3, 2019. Pretrial. Sam Hardy and his two associates entered Judge Wagner's courtroom just prior to our 9:00 a.m. pretrial conference. The courtroom was moderately full. Mostly media. Maybe the Second Amendment crowd was sleeping in.

I hadn't forgotten how huge Hardy was. He was a presence just by walking into the courtroom, and he reveled in the attention. He dumped his briefcase on counsel table and walked over to me, extended his catcher's mitt of a hand, and boomed, "Counselor, you're not seriously going to take this turd of a case to trial? I was hoping you would come to your senses." I'm certain his bluster was intended for the attentive media.

I stood and shook hands, my hand swallowed by his paw. "What can I tell you? I've got a hard head when it comes to doing the right thing." Looking up at the prominent ridge above his eyes and his shaved head, I added, "Maybe I'll even learn something about trying cases by watching your brilliance."

Hardy's laugh ricocheted off the walls. "You're a feisty sonofabitch, Clearwater. I like that and I'm going to enjoy knocking you around the courtroom."

I trusted that was metaphorical.

Our exchange, as delightful as it was, was cut short as the bailiff called court to order and Judge Wagner took the bench. Wagner was a handsome, courtly older man with striking silver coiffed hair set off against his golfer's tan. "Gentlemen, I understand we are here for a pretrial conference. Please make your appearances."

"Jake Clearwater for the State, Your Honor."

"Sam Hardy on behalf of Don and Kay Pouse. Your Honor, before we go any further, I'm filing a challenge against this court." Attorneys can challenge a judge for any reason whatsoever. Such challenges are limited to one per trial. Should a lawyer have concerns about a judge, this is the tool. It can be problematic, judges often take such challenges personally, and in the future, should the challenging lawyer draw that judge again, it may not go so well.

It could be hard for a judge not to take a challenge personally.

Occasionally, a district attorney's office or a public defender's office will file a blanket disqualification of a particular judge. It is rarely done but may be the only remedy for a judge who consistently makes poor rulings against a particular side. When I was a prosecutor in San Arcadia, my office made a blanket challenge of a judge who consistently ruled against the prosecution in suppression hearings. The effect of our blanket challenge was to reduce that judge to presiding only over civil matters. A fairly drastic remedy, but an effective one.

I understood why Hardy challenged Wagner. He had a reputation for running a tight courtroom. Hardy would chafe under that kind of authority. As I had learned during the two prelims, he would always attempt to assert his control over the courtroom. With someone like a Judge Wagner, that may not be possible. Hardy was rolling the dice that whoever was slotted as backup would be someone he could have his way with. But that was a crapshoot.

Wagner didn't seem to take the challenge personally. Without missing a beat, he replied, "Okay, Counsel, I'll put this case over to the afternoon calendar with another judge. You will both receive a text as to which courtroom." He gaveled and retired. Wagner was free to return to the links.

As I packed up, I looked over at Hardy. "Looking for somebody you can bully?"

"I'm looking for a judge who will let me try my case. I've read up on Wagner. I don't want some hard-ass retired judge."

We were assigned to Department 402 with Sarah Winchell presiding. I did a quick search on her. In contrast to Wagner, she was on the younger side, forty-two. She had been a deputy public defender before being appointed to the bench only eight months earlier. Not much of a track record for Hardy or me to get a handle on. I had checked in with Nancy Seah when I learned who we had drawn, to see if she had any insight on whether Winchell was a good fit.

"From what I hear, she seems competent," Seah said. "I've heard no complaints from any of our deputies."

"Formerly a public defender. Should I be concerned?"

"I don't think so. If she was acting as a defense lawyer from the bench, I would have heard about it," she said. "And Jake, I don't want to be in the habit of challenging judges. Given her age, she's likely to be around for the long haul, and we can't afford to be on her bad side. My sense is that you go with her."

"You're the boss. I do worry, with her relative lack of experience, whether she's tough enough to keep Hardy in check."

In an annoyed tone she admonished, "Surprisingly, Jake, women can be as tough as your gender. Take me, for example. Am I tough enough?"

"Wait a minute," I explained, "I wasn't referring to her gender but to her experience and having to deal with the likes of Hardy."

"Point taken. She's your judge, for better or worse. Good luck, Jake."

Winchell had several other matters on calendar. Hardy and I waited for her to call our case. Once again, the room was moderately full, mostly with media waiting for the Pouse case to be called.

Winchell was an attractive woman with strikingly blond, almost-white hair that fell to her shoulders. In dealing with the matters before calling our case, she was polite and respectful to counsel. She seemed poised and thoughtful. But, I suspect, she had yet to deal with the looming hurricane that was Hardy. How would her poise hold up, once he started leaning in?

She called our case and we made our appearances. She was all business, no pleasantries. "Counsel, have there been any discussions toward a disposition?"

Hardy jumped in. "There's no chance of a resolution short of the prosecutor dismissing all charges against my clients. Their case is a travesty and not worthy of taking up valuable court time—" He attempted to go on, only to be cut off by Winchell.

Blocking Hardy's first volley.

"Mr. Hardy, I'm not interested in your editorial asides." She turned to me. "Mr. Clearwater, do you share counsel's opinion that any talks aimed at disposition would be fruitless?"

"Unfortunately, I do, Your Honor. This case will only be resolved through trial."

"Very well, we therefore won't take up any valuable court time with talk," she said, "but get right to it. All motions to be filed by this Friday and heard one week from today." She stopped and studied Hardy. "I note, Mr. Hardy, that you represent both defendants. Has there been a waiver by both as to any potential conflicts that might arise? This concerns me. In the public defender's office, we were reluctant to represent two defendants in a single trial."

"Judge, I appreciate your concern, but my clients have waived any conflicts."

Winchell shrugged and said, with a dismissive tone, "Okay." She seemed tough enough. I suspect she and Hardy were destined to scrap.

I filed no motions. Usually motions are made to exclude testimony. I wanted the whole ugly mess in. Hardy, on the other hand, had motions to exclude. As he had attempted during the two preliminary hearings. He moved to exclude the actual murders. He continued to maintain that any culpability by the parents ended when they left the school on the day of the shooting. That motion would never fly, yet Hardy kept pushing it. He also moved that any photographs of the murder scene or of the autopsies of the victims be excluded as overly prejudicial.

Wednesday, October 10, the date set to argue motions. We were first on Judge Winchell's calendar. As Detective Otto Cipolla and I approached Department 402, we were greeted with a chaotic scene outside the courtroom. Hardy's voice stood out as he denounced the prosecution's case to an array of reporters and cameras. "This abuse of the legal system has got to be stopped. This prosecution is nothing but a political stunt by the DA himself to appeal to those who are hell-bent on the destruction of the Second Amendment and the freedom of the family to raise their children as they will."

Several members of the media broke off from the pontificating Hardy and thrust their microphones at me. I was urged to respond to Hardy's bombast. I waved the microphones away and Cipolla and I entered the relative calm of the courtroom.

I preferred to try my case to a jury. The histrionics belonged to the blowhards. The courtroom was packed. I'm certain Hardy had beat the drum for his Second Amendment acolytes to show their support.

As we settled in at our table, we caught some derisive comments. Apparently, I was the latest villain to the Gun-Toting Right. Hardy entered with a couple of his minions in his wake. The crowd hushed as he lumbered to his counsel table. There was a sense of awe from the assemblage as he shook some hands and actually blew one woman a kiss.

The man had a presence. I wouldn't be surprised if one day he ran for the Senate. Idaho? Wyoming, maybe? California, no.

I turned to take in the families of the three murdered boys, sitting directly behind me. They looked shell-shocked at witnessing Hardy's entrance. I got up and went to them. I held hands with one of the mothers and murmured assurances that the trial was not in the hands of the crowd but would be decided by a jury. I got some nods and thank-yous. Since Devon was in a psychiatric facility and may well be there for years, the trial would be the only outlet for the families of the victims to receive any small measure of justice.

The clerk called the case and we made our appearances. The formalities over, Winchell turned to Hardy. "Mr. Hardy, seems as if you are the only moving party. I have read your motions. You may proceed."

"Yes, Judge." All six-foot-eight of him rose and, in a deep baritone, began. "As I'm certain this court is aware, this trial is about an attempt by the State to attack my client's Second Amendment rights."

What crap. He was stoking the crowd.

Winchell put up a hand, commanding Hardy to stop. "This is not the time to make speeches, but rather to hear and rule on your motions," she said, in a tone that broached no dissent. "I understand your first motion is to exclude any evidence of the events once the defendants had their last contact with their son. Is that correct?"

"Yes it is," Hardy acknowledged. "What I was attempting to do was give the court context to better understand the intricacies of this trial."

"Mr. Hardy"—she offered an insincere grin—"I appreciate your concern for my understanding. But I've read the preliminary hearing transcripts of both prelims and feel sufficiently versed in the context you refer to. And now I want you to tell me why I should exclude any evidence following the defendants' last interaction with their son."

She was tough enough!

Hardy heaved a sigh of exasperation and went on to make the same argument he had made at the prelims, concluding with, "The events following my clients' departure were completely irrelevant to the issue at hand and additionally are unduly prejudicial."

Winchell, instead of asking for my response, gave Hardy a perplexed look. "Mr. Hardy, this is an involuntary manslaughter case. We've got three victims. How can their deaths be irrelevant to such a charge?"

Hardy tried to interject, only to be cut off by the judge. "Mr. Hardy, I understand your desire to avoid any difficult and frankly emotional testimony about the deaths of three boys, but your argument is ludicrous on its face. Of course there has to be evidence presented as to the deaths—it's a manslaughter case."

Hardy put up his hand. "With respect," he countered, "you're dead wrong."

Here we go. We hadn't even gotten to trial yet.

Winchell's voice took on icy tone. "Be that as it may, Mr. Hardy, that's my ruling." She then added, with steel in her voice, "For your edification, henceforth you will show respect to this court."

Hardy stood transfixed, staring at Winchell before finally turning to me and, with every effort of composure he could muster, said, "Given the court's ruling, Mr. Clearwater, I'm willing to stipulate to the deaths to satisfy the court's concerns."

I didn't look at Hardy but kept my focus on the judge. She studied me, waiting for my reaction. "Judge, as you pointed out, this is a manslaughter case, and this trial is about the defendants' role in these deaths. The jurors need to understand the connection between the conduct of the defendants and the shooting deaths of three innocents. I'm not willing to simply stipulate as per counsel's suggestion. The jurors need to hear the entire scenario to properly evaluate the role of the defendants in these murders."

Hardy blustered in. "Judge, he just wants the blood and guts to emotionally charge the jurors, to divert them from the real issues."

"Mr. Hardy, when I seek your thoughts, I will ask for them. Otherwise, you will maintain a professional demeanor and only speak with the court's permission. Am I understood?"

Hardy took an uncomfortably long time to formulate a response. "I understand the court's words." Through clenched teeth, he went on. "When I feel the court is making a mistake, I will not shy away from calling attention to that mistake."

Winchell, far from shrinking under Hardy's half-assed acknowledgment of her authority, replied, "Mr. Hardy, we are going to work through what figures to be a difficult trial, and while I respect your right to raise concerns and objections, you will understand this is my court and I will run this trial as I see fit." She offered a piercing look at Hardy, waiting for a response.

Hardy didn't disappoint. "In light of the court's ruling, my second and third motions are to exclude photographs of the murder scene and any autopsy photographs as not only irrelevant but extremely prejudicial."

"I will certainly evaluate any such photographs as to whether they are unduly prejudicial." She turned to me. "Mr. Clearwater, please present any photographs you plan to use to me prior to their use."

"Certainly."

Judge Winchell shuffled some papers and looked at a young

woman seated behind me on the bench reserved for lawyers. "Ms. Kellerman, I take it?"

She looked about twenty and was dressed in a stylish skirt suit that accentuated her fit body. "Yes, Your Honor. I am here representing Court TV. May I proceed?"

"Ms. Kellerman, welcome to my courtroom. I read your motion requesting that Court TV televise the trial. You may speak to the motion."

She nodded deferentially. "As noted in my brief in support of the motion, there is extensive support for my motion. Especially in a trial like this with issues involving matters of great public interest."

Winchell cut her off. "Ms. Kellerman, I read your brief, and I applaud your effort. However, I'm concerned that allowing cameras into the courtroom will distract the advocates and the witnesses. This trial already has a number of built in distractions and I don't want to feed the beast. Accordingly, I must deny your motion."

Hardy stood and without asking leave to weigh in, said, "Judge, this young lady is correct. There are real issues that should be brought to the greater public arena. And I, on behalf of my clients, would welcome the exposure of those issues."

"Mr. Hardy, that's the second time you've shared your unsolicited thoughts. I will seek your counsel when I feel it appropriate for you to weigh in. Until then, you will seek my permission before speaking. I trust this second warning has made my point abundantly clear."

Hardy remained standing without comment. An uneasy silence filled the courtroom. Finally, Hardy, with his eyes locked on the judge, sat without uttering a word.

Winchell, having again asserted her authority, shifted from Hardy to Kellerman. "Ms. Kellerman, you are dismissed."

For what it's worth, I agreed with the judge. Televising trials alters the trial dynamic. I understand the public interest, but I'm more concerned that the distractions and occasional theatrics may interfere with the essential business of trials.

Speaking of theatrics, did I mention Hardy was defense counsel?

Thursday and Friday, I worked from home. Lisa was off to work, and I had uninterrupted time to refine my voir dire and opening statement. We had been blessed with unseasonably mild weather, allowing me to set up shop on the balcony. Our unobstructed view of the Channel Islands provided welcome breaks from my prep.

Bruno Keys, the good life.

Lisa and I drove to the Ojai Valley Inn that weekend, where Lisa luxuriated in their world-class spa. I learned how to play pickleball. All talk of the Pouse trial was, by mutual consent, forbidden. We returned late Sunday, and I was back in the office Monday for two more days of trial prep, but there wasn't much more to do. I had reconciled myself that my efforts to convict the Pouses might well fall short, but I believed I was on the side of the angels.

CHAPTER 54

Wednesday, October 17, 9:00 a.m. Hardy's folks, the media, the curious, the families of the victims, and not least of all, fifty prospective jurors, filled the courtroom. News coverage of the timely and pressing issues at the heart of the trial were about to be pushed front and center. Could and should society condemn parents for the deadly consequences of their minor children? Lurking within that issue was the Second Amendment.

Prior to turning the questioning over to Hardy and me, Judge Winchell took any hardship concerns from the prospective jurors. That weeded out sixteen of the prospective jurors. She then gave a general overview of the facts before turning to her clerk, who pulled out twelve chits and filled the jury box. Winchell then questioned each on general biographical information and, when finished, looked at Hardy. "Mr. Hardy, you may inquire."

"Thank you, Your Honor, and good morning, ladies and gentlemen." He was upbeat but with a serious demeanor. "As the judge has already told you, my name is Sam Hardy, and I have the responsibility of representing Don and Kay Pouse."

He stood between the Pouses. Kay Pouse sat tall and erect. She was dressed professionally, with a pearl necklace and matching earrings which seemed, at least in my view, over the top, given the circumstances. Her husband sat hunched forward, elbows on the table. He sported a blue blazer and a white turtleneck over gray slacks. "They're good people. Don is a commodities broker, and Kay is in real estate. These folks have been blessed with one child, Devon. Devon is sixteen and won't be with us here in this trial."

Finished with the personalization of his clients, he worked his way to the jury. "You've already learned some of the facts from the summary Judge Winchell gave you. Let me fill in the rest of the story so that you have a proper context to assist you in answering some questions about your suitability to serve on this jury." He was pleasant and even a bit charming, in a gruff sort of way.

"You've already heard from Judge Winchell that on September 13 of last year, Devon Pouse, the defendants' son, suffered a psychiatric break and shot and killed three of his classmates." He paused, his face pained by the words. "That's a very hard fact, a tragedy that has caused incalculable pain and suffering. We've got the families of those boys with us here in court."

He took several steps toward the families, extending his arm to them. "It's difficult to imagine how they feel. Our hearts go out to them."

"Bullshit, you hypocritical ass!" screamed the father of one of the murdered boys, as he stood and pointed an accusatory finger at Hardy. "You fuckin' hypocrite!"

Hardy stood transfixed, gaping at the man. Complete silence in the courtroom. Winchell gaveled and ordered her bailiffs to remove the man, as he was pushing through the other family members to get at Hardy. The bailiffs wrestled him to the ground and carried him out as he screamed, "You have no idea how hard this is! That was my boy!" He finally collapsed in the arms of the bailiffs, sobbing as they carried him through the doors.

Winchell was hot. "I will tolerate no outburst in this courtroom. Any disruptions from this point forward will result in arrest." She stared at the audience for a long, poignant moment before turning to Hardy. "Mr. Hardy, you may resume."

Hardy, his face beet red, a prominent vein throbbing in his forehead, walked to his table and accepted water from his investigator. He drank with his eyes downcast and, without moving back to the jury, in a low, quiet voice, began. "I don't blame him for his conduct. He lost a child." Brief hesitation. "He lost a child." He repeated. "He needed to vent his despair. Hard to blame him for that. If our roles had been reversed, I might have done the same."

He slowly made his way back toward the jury, but then stopped and turned back to the families of the slain boys. "I owe you, the families of those boys, an apology. It was not right of me to presume to understand your pain. I'm sorry for that." He bowed his head and resumed his slow trek toward the jury. "As we have just seen, this trial will be emotionally charged. How could it not be?" He let his rhetorical aside hang in the air before going on.

Brilliant lawyering. He took what could have been a hard blow and turned it around. Brilliant.

"In a few minutes, I'm going to talk with each of you about the emotional aspect and how well each of you will be able to deal with it. But first I need to return to Don and Kay."

First names.

"They are devastated that their son took the lives of three other boys. I'm not in any way going to compare their pain to the pain of those families. But I can assure you of this. These parents are in pain, and they're at a loss to explain what happened."

A long, thoughtful look at the prospective jurors. "This trial will work toward an understanding of how this tragedy happened. And ultimately, that question will be left for you jurors to decide. But that question cannot be made with your hearts, it must be made with your intellect. Emotions and sympathies are not to play a part." He paused.

"Easy to say, tough to do. So my first question for the twelve of you is, can you do your best to somehow put your feelings of sympathy and even pity aside and take in the facts and make your judgment on the facts and the law you will hear during trial?"

He took a breath, then called on Juror Number Four, a man who, we earlier learned, worked in construction. "Sir, I apologize for not referring to you by name, but as the judge explained, we can't get into names, for security reasons." The man nodded his understanding. "Can you put your emotions aside and let the facts and law guide your decision?"

He cleared his throat. "All I can promise is that I'll do my best." His voice, rusty as an old iron gate. "These schoolhouse killings have gotten out of hand. It's not just my emotion that I will work on but my anger that this stuff keeps happening."

"I understand your concern, your anger. Everyone in this courtroom is struggling with those same concerns. As a juror, you will take an oath to follow the law. To somehow put the anger you feel about shootings aside and try this case only on the facts and law you will be presented with." He paused, then asked, "Can you do that?"

"I'll do my best." He didn't flinch under the scrutiny.

"That's all we can ask." Hardy nodded thoughtfully at him. "Now let's turn from thoughts of anger and return to thoughts of sympathy. The families who lost their boys are going to be here with us throughout this trial. The sympathy we feel for their loss is acute. But just as we must put our anger aside, we must also put our sympathy aside. Can you do that?"

Number Four didn't respond immediately but appeared to be

carefully considering. "I honestly don't know. Like I said, I will try very hard to do so. I'll try my best."

"Sir, that's the best answer any of us could hope for. I appreciate your thoughtful consideration." Sincerity graced with charm.

Hardy parked on these first points and worked through the jury box with mixed results. Two of the jurors admitted what I'm certain the others were thinking, that it would be nigh impossible to keep emotions from entering into their deliberations. Those two were excused for cause and others were called to fill their seats.

Winchell called for a morning recess, reminding the prospective jurors not to discuss this case or access any social media sites concerning the trial.

We resumed mid-morning. Hardy was still up. "We need to talk about guns and gun ownership. Don and Kay are gun owners; they have several guns. They like the protection guns provide. They also enjoy the recreational aspects of gun ownership. They target shoot and enjoy the benefits as members of a gun club."

He stopped and took an appraising look at the twelve faces. "Now there are lots of people in our society that detest guns, they wish there were no guns, and they might harbor hard feelings about gun owners. So in order for this trial to be true and fair, we need to know how each of you feels about guns and gun ownership." He put up his hands in an I'm-not-passing-judgment gesture.

"Juror Number Six, let's start with you. I noticed a disdainful look when I started talking about guns. This is your opportunity to tell us how you feel on the subject."

She didn't hesitate. It was as if she was waiting for a chance to go off. "I hate guns. I hate the violence and deaths they cause. Especially those automatic weapons we hear about. Since your clients permitted guns into their house, I'm inclined to believe they would be responsible for any evil that occurred." She spoke with the fervor of the righteous.

Hardy, with an understanding nod, replied, "Ma'am, thank you for your honesty. Your feelings are shared by many. You would probably agree with me that this trial may not be the right fit for you."

She took a breath, shrugged, and said, "I guess not." She was excused for cause.

That exchange was again brilliantly handled by Hardy. Instead of getting into it with her, he acknowledged her opinion and, in so doing, displayed his tolerance and understanding. This guy wasn't all bombast and ego. There were layers to this skilled trial lawyer.

Once he had finished working the gun issue, four other jurors and two replacement jurors were excused for cause. Guns and gun ownership were polarizing issues in this trial, as they are in society in general.

Hardy adroitly shifted gears. "Let's move from one difficult area to another. Devon's mental health. There will be testimony from a psychologist who spent hours with Devon, and she will testify that Devon suffers from a delusional disorder which included a paranoid episode on the day of the shootings." Hardy paused; he knew he was getting into murky waters.

"Now there are some who are skeptical about such matters. 'How convenient,' they'll think. So I need to ask, will each of you be willing to carefully consider such evidence? Will you be able to keep an open mind when a highly qualified psychologist is telling you how she came to her findings? Ma'am," he said, looking at Juror Number One, a middle-school math teacher, "will you be willing to consider the mental health of Don and Kay's son, which preceded the shootings?"

She looked confused. "I'll consider it, but I'm not clear on why that matters, since we're considering whether the parents are somehow responsible for their son's conduct."

"That's a fair point. My question wasn't focused enough. If, for instance, you find that Devon shot those boys out of some delusional paranoid episode, you might find that he acted without his parents' involvement."

Juror Number One, still with a perplexed look, replied, "I see your point. But wouldn't the parents know about their own son's mental health and do something about it?"

"Point taken, but that would presuppose that the parents were aware of his condition, and that will be an issue that will come up during the trial." The juror wrinkled her face. Hardy went on. "Let's return to the question I started with. Will you keep an open mind when you listen to the expert's testimony about Devon's mental health?"

"Of course I will."

There was no way in hell Hardy would leave her on the jury.

"Thank you." Hardy had managed to keep any exasperation out of his voice or his face, despite the difficult interaction. And now he was obligated to open the question of Devon's mental health to the balance of the panel. He slugged through it, encountering some headwinds.

There was always skepticism over psychological testimony, and perhaps of even greater concern to Hardy was the question voiced by the woman who raised difficult questions about such testimony. If Devon's condition was so deteriorated, how come his parents didn't recognize his problems and do something about them? It was not Hardy's finest hour. Nonetheless, the mental-health issue was out there, but it would force Hardy to thread a fine needle: Devon suffered a psychic break and yet his parents either never knew about it or knew about it but took no action.

Battered and bruised, Hardy persevered. "Folks, I appreciate you bearing with me. The trial we are embarking on, as you can tell, has several layers. We've covered a few of them: sympathy, guns and gun ownership, and mental health. There's still one layer we need to explore: parental responsibility. The prosecutor will assert that the parents acted criminally in failing to prevent this tragedy." He stopped and repeated, "Parental responsibility for the conduct of their sixteen-year-old son. In other words, should the defendants be responsible for the actions of another?"

"Objection, Your Honor. Counsel is mischaracterizing."

"How so, Mr. Clearwater?"

"These are not some generic defendants. The issue is about whether these two parents acted irresponsibly, which led to their minor child committing murder."

Hardy asked, "May I respond?"

"Mr. Hardy, rephrase your statement."

"You won't let me respond?"

"Rephrase, Counsel." It was indeed Winchell's courtroom.

Hardy's face evidenced incredulousness. He held Winchell's look, finally shrugged, and turned back to the jury. "I trust you folks understand what I'm saying." He grinned indulgently for their benefit. "We know from the judge's earlier questioning that many of you have children. From babies," he looked and smiled at Juror Number Eleven, who we earlier learned was a young mother, "to teenagers," he nodded to Juror Numbers Two and Nine and got nods in return, "to adult children." His charm and command of such detail without referring to his notes was exceptional. "So let's talk about parents and their children. Ma'am," nodding at Juror Number Two, "we earlier learned that you have two teenage daughters. How old are they?"

"One is seventeen and one is thirteen."

"Let me ask you about your thirteen-year-old. How important is your advice and guidance to her?"

"I hope it is very important to her. And I think that's how she feels."

"I understand. Let's contrast that with your seventeen-year-old. How important is your advice and guidance to her?"

"Oh, I think it is still important."

"Do you find that she is more independent than she was at thirteen?"

"Of course. I trust her to make her own decisions. She's much more out in the world. She's pretty independent."

"So you can't watch over all her decisions?"

"Objection. Is there a question in there somewhere that goes to the exercise of a challenge for cause?" Ostensibly, voir dire inquiries are to determine whether jurors should be disqualified due to some belief, association, life experience, and so forth. The reality is far different. Judges, at their discretion, may allow inquiries that run far from cause challenges. In my view, Hardy's last area ran too far afield.

Winchell didn't agree. "Objection overruled. However, Mr. Hardy, tie your inquiry back to this case." She was throwing Hardy a bone.

"Happy to do so. In your view, ma'am," he said, again directing himself to Juror Number Two. "Are older teenagers more likely to take on important decisions on their own? Do they always tell you what's going on in their life?"

"Sometimes, but certainly not always."

That response couldn't have been better scripted for Hardy. He wanted to establish some independence of a teenager like Devon from his parents. He worked that answer around the jury box, to mixed results.

"Your Honor, I have no further questions. Pass for cause."

CHAPTER 55

Following the lunch recess, it was my turn.

"Good afternoon." I made a come back motion with my hands. "I want to reel us back a bit from defense counsel's efforts and return to the basics. Amidst all the topics mentioned by defense counsel, we must keep in mind that this trial involves three deaths. The charge against the defendants is involuntary manslaughter. Now, that's a phrase we've all heard from time to time, but let's flesh it out a bit. A charge of involuntary manslaughter is appropriate when an individual engages in criminally negligent conduct which leads to someone's death."

I paused and again put up my hands. "Criminally negligent conduct? That involves a person or persons acting not just unreasonably but grossly unreasonably. It involves reckless conduct. And when that kind of conduct leads to death, that constitutes involuntary manslaughter." I stopped and studied the faces.

"Sir," I said, nodding to Juror Number Three, who we had learned was an electrical engineer, "can you accept the idea that if a person with no intent to hurt anyone is found to have acted criminally negligently or recklessly, they can be found guilty of manslaughter?" I needed a sharp individual to work through involuntary manslaughter. An electrical engineer qualified.

"I can accept that," he said, and nodded thoughtfully.

"And just to follow up, the person need not even intend that someone might die?"

"I understand," he said. "This is like when someone does something really careless while driving."

"Exactly. The guilty person doesn't have to intend harm, they only need to have undertaken conduct which led to the death."

He nodded his agreement.

"Let me stay with you one more moment. If the evidence convinces you that the defendants were criminally negligent in failing to supervise their son and that led to the deaths of three boys, will you be able to follow the law and convict?"

"Objection! He's asking this juror to prejudge the evidence."

"I disagree. It's a fair question," ruled Winchell. "Overruled."

I turned back to Number Three. "Sir?"

"Yes, if I was convinced that the evidence supported your point."

"Of course. Thank you, sir." I stepped back from Number Three and took in the whole jury. "How about the rest of you? If the facts are there to prove criminal negligence that led to death, will you hold the defendants accountable?" I worked some version of that question to the rest of the jurors and, with only a couple of minor questions, got the agreement I needed.

"Let's turn to another aspect of this case. This trial is only about these two defendants. Not about anyone else who was involved. For instance, you're going to hear testimony about the school where the shootings took place. About what the school principal did or didn't do. That testimony may get in the way of the focus of this trial. Now, there surely will be other lawsuits that will arise out of this tragedy, but they have no bearing on this trial. I need your assurances that you will keep your focus on whether these two defendants are guilty of manslaughter.

"Juror Number Eight" —a bus driver for LA Metro—"let's start with you. Will you be able to put any feelings you may have about the involvement of others aside and keep your attention only on the involvement of the defendants?"

"I get that," she said. "You're telling us that this is going to get complicated, right?" She smiled, completely at ease, in sharp contrast with most of her panel peers.

"It will. That's why I need you and the others to keep in mind only what this particular trial is about."

"That seems fair enough to me," she said, nodding agreeably. "So even if I think someone else might also be responsible, I'm only to decide whether the parents are responsible?"

"Well said, ma'am."

Juror Number Five, an accountant, broke in. "But what if we find that others may have had something to do with the deaths, do we just ignore that? That doesn't seem right."

"Great question. I don't want you to ignore any evidence. But your job, if you are selected as a juror, is to only assess the criminal liability of these defendants. If others should be charged or sued, that is for a different jury in a different trial." I moved over directly in front of him. I needed to nail this point down, especially in light of the school principal's failures. "Will you be able to keep your focus on these defendants and what they're charged with?"

"All right," he said cautiously, but seemed settled on the point. Once again, I worked my point through the prospective jurors. I received agreements. So far, so good.

"I have one final area I'd like to explore. That's about guns and gun ownership. Defense counsel went to great pains to explore gun ownership. I suspect that during the trial, he is going to suggest that a conviction in this case somehow will violate the Second Amendment."

"Objection!" Hardy was up and angry. "I suggested no such thing. However, Counsel—"

Winchell cut him off. "No speaking objections, Mr. Hardy." She gave him yet another admonishing look. "Let's hear from Mr. Clearwater."

"Thank you. The clear thrust of Counsel's questions implied that this case involves the Second Amendment. It doesn't, and to suggest otherwise mischaracterizes what this trial is about."

"I need to respond," boomed Hardy.

"No, you don't," Winchell responded in a commanding voice. "It's my job to explain what this trial is about and to keep it on the right track." She turned to the jurors. "Your verdict in this case has absolutely nothing to do with the Second Amendment. This is not a referendum on gun rights. The issue, the only issue in this trial, is to determine whether the defendants were criminally negligent in supervising their son, and should you find they were criminally negligent, whether their conduct was a cause of the deaths of the three victims." She took a steady, appraising look at the twelve. "Is that clear to all of you?" She got nods from everyone.

She turned to me. "Mr. Clearwater, in light of my comments, do you care to pursue your line of questioning?"

"No, you've done what I believed needed doing."

"Would you care for my reaction?" asked Hardy.

"Mr. Hardy, that won't be necessary."

"May we approach?" Hardy was intent on weighing in.

"Come." She waved us up.

"Judge, I feel like it's two against one here. You are consistently denying me opportunities to address rulings. In my experience, that's not how trials work."

"Counsel, I'm calling it straight down the middle. I understand you may not like some of my calls, but they're my calls." She looked him dead in the eye. "Is there anything else you want to discuss?" Getting no reaction from Hardy, we were waved back.

"Mr. Clearwater, do you have further inquiries of the panel?"

"No, Your Honor." Facing the jurors, I said, "Panel members, your patience in answering my questions is appreciated." Back to Winchell, I said, "Pass for cause."

And with that, Winchell gaveled us into the afternoon break.

Following the recess, we exhausted the cause challenges and were into the peremptory challenges. "Mr. Hardy, it's back to you. Do you have a peremptory challenge?" He challenged the Metro bus driver. Another prospective juror filled the seat. She was subjected to the same questioning as the others. And on it went. By 4:40, Hardy and I were down to one peremptory challenge apiece. Both of us were concerned that, should we burn our last challenge, we might catch a juror we would regret. Out of an abundance of caution, we both accepted the jury.

CHAPTER 56

The following morning, I stood, sans notes, took the gun from the evidence bag sitting on my desk, and placed it flat on my open hand. In a matter-of-fact voice, I began my opening statement.

"This is a Glock 19 semiautomatic. It holds eleven cartridges. It can fire all eleven rounds in seconds. It was purchased August 31 of last year by Kay and Don Pouse for their son Devon. Fourteen days later, this gun was used by the defendants' sixteen-year-old son to murder three of his classmates." I waited a bit, to let that sit.

Still holding the gun, I resumed. "As you already know from voir dire questioning, the boy who murdered Lincoln Riddel, Josh Fellows, and Mark Ivey is not on trial in this case. He will be tried separately. This trial is about that boy's parents, the defendants. They," I gestured at the parents, "not only bought him this weapon but ignored his cry for help and then completely abandoned any effort to supervise his use of this weapon of war."

"Objection to the 'weapon of war' characterization. That is complete nonsense."

Winchell gave me a discerning look. "Counsel?"

"How else should we characterize a weapon that can rapid-fire eleven bullets and kill three people in a heartbeat? A hunting weapon?" I couldn't help myself.

"Your sarcasm is not appreciated, Mr. Clearwater," Winchell admonished. "You've made your point, now move on."

"My apologies, Judge." I turned back to the jurors. "There is one thing that I insist we must do in this trial, and that is to keep in mind the three boys who were killed. I will not let them simply be referred to as victims." I walked over to where the families were sitting. "They had personalities, they had friends, loving families. They had their whole lives to live. They had dreams." I nodded to the families.

"Lincoln Riddel," I said, looking at the Riddels. "Lincoln's family, his mom and dad and his two sisters, are here. Lincoln was a popular guy who played on the basketball team. He wasn't a starter but he was a hustler and a scrapper, and everybody loved him. He planned on going to community college when he graduated and then hoped to get into a UC school."

I shifted and locked up with the Fellows family. "Josh Fellows. Josh's mom is here. His dad, you saw, was present before he was excluded for his outburst. You all witnessed his pain. Josh's older brother, Marc, is here. He's in the Marines. He got leave to be with us here during this trial."

Hardy stood and heaved a heavy sigh. "May we approach?"

We were motioned up. Winchell clicked off her microphone and looked at Hardy.

"There's only one reason he's introducing the families and that is to generate sympathy. It serves no purpose beyond that. It's irrelevant and unduly prejudicial."

Winchell gave Hardy a steely look. "I suppose when you make your opening remarks, you will have some personal things to say about your clients. Am I correct?"

"The families are not parties to this lawsuit."

With a simple "Overruled" from Winchell, we were motioned back. I took my time and resumed my place near the families. "As I was saying, Josh planned to follow his brother into the Marines." I shrugged. "He never got the chance."

I gestured at the mother of Mark Ivey. "Mark's mother is here; his dad passed away years ago. Mark was an only child. He was on the staff of the school's newspaper. He loved writing and always told others that his hero was Bob Woodward of Watergate fame. Even though the Watergate scandal happened years before he was born, he studied the events and was a bit of an expert on the details." I offered two small soft claps to the families. "Thanks for being here, all of you. Your boys will not be forgotten."

I made my way back to the jurors. "I'm going to be very meticulous as we work through the fourteen days from when the defendants purchased the gun for their son to the day he used that gun to kill."

"Objection! May I be heard?"

"Go ahead, Mr. Hardy."

"The gun was not purchased for Devon. Counsel's statement misstates the evidence that will be produced."

"Response?"

"The evidence will be unequivocal that the gun was purchased for their son," I answered matter-of-factly.

"Given that representation, the objection is overruled."

Fortified by the ruling, I doubled down on the point. "The evidence will be clear—that Glock was Devon's. It was purchased for him and he was obsessed with it. He knew about guns. His family was a gun family. The three of them were members of the Santa Inez Gun Club, where they would target shoot. The Pouse family was very familiar with guns. Devon was raised around guns."

I went back to counsel table and picked up the Glock again. "One of the questions that may surface during the trial is why Devon insisted and why the parents acquiesced in buying their sixteen-year-old a handgun. Handguns, as we all know, are easily concealable. In a pocket, a backpack, even a lunch box. Why a handgun? And why a handgun as potentially lethal as a Glock 19? The folks who know guns characterize this gun as a semiautomatic. That means the trigger has to be pulled for each shot. But it doesn't need to be recocked each time." I held the gun flat in my left hand and with my right, pulled an imaginary trigger five times. "Five shots, mere seconds, three bodies."

I walked back to the counsel table, laid the handgun down, and made my way back to the jurors. "Let's track the fourteen days from purchase to mass murder." There was some uneasy shifting in seats by several jurors, perhaps in anticipation of the hard facts they knew were coming.

I nodded for Detective Cipolla to illuminate the first PowerPoint.

AUGUST 31, 2018—14 DAYS FROM MURDER
MOM BUYS DEVON THE GUN

"August 31 began the countdown to murder. The clerk who sold the murder weapon will testify about his interaction with Kay Pouse and Devon. Since Devon was too young to buy a gun, it was his mother who supplied the necessary paperwork for the background check. She used her credit card for the purchase. The clerk will testify that it seemed clear to him that the gun was being purchased for Devon." I waited for a Hardy objection. Having already lost that scrimmage, he remained seated.

Cipolla clicked to the next PowerPoint.

SEPTEMBER 3, 2018—11 DAYS FROM MURDER
"JUST GOT MY NEW BEAUTY TODAY"

"Following the three-day background check on Kay, she and Devon picked up the Glock. The clerk handed the gun to Kay Pouse, and she promptly handed it to Devon. In addition to immediately posting on several social media sites that he 'just got his new beauty,' he sent photos of himself aiming the gun at the camera." A boy with his new best friend. The next PowerPoint popped up.

SEPTEMBER 6, 2018—7 DAYS FROM MURDER
"LOL, I'M NOT MAD AT YOU. YOU HAVE TO LEARN NOT TO GET CAUGHT"

"Let me put that statement by Kay Pouse in context. Seven days before Devon shot his classmates, he was sitting in class, and instead of being focused on schoolwork, he was searching his phone to buy ammunition for his Glock semi. That's right, sitting in a math class, searching for ammunition." I paused to let that register. "His teacher noticed what he was doing and called him out. He was sent to the school office, where the principal tried to talk to him, but Devon refused to talk. His parents were called and were requested to come to the school. They refused. That's right, neither defendant came.

You will hear from the principal that in speaking to both parents, neither seemed overly concerned about their son's conduct. To demonstrate their lack of concern, that very afternoon Devon's mom sent him this text. 'LOL, I'm not mad at you. You have to learn not to get caught.'" I felt no need to elaborate. Cipolla illuminated the next slide.

SEPTEMBER 13, 2018—TWO HOURS BEFORE THE MURDERS
DEVON'S CRY FOR HELP

"Seven days later, during third period on the day of the murders, the same teacher who earlier had caught Devon searching for ammunition saw Devon with a drawing he had made of a gun pointing at the words 'I'm useless, help me. I hate them all.' Once again, the parents were called, and this time they came to the school. The principal showed them the drawing and insisted they take Devon home and encouraged them to get their son help—some counseling.

"The defendants spoke to Devon. But somehow, Devon convinced them he was just having a bad day and that he was all right. And the parents refused to take him from school over the strong request, or should I say demand, from the principal. They both claimed work responsibilities. They left." I gave a perplexed shoulder shrug. "They left," I repeated, "and Devon was sent to his next class. And that semiautomatic Glock, all the while, was in Devon's backpack."

I stepped back. "Some of you are no doubt thinking, Why didn't the principal do something? And that's fair enough. However, as we discussed during voir dire, there will be other lawsuits. But this trial is about only those two." I pointed at the parents. "Only about their conduct, their part in this tragedy. With that in mind, let's resume our countdown to murder."

I motioned to Cipolla.

SEPTEMBER 13, 2018, 2:37—THE MURDERS
THE MURDERS OF LINCOLN, JOSH, AND MARK

"Just a little over an hour after the defendants refused to take their son home and get him the help he so desperately needed, Devon took his new beauty, followed the boys into the bathroom, and murdered Lincoln, Josh, and Mark. Lincoln with two shots, Josh one shot, and Mark two shots."

I motioned for Cipolla to turn off the PowerPoint and I moved up close to the decision-makers. "At the conclusion of the evidence, I'm confident that you twelve will find that the defendants facilitated these murders by buying their sixteen-year-old a murder weapon and then utterly abandoned any responsibility for their troubled son, leading to the murders of Lincoln, Josh, and Mark."

CHAPTER 57

Following the morning recess, Winchell signaled for Hardy. He heaved his bulk to his feet, shaking his head, and in a low rumble, began.

"This was a tragedy. A tragedy that these families"—nodding toward the families—"and students and staff at that school will live with for the rest of their lives." He stood back from the jurors so as to not overwhelm them with his size.

"And when we are confronted with a tragedy such as this, we want to lash out, to cast blame, to seek vengeance on those we feel were responsible. That's just what we do; we can't help ourselves." He cast a sidelong look at the families. "Isn't that what we do, isn't that our reaction?" He shook his head, his unibrow scrunched over his eyes.

"Who's to blame? Who is responsible?" He shrugged. "Those school officials who did nothing to intervene. Who didn't call in a psychologist? Who didn't suspend Devon Pouse and send him home? Who didn't check his backpack? How about the clerk who sold the gun? Should he have let the sale go through?"

Holding out his arms, "How about the gun manufacturer who built, promoted, and sent this gun out into the public? After all"—he gestured in mock disbelief—"who needs a semiautomatic handgun? And while we're at it, let's not forget the parents. After all, they bought the gun, and as the prosecutor likes to point out, they didn't pull him from school."

"Objection. May I be heard?"

"Go ahead."

"His comments are misleading. The defendants are the only ones on trial here today." Hardy's argument was fair. I just wanted to interrupt his momentum. Tactics.

"Overruled. Fair comment. Mr. Hardy, you may continue."

Hardy arched his unibrow, perhaps surprised that he got a call from Winchell, and resumed. "Or should we consider that the sixteen-year-old suffered some unforeseen delusional psychotic break, which led to this tragedy? We can cast a wide net for those responsible, but the evidence will establish that Devon Pouse just broke." He held up his hands as if to say, It's as simple as that.

"You're going to hear from a prominent psychologist who thoroughly examined and studied this troubled boy, and he's going to tell you that Devon suffered a paranoid delusional episode, which rendered him incapable of rational thought. Simply put, she will testify, Devon believed those around him were threats, deadly threats. He was confused and scared. And the evidence will establish that his parents didn't realize their son was struggling. He was sixteen; don't sixteen-year-olds have problems? Should his parents have done more? In hindsight, we can all agree they should have. But they just didn't know."

He stepped back. "Now we," motioning to the jurors, "discussed Devon's struggles during voir dire. Now I know there is a tendency to disregard evidence of mental and emotional problems. Some see it as an excuse for behavior. But you all agreed when I had a chance to talk with you that you would listen and evaluate all the testimony before passing judgment." Hardy paused, drawing up as close as his bulk would allow. "I'm counting on you to hold to your oath."

Hardy moved over behind me as I sat at counsel table. I think he wanted me to turn and face him but I resisted, even though it felt uncomfortable having this brute of a man hovering at my neck. "I'm going to suggest to you folks a possible agenda at issue in this trial. This prosecutor, doing the bidding of his office, knowing full well that Devon suffered some kind of mental break, is attempting an indirect attack on our constitutional right to bear arms, to own guns."

I was up and turned at Hardy, not more than three feet away. "Objection! He is impugning my motives. This is a personal attack; counsel should be censured."

Hardy, jabbing a finger at me, began to respond, only to once again be cut off by an angry Winchell. "I will see counsel in chambers immediately. We are in recess. Bailiff, please escort the jurors out." She jerked from her chair and stormed to the door leading to chambers.

Hardy and I held our positions, staring at one another. One of the bailiffs stepped over. "Gentlemen, chambers."

Winchell stood waiting for us and slammed the door after we entered. "What the hell! Are you two going to have a fist fight?" She took in a huge, stabilizing breath and slowly walked to her chair. We assumed seats. "Your behavior is not just unprofessional, it is despicable. You two can brawl on your own time but not in my courtroom. I'm holding both of you in contempt of court and fining you each $1,000." She let that take hold.

"Mr. Hardy, your personal attack was reprehensible. How dare you so flagrantly cross the line." Turning to me, "Counsel, you handled the exchange in an unprofessional manner. Instead of a simple objection, you virtually offered a physical challenge. I will not have it."

No one spoke. There wasn't much to say in our defense.

Winchell filled the vacuum. "Mr. Hardy, your opening statement is concluded."

Hardy registered disbelief. "I wasn't finished, Judge." His voice was mean, on the edge of threatening. The dressing down hadn't cooled him.

Winchell didn't flinch, and in a take-no-crap voice, repeated, "Your opening statement is completed, Mr. Hardy."

Leaning forward, Hardy said, "Judge, you are generating a rash of issues on appeal."

With a derisive grunt, she replied, "So be it. But I will maintain control over this trial. Appeal away, Counsel." She held Hardy's eyes. "I'm going to announce the lunch recess. When we resume, the prosecution will call its first witness."

CHAPTER 58

Jonathon Moore was the assistant manager at Dick's Sporting Goods. He was older than one might expect of an assistant manager. He was not pleased to have been subpoenaed to testify; he had made that known to Detective Cipolla when being interviewed. He had most likely been warned that he may be vulnerable in some later civil suit for selling the Glock to a minor. My examination of this uncooperative witness would be a slog.

Following brief preliminaries, I got to it. "Mr. Moore, now that we understand where you were working last August and September, let's focus on August 31. Tell us what you recall about the sale of this Glock semiautomatic I'm holding in my hand." I wanted to keep the gun visible for the jurors.

"It's been a while, and I'm not real clear on a lot of detail."

A classic chicken-shit I-don't-remember response. I knew this guy was going to make me work. His voice had a nervous edge, and he couldn't help but stare around the crowded courtroom—obviously, that he wished he were anywhere but where he was. It was time to dig in.

"Let's see what we can do, Mr. Moore," I said, shaking my head dismissively. "You certainly do recall the Pouse family coming into your store on August 31, correct? Just to confirm the actual date, you've seen the receipt of the purchase."

"I have."

"And you were the associate who sold the Glock on that day?"

Hardy said, "Counsel is leading the witness."

Indeed I was, and indeed I had every right to do so. During direct examinations, counsel are typically forbidden to lead their witness, the rationale being that since the examiner called the witness, the witness should and would be cooperative during the exam. However, as Hardy and the judge well knew, if during the direct examination the witness proved uncooperative, the examiner could resort to leading questions. It was obvious this guy wasn't going to play ball with me.

"Overruled. I'll allow it, as it seems there is some reluctance on the part of the witness."

I was right back at him. "Mr. Moore, do you have the question in mind or should I ask again?"

"I was the one who sold the gun." He stared defiantly at me. *If looks could kill.*

"Who first approached you?"

"It was the boy with his mother."

"That would be Kay Pouse and Devon Pouse?"

"Yeah."

"Was Don Pouse, the father, with them during the sale?"

"No, it was the mother and the boy."

"Between Kay Pouse and her son, who did most of the talking concerning the purchase?"

Moore shrugged. "I don't recall. They were both there."

"Is it your testimony that you don't recall who did most of the talking during the interaction?"

"Yeah, like I said, it's been awhile."

"If you had an opportunity to review the statement you gave Detective Cipolla, would that refresh your memory?" He damn well knew the answer and hoped I'd let his non-response slide. Fat chance.

He caved. "The boy was asking the questions."

"To be clear, that was about the Glock handgun that was eventually purchased?"

"That's right. The boy knew a lot about the gun but he kept asking questions."

"Did Kay Pouse ask many questions?"

"Yeah, she was involved."

"Is it your testimony that she was actively involved in the discussion about the gun?"

"Yeah, I'd say so."

"Mr. Moore, let's turn back to the statement you gave the detective following the shootings of the three boys. You understood that he was investigating the shooting deaths of three boys, correct?"

"I did."

"And you understood he was a law enforcement officer, correct?"

"I did."

"And further, you knew that it was a crime to supply false information to law enforcement, isn't that true?"

"I told him what I knew."

"That's right. You told him that almost all of the interaction that day was between you and Devon, correct?"

Hardy made no effort to stop my impeachment of this evasive—lying—witness.

"I guess that's what I said."

"You had no reason to lie, did you?"

"No, I didn't."

"Mr. Moore, it was your opinion that gun was being purchased for Devon, isn't that right?"

"Mrs. Pouse paid for the gun with her credit card."

How's that for a stupid response?

"Let me repeat my last question. It was your opinion that the gun was being purchased for Devon, wasn't it?"

"That's what it seemed like. But she paid for it."

Doubling down on stupid.

"You knew at the very time of the purchase that it was illegal to sell a gun to a minor, correct?"

"Like I said, I sold it to Mrs. Pouse."

"I understand your need to qualify your answer, but to be clear, you were well aware that you couldn't sell to a minor?"

"I was aware."

"After the three-day waiting period, Devon and Kay Pouse came in and picked up the gun, right?"

"Yes." It seemed that some of the starch had left Mr. Moore.

"And in your opinion, Devon was very pleased."

"I handed the gun to Mrs. Pouse."

Maybe a little starch was left.

"Mr. Moore, you saw her hand the package containing the gun over to her son, true?"

"Don't recall."

Unbelievable! Didn't this dolt realize he would just get impeached once again?

"Do we need to return to your earlier statement once again?"

Shaking his head, he said, "Seems like I recall her handing it over to the boy."

"Thank you, Mr. Moore. Your testimony has been enlightening."

Winchell looked expectantly at Hardy. "Mr. Hardy, cross-examination?"

From his seat, he replied, "If you'll permit it." Insolence was dripping from Hardy, still stinging from having his opening statement cut short. The skirmishes between Hardy and Winchell had escalated to a shooting war.

Winchell paused, considering whether to rebuke Hardy or again cite him for contempt.

My money was on another $1,000 contempt citation.

She stared at him, disbelieving his intransigence, the moment pregnant in anticipation, and finally she opted to exercise restraint.

Hardy acknowledged the pass and finally stood. "Mr. Moore, who did you sell that gun to?"

"Mrs. Pouse. It was always Mrs. Pouse. I don't sell to minors."

"Why not?"

Moore, relaxed now in Hardy's embrace, displayed perfect recall.

An amazing coincidence.

"It's against the law."

Hardy sat down after his perfunctory two-question cross.

Winchell called us up. "Mr. Clearwater, how long do you anticipate your next examination to take?"

"It could be lengthy; it's the school teacher."

"Okay, we're going to recess and pick up with your witness tomorrow."

The following morning. "Your next witness, Mr. Clearwater."

"The state calls Ken Green."

Cipolla retrieved Green from the hallway. The witnesses had all been excluded from the courtroom until called. Green looked like what he was, a high school math teacher. He was the perfect stereotype: tall, slight, gawky, and wearing glasses and an unfortunate tie sporting liberal doses of purple and green. The tie would clash with anything Green chose to wear. He sat in the witness chair with a self-deprecating smile. He reeked sincerity. I couldn't help but smile back at him.

"Mr. Green, before we get into the reason you've been called, tell us a little about yourself. Let us get to know you a bit." Some judges won't let the examiner engage in a little personalization, finding it irrelevant. I disagree. One of the toughest jobs for jurors is to ascertain which witnesses are credible. Who they can trust. It is my belief that getting some personal background on a witness helps the jurors in their evaluation of a witness's credibility.

"Certainly. I'm a high school math teacher." He missed my point and went right to his job. Happens all the time. People are not defined by their jobs.

I held up my hand. "Mr. Green, apart from your profession, tell us a little about yourself."

He looked a bit sheepish. "I'm sorry, I now understand what you were asking. I'm twenty-eight. I got married to a fellow teacher last year. My husband and I are in the process of adopting a child."

"Good for you, Mr. Green."

"Objection." Hardy had had enough of the personalization.

Winchell threw me a look.

I moved on. "How long have you been a teacher at Excelsior High?"

"Four years, teaching algebra and geometry to mostly juniors and seniors."

"Devon Pouse was in your third period algebra class, during the fall semester of 2018?"

"Yes."

"So obviously, you've had some interaction with him. What can you tell us about him?"

"Devon's bright. He was one of the top students in the class."

"Can you tell us from your observations how he got along with the other students?"

"He's kind of a loner. Looked to me like he didn't do much socializing. Kept to himself."

"What about his interactions with you?"

"We talked. Mostly about course stuff. Nothing personal."

"Did anything about Devon's behavior prior to the shootings strike you as odd?"

"Objection," said Hardy. "Calls for opinion testimony. This witness is not a psychologist or psychiatrist."

"Overruled. He can testify to his specific observations."

Green looked unsettled. I prodded. "Do you have the question in mind?"

"Yes. He often seemed distracted. A couple of times I had to call him back from wherever his mind had drifted." He then added, smiling, "But that's not terribly unusual with high school students."

"I want to now focus on two particular days during September of last year. The first is September 6, Wednesday, a week before the shootings. During the third period class, tell us what you observed."

"The students were doing an exercise I had assigned. While they were working on it, I walked around the room to monitor their work." He hesitated, looking troubled. Difficult memories.

"Go on, Mr. Green."

"When I got to Devon, he wasn't working the assignment. He was on his phone, looking at a website advertising guns and ammunition."

"What did you do?"

"I pointed to his phone and asked, 'What's this?'"

"Did he respond?"

"He looked at me and in a matter-of-fact-voice, said he was looking to buy ammunition for his gun."

"Did he say his gun?"

"He did."

"Did that concern you?"

"Yes. We're instructed to be vigilant when it comes to guns and such."

"Then what?"

"I took his phone and told him to report to administration."

"Did you go with him?"

"I did. I turned my class over to my student intern."

"While the two of you were walking to the administration building, did you talk?"

"No, it only took a minute or so to get there. I told the front office that I needed to talk to Principal Conklin. She wasn't busy, so we went right into her office. I told her what I had seen and handed her Devon's phone."

"Then what?"

Green shrugged. "I left it with Ms. Conklin and went back to my class. I've got to confess, I was a little shook up."

"Why?"

"There've been so many school shootings. I guess I was worried."

"Did you see Devon later that day?"

"No, I didn't."

"Did you talk with Principal Conklin about it?"

"No, I figured she had handled things."

"Did Devon return to your class the next day?"

"He did. Seemed like everything was more or less back to normal."

"Were you at all apprehensive about Devon?"

"Apprehensive is too strong. It was difficult for me to completely erase what had happened."

"Okay, I want to move forward seven days to September 13,

the day of the shootings. Devon's in your third-period class. Tell us what you observed."

Green took a deep breath and looked off to his side at nothing. He was working to maintain his composure. School shootings weigh heavy.

"Do you need a moment, Mr. Green?"

He hunched his slight shoulders and made an effort to lock onto me. "I'm okay."

"What did you observe?"

"I was walking around the room, monitoring exercises, and saw Devon drawing on a piece of graph paper."

"Could you see what he was drawing?"

"It was a crude drawing of a gun pointing at the words 'I'm useless, help me. I hate them all.'"

I retrieved a document encased in a plastic sleeve from my table. "Mr. Green, would you recognize that drawing if I showed it to you?"

Nodding yes, he said, "It's imprinted on my mind."

"Your Honor, I have what's been pre-marked as People's 1 for identification. May I approach the witness with Exhibit 1?"

Winchell gestured her assent.

"Mr. Green, I'm showing you People's 1 for identification. Do you recognize it?"

"I do. That's Devon's drawing."

"Move People's 1 into evidence."

"Any objection Mr. Hardy?"

"No objection." Hardy didn't bother standing.

"Leave to post an enlargement of the Exhibit 1 on PowerPoint?"

"You may."

Cipolla lit up the exhibit. I watched the jurors absorb it.

"What did you do at that point?"

"I was very concerned for Devon's well-being. Especially after the first incident with the ammunition. I took the drawing and told Devon to come with me to administration."

"Describe Devon's demeanor."

He grappled for an answer. "Apathetic, listless."

"What happened when the two of you got to administration?"

"I pretty much barged into Ms. Conklin's office with Devon. I showed her the drawing. She asked me a few questions that I don't recall."

"And next?"

"That's the last time I saw Devon."

I let that sit. "Mr. Green, thank you for your testimony. I know it was difficult, but you hung in there. I appreciate that."

Winchell: "Ladies and gentlemen, we'll take our morning recess at this time."

Winchell: "Mr. Hardy. Your witness."

Hardy rose and strode over near the jury box. "Mr. Green, your answer about being concerned for Devon struck me. When you saw that note, your thoughts were for Devon's well-being. Did I hear that right?"

Nodding yes. "That was my first thought."

"Your thoughts were not about Devon being potentially dangerous?"

"No."

"Your thoughts weren't about Devon possibly hurting anyone?"

"No. Like I said, my concern was for his well-being."

"Mr. Green, as a high school teacher with some experience, would it be your opinion that the actions of high school kids can sometimes be difficult to understand?"

"Sure." It was clear that Green didn't want to disagree with Hardy.

Couldn't blame him for that.

"I imagine from time to time, some of your students have done something unpredictable, true?"

If Green was going to offer any resistance, this would be the place. For instance, nothing as unpredictable as murder. But the compliant Green went along with Hardy. "Sometimes you just don't know what's going on in their heads."

"I agree, Mr. Green." Hardy's use of Green to showcase that teenagers were sometimes unpredictable, even flaky, was well done. And by extension, it wasn't just high school teachers who were occasionally baffled by their behavior, but also their parents.

CHAPTER 59

Friday afternoon. "Next witness, Mr. Clearwater."
"The people call Juliet Conklin."

Conklin was wearing a conservative business suit. She was ushered in by Cipolla and looked ready to pass out. She had been chewed up by Hardy at the second preliminary hearing and clearly feared another onslaught. Eyes huge, darting everywhere. She couldn't have been more stressed if she knew the witness chair was electrified. I tried to ease her anxiety by working through a brief personalization, which only exacerbated her distress. I cautiously moved to the preliminaries concerning her job before settling on September 6, the first time Green ushered Devon into her office.

"Ms. Conklin, describe Devon's demeanor when he was brought to you that day?"

She hesitated, sipped some water. "He was withdrawn. I tried to get him to talk to no avail. I told him that his behavior was inappropriate, He just sat there, unresponsive."

"And next?"

"I called his parents. I reached Mrs. Pouse and explained what had happened."

"Her response?"

"She didn't see Devon's behavior as a serious concern. When I suggested that she or her husband pick Devon up, she laughed and said, 'Don't make a big deal out of it. He didn't do anything wrong.'"

"She laughed?"

Nodding. "Yeah, laughed."

"How did her reaction to your call strike you?"

"Objection." Not relevant.

"Sustained. Mr. Clearwater, move on."

"Did she or her husband come to school to pick Devon up?"

"No, they didn't." She shook her head and went on. "I debated about what to do. Finally, I sent him back to class. I did keep his phone. I wanted to eliminate the distraction."

"You didn't hold him in the office for the rest of the day?"

"No. I didn't see the point."

"Tell us about the text message that appeared on Devon's phone later that day."

She licked her lips before speaking. "A little before two o'clock, there was a text message from his mother."

"Go on."

"Objection." Hardy was up. "This witness had no right to look at a private message on Devon's phone. That's a violation of his Fourth Amendment rights."

I was ready. Frankly, I was surprised Hardy hadn't raised his objection during the pretrial motions. "May I speak to the objection?"

"Counsel approach."

Winchell nodded for me to respond. "As this court is well aware, the Fourth Amendment only restricts law enforcement, not school officials."

Hardy looked at Winchell and got the go-ahead. "The Supreme Court has found that when school officials assume the role of law enforcement, the Fourth Amendment against unlawful search and seizure applies to them."

Winchell turned to me. "The principal had not assumed the role of law enforcement. She was merely functioning to maintain a proper environment in her school. There was no law enforcement purpose being served here."

Hardy broke in. "How was a proper school environment served by snooping on a student's phone?"

Ignoring the interruption, I went on. "The student's use of the phone had already proved disruptive." Winchell's skeptical look was not encouraging. I switched tacks. "Beyond that, even should this court find that the principal was somehow acting in a quasi-law enforcement capacity, Mrs. Pouse has no standing to assert her son's Fourth Amendment rights. The only one who could assert Devon's rights is Devon. It was his phone." Standing is a constitutional restriction limiting those who could assert a violation. Only the person who allegedly suffered the violation can raise an objection to that alleged violation.

Hardy, without seeking Winchell's permission, replied, "Judge, this was a private communication between a mother and her minor son. What could be more privileged than that?"

Winchell looked thoughtful. "Mr. Hardy, I take your point. But Mr. Clearwater raises standing. Even if the Fourth was violated, she can't assert. The objection is overruled."

Hardy was livid. He slowly walked back into his chair and slapped the table. Winchell let the tantrum go unpunished.

Hardy had erred. First by not bringing a pre-trial motion to exclude the text, and second by not objecting when I posted it during my opening statement. Unforced errors. By my reckoning, Hardy's forceful objection only called the jurors' amplified attention to whatever he had been trying to exclude. Even though the jurors had already heard about Mrs. Pouse's text, they had to realize it must be particularly significant to provoke Hardy's effort to keep it from them.

Having beaten back the objection, I had a clear path. I slowly walked toward the jurors and, savoring every word, asked, "Principal Conklin, what did the message from Mrs. Pouse to her son say?"

Conklin, seeming a bit more relaxed, replied, "LOL, I'm not mad at you. You have to learn not to get caught."

Twelve sets of eyes, actually thirteen sets of eyes, including Judge Winchell's, flashed at Kay Pouse. She looked down, staring at nothing. Even though her text was no longer a surprise, it still reverberated.

"Ms. Conklin, what did you think when you read that text?"

"Judge, calls for the witness to speculate."

"Your Honor, I'll withdraw my question. The jurors can draw their own conclusions." Conklin's answer was unnecessary; it had been my intention to park on the text to allow the full impact to hit the jurors. It already had.

"Very well."

"Okay, let's move forward," I said to Conklin. "Did you have any interaction with Devon from that day to the day of the shootings?"

"No, I didn't." She hesitated and stared hard at me. "I wish I had. Maybe I could have helped him."

"How so?"

"I don't know, exactly." Her eyes were suddenly wet, her voice husky. "Based on what happened," she labored on, "he certainly seemed troubled. Maybe by talking with him, counseling with him, I could've helped." Her voice trailed off.

"Ms. Conklin, do you need a moment?"

"No, let's just get through this." She let out a long breath.

I gave an understanding nod. "As you wish. Let's turn to September 13, the day of the shootings. We've heard from Ken Green that he again brought Devon to your office during third period. Describe what happened."

"Ken walked into my office with Devon. It was obvious that something had happened. Ken didn't even knock. He pointed Devon into a chair and handed me his drawing."

"What did you think when you saw that drawing?"

"Objection!" Hardy, against all his instincts, waited for Winchell's permission.

"Basis, Mr. Hardy."

"Lack of foundation. He's asking this witness to testify outside the witness's expertise."

Winchell looked at me to respond.

"I'm not going to ask Ms. Conklin for any psychological or psychiatric observations but rather what she thought in her role as a high school administrator."

"The objection is sustained. Rephrase your question."

"Ms. Conklin, share with us your thoughts from your perspective as a high school principal."

She took in another deep breath and swallowed. "Devon was obviously troubled. This, in my view, was a cry for help."

"Did you and Mr. Green try to talk to him?"

"We did, but he refused to respond."

"He just sat there?"

"Yes."

"What happened next?"

"Ken Green left to go back to class and I called Devon's parents."

"Did his parents come to the school this time?"

"They did. After I explained what had happened, I showed them the note and left them alone with Devon in my office. After about twenty minutes, they came out and reported that Devon was responsive and wanted to explain his conduct."

"Tell us about your conversation with the parents outside Devon's hearing."

"I expressed my concerns about Devon's stability and suggested in clear terms that he needed professional counseling."

"Their response?"

"Mrs. Pouse accused me of overreacting. She said that if her son was sent to counseling, it would permanently brand him as a person in need of psychiatric care. She was concerned that it would affect the rest of his way through high school, and more importantly, it could hurt his ability to get into a good university."

"Your response?"

"I explained that any treatment or counseling would be confidential and that her concerns were unfounded. She was not convinced."

"Anything else discussed?"

"Again I stressed that they take Devon home and get him counseling."

"Were they receptive to that?"

"No, they weren't."

"So what happened then?"

"The three of us went back into my office. Devon seemed more alert. With some coaxing from Mrs. Pouse, Devon gave assurances that he was all right and that we were all making a big deal out of nothing. He said he was just having a bad day." Conklin shrugged. "The four of us sat in the office talking, trying to get a sense of Devon's well-being."

"What happened next?"

"His parents explained that they needed to get back to their jobs and that Devon should finish the school day."

I held up my hands. "They wouldn't take him home?"

"No, they stressed that they needed to get back to their jobs."

"Did they leave?"

"They did. Over my protest."

"What do you mean?"

"I again stressed that despite Devon's assurances, he needed counseling. But they ignored me and left."

"What happened then?"

"Frustrated and against my professional instincts, I told Devon to go to his fifth period class."

"We need to pause here. That decision obviously proved fateful. Tell us why, from your perspective, Devon was allowed to go back to class."

"I was at a loss. His parents wouldn't take him, he hadn't broken any laws, there wasn't anything to warrant getting law enforcement involved."

Incredulous, I put up my hands. "So you sent him back to class?" My challenge question was intended to give the witness an opportunity to explain her conduct.

"In hindsight, that was catastrophic," she said, in frustration. "Even after I had strongly advised his parents to take him home and get him some help, they refused." She gushed on, wanting to somehow justify her actions. "At that point, he seemed rational. He hadn't done anything to call in law enforcement. So, God help me, I sent him back to his classes."

With her head down and seemingly only to herself, she continued, "I'm going to have to live with my part in this tragedy for the rest of my life."

"At the time you allowed Devon to go back to class, were you aware that he might have access to a weapon?"

"Of course not. Had I known that he had access to a gun, that would have changed everything."

"How so?"

"I would've checked the backpack."

"Thank you, Ms. Conklin. No further questions."

CHAPTER 60

How would Hardy undertake his cross? Would it be in his best interest to beat up on the principal who had exhibited remorse for her failures? He had certainly done that during the second prelim, with devastating effectiveness. However, the prelim was before a judge, not twelve jurors. A sharp cross of this woman could well alienate some of the jurors. Conklin was certainly an easy target; however, her vulnerabilities didn't necessarily exonerate Hardy's clients.

Hell, there was blame enough to go around.

Another approach would be to play nice and work the angle that if this school professional was at a loss at how to deal with Devon, what could be expected of the parents? Was it reckless conduct for the parents to not understand their son's conduct and take appropriate action?

Hardy began nice and easy. "Ms. Conklin, I appreciate how poorly you feel about this tragedy. Your remorse does you credit."

Plan B, playing nice. At least to start.

"During your first encounter with Devon on September 6, you were made aware that Devon was on his phone, checking out sites to purchase ammunition, correct?"

"Yes," Conklin warily replied, intimidated by the prospect of Hardy once again tearing into her.

Hardy continued in an understanding, even sympathetic, voice, "When you learned that Devon was looking at ammunition sites on his phone, you weren't worried that this boy was dangerous, were you?"

She hesitated, worried about some kind of trap. "No, it didn't occur to me that he was dangerous."

Nonchalantly, Hardy shrugged. "You probably thought he was acting inappropriately, given the school environment?"

Conklin, still guarded, replied, "I did. Like most schools, we have a no-phones-during-class policy." She gave a short nervous laugh and added, "Phones are not conducive to a learning environment."

"That makes perfect sense. You've most likely had to discipline other students using their phones during class?"

Conklin was loosening up, but still on guard. "Happens every day."

"So phones in class are a frequent event?"

"They are," then added, "but in Devon's case, he was on a gun site. That was unusual." Finally an answer that didn't acquiesce to Hardy's question.

"I appreciate you pointing that out. But as we agreed earlier, you didn't consider him dangerous."

"But it was unusual enough to call his parents." Again, mild pushback.

Hardy nodded understandingly. "But to return to my question, you didn't consider his conduct as presenting any kind of a threat?"

"No, I didn't."

"Ms. Conklin, as the school principal of Excelsior High, you have an understanding of who the problem students are, correct?"

Conklin nodded. "We have 1620 students. I don't know all of the problems that crop up on a daily basis, but I have a pretty good grasp of problems and problem students."

With a questioning look, Hardy asked, "To your knowledge, Devon has never presented a discipline issue to you or, to your knowledge, to anyone at the school in his two-plus years at Excelsior?"

"To my knowledge," she replied.

"And just to be clear, any serious discipline problems would have been brought to you?"

"That's correct."

"And to your knowledge, Devon had not had any fights or any kind of altercations with any fellow students, correct?"

"I'm not privy to everything that happens at my school. I'm sure there are minor conflicts happening all the time. Bullying and such."

"So to conclude the point, Devon had never been a discipline problem?"

"That's correct."

"Principal Conklin, let's move to September 13. That drawing Devon made concerned you?"

"Of course it did."

"That drawing depicted a gun?"

Conklin tensed and hesitated, perhaps sensing that Hardy was moving into attack mode. "Yes, there was a drawing of a gun and some disturbing words."

"As a school principal, you are hyper-aware and concerned about school-place shootings?"

"I think we all are."

Pushback.

"But as the ultimate authority figure at the school, you, more than anyone, bore the responsibility to keep your students and staff safe from violence, right?"

Conklin's face hardened, her eyes locked on Hardy. In a bitter tone she said, "I am the principal and, of course, I'm focused on preventing violence in my school." She paused; her initial trepidation of Hardy was giving way, and a spark of anger was lit. "As I said during my earlier testimony, I have taken responsibility for my conduct. I made a serious mistake. But the responsibility, Mr. Hardy, to ensure that our schools are safe, doesn't just rest with me and my teachers and my counselors. It also rests with parents and caregivers." She took a breath but wasn't finished. "We at school may see only the tip of the iceberg; parents see and understand so much more."

Whoa! Conklin making a stand.

In response, Hardy jerked off the gloves.

No more Mister Nice Guy.

His voice firmer, a notch louder, he stepped up closer to Conklin. "Principal Conklin, you would agree, as the school principal, your knowledge that Devon was fixated on guns and appeared to be unstable on the very day of the shootings presented real concerns, yet you failed in your most important job—to ensure the safety of your students and staff."

Conklin, leaning forward, shot back. "Had I known he had an easily concealed handgun, I would have handled things differently. They"—looking at the Pouses—"had that knowledge." She hesitated, gathering her thoughts, and went on. "I've admitted my failing. It's time for others who had the most critical information to admit their failings."

Score six for the principal.

Hardy was right back at her. "You made no effort to counsel him, to reach out to him during those seven days before the shooting?"

"That's on me. I wish I had."

"To be clear, you made no effort for that entire week?"

"I didn't."

"Nor did you instruct your school counselors to bring Devon in to discuss the incident?"

"Like I said a number of times, when he was released to go back to class, he seemed okay. I still felt he would benefit from counseling, but that was his parents' responsibility."

"So, not only did you make the decision to not counsel with him during those seven days, but you allowed him to return to his classes for the next day and on through the week.

"I've explained why."

"I want to examine some other options available to you during those seven days. You had two counselors at your school, correct?"

"Yes, I did. They were tied up with other matters that day and not available."

"Correct me if I'm wrong, but those counselors are trained to deal with students who appear to be troubled, isn't that right?"

"As am I."

"But you didn't call in either counselor that day?"

"Objection. Asked and answered." I wanted to give Conklin a brief reprieve.

"Overruled. Different question."

"Like I said, they were unavailable."

"But you could have delayed your decision to return Devon to class while you waited for one or both to confer with, isn't that right?"

"I made my decision based on the information I had."

"But you could have waited for their input?" Hardy wouldn't be put off.

"Yes."

"Another option available to you was to call the school district's central office and ask for help?"

"I didn't think that necessary." Conklin bit off her response. She was holding her own. Anger can be an equalizer.

"In fact, Principal Conklin," queried Hardy in his take-no-prisoners voice, "you were fully aware that there was a psychologist trained in adolescent behavior on call to deal with serious problems, weren't you?"

"I was aware. Given my limited knowledge of the facts at the time, I didn't think it was necessary."

"So despite Devon's fixation with guns and despite evidence in that drawing of a troubled and unstable teenager, you felt that it was not necessary to call in a trained, qualified psychologist?"

"In hindsight, I wish I had."

"So do the families of those three boys."

Hardy had crossed the line.

"Objection!" I shouted, jumping from my chair. Excited chatter broke out in the courtroom.

An angry Winchell, her face flushed, ordered silence, then motioned us up.

"Mr. Hardy"—barely getting the words through her gritted teeth—"you are once again in contempt. This one is going to cost you $5,000, and I'm going to report you to the State Bar. Your comment was despicable."

Hardy grunted but had enough sense to shut up. Yet another death stare between the two. Finally, Winchell motioned us back.

Winchell turned to the jury. "As you most likely ascertained, Mr. Hardy's comment was highly improper, and to the extent you can ignore his comment, I urge you to do so."

Bells are indeed tough to unring.

Hardy's cheap shot didn't buy him any goodwill with the jurors. Most were eyeing him with disapproval. The good guy approach he had started his cross with had been trampled in the dust.

Hardy then offered one of the most insincere apologies ever uttered on the North American continent. "If my comment offended anyone, I apologize."

"If my comment . . ." When is an apology not an apology?

Seemingly unfazed, and protected by rhino-thick skin, Hardy dared to go on. "Ms. Conklin, you had yet another option available to you before you released Devon back to the class. And that was to simply hold him in your office for the rest of the school day. But you didn't take that option either, did you?"

"No, I didn't. His assurances that he was just having a bad day seemed sincere. His parents, who I had to believe knew him better than I did, felt he was okay." She gave an equivocal shake of her head. "I let him return."

"Yes, you did," he said. "I have nothing further for this witness."

"Mr. Clearwater, let's take a brief recess before your redirect examination."

Cipolla and I retired to the attorney conference room. I was hot. "I'm going to jam Hardy's cross down his throat."

"This should be entertaining," Cipolla said, grinning.

CHAPTER 61

"Just a couple of questions," I began. It was time to turn the focus back on the Pouses. "Principal Conklin, let's talk about what you didn't know. Did you play any role in purchasing the Glock semiautomatic handgun used to kill the three boys?"

"Objection."

Winchell: "You put the principal's conduct at issue. Overruled." Winchell was going to let me ride it out.

Giddy-up.

"Of course not," Conklin answered, without me repeating the question.

"Did you have anything to do with leaving that weapon in a place in the Pouse home where this sixteen-year-old could access it?"

"No, I had nothing to do with how Devon got hold of that gun."

"Were you aware that the weapon we are talking about was an easily concealed handgun?"

"No idea."

"Were you aware that that handgun could fire eleven times in mere seconds?"

Conklin shook her head no, before answering no.

"On September 6, the day Devon was caught searching for ammunition, did you call his parents?" I was mirroring my redirect from the second prelim. It was effective then and I believed it was proving effective now.

"I did."

"Did you urge them to come to school and discuss their son's conduct?"

"I did."

"Did they come?"

"No."

"On the day of the shootings, just an hour or so before the shootings, did you urge the defendants to take their son home?"

"In the strongest possible terms."

"On that day, did you show them Devon's drawing?"

"I did, and again, in the strongest words, I urged them to take Devon home and get him some help. They refused. They accused me of overreacting."

"One last point. Did you check Devon's backpack, which contained the Glock, before you released him back to class?"

"No."

"Why not?"

"I assumed his weapon was some kind of rifle. If I had known it was a handgun, that would've changed everything."

"How so?"

"If I'd known it was a handgun, I would have checked his backpack. I would've found the gun, called the police, and none of this would've happened." She flashed to Kay Pouse, "Three boys would still be alive."

"Objection. I ask that the answer be stricken. He's asking this witness to speculate."

"Overruled. The witness can testify as to what her actions might have been. She's not speculating."

I looked at the twelve in the box. Several were nodding. It's a comforting feeling to end the week of testimony on a high point.

CHAPTER 62

Monday morning, I called Jesse Blank to the stand. Blank was the first deputy on the scene. He was young, with only one year on the job. He was tight creases and close-cropped hair, a military bearing.

Following brief preliminaries, I asked, "Deputy Blank, you were the first law enforcement officer to respond to the shooting on September 13 at Excelsior High. When did you arrive?"

"I received a dispatch at 2:46 p.m. So, within minutes of the dispatch."

"What did you do upon arrival?"

"I was contacted by a school custodian in the parking area, who pointed in the direction of the north annex."

"Go on."

"I had my service revolver out and cautiously made my way to where he directed. As I came around a building, I saw an individual slumped against the side of a building. There was a handgun lying at his side."

"What happened next?"

"At gunpoint, I ordered the individual to lie on his belly."

"Did he comply?"

"No. He just continued to sit there. He was unresponsive. Out of it."

With a nod, I urged him to go on.

"I approached and held him at gunpoint and retrieved the weapon."

"Then what?"

"My sergeant arrived and took over."

"Your Honor, I have a photograph of Devon Pouse marked as People's 2. May I approach the witness?"

"Yes."

"Deputy, is this the individual you took into custody that afternoon?"

"It is."

"Move People's 2 into evidence."

"It's received."

I retrieved the Glock and handed the gun to Blank. He checked the ID tag and confirmed that it was the gun he took from Devon. The gun was also received into evidence.

"Thank you for your service, Deputy. I have no further questions."

Judge Winchell: "Mr. Hardy."

Hardy, from a seated position, "You described Devon as unresponsive. In your words, 'out of it.' So I take it he didn't interact with you in any way?"

"That's correct sir."

"Even as you were holding a gun on him, he didn't follow your command?"

"That's correct."

"Did he put up any resistance whatsoever?"

"No, sir."

Hardy put up his hands in an "I'm finished" gesture.

The judge nodded. "Okay, let's take our morning recess."

"Mr. Clearwater?" Winchell asked, following the recess.

"Call Sergeant Roger Hence."

Cipolla ushered Hence in. From my prelim hearing preparation, I learned that Hence was a former Marine and a twenty-two-year veteran of the LA sheriff's department. He looked the part. He was a solid five ten or so with a crew cut and a hard face. A smile might crack his stony countenance. After scant time on the preliminaries, I got right to it.

"What time did you arrive at the scene that afternoon?"

"Right at 1500, or 3:00."

"Describe the scene at the school when you arrived."

"It was in lockdown."

"Your actions?"

"I pulled in next to Deputy Blank's vehicle and was directed to his location."

"Describe what you saw."

"Blank and two other deputies had a suspect in custody. I radioed our position and directed arriving deputies to fan out and secure the surrounding area."

"Why?"

"At the time, I didn't know if the suspect was the only shooter."

"Then what?"

"Then Deputy Blank reported that a custodian"—he checked his notes—"a Mr. Perkins, told him the shots came from the boy's restroom fifteen feet or so from where the suspect had been taken into custody."

"Go on."

"I moved to the door of the bathroom and yelled for anyone in there to come out. I was concerned that another shooter or shooters might be inside. No one responded. After repeated calls for anyone to emerge, I pushed open the door and immediately saw an adolescent male on the ground who appeared to be unresponsive. I entered and found two other adolescent males. All appeared to have been shot. None were responsive."

It was one of those moments when everyone in the courtroom collectively took a breath. Some, most likely family members, audibly sobbed. The Second Amendment folks, confronted with the reality of three dead teenagers, were subdued. Some of that crowd left the room.

I noticed that Hence's eyes glistened.

"Sergeant, are you okay to continue?"

"I am." He looked up at me. "In my time in the Marines, I've seen my share of bodies. But I never expected to see three boys, right here where I live, gunned down and killed." He took another breath. "It's something I'll never get over."

I nodded my understanding. "Please go on."

"The scene was secured. EMTs confirmed that the three individuals were deceased. The deputy coroner arrived and began her initial investigation. I then ordered in the forensics team and contacted the DA's office to apprise them of the situation. Shortly thereafter, Detective Cipolla arrived on scene to assist with the investigation."

"Your Honor, I have no further questions of Sgt. Hence."

Hardy passed on cross-examination.

Winchell ordered a lunch recess and ordered us back to her chambers. We settled in, but no one spoke. Hence's testimony had been hard on everyone. Winchell broke the silence, looking at me. "Where do we go from here?"

"I'm going to bring in the coroner to identify the victims and testify to the causes of death. Then we'll hear from the forensic analyst who will link the Glock to the fatalities."

"Let's not do that," said an uncharacteristically subdued Hardy. "This is what I was most concerned with. The anger and the sympathy. Judge, the prejudicial impact of dwelling on the causes of death, which I assume will include autopsy photographs, is just too great. We can avoid that. I'm willing to stipulate that Devon fired all the shots that caused the three deaths. God help us, we don't need photographs of the dead boys. And I say this as much to spare the families of the boys as anything else. They've suffered enough."

Winchell looked at me.

I hesitated, thinking through the ramifications. Hardy was right, it would be devastating for the families. "If the stipulations include that Devon Pouse was the shooter. That he killed the three boys with the Glock purchased on August 31st. Also, I want yearbook-quality photographs of the three boys displayed to the jury."

Hardy agreed. Winchell wrote out the stipulations to the jury and then read them back to us.

Following the lunch break, Winchell read the stipulations and explained their impact. I felt a release of tension in the courtroom. No one wanted to see the horrific photographs of the three murdered boys.

As Winchell concluded reading the stipulations to the jury, a bailiff came over to Cipolla and pointed to the courtroom door, where a sheriff's deputy waited. Cipolla slipped to the door and returned just minutes later. He leaned over to me. "Devon Pouse is dead. Hung himself at the psych hospital."

I sat dumbfounded. I looked hard at Cipolla and stupidly asked, "Is there any doubt?"

"No. It happened an hour ago."

I stood. "Judge, we need to retire to chambers."

Winchell looked puzzled but then nodded. "Ladies and gentlemen, my apologies, but I need to confer with the lawyers."

Before we even sat, I said, "I've just been informed that Devon Pouse is dead. He hung himself an hour ago."

Hardy's body jerked. He stretched out an arm and groped for the couch against the far wall and collapsed into a seated position. Winchell leaned on her desk. I took a chair. Silence.

As the shock wore down, my mind was working. Grief for the Pouses. Quickly followed by what this means for the trial. I know it sounds callous, but I was calculating how Devon's death would impact the jurors. Sympathy for the Pouses? Was there any other way the jurors would react? Or might some harbor even more disdain for the parents, since they didn't get Devon any help? The entire trial could turn on its head.

Judge Winchell was the first to voice her thoughts. "How can a person in a psychiatric facility hang himself? How could that happen? Isn't everything they could use to hurt themselves taken from them?"

"No place is absolutely foolproof." Hardy quietly spoke as he was slumped on the couch. "Several years ago, up in the Bay Area, I had a client who hung himself in a jail cell. He tore his uniform into strips, made a noose, tied the end to the frame of his cot, and hung himself in only a foot or so. I'm told it's extremely painful. The person actually suffocates."

"How terrible," Winchell said, as she walked around her desk to her chair. "Isn't that how Robin Williams died? I think I recall he hung himself from a doorknob."

Hardy shrugged yes, and worked his way up from the couch. "I've got to tell Kay and Don."

"Wait a minute," I said. "We've got to think this through. If the jurors learn of this, it could compromise the trial."

"Screw that, Clearwater. These parents just lost their child. I need to tell them."

"Hold on, Mr. Hardy," Winchell demanded. "He's right. We

need to assess. If you have to wait a few minutes to inform the Pouses, so be it."

Hardy was incredulous. "They just lost their only child. The trial be damned."

"No, it will not be damned," Winchell said, and told Hardy to resume his seat. "Mr. Clearwater, your thoughts?"

"If the jurors learn of this, any chance of a fair result is compromised."

"So now the shoe is on the other foot." Hardy was incensed. "You're afraid the sympathy will now flow to my clients. Didn't bother you when you had all the sympathy."

"Sympathy should not weigh in on this trial on either side," Winchell intervened.

"I think we need to sequester the jury for the duration," I said. "I'm ready to rest my case. We're only talking a couple of days."

Hardy rose. "You two have been conspiring against me and my clients since this trial got underway. I'm certain any input I offer will be disregarded."

"Mr. Hardy, given the circumstances, I'm going to let that statement slide. But that's it." She stared at him. "I see no option other than to sequester the jurors. Should they learn of Devon's death, it will impact the jury." She waited for Hardy's reaction. Hardy just shook his head. Winchell went on. "Mr. Hardy, I'm certain your clients would like to have some time off. We'll adjourn for the day and tomorrow and resume Wednesday."

"Can I go now?" Hardy asking permission like a high school kid asking to leave the vice principal's office.

"Of course. But wait until I adjourn before you inform the Pouses."

We re-entered the courtroom. Winchell told the jurors that due to unforeseen circumstances, they were to be sequestered. They were understandably upset and, of course, had questions and concerns, which Winchell deftly fielded. She explained that they would remain sequestered in a nearby hotel for the balance of the trial. She also announced that she would hear any concerns from any of the jurors who felt that being sequestered presented an undue hardship. The next hour was taken up with two jurors claiming hardship. Winchell found one concern pressing and dismissed that juror. The second claim was denied. The first of the two alternate jurors was sworn in. Both alternate jurors would also be sequestered. The trial was adjourned until Wednesday. The jurors were to be bused to a nearby hotel. When we concluded, I watched as Hardy escorted Don and Kay Pouse to the adjoining conference room.

I didn't envy him.

CHAPTER 63

On the way home, I phoned Lisa and filled her in. "Oh my God. Those poor people. I can't imagine losing a child." She took a breath. "And now these parents are undergoing a trial for their conduct. Life can be cruel."

In light of her previous misgivings about my prosecution, I hesitated before responding, picking my words carefully. "They certainly didn't deserve this. How tragic this whole ugly chapter has been." I paused. "As badly as I feel for them, I keep thinking if they had just gotten some help for Devon, could this have been avoided?"

There was a long silence. "Jake, it's not for us to know. Maybe counseling would have helped. Maybe. Maybe not."

"We'll never know. I'm still processing what happened and what's still to happen." I took a deep breath. "I should be home in an hour."

I stayed home Tuesday. Paddle-boarded on the glassy ocean for several hours, letting my mind go wherever it would. It didn't drift far from the trial. Nor far from the four dead teenage boys, now that Devon Pouse had been added to the carnage.

Wednesday morning in chambers, Hardy informed Judge Winchell and me that Don Pouse had fired him. That's right, fired him. According to Hardy, Pouse felt he was being vilified because of his wife's conduct. He wanted a lawyer who would represent his interest instead of being brought down by his association with Kay. He didn't want to be lumped in with her.

How noble of him, lay it off on the wife.

However, as I thought about it, maybe Pouse had a point. Even though he was Devon's father and presumably had acquiesced to the Glock purchase, the testimony from the clerk didn't put him in the store for the purchase. Kay, it seemed, was the prime mover. It was Kay who immediately turned the Glock over to Devon. It was also Kay who sent Devon the LOL text message excusing his behavior in searching for the ammunition.

On the other hand, Don, along with Kay, had refused to come to school following the ammunition incident and, more alarmingly, had refused to take Devon home on the day of the shootings. Beyond that, Don, as one of two adults in the household, apparently didn't monitor his son's access to the gun. His conduct was far from exemplary—however, in comparison to his wife's conduct, not as egregious.

Infuriated by Hardy's bombshell, Winchell ripped into him through clenched teeth. "At the very outset of this trial, you assured me there would be no problems with you representing both parents." She checked herself, laboring to maintain composure. "Yet here we are in the closing days, and one of your clients wants out." She slapped her desk. "This is unacceptable on so many levels."

Hardy, not one to back down or admit a mistake or, for that matter, to apologize, responded, with a complete lack of contrition, "No one could have foreseen this eventuality. No one." He flexed his massive hands before responding. "Devon's death is the catalyst of Don's request. He doesn't want to be seen as the cause of his son's death."

What? I didn't follow that logic.

Winchell's face contorted in confusion. Apparently, she too, didn't follow Pouse's logic. "I'm not sure how he reasoned that." She became angrier as the exchange went on. "Back to my point. Despite your assurances to the contrary, we have a serious problem, and as far as I can see, you are the cause!" *Judicial temperament be damned.*

Hardy put out his hands in a mollifying gesture. "I have a solution."

The architect of the problem had a solution. Give me a break.

Winchell would not let go. "Yeah, the solution should have occurred to you weeks ago when you represented that there would be no problems with you representing both parents."

"Let me suggest a solution," he persisted.

Winchell leaned back in her chair. "What?" she snapped.

"I will continue to represent Kay, and I reached out to Tom Strong. He's willing to represent Don."

Winchell looked confused.

"Isn't Strong doing television commentary on the trial?" I said, surprised.

"That's right." Hardy rushed to follow up. "Just like you did on the Cort trial." Apparently Hardy had done his homework on me. I had done commentary during the first Cort murder trial, which resulted in a hung jury. Following the mistrial, I had then been appointed by the DA to prosecute the retrial. "That makes him a good choice to step into the trial. He's been watching it from the beginning. He shouldn't need much time to get up to speed."

Winchell shook her head dismissively. "This seems too bizarre. Is this some kind of manipulation, Mr. Hardy?"

Hardy's credibility was below the water line.

"Because I feel like I'm being manipulated." She stared hard at

Hardy, radiating skepticism. "So let me see if I have this correct. Just since Monday, two days ago, after the Pouses learned of their son's death, Don Pouse decided he needed a new lawyer, and you and he have already made arrangements for him to retain a replacement lawyer? This just doesn't smell right."

Winchell shook her head and looked at me. "Mr. Clearwater, you've been remarkably quiet. Your thoughts."

I put up my hands. "This is not a problem of my making."

"Nor mine," Winchell snapped at me. "Yet here we are. And just for the record, Mr. Clearwater, if we can't get this resolved, we could have a mistrial on our hands, and that's not good for anyone. So, back to my question. Does bringing in a new lawyer this late in the trial raise reversible issues?"

"I don't think so," I said, thinking it through, "as long as we get the appropriate waivers. And there is some merit in bringing in a lawyer who is already steeped in the details of the trial. I don't know Mr. Strong, but since he is doing commentary, I assume he is up to the job."

Fair assumption?

"I can vouch for him. He's an experienced trial lawyer," Hardy assured us. Hardy's assurances didn't carry much weight.

I ignored Hardy's comment. "Assuming he can step right in," I said to Winchell, "that's a real plus, since we have a sequestered jury sitting on their hands in hotel rooms."

Winchell was still slumped in her chair and working to adjust to the new reality. "Maybe this is our best path forward after this completely preventable development." She looked at Hardy. "Can you get him, whatever his name is, in here tomorrow morning?"

"I think so."

"Okay, we'll adjourn to tomorrow. I'm going to send the jury back to their hotel and tell them that the trial will most likely resume

Monday. I want to give this replacement lawyer, if he is going to come in, time to acclimate."

She looked at Hardy and shook her head. "I'm uncomfortable with this plan, but I want to avoid a mistrial and keep this trial on the tracks."

I filled Nancy Seah in on the morning's developments, asking if she saw any landmines I might have overlooked. Her advice was to get appropriate waivers. Neither one of us wanted any conviction we might achieve thrown back on appeal. Guarding against the machinations of a win-at-all-cost lawyer like Hardy, always a good strategy.

Thursday morning, the courtroom was half-empty. Strong was present. He looked like a lawyer you'd see on television, right down to his perfect pocket square that matched his perfect tie. He was on the shorter side, goateed, with dark hair brushed straight back. He had a confident swagger.

"Welcome, Mr. Strong," said Winchell. "I'm sure Mr. Hardy filled you in on developments."

"He has, Your Honor."

"I understand you've been following the trial quite closely."

"I have. I've been in the courtroom from day one. I'm doing commentary for Channel 6."

The same station I had given commentary during the first Cort trial.

"Are you willing to give up your commentary and represent Don Pouse?"

"I am."

"This will not be at the state's expense. You'll need to make arrangements with Mr. Pouse."

"Already done."

"As you are then aware, Don Pouse has asked me to terminate his representation by Mr. Hardy and appoint you as his counsel for the balance of the trial," said Winchell, keeping the record in mind.

"I am aware of the circumstances, and should you allow me to substitute in, I stand willing and ready to step in as Don Pouse's lawyer."

"Mr. Pouse, please stand," Winchell ordered. "I need to make certain you fully understand the consequences of terminating the services of Sam Hardy and requesting that I allow Tom Strong to step in as your attorney."

"I do."

Winchell then went through a lengthy process that I hoped would withstand appellate review. Of course, appellate review would only be an issue if there was a conviction. No guarantees there. Once Pouse acknowledged his understanding, Strong was appointed. Strong said he would be ready to proceed Monday. Winchell got further assurances from Pouse and Strong that the short window for preparation was adequate. She was guarding against an ineffective-assistance-of-counsel claim on any possible appeal.

CHAPTER 64

Unexpectedly, I had some time on my hands. Friday morning I stayed home, got up before Lisa, made us breakfast, and volunteered to drive her to work. I called Duke and invited him to lunch. It had been several months since we had caught up. He lived in Santa Paula, a half hour inland from San Arcadia.

Noon, Emelia's Mexican just outside Santa Paula. I had several hours to kill before lunch and killed them at Vintage Books.

Duke beat me to Emelia's and greeted me with a smile. "What brings you out to the hinterlands? Aren't you in trial?" he asked, with a good-natured shake of his mostly bald head. "I saw on the local news that you're in a controversial trial. Something about stiffing the Second Amendment?" That brought a laugh.

Duke was a longtime friend. We had met while I was a DDA in San Arcadia and he was a district attorney investigator. He was the best investigator I ever worked with or most likely ever would work with. We worked four or five trials together while still in the DA's office before I left for Pacifico. About that time, he hung his private investigator shingle. I hired him a few years later to assist me in our successful defense of Duane Durgeon. And more recently, I lured him to Los Angeles last summer to help with the high-profile Cort murder prosecution.

Duke was dressed as he usually dressed. A checkered short-sleeve button-up shirt a size too small. The buttons strained to contain his belly. He had on blue jeans and white Converse high tops.

"There's a lull in the trial, so I'm taking the day off. I drove Lisa to work, and here I am."

"Glad you called. Tell me about this controversial trial." He smiled good-naturedly. "Apparently you're really pissing off the gun crowd."

We ordered Coronas, chips, salsa, and Emelia's famous chili rellenos. Occasionally you find a restaurant that does something better than anyplace else: Emelia's rellenos.

"I didn't set out to piss anyone off, it just sort of happened. Since you've been following the news, you know that I'm prosecuting the parents for providing their troubled sixteen-year-old with a Glock semiautomatic that he used to kill three classmates."

"Sounds pretty controversial to me." Duke grinned as he was wiping salsa off his shirt from an overloaded chip. "So why the days off mid-trial?

"It's a mess." I explained the circumstances.

"Why was this dumbshit trying to represent both defendants? That seldom goes well. Starts off okay but frequently ends up in a ditch."

"We're in the ditch now. I'm hopeful we can get back on the road."

"I've got to say that going after the parents is bold. And now with the kid killing himself, I don't know."

"The jurors don't know the boy killed himself. We're keeping that from the jury."

Duke sat back. "You're right, it's a mess."

"And to make it even more of a mess, at least for me, I'm getting some pushback from Lisa."

"She didn't want you to go after the parents?"

"Yep."

He took a healthy swallow of beer. "I'm not sure I disagree with her."

"Come on, Duke, a disturbed sixteen-year-old with a semiautomatic handgun?"

He leaned back and put up his hands defensively. "I know, but still. Tough case."

Lunch arrived and we dug in, letting the discussion wane. Between bites, Duke asked, "So other than the trial being a mess, how's it going?"

"Bought a house in Bruno Keys."

He dropped his fork. "You buried the lead." He gave a disbelieving look. "Bruno Keys is blue blood. You win the lotto?"

"Actually, Lisa bought a house in Bruno Keys."

"I'm lost."

"My brilliant and talented wife is loaded."

With the briefest of hesitations, he said, "Her paintings?" Duke put things together quickly. Nice trait for an investigator.

"Yep."

Duke pushed back and laughed. "You sonofabitch. Not only is she gorgeous and sexy as hell, but also rich." He continued laughing. "You're living the life, Jake."

"I'm well aware of that." I beamed in agreement.

While I was still enjoying the moment, Duke suddenly switched back to the trial. "So the trial ain't going so well?"

"Got a real piece of work as defense counsel."

"Who is it?"

"Sam Hardy, a real ass. He's wrestling for control of the courtroom."

"I'm sure you're holding your own."

"I don't know, it's a daily battle. Got a pretty tough judge who is working to keep him in check."

"You gonna win this thing?"

"I don't know," I said, forking in a mouthful of incredible rellenos. "I just don't know."

We let that set for a while.

"Let me throw out a stupid idea."

I eyed him carefully. Duke never had stupid ideas.

"First, let me back up a bit. It strikes me that since you took a leave from teaching to get back into trials, maybe you've worn out your appetite for teaching and want to be back in the courtroom, even after your current gig is up." I carefully put down my fork, took a drink of Corona, and stared at him. He wrinkled his ample forehead questioningly. "Have you given any thought to hanging a shingle in San Arcadia?"

"Where in hell did that come from?"

"I'm a trained investigator. Just assessing the facts. Your move north to Bruno Keys, your leave from Pacifico, and getting back in the courtroom seemed to suggest to me that something was brewing." He put up his hands in an I'm-just-saying gesture.

"Duke," I said, smiling, "you're a piece of work. The idea never crossed my mind. At least till now." I brushed the thought away. "Beyond that, I don't think I could do full-time defense work."

"Hey, I'm not pushing you. Just putting the pieces together. Besides that, tell me you didn't get off on representing Durgeon in the death-penalty case a while back."

"Durgeon was a one-off. If I ever change my mind, you will be the second one to hear about it."

"Right behind Lisa."

"Exactly."

Lisa and I shared some appetizers for dinner on San Arcadia's wharf. I wasn't hungry after that heavy lunch; neither was she. Over dinner, I mentioned Duke's comment about moving back north and opening an office, gauging her reaction.

Her beautiful face framed her question. "Where did that come from?"

I explained Duke's thoughts.

She considered, cocked her head, and asked, "Would that ever happen?"

I gave a dismissive shrug. "I'm real happy at Pacifico and as I've said, I'm not built for defense work."

CHAPTER 65

Monday morning. Judge Winchell introduced Tom Strong and explained to the jurors that he was now representing Don Pouse. Winchell cautioned that they were not to speculate why Strong was now representing the husband. Even as they were being cautioned not to speculate, they were busy speculating.

The judge turned to me. "Mr. Clearwater, any more witnesses for the state?

"No, Your Honor, the state rests."

"Very well. Mr. Hardy, the defense case on behalf of Kay Pouse?"

"Before we proceed, I have a motion to be heard outside the presence of the jury."

Winchell: "Ladies and gentlemen, I apologize once again, but I need you to return to the jury room." Some of the jurors shook their heads as they filed out. I couldn't blame them. Especially after days spent in a hotel. Some, if not all, had to be surly at what they perceived as their mistreatment.

Hardy, as was his due, made his motion for acquittal, arguing I had not met my burden. Winchell listened patiently and, after Hardy's steam had played out, looked at Strong. "Mr. Strong, any motions?"

"I join in the motion articulated by Mr. Hardy."

I stood to respond.

"No need, Mr. Clearwater. I'm not taking this case from the jury. The motion to dismiss is denied."

Hardy, with attitude: "Were you even listening?" He punched out each word.

Winchell didn't flinch and was back at him in a heartbeat. "That remark will cost you another $5,000, Mr. Hardy. Payable to the clerk by the end of the day."

I don't know what Hardy was charging, but the contempt fines had to be cutting into his fee.

Hardy remained standing in defiance.

Winchell said, "Mr. Hardy, at the risk of yet another contempt citation, do you care to be heard further on the matter?"

Without answering, Hardy slowly sat.

"Bailiff, please bring the jurors back."

They filed in. A disgruntled lot, from their looks. They had been tossed and turned, shuttled in and out of the courtroom, and taken from their homes.

Addressing Hardy, Winchell asked, "Now that we are back with our jurors, will there be a defense case on behalf of Kay Pouse?"

Hardy turned to the jury. "Ladies and gentlemen, there will be no defense case on behalf of Kay Pouse. We'll stand on the evidence."

Hardy's decision to present no witnesses and not put his client on the stand made sense. He was protecting her. Once she had testified, attempting to justify and rationalize her conduct, I could have at her. And he knew that would be a bloodbath. She presented a target-rich environment. I would have enjoyed the cross.

While keeping Kay from testifying made sense, not calling a mental health expert was stunning. He had promised the jurors during voir dire and during his opening statement that they would hear from an expert that Devon had suffered a psychotic break. I could only surmise that whoever he had retained had not delivered on what Hardy needed. Either the evaluation had not gone far enough to conclude that Devon had suddenly suffered some kind of breakdown, as Hardy had promised, or the expert had diagnosed Devon with a pre-existing psychological condition that would most likely have been apparent to those around him, including his parents. In either case, Hardy apparently didn't have an oar to paddle.

Winchell, nonplussed at Hardy's decision, turned to Strong. "Mr. Strong, will there be a defense case on behalf of your client?"

"Yes, there will be, Your Honor. Don Pouse will testify." That elicited a stir from the assembled, which Winchell quickly stifled.

Hardy lumbered to his feet. "This comes as a surprise and also presents some complications." And in an overly contrite tone, "May I be heard?" Perhaps the contempt fines had finally hit their mark.

While Winchell briefly considered the request, Hardy plowed on without leave. "There are privileges that will be compromised." Hardy had spoken out of school. His comments in front of the jurors were provocative and could only increase the jurors' desire to learn what they might be precluded from hearing and who was responsible for precluding them.

Fundamental mistake. Hardy's antagonism with Winchell again clouding his judgment.

Winchell held up her hand for Hardy to stop. She turned to the jurors and apologized to them and again ordered them back to the jury deliberation room. There was some subdued exasperated laughter from several of the jurors. Their plight was taking its toll.

We adjourned to chambers and Hardy went after Strong. "You put him on the stand, he's going to blame his wife, and in the process, violate marital privilege. There's no way that's going to work."

Strong looked at Winchell for permission to respond. She nodded. In a voice not in the least cowed by Hardy, he responded,

"My allegiance is to my client, and my client demands that he be allowed to testify. That decision rests exclusively with him." Turning to Hardy, "I need not clear it with anyone. Including you, Sam."

"Dammit, Tom. We rest on the facts and argue no culpability at closing. That's the correct path. Don's testimony jeopardizes both Kay and Don."

Strong shrugged. "He insists on testifying."

Winchell let the dust settle. "Mr. Strong, might your client's testimony raise marital privilege concerns?"

"That is a concern I've raised with Mr. Pouse. He understands that he cannot testify in any way against his wife, and he will not testify about any conversations with his wife. He will simply explain his conduct and how it relates to the events leading to the shootings."

"What fantasy are you living in, Tom?" Hardy was adamant. "Marital privilege won't allow one spouse to testify against the other. How do you propose to get around that?"

"He's not going to testify against Kay. He's simply going to testify as to his own conduct, not Kay's." Strong appealed to Winchell. "I understand Sam's concern. However, my client's got an absolute right to testify in his own defense. He can't be denied that."

"I take your point, Counsel." Turning to me, Winchell asked, "Mr. Clearwater, any thoughts?"

"I think Mr. Strong is correct. Pouse can't be precluded from testifying. But with that said, his testimony will be walking a fine line. Every answer must be free of any testimony implicating her in the shootings, as well as free of any confidential communications with his wife."

"Fair comment and fair warning," said Winchell.

"May I comment?" asked Hardy.

"Go ahead."

"I'm putting everyone in this room on notice that, should

my client be convicted, you all are providing excellent grounds for appeal."

Winchell sat back and grinned. A genuine grin, not an incredulous grin, not a sardonic grin, but a genuine grin. Seems she had worked her way to being Hardy-proof. "It occurs to me, Mr. Hardy, that had you not taken on both Pouses at the outset of this trial, we wouldn't be dealing with the number of issues your foolish decision has created."

Hardy sat back, his mouth agape. He was speechless.

That was a moment to savor.

"All right, Mr. Strong, we'll take your client's testimony following our morning recess."

CHAPTER 66

Following the recess, and with the jury once again in attendance, Winchell said, "Mr. Strong, will there be any witnesses of behalf of Don Pouse?"

"Yes, Your Honor, Mr. Pouse will testify."

Pouse stood from the end of the defense counsel table and walked hunched over like a man taking his final steps to the gallows. He wore his grief, worry, and anxiety like fifty-pound sacks of sand lashed to his back.

Following the oath, Strong began, "Don, please tell the jurors why you are testifying."

Looking down and speaking almost too low to hear, he replied, "First, I wanted to express my apologies and regrets to the families of the boys lost. I know that doesn't help, but I needed to say it."

Strong nodded earnestly and asked, "Are there any other reasons you are choosing to testify?"

"Yes, I need to try and explain my conduct leading up to all this." Carefully avoiding eye contact with his wife, he added, "I'm not going to cast any blame, but I want to explain my own unforgivable part in this terrible tragedy."

"Okay, let's begin with your relationship with Devon."

Following a fortifying breath, Don began. "I tried to be a good father, but looking back, I now realize I spent too much time on my career and not enough on my son."

"Describe the interaction with your son."

"I didn't do enough father–son things with him." A long pause. "I should have done better. Much better." He dropped his head. "I loved him but didn't take time to show it."

"How so?"

Pouse gave Strong a weary look before reluctantly answering. "We didn't spend much time together. When he was younger, I wasn't there to watch him play soccer or basketball. Seemed like I was always too busy with work." He hesitated, and Strong waited to see if there was more.

Shaking his head, Pouse went on. "I'm in a high-stress job. I'm a commodities broker, which demands a great deal of time, along with the stress of the job." He took a fortifying breath. "I was a poor father."

"I appreciate your candor, Don. Let's talk about your family's membership in a gun club. Why a gun club?"

Flexing his jaw and looking down and off to the side, his voice still husky and low, he said, "When I was a kid growing up in Bakersfield, my father had several rifles. He would take me out to the desert and teach me how to safely handle guns. I wanted my son to be familiar with safe gun ownership, so we joined a gun club. I hoped he would learn gun safety. It was one of the few things we did as a family."

"You mentioned rifles; any handguns?"

He shook his head.

"Don, you have to answer out loud."

"Sorry. No, my experience was always with rifles, not handguns."

"We've heard testimony that back before the shootings, a handgun was purchased. Were you present when the gun was bought?"

An emphatic "No."

"Were you even aware that it had been bought?"

"No."

"Were you aware that the handgun was in your house after it was purchased up until the time of the shootings?"

Shaking his head, he said, "I had no idea." His eyes flicked to Kay. "Like I said, I work a lot of hours, and sometimes I wasn't aware of what was going on in my own home."

"Were you aware that in early September, Devon sent a text saying, 'I got my beauty today' with a photograph of the handgun?"

Becoming more assertive, Don replied, "If I'd seen that, I would've taken the gun away."

"Why?"

"That's a semiautomatic weapon. It's dangerous. It's not something that I wanted around the house, especially with a teenager."

Strong picking up the cadence. "We've heard testimony that on September 6, a week before the shootings, Devon was caught using his phone to search for ammunition during class. You were contacted by the school to come in and discuss Devon's behavior. But you didn't go to the school and meet with the principal. Why not?"

Pouse leaned forward, eager to explain. "When I heard Devon was looking at ammunition, it didn't seem like that big a deal. I mean, we have several rifles. I guess I assumed he was looking at ammunition for the rifles." Pouse stopped and once again shrank back in the witness seat. "I wish I'd gotten more involved."

"What do you mean?"

Pouse took some steadying breaths and fidgeted with his hands. His voice was low again, husky with emotion. "I should have gone to the school and had a better idea of what Devon was doing." He dropped his head.

Strong let Pouse collect himself. His eyes glistened. Finally Pouse mumbled, "If I'd been a better father and not so focused on my job, those boys and my boy might still be alive."

Dammit! Devon's death was now out there. I was on my feet, my hands out to the judge in a what-are-we-going-to-do now gesture. I then flashed to the jurors. Pouse's revelation was not lost on them or on the packed courtroom. They were stunned, trying to fit Devon's death into the greater picture. The trial had tilted at its core.

Winchell gaveled. "We are in recess. I'll see counsel in chambers."

As I walked back to chambers, I thought back to Murielle Ramirez's testimony in which she inadvertently referred to "boys" instead of just "Oscar." In that trial, Murielle's slip seemed to have been missed by most of the jurors. No such luck this time. Would learning of Devon's death fundamentally change the trial? Would it generate sympathy for the parents? Winchell had agreed with me that Devon's death should be excluded for that very reason. Or would it make them seem even more neglectful? Were my chances of conviction compromised? Enhanced?

I certainly had grounds to move for a mistrial, which I'm certain Winchell would grant. But prosecutors rarely take such action. We'd invested better than two weeks on this trial. I didn't want to lose that.

We settled into chairs. Winchell unzipped her robe and carefully hung it. I think she figured this was going to be a lengthy discussion. She sat and studied me. "Jake, let's start with your reaction."

I shook my head and gave a bitter grunt and looked at Strong. "Mr. Strong, I don't hold you responsible. Witnesses caught up in emotions, especially such hard emotions as dealing with a child's death, can't always be counted on to do as promised."

"I appreciate that. I thoroughly discussed that with him. It just came out."

"I agree," said Winchell. "Nonetheless, here we are at yet another crossroads. Where do we go from here? Jake, back to you."

"I'd hate to lose two weeks of trial, but I'm still mulling over how this plays with the jurors." Hardy was conspicuously quiet. He stood to win either way. With a mistrial, it would be months before a second trial. That's if the DA's office opted for a second trial.

Would the Elders opt to burn another couple of weeks on this difficult and controversial trial, where convictions were uncertain at best? However, if the trial continued, Hardy and Strong had some sympathies working in their corner to offset the sympathies of the three dead boys.

I studied Hardy, who was earnestly staring out the window at nothing. "Let's go forward," I said, "but under certain conditions." Hardy didn't move and kept his gaze out the window. He had to be sensing an advantage.

"First condition, we draft a stipulation to be read by the judge informing them of Devon's death by suicide. But no particulars. Second, there will be no mention of Devon's death during any examinations or during closing arguments."

A surprised Winchell studied me and without a word turned to Hardy.

Hardy, ever so casually, said, "I can live with that."

Strong: "Okay by me."

"Okay, we'll take our recess." Winchell looked at me. "Jake, you draft the stipulation, and once it's approved by defense counsel, we'll resume."

"One more thing," Hardy said. "Now that Devon's death is out there, I see no further need to sequester the jury."

Winchell nodded. "Thank you for reminding me, Mr. Hardy. I'll release them to return to their homes when we finish for the day."

Winchell read the stipulation to the jurors. It included language that they were not to consider Devon's death in their deliberations. I felt obliged to include that instruction, knowing it was pointless. It was fiction, but the courts treated it as gospel. However, if I did get convictions, I didn't want an appellate court to consider that Pouse's revelation worked in my favor and should have been excluded.

Pouse was recalled and Strong resumed his direct examination. "Mr. Pouse, from the time of learning that Devon had searched for ammunition up to the day of the shootings, were you aware the handgun was in the house?"

"No," Pouse said, his voice unsteady.

"Let's turn to that terrible day. You came to the school that day. Why?"

"It was the second call from the school in just over a week. I couldn't ignore that."

"You were shown Devon's drawing with his words 'I'm useless, help me. I hate them.' You talked to Devon about that drawing and those words?"

"I did." A tear worked its way down his face, and his nose ran. He wiped his face with the sleeve of his jacket, sucked in some air, and went on. "When I talked to him, he seemed to have pulled himself together and told us he was just having a bad day. He seemed okay. I told him we would talk that evening." As his voice trailed off, he added, "I honestly thought he was okay."

"Thank you, Don. Is there anything else you want to say?"

Through his tear-stained face, Pouse looked up at the cluster of the victims' families and in a voice choked with anguish said, "I am so sorry for what happened. I know it doesn't help, but I need to say it." I felt some disturbance behind me. It was Lincoln Riddel's mother standing, with tears of her own.

"Don, I forgive you. I accept your apology," she said in a choked voice. There was a shocked silence throughout the courtroom. No one moved. Then two other parents of the victims stood and reached over to embrace Mrs. Riddel.

I felt my eyes moisten. I turned back to Pouse. He stood from the witness chair with his arms extended to Mrs. Riddel, making no effort to brush the tears from his face.

Winchell let the extraordinary moment play out. Mrs. Riddel and the others resumed their seats after hugging each other.

Strong, sensing the moment, "Your Honor, I have no more questions."

Winchell looked at Hardy. "Mr. Hardy, do you care to cross-examine the witness?"

In trials with multiple parties, each party has an opportunity to cross-examine any other party's witnesses.

"I have no questions," said Hardy. Of course that made sense. There was nothing useful Hardy could get from Don Pouse. Strong and Pouse had been careful to not implicate Kay.

"Mr. Clearwater?" Winchell asked.

Pouse had fallen on his sword, but only to the extent of failing to act reasonably. His testimony suggested that he was most likely negligent, but perhaps not negligent enough for criminal liability. For me to prevail, I needed to prove criminal or gross conduct—in other words, reckless behavior. Cross-examination would be my opportunity to determine whether his behavior was reckless.

"I have a few questions of Mr. Pouse." Given the raw emotions that had just played out, I was calculating how to proceed. I had to be careful but I wondered if Pouse and Strong had sanitized his testimony. Could he have been truly ignorant of the gun purchase and consequently ignorant that the gun was in the house? His testimony had, from what I judged, the ring of truth. Cross-examination has been referred to as the ultimate test of truth. It was time to test that maxim, but oh so carefully. I couldn't be the bully.

"Mr. Pouse, you were called by the school on September 6, correct?"

He studied me before answering. "I was."

"You received the message that your son's conduct was significant enough to provoke the principal to reach out to you to come and discuss Devon's behavior, correct?"

"Yes, and I should have come to the school."

"Correct me if I'm wrong, but that was the first time you had ever been called by the school to come in and discuss your son's conduct, right?"

"That's right."

"You would agree with me that such a summons most likely wouldn't be over something trivial, wouldn't you?"

"You're right, of course. I was at work in the middle of an important transaction. I felt I couldn't break away." He looked off, reflecting on his failure.

"Since you'd never been called to come to school before, you had to believe that it probably involved something significant, wouldn't you say?"

"I should have come."

"So that's a yes, something significant?"

"Yes."

"Maybe something more significant than the business transaction you were involved in?"

"I should have come." He said with bowed head and closed eyes.

"Now, that evening, or for that matter, over the entire next week leading up to the shootings, you learned that the incident involved your son searching for ammunition, right?"

He deflected. "I thought it was ammunition for our rifles."

"Is it your testimony that for that entire week, you never learned he was searching for ammunition for his Glock handgun, his 'new beauty'?"

He sucked in his bottom lip. "Like I said, I thought it was for the rifles."

"Are you telling us you didn't discuss any specifics with your son regarding the ammunition?"

Again with the lip. "No, like I said, I assumed it was for the rifles."

"Let's move to the day of the shootings. Once again, you were called by the school principal, correct?"

"I was."

"But you showed up this time?"

A trace of exasperation. "I did."

"Judge, leave to post the drawing which I believe is Exhibit 3?"

"You may."

Cipolla got it up on the PowerPoint.

"That drawing is downright scary, isn't it, Mr. Pouse?" Scary was the word Hardy used when crossing Conklin.

"It is disturbing and heartbreaking," Pouse agreed.

"In addition to your son drawing a picture of a gun shooting, he wrote, 'I'm useless. Help me. I hate them all.' Isn't that right?"

"Yes." He said through a choked voice and dropped his head into his hands.

I let him collect himself before continuing. "When you saw that picture and read those words, you knew your son was troubled, didn't you, Mr. Pouse?"

"Yes."

"Those two words, 'Help me,' were particularly concerning, weren't they?"

"They were."

"You believed this was your child screaming for help, isn't that right?"

Pouse again dropped his head, and in almost a whisper said, "But as I talked to him, he calmed down and explained that he was just having a bad day."

"I know this is difficult, Mr. Pouse, but we all need to fully understand what happened at the school just an hour or so before the shootings."

Taking in breath, he replied, "I understand."

"The principal begged you to take him home and get him the help he needed, didn't she?"

"But, like I've said several times, he explained that he was doing okay, it was just a bad day." Then he looked squarely at me. "Mr. Clearwater, I know you're just doing your job. But I'm agreeing with you that I completely failed my son. If I had done the right thing, four boys would be alive today."

I had my answers. "Your Honor, I have no more questions."

After Strong indicated he had no redirect, Winchell motioned for Pouse to step down. But he didn't move, and every eye in the room was riveted on him. Finally, a bailiff took his arm and guided him back to the defense table.

Cipolla leaned to me as I sat. "You hit him pretty hard, Jake."

"He had it coming." When I measured his misery against the families who had lost their boys, I had no regrets for beating on him. But beyond just making him pay for his conduct, I wanted to gauge his sincerity and his sense of remorse. I didn't think he had lied, and I did sense a deep level of remorse. I thought him a poor father, a non-engaged father. A man who prioritized his career over his family.

I believed him when he said he didn't know about the gun. Although a responsible parent should have known. A responsible parent would have pulled Devon from school and got him help. It baffles me that his wife didn't tell him about the gun. His ignorance was careless; he should've known.

With all that said, I don't think his conduct rose to the level of criminal negligence necessary for involuntary manslaughter. He should face consequences in a civil trial because he was surely negligent, but not here, not in this criminal prosecution.

Strong stood. "I have no further witnesses, Your Honor. At the court's convenience, there will be a defense motion on behalf of Don Pouse to be made outside the presence of the jury."

I stood. "Your Honor, may I have a moment?"

"Certainly."

I leaned over to Cipolla and whispered, "Otto, I don't think he knew about the Glock. What's your take?"

"I think you're right. What are you thinking?"

"I'm thinking he's not criminally negligent."

Cipolla gripped my shoulder. "You going to dismiss him?"

"I am."

Cipolla leaned back, studied my face, while thoughtfully considering, and finally nodded. "I agree."

I stood. "Judge, counsel's motion will not be necessary. On behalf of the State, I move to dismiss the charges against Don Pouse."

That jerked Judge Winchell forward. There were murmurings throughout the courtroom. I flashed to Don Pouse. No reaction. He sat motionless. I don't think my words had reached through his grief. I felt the stare of Juror Number Eight, a middle-aged high school teacher. I glanced at him, and he offered an almost imperceptible nod of approval.

I glanced at Hardy. He didn't react, his face impassive. No doubt he was immediately calculating the impact on his client.

Winchell: "Do I understand, Mr. Clearwater, that you are dismissing the three charges of involuntary manslaughter against defendant Don Pouse?"

"I am."

Winchell took that in and leaned back in her chair. "So be it. Mr. Pouse, you are discharged."

And to the jury, she said, "We will take our recess for lunch and resume at two o'clock. At which time I will instruct you on the law and we will then proceed to closing arguments."

During the break, I huddled with the victims' families. I explained my action in dismissing Don Pouse. I expected some anger, some pushback, but instead got reassurances. Mrs. Fellows said, "I believed him. He didn't know. And he lost his boy." That seemed to be the general consensus. I was relieved.

CHAPTER 67

"How do we process what we've heard over the past two weeks?" I said, as I made my way to the jury and began my closing argument. During the break I had changed out ties and now wore my Lisa-bought Gucci tie. No notes. No podium. Maximum eye contact. Nothing between me and my audience. "How do we make any kind of sense of this tragedy? This entirely preventable tragedy. How?" I paused and scanned their faces.

"What would it have taken to prevent the slaughter of the three boys? Were there times during those fourteen days leading up to the murders when this tragedy could have been averted?

"Let's start with not allowing a sixteen-year-old an easily concealable semiautomatic weapon of war. How about having an adult securely storing that weapon, preventing an obviously obsessed teenager from getting his hands on it? How about the parents asking questions when their son was hunting ammunition during class? How about after reading 'I'm useless, help me. I hate them all' and recognizing their own child's cry for help and simply walking away?

"And, of course, the last and final opportunity to prevent the slaughter, telling someone, anyone, that he has access to a Glock handgun." I stopped and studied my audience. "Who was there every step of the way?"

I moved to the far right of the jury box and briefly glanced back at Judge Winchell. "We've just heard the judge give the guidelines you'll use in reaching a verdict. A defendant is guilty of involuntary manslaughter when she acts with criminal negligence and that criminal negligence caused the death of another. She explained, and I quote, 'Criminal negligence involves more than carelessness, inattention, or mistake in judgment. A person is criminally negligent when she acts in a reckless way that creates a high risk of death or great bodily injury to another.' That's a mouthful, isn't it? It boils down to two questions. First, was Kay Pouse criminally negligent? Second, if she was, did her criminal negligence lead to the deaths of Lincoln, Josh, and Mark?

"Criminal negligence. The judge was careful to tell you that the conduct must be more than simple inadvertence. Or a simple lapse of judgment. For example, let's take running a red light, causing an accident. That is a lapse of reasonable conduct and can never be the basis for criminal conduct, even if it leads to serious injury or even death. But what if instead of just running a red light, an individual ran that light traveling eighty miles an hour through a busy intersection? That's criminal negligence. And if that driver struck and killed someone, that's involuntary manslaughter. That's criminal negligence leading to death." I stepped back and took in the whole group, looking for signs of confusion or pushback. They were with me.

"How sure do you folks have to be in determining whether Kay Pouse was criminally negligent?" I nodded once. "You have to be sure beyond a reasonable doubt. Now there's a phrase we've heard throughout our lives. Reasonable doubt. Surprisingly, that simple phrase is often misinterpreted and confused. Some think it means beyond all doubt or even beyond a shadow of a doubt. Right?"

I got several nods and smiled. "Well, it's time to put those notions aside. It's simply beyond a reasonable doubt. When you examine the defendant's conduct, you must be convinced beyond a reasonable doubt that her conduct was criminally negligent and caused the death of another. Was she reckless when she allowed her clearly troubled teenager access to an easily concealed handgun and just simply walked away?" I paused to let that resonate.

"Okay, now that we're squared away on the law, let's go back through the evidence and take a hard look at Mrs. Pouse's conduct over the fourteen days leading up to the murders. Day one, buying her sixteen-year-old a gun."

I picked up the gun and placed it in my coat pocket. "And not just any gun, but an easily concealed handgun. We also learned that gun was a semiautomatic, which permits the shooter to fire up to eleven shots as quick as your finger can twitch.

"We also learned that Devon was obsessed with his gun."

"Objection. The testimony is that Mrs. Pouse bought the gun for herself."

"Mr. Clearwater, response?"

"The evidence was quite clear. The defendant bought that gun for her son."

"I'm going to overrule the objection." Turning to the jury, Winchell instructed, "You, ladies and gentlemen, heard the evidence. It is your understanding of the evidence that matters."

I turned back to the jury. "Whose gun? Think back to his social media post. 'I got my new beauty today.'" Again, several nods of agreement.

"Should Devon's insistence on and obsession with that easily concealable semiautomatic handgun have raised some concerns in her mind?" Rhetoricals work best when you allow the audience to reach their own answer.

"Moving forward to Day 6. Devon's caught searching for ammunition while at school. Now, given that the Pouse family had guns, that alone doesn't raise serious red flags, but it's further evidence of Devon's obsession with guns—and with his Glock in particular, should that have concerned Mrs. Pouse? What was her response? You heard it. 'Don't get caught.' I stopped and slowly repeated. 'Don't get caught.' Did her words strike you folks as hard as they struck me?" I let that linger.

"And how did it strike you twelve when the school summoned the parents and they just blew off the principal? Did that concern you? Should the parents have gotten involved? Should they have left their jobs and come to find out if their teenager was acting out, that something might be wrong?

"Were you concerned that Devon had access to the Glock from Day 1 to the day of the murders? We never learned where that gun was kept. Was it locked away or in the care of the adults, or was it under Devon's control?

"Day 14. That hand-drawn picture." I motioned for Cipolla to bring it up on the PowerPoint, and I stepped to the screen. "What's our takeaway here? What must Kay Pouse have been thinking when she was confronted with this? This is that car hurtling along at eighty miles an hour just before it got to that busy intersection. She could have braked. She was in a position to stop it. She knew about the gun. She had the ability to stop this tragedy. Who was the only one who knew her troubled child had access to the weapon?"

I could feel my anger building, my voice rising. "The father, the principal, didn't know. She was the only one standing between Devon and the murdered boys. She, and only she, had the ability to slam on the brakes. She, and only she, had the knowledge that could have stopped that out-of-control car from bursting into that busy intersection."

I shook my head in disgust. "She let that car career into the intersection and into multiple fatal collisions." I put up my hands in exasperation. "You'll have to excuse my vehemence. She knew he was troubled, that he was screaming for help, and that he could've been armed, and she did nothing." I stopped again. "Criminal negligence? Yeah! Involuntary manslaughter? Yeah!

I walked to my table and sipped water while Cipolla shut down the PowerPoint. I made an effort to dial it down, willing my voice back to an even timbre. "I would like to address a couple of things Mr. Hardy has raised during the trial. Why not prosecute the principal and the school? Without question, Principal Conklin bears serious responsibility for not pulling Devon from his classes. That was a foolish, thoughtless, and ultimately tragic decision. So why didn't I bring criminal charges against her? What didn't she know that only Kay Pouse knew?"

I didn't have to answer my question. It was written all over their faces. "Principal Conklin will most likely be sued in a civil trial and she should. She failed to do what her job demanded. She bears heavy responsibility. The only reason she's not sitting next to Mrs. Pouse is that she didn't know Devon had access to the handgun.

"How about Don Pouse? Why'd I dismiss the criminal charge against him? Like the principal, he didn't know about the gun. He should've known, but he didn't. He's guilty of being a lousy father. His priority was his job. Devon wasn't nearly so important. He's going to have to deal with his own demons for the rest of his life." My voice was mean and bitter. I wasn't about to spare his feelings. "In all likelihood, he'll also be held accountable in a civil lawsuit. And just like the principal, he should be.

I walked over to my table and accepted more water from Cipolla. Gathering my thoughts, I returned to the jurors. "Defense counsel has insinuated that somehow this prosecution is an attack on the Second Amendment. How wrong could he be? It's not, and you all know that. It's not an attack on the Second Amendment, it's an attack on criminally stupid conduct," I said. "That's right, criminally stupid conduct. I don't apologize for being so crass and graphic, but there it is. It's about flagrant criminal conduct which led to three families losing their sons."

I took in a breath and then slowly let it out, again releasing some of my anger before continuing. "I feel for Mrs. Pouse, I do. I sympathize with her. She's going through a very tough time. But that can't absolve her and cannot stand in the way of convicting her." I clenched my fists. "Don't do that." I walked to counsel table and sat. The room was stone-cold silent.

"Thank you, Mr. Clearwater. We'll take our afternoon recess. Then we'll resume with Mr. Hardy's closing remarks."

Cipolla and I walked to the attorney conference room. I studiously avoided any eye contact with anyone as we made our way. "Jake, you okay?" asked Cipolla, once he'd closed the conference room door.

"Yeah, give me a minute." I sat, while he turned on the Keurig. "I guess I hadn't realized how angry I am about the absolutely senseless deaths of those three boys." I looked at him. "Was I over the top?"

"Nope. You crushed it, Jake. Crushed it. That was awesome. I was feeling a little queasy about our chances of conviction until you just did what you did. Those jurors felt it."

I lifted my cup. my hand was still shaking. "Otto, I appreciate that." I gripped the cup with two hands and managed a drink. "Now we've got to sit through Hardy's close. We've got a ways to go."

CHAPTER 68

Hardy unfolded from his chair and slowly walked behind me, stopped, and in a commanding voice, began. "There's a huge difference between making a mistake in judgment and engaging in criminal conduct. Despite what you just heard, a mistake in judgment is not manslaughter. And despite that emotional appeal from the prosecutor, it wasn't a mother's love and support for her son that's responsible for what happened.

He moved from behind me and stopped squarely before the jury and dropped his voice. "Let me double down on that. She supported him and she loved him. And now this prosecutor is screaming that we should vilify her for the conduct of her son."

Hardy shook his huge bald head and turned and pointed at me. "He's tried to make it sound like everything this mother did was not just wrong but evil. She bought a gun. A perfectly legal thing to do. The family likes to hunt and they like target practice. And like so many of us, they feel safer and more secure having some guns in the house. But to hear the prosecutor rant and rave, buying that gun was one of the greatest sins ever." He stopped to study his audience.

"Folks, that gun was legal. It is even legal in a gun-hating state like California. Yet," he said incredulously, "it's the linchpin of the prosecutor's argument. I guess he figured if he screamed 'Glock' and 'semiautomatic' often enough, he'd scare you into a conviction.

"What else did Kay Pouse do that should convict her? She sent that text supporting her sixteen-year-old." He shrugged skeptically. "That's certainly another black mark against her. He was looking at ammunition on his phone. Kay didn't think that was a big deal. After all, it's a family that has guns. She sent that text in support of her son. Yet, once again, the prosecutor assigned the most sinister connotation. Another piece in his mythical case. Evidence completely disconnected from later events."

Hardy stood at his table and put his hand on Kay Pouse's shoulder. "Let's continue on with Kay's sinister path to manslaughter. What was the next terrible and certainly incriminating action Kay undertook? After coming to the school and talking to her son, she left. Why'd she leave? Devon assured her he was okay. He was just having a bad day. She trusted him." Hardy repeated, "She trusted her son."

Hardy let that resonate a long while before continuing. "She trusted him. She believed him. But she wasn't the only one. Devon's father believed him. You know who else believed him? The principal. Her action in letting Devon go back to class speaks louder than her testimony. Would the principal have done that if she believed him capable of murder?" Hardy paused, allowing the gravity of his rhetoric punch to weigh on the jurors.

Hardy worked his way to the far end of the jury box, nearest the witness chair, right in front of Juror Number Eight.

No accident there. Hardy was thinking, as I was, that Number Eight was a likely foreperson candidate.

"This has never been about manslaughter. This trial is about the DA's office trying to send a message. Their message? Guns are bad. And the deaths of those three boys gave them the perfect opportunity to send that message. Admittedly, there are lots of guns out there. Should adults be vigilant in securing them from kids?

You bet. We have laws about that. About securing guns in a safe manner. The Pouses are certainly guilty of not doing that. But does it logically follow that, should a teenager get hold of a gun, the adult should be responsible for his unforeseeable conduct? Do you see a disconnect there?"

Hardy stepped back, considering. "How about if a parent left her car keys on the kitchen counter and her underage daughter takes the keys and drives off and recklessly runs over and kills a pedestrian? Is that parent liable? Is there a disconnect?

"When you folks retire back to deliberate, I ask you to stop and consider the critical moment in this tragedy." Hardy leaned in at Number Eight. "That moment occurred after Devon was sent back to class. Recall, sixty, seventy, eighty minutes passed. And in that time, something happened in the mind of the teenager, this unpredictable and, yeah, troubled sixteen-year-old. He broke. He snapped. No one saw it coming. Not his mom, his dad, not his principal. It was a bolt out of the blue. It was completely unpredictable." Hardy again shook his head dismissively. "She can't be held accountable for the unforeseeable."

He walked over and poured himself water and took a long, contemplative drink before continuing. "Now, when I finish my remarks, the prosecutor is going to have the last word. I challenge him to explain the disconnect. The unpredictable. I also want the prosecutor to establish how Kay Pouse somehow knew Devon had the gun that day. Think about that. Without that gun, was Devon a danger? Was he harmless? He was a skinny, undersized sixteen-year-old. You heard the judge's instructions: the defendant's conduct must create a high risk of death or great bodily injury."

Hardy boomed, "No gun, no risk of death! As far as Kay knew, he was harmless. Ladies and gentlemen, that's a trump card. When you weigh Kay's lack of knowledge about the gun, you twelve need to bear in mind this business of reasonable doubt. How can you be certain beyond any reasonable doubt that Kay Pouse is guilty of manslaughter if she had no way of knowing that he had a gun with him? How in the hell did her conduct create a high risk of death?"

The jurors sat stunned. The courtroom was eerily quiet. Hardy had earned his keep. I could feel the momentum sliding toward the defense table.

CHAPTER 69

Judge Winchell: "Mr. Clearwater, it's 4:40. Would you prefer to make your rebuttal tomorrow morning?"

"No, Your Honor. I'll go now." I couldn't let the jurors stew on Hardy's close.

"Very well."

I strode to the jurors as if Hardy's close hadn't laid a finger on my case. "Unpredictable? Unforeseeable? Maybe Devon's words didn't register with defense counsel. 'I'm useless, help me. I hate them all.' Are we stunned and surprised that he acted out? We may not know precisely how he might act out, but given his words, are we surprised that this gun-obsessed teenager with access to a semiautomatic weapon would act out? The only thing unforeseeable was the precise nature of what he would do. And that gun, his beauty, was certainly going to be a part of it.

"There were three adults in that school office who saw Devon's drawing and read his disturbing and hateful words. All three were concerned that they had a very troubled teenager on their hands. But, and this is critical, only one of the three knew the ultimately damning information." I paused for emphasis. "Only one of the three knew he had access to a gun. Only one in three knew he was completely obsessed with his gun. Only one in three knew that gun was a semiautomatic capable of rapidly firing eleven rounds. And only one in three knew it was a handgun, a handgun that could be easily concealed." I paused. "That one is sitting right in front of us. Her reckless knowledge created a high risk of death. The twelve of you know that. You know that without any reasonable doubt." I studied them one last time. "Do what you have taken an oath to do."

Winchell gave the jurors the concluding instructions and ordered them back on the morrow to begin their deliberations.

CHAPTER 70

I couldn't sleep that night. Lisa was kind and sat up with me until about two o'clock, when she fell asleep on the couch with her head in my lap. Hardy's closing kept ringing in my head. The logic of his argument—as far as Kay knew, he was harmless—had hit the mark. I kept mentally replaying my rebuttal. Could I have responded better?

Losing was hard on the ego. But I would be okay. This wasn't about my ego. This was about accountability. Placing blame where it was so richly earned. I'd lost before and could very well lose again. What would hurt most was that Kay Pouse, who I fervently believed bore significant fault in the three deaths, would be criminally exonerated. That would be an injustice. That would be hard to live with.

I took my time driving into the office Tuesday. There was no urgency. The jurors had a lot to consider, and it would take a while. I thought about Juror Number Eight, the teacher who had given me that slight nod when I dismissed Don Pouse. He was sharp and focused. I think he was with me. I hoped he would be the foreperson and have the wherewithal to bring over any dissenters.

At a little past one o'clock, I drifted down to the cafeteria. I was killing time. I'd already haunted Nancy Seah's office and wasted part of her morning. She was encouraging but acknowledged it had always been a difficult case. Maybe Roger Hawthorne had been correct from the beginning.

Nursing a coffee and an uneaten piece of pecan pie, I felt a hand on my shoulder. I looked up to see Hardy towering over me. "Mind if I join you?"

"Why not," I grinned. "Have a seat. But stay away from the coffee. It's terrible." He was alone, none of his retinue in tow.

"Never touch that shit." He pulled up a chair. "Excellent closing, Clearwater. That rebuttal was spot on."

"Get out, I was sitting here thinking you kicked my butt with your closing."

He leaned back and burst out laughing. "You could be out there making some serious money from the defense side. Serious money."

"Actually, my real job is teaching law at Pacifico."

"So what in the hell are you doing prosecuting?"

"A year leave and then back to the classroom."

Hardy studied my face as if looking for signs of intelligent life. "Passing up a big career and buckets of money. You're too good to waste it in some classroom." This conversation with this man seemed surrealistic. We had fought hammer and tong.

"I appreciate that, Sam. But I'm doing what I think I need to be doing."

"You gonna eat that pie?"

I shoved it over. He picked it up and finished it in two bites.

"Sam, you didn't call a shrink. How come? I was waiting."

He smiled, remnants of pie at the corners of his mouth. "I'll bet you were. I can't tell you about that. What happens if this puppy hangs and you're foolish enough to get after it again?"

"Think it's going to hang?"

"Fair chance." He grunted. "Damn, I don't want to try this thing again. I'm sick of the Pouses. Dumbshits that they are."

"A kid with a Glock."

"Yeah, a kid with a Glock and three dead teenagers," he said somberly. "If it hangs, maybe you'll settle for misdemeanor manslaughter, with a suspended sentence, and some jail time."

"You forget the three dead boys?"

"Yeah, I know." He stood. "Thanks for the pie."

No word that day. The following day the jury sent a note. We reconvened. Number Eight was the foreperson. "Your Honor, we seem to be stuck," he said. "I'm not sure we can reach a verdict."

Winchell surveyed the jurors. "You have only been deliberating a short time. I'm sending you back to keep trying. You twelve are in the optimum position to decide this case. Each of you took an oath to carefully deliberate, to talk to one another, and reason with one another. We need that commitment. I urge you to redouble your efforts." Then, with emphasis, "Go back and try again."

After the jurors were ushered out, Hardy came over. "Let's talk," and motioned me to the attorney conference room. "They're going to hang this thing, and neither one of us wants to do this again. What say you let Kay plead to misdemeanor manslaughter with some jail time?"

With a disbelieving look, I said, echoing myself from the day before, "Three dead boys."

Hardy started to say something but caught himself. A very unlike Hardy thing to do.

"Say what you have to say," I said.

"Okay," he said, staring me dead in the eyes. "What are you trying to prove, Jake? Is convicting Kay Pouse of felonies the end game? Keep in mind those families aren't the only ones who lost a boy. Kay is hurting too. Her hurt is her boy's suicide. That's as rough as it gets. She's racked with guilt. She's damn near suicidal herself. If this trial hangs, I don't think she'll be around for a retrial."

"Trying to lay some guilt on me, Sam? It's hard to work up sympathy for her. She's the reason we're here."

"That may be. But that's in the past, we can't change that. I'm thinking about what's right going forward. What does justice look like right now?" He hesitated. "You take felonies off the board, so that she's not looking at prison, maybe we can get to a place that's far from ideal but which has a touch of compassion and a dose of reality." Hardy's bombastic style had morphed into thoughtful reasoning.

I didn't especially want Kay Pouse in prison. I wanted accountability. But did I need felony convictions to get there? Was my ego in the way? Was Hardy right? Were misdemeanors and jail time instead of felonies and prison the way to go? Did I need to relent?

"Sam, let me think about it. But before I do anything I'll need to talk to the families. If they say no deal, it's no deal."

"I understand."

Cipolla set up a conference call from my office. I had all five parents on the line. I began. "I'm pretty sure the jurors aren't going to reach a verdict. They've already told the judge, but she sent them back to keep trying. But I don't think it's going to work. So there are decisions to be made. Without question, we can try it again. A retrial will take months to happen. And even if we retry it, there are no guarantees the second trial will go any better."

"You're not saying that you'll drop the case?" Mrs. Turner asked, with an accusatory tone.

"Not at all. If the five of you want to go through another trial, I'm there."

"Mr. Clearwater, this is Mel Turner. What are you suggesting?"

"There is another way to go. I reduce the charges from felonies to misdemeanors, which Pouse will plead to and receive jail time."

"A plea bargain?" said Mrs. Turner, as if it was the worst possible outcome.

"Yes, but I won't do that unless you five all agree."

"Mr. Clearwater, this is Harold Fellows. You've been straight with us from the beginning. I understand a lot of prosecutors wouldn't have even pursued this case. Is this plea bargain your best advice?"

"I think so. By her pleading guilty, we have an acknowledgment of wrongdoing and some closure. She'll spend some time in jail."

"It doesn't seem fair," said Mrs. Turner. "Like you said during your argument, she knew, she could've stopped it."

Mr. Fellows was back. "Nothing's going to bring our boys back." And then, "I don't want this to drag on for more months. I think we ought to take Mr. Clearwater's advice so we can all move on."

There was more discussion. I stayed out of it. But finally, they grudgingly agreed. Even Mrs. Turner.

Back in chambers, Winchell studied Hardy and me as we laid out the plea. She didn't seem surprised. "Has there been any discussion as to how much jail time?"

"No," said Hardy. "We didn't discuss it. I'm okay leaving it up to you."

"Very well, we'll reconvene without the jury at two o'clock."

Word had spread. The courtroom was packed. Onlookers and media. The families of the boys were, of course, there.

Winchell ascended the bench and looked at Hardy. "Mr. Hardy, I understand there is to be a plea."

"That's correct, Your Honor."

"Mr. Clearwater?"

"Judge, I met with the families of the slain boys, and out of an abundance of compassion, they have agreed to allow me to reduce the felony manslaughter charges to misdemeanors."

Winchell looked at the three families and gave them a grave nod.

"Very well." Winchell stared at Kay Pouse. "Mrs. Pouse, please stand. How do you plead to misdemeanor manslaughter in the death of Lincoln Riddel?"

In a weak voice, "Guilty."

"How do you plead to misdemeanor manslaughter in the death of Josh Fellows?"

"Guilty."

"How do you plead to misdemeanor manslaughter in the death of Mark Turner?"

"Guilty."

Winchell began. "The pleas are entered and accepted by the court." She stared hard at Kay Pouse. "Mrs. Pouse, it is the usual practice to refer matters to probation to perform a workup and recommend sentencing. I'm going to forgo the referral and impose sentence at this time. But first, I feel compelled to offer my thoughts as I listened to the testimony."

Turning to the families of the victims, she said, "First, I offer my heartfelt condolences to the families and friends of Lincoln, Josh, and Mark. I can't imagine your pain and suffering. I can only trust that this plea will help in some small way to bring you closure."

Winchell turned to Kay Pouse and Don Pouse, who was sitting directly behind his wife. "I also offer my condolences to the two of you for the loss of your son." The judge unnecessarily shuffled some papers, perhaps thinking through what she wanted to say. "I'm going to address both Kay and Don Pouse. What struck me in listening to the testimony were your failures as parents. As important as your jobs are, they must pale in importance to the care of our children. If there is one lesson that emerged from this horrific tragedy, it is that. Our children need us. They need our love and our guidance. They need us through the happy times and through the troubled times. You two," she said, "abandoned your son during his troubled time. That failure in large part led to this horror."

Winchell leaned forward and brushed back the sleeves of her robe. "Kay Pouse, I sentence you to six months in the county jail on each count of involuntary manslaughter, the times to run concurrently." She then zeroed in on Don Pouse. "Sir, if I had it within my authority, I would have you sitting beside your wife in her jail cell as she does her time." She watched for reaction from either Pouse, and got nothing.

After Kay Pouse had been led off, Winchell ordered the jurors back into the courtroom. Once again, they had been excluded from so much of the trial. "Ladies and gentlemen, your services are no longer required. The defendant has pled guilty to three counts of involuntary manslaughter." Their surprise was quickly followed by the relief registered on their faces. Juror Number Eight bowed his head and closed his eyes before looking up at me and again giving me a slight nod. "You are released from service, with the court's thanks."

EPILOGUE

Juror Number Eight—Frank Connelly—waited for me outside the courtroom and informed me that the jury was hopelessly split ten to two for conviction. "The two holdouts for the defense were older men. They were gun advocates and believed Hardy's pitch about this being an attack on the Second Amendment."

"That had to be frustrating."

"It was. From the first straw vote, it was clear that they would not move from their position."

"I'm sure you tried."

"I did. I want to thank you for dismissing the husband. He was only on the fringe of this thing. Like you said, a lousy father, but not really involved." I nodded my agreement. "I do have one more question. How'd the families of the boys handle Pouse's plea?"

"I got their agreement. It should have been their call. If they had wanted to go again, I would have retried the case."

Kay Pouse was released from jail after serving four months.
Don Pouse filed for divorce while Kay was still in jail. I later learned that he quit his job and left the state.

Gil Haines, the Los Angeles District Attorney, resigned following the disclosure of illicit campaign contributions received during his campaign for DA. Nancy Seah was appointed acting district attorney.

Lisa and I took a second honeymoon to the Bahamas. And I returned to the classroom for the spring semester.

ACKNOWLEDGMENTS

Writing a novel requires much more than the novelist. There are, of course, the behind-the-scene experts. Jose Ramirez at Pedernales Publishing and Kathleen Kaiser at Kathleen Kaiser & Associates, who personify professionalism. And there are the loved ones with their support and constant encouragement. Thanks, Julie, Louie, MacKenzie, Eric, Lee, and Otto.

ABOUT THE AUTHOR

HARRY CALDWELL is a Pepperdine/ Caruso School of Law law professor and teaches Criminal Law, Criminal Procedure, and Trial Advocacy. He writes extensively in the areas of his expertise, having published over forty law review articles. Caldwell is the co-author of several trial advocacy textbooks, including *The Art and Science of Trial Advocacy*, which law schools across the country have adopted, and the LA Times awarded *Ladies and Gentlemen of the Jury: Greatest Closing Arguments* a best non-fiction book of the year. *Cost of Malice* is the third in the Jake Clearwater legal thrillers, including *Cost of Arrogance* and *Cost of Deceit*.

Milton Keynes UK
Ingram Content Group UK Ltd.
UKHW022253280924
448873UK00012BA/125/J

9 781737 512370